ELIXIR OF IMMORTALITY
and the
WHORE OF BABYLON

A KINE

Grail Publishing House

A Kine / Grail Publishing House

Printed in the United States of America by Kindle direct printing

Publisher's Note: This is a work of fiction. Names, characters, places, and incidents are a product of the author's imagination. Locales and public names are sometimes used for atmospheric purposes. Any resemblance to actual people, living or dead, or to businesses, companies, events, institutions, or locales is completely coincidental.

Elixir of Immortality and the Whore of Babylon/ A Kine -- 1st ed.
ISBN – 9780473509774

Authors Note:

This book is based upon a lucid dream that both intrigued and plagued me for many years. If there is such a thing as channeling, then much of the content in this book was obtained via it.

I spent many years researching elements of my dream and I've included a condensed version of that research in this book. Mythology, biblical lore and religious texts from the Vedas and ancient Egypt appear on the following pages alongside a fictionized version of my dream.

For your own enjoyment, it would be best if you read the previous book, *White Harvest,* first.

Other books by A KINE
Series: Beyond the veil of propaganda
WHITE HARVEST

I charge you, O daughters of Jerusalem, that you stir not up, nor awake my love, until he please. Thou art all fair, my love; there is no spot in thee.

The roof of your mouth is like the best wine that goes down sweetly, causing the lips of those that are asleep to speak.

I sleep, but my heart wakes: it is the voice of my beloved that knocks, saying, open to me, my sister, my love, my dove, my undefiled: for my head is filled with dew, and my locks with the drops of the night.

Let him kiss me with the kisses of his mouth: for his love is better than wine. Because of the savor of His good ointments, his name is as ointment poured forth, therefore do the virgins love him.

I come into my garden, my sister, my spouse: I have gathered my myrrh with my spice; I have eaten my honeycomb with my honey; I have drunk my wine with my milk:

Eat, O friends; drink, yea, drink abundantly, O beloved.

CONTENTS

CHAPTER ONE

Creation story

Wolf leaned back against his latte, velvet headboard with Lilly. "Comfy?" he said.

Lilly nodded absentmindedly, her gaze remaining on the archway in front of them that opened into the living area. Waterfalls trickled down either side of it before pooling into rocky crevices.

"I'm going to tell you a story," Wolf said.

"Cool," Lilly said, her eyes wandering to a tapestry hanging on another wall featuring a naked lady staring off into the distance over one shoulder. She had a large pregnant belly and plentiful breasts.

"Once upon a time, there was an intelligent humanoid race that changed the world. After learning to make mechanical wonders and fly to the heavens in marvelous flying contraptions, they mastered the art of terraforming worlds and making flowers and animals. Much did they learn and much did they create, but their efforts were always hampered by their warring natures; repeatedly, their societies were destroyed by war."

"I can see how that might happen," Lilly said, thinking of man's exploits. "Humanity suffers from the same affliction. We spend more time and money on finding new and inventive ways to kill each other than we do on making anything constructive."

"Indeed. Following a particularly spectacular crash, the humanoid race sought a solution to their problem. After much deliberation, they decided to breed a superior ruling class to govern them. Highly intelligent men and women were selected in childhood and trained. Later, the best of them were paired in the hopes their offspring would be smarter and more logical than the average man, and do a better job of managing society."

Lilly rolled her eyes. "Right—"

"Over time," Wolf said, somewhat impatiently, "progress was made, but it was never enough. The smart leaders were still men— still fallible. More was needed. Turning to genetics, they decided to genetically engineer their superior leaders."

"Um ... that doesn't sound like a good idea."

Wolf nodded. "That's exactly what the populous thought. Warning bells rang out and protests raged. People feared genetically engineered leaders would turn on them, but chaos couldn't be allowed to reign so control systems were devised, including rendering the new leaders incapable of independent existence."

Lilly frowned. "How did they do that?"

"The new leaders were given specialized culinary needs and feeding adaptations. While still able to eat normal food, they were engineered in such a way that if deprived of specialized food their brains wouldn't function at an elevated level."

Lilly clicked her tongue. "This is all starting to sound like mad scientist stuff ... Frankenstein springs to mind."

"As an added safeguard, the new beings were also rendered incapable of independent reproduction."

Lilly blinked several times. "Isn't that a design fault?"

"They weren't created alone. Rather, they were created in unison with a smaller humanoid race; a race they'd feed off and in whose wombs they'd reproduce."

"What?" Lilly's eyes whizzed to Wolf's, her interest peaked. "They were designed to behave like cuckoos? You're talking about your kind?"

"I am, yes—"

"And my kind!"

"Yes."

Lilly felt sick. "My son is your son! That's why his placenta was different ... Why it didn't come out?"

"Indeed."

"Oh my God!" Lilly's mind whirled. How could such a secret be kept from her, kept from humanity? People had long suspected malevolent aliens were flying around in saucers, but this was too much. She felt faint.

"You're all right. I'm not going to hurt you."

"You already have! Your baby was enormous and you guys have been messing with my head and emotions!"

"Only a little," Wolf said dismissively.

Lilly blinked rapidly. *Is he really going to carry on with his story after that?* Trying to focus, she took several deep breaths.

"After our creation, controversy reigned and there was much indecision because the first of my kind grew to enormous proportions and were viewed as a threat of the highest order. As a safeguard, a solitary individual was selected for further study and the rest terminated. Your kind, on the other hand, were viewed more favorably because you were also created to be slaves. Much of the warring that had gone on had happened because of the enforced slavery of portions of the populous, either literally or via low wages. So, there was almost a hundred percent agreement when it came to creating a smaller humanoid race with limited intelligence to serve as slaves. ... The masses liked slaves ... especially sexual slaves."

"So!" Lilly scowled. "What went wrong? How did the genie get out of the bottle?"

"In an act of desperation, when the first of my kind went on heat in his adolescence, he ejaculated into his own hands and pushed his semen into the mouth-like opening of his womb, his vagina, to inseminate himself."

When Lilly first met Ox, an enormous Bigfoot similar to Wolf in looks, only larger and a darker colour, she'd mistakenly thought he had limited intelligence. She was wrong, he was smarter than her. She imagined the first of Wolf's kind to be like him, sensual and intelligent and she could almost feel his pain; sense his desperate need to fulfill an urgent biological need, and his desire for a companion that cumulated in an attempt to replicate himself.

"After his self-mating, his womb filled with self-fertilized eggs that would largely be held in suspended animation for the rest of his life via an adaption obtained from the genes of a queen bee."

Lilly frowned. "Queen bees keep their eggs in suspended animation?"

"They do, yes. A queen bee will only mate once in young adulthood, but she'll produce eggs throughout her lifetime."

Blinking rapidly, Lilly wondered what the next revelation would be.

"After his self-mating, the first of my kind's vagina shrank to become an opening for a small injector probe as per design. His self-fertilization was observed on hidden cameras, but the highly intelligent leaders who came from generations of carefully selected progeny, didn't inform the populous. Instead, they secretly introduced one of your women to him. Everything went as planned; better than imagined in fact because he was a charming Romeo. He wooed and comforted the smaller humanoid before probing her womb and inserting a fertilized egg stimulated to develop by her pheromones."

Lilly's brow furrowed. "Was she injured?"

"No, the specially designed injector probe had worked perfectly and he was a gentleman throughout the whole affair, but her obvious attachment to him alarmed the leaders; he was as cunning as an old fox."

"So, what happened next?" Lilly said impatiently.

"The leaders didn't act on their reservations. After the woman was removed from his cage, they introduced another to see how he'd react to her. He obligingly wooed and impregnated her too. Later, the women gave birth to healthy sons."

"Is this knowledge in the world? In my old society I mean ... do people know about this?"

"Of course," Wolf said. "In Greek mythology, the first-born, a primeval deity of procreation and life generation was called Phanes. With broad golden wings and a helmet, he was frequently depicted as a deity emerging from a cosmic egg entwined with a serpent. Like ourselves, Phanes was a hermaphrodite. A deity of light and goodness, his name meant 'to bring light' or 'to shine,' and he's said to have emerged from a void or watery abyss and given birth to the universe."

Phanes with wings and a serpent

"Is the story of Phanes the only such story in mythology?"

"No. The god Amen-Ra also generated life through masturbation; creating Shu and Tefnut. In that creation story, Amen-Ra said:

> *I had union with my hand, and I embraced my shadow in*
> *a loving embrace. I poured seed into my own mouth, and I*
> *sent forth from myself issue in the form of the gods Shu*
> *and Tefnut."*

Lilly mulled over her own pregnancy. "It still makes no sense to me," she said at last. "My baby was big, yes, but surely any infant of yours would be so enormous a human couldn't carry it? Especially not a little woman like me. I'm small for a European woman."

"Humans have huge babies with large heads. A newborn ape weighs a mere three percent of its mother's weight, whereas a human baby weighs six. Ape's penises are also tiny in comparison to humans. You were designed to go with me … to carry and birth an enormous infant. Such births are difficult for you, granted, but you're capable of them, and our newborns are tiny in comparison to us and quite immature. Their head shape allows them to escape your wombs with ease."

"Really? Is that what that verse in Genesis is about?

> Genesis 3:16 I will greatly multiply your sorrow and your
> conception; in sorrow, you shall bring forth children."

"Of course," Wolf said. "Birthing a large baby with a big head is both hard work and painful."

"Well, I think it's disgusting! You should be ashamed of yourselves!"

"Why? We had nothing to do with it. We were created in unison with you and we're designed to enjoy a mutually pleasurable symbiotic relationship."

Lilly groaned. "So, what did the populous think when they found out about the babies?"

"They protested loudly of course, demanding the father and sons be terminated forthwith."

"Grab your pitchforks boys!"

"Yes, that was the sentiment."

"Well, why weren't they killed?"

"Shortly after the women gave birth their placentas came away and the leaders were mystified as to why. The loss of the placentas was a huge disappointment because they'd hoped to milk them. Further experiments and tinkering were required, so more women were brought to the father and sons to impregnate. Over time, the populous realized my kind was not only a valuable resource, but also a necessary one and the rules were relaxed."

"So, you're all clones?"

"No," Wolf said. "Sperm carries a split of genetic material that varies from one another."

"Surely, the father and sons must have been near on identical?"

"DNA is shuffled. The father was unique but his genetic material was largely sourced from the generous gene pool of the superior leaders. This gave his sperm and eggs sufficient material to contain a random selection of DNA, and allow mutations not seen in his body to emerge."

"And the resulting offspring—"

"Stable and carrying a suitable level of genetic variation."

"And the specialized food your brains require to function at a superior level ... what's that?"

"The wine in your inner womb isn't recycled from Ox ... When you became a conjoined female, a woman within whom one of our placentas is attached and thriving, you started producing a unique substance in your brain. After it circulates in your blood your placenta absorbs it. Commonly called wine, I extract it with my wine probe, and my brain requires it to function at an elevated level."

"Were Bigfoots like Ox created at the same time as humans—designed to carry and nurture us?"

"Of course:

> *Job 40:15 Behold now behemoth, which I made with you;*
> *he eats grass as an ox. 16 Behold now, his strength is in his*
> *loins, and his force is in the navel of his belly."*

"But the verse says behemoth eats grass."

"It does, yes. Grass is yet another code word for your kind in the Bible, as is 'Son of man.'

> *Isaiah 51:12 I, even I, am he that comforts you: who art*
> *thou, that you should be afraid of a man that shall die, and*
> *of the Son of man which shall be made as grass.*

"Ox told me his kind only feed and carry Caucasians."

"Some Caucasians," Wolf clarified. "Seed that's bred true ... it hasn't corrupted over time."

"Why do you call it seed? The Bible uses this term too, but it seems odd to me."

"The word 'sperm' is derived from the Greek word 'sperma,' meaning seed."

"Where did humans' genetic material come from?"

"Mostly from Homo erectus," Wolf said. "Our creators made us primarily from their own DNA, and after they divided humanity into two strains, a prey species and a slave species, they inserted a small amount of our DNA into yours to link us together, and it increased your intellectual abilities. The DNA is known as 'Sin' and it's said to be responsible for the fall of man spoken about in Genesis in the Bible."

Lilly wondered about the legitimacy of engineering slaves, but leaders make the rules, so, obviously, it would've been up to them to deem it legal or not.

"The new humanoid species with its two strains pleased their masters because they were smarter than pre-man, and humans took instruction well and performed tasks adequately."

"Was Homo erectus similar to a chimp?"

"A close relative. Are you aware you share 98.8 percent of your DNA with a chimpanzee, but you have two fewer chromosomes."

"Two fewer chromosomes! Forty-six in comparison to forty-eight? If that's true, how can a human be anything like a chimp?"

Human
Chromosome 2

Chimp
Chromosome 2p
and 2q

"The information in your DNA is largely the same as theirs ... To connect with your creators' DNA and ours, two of your chromosomes were fused or spliced together in a laboratory. The genetic material contained on the conjoined strands is largely as previous. At least 100,000 Sumerian clay tablets have survived to this day, and they speak of superior beings called gods living among humans and ruling over them as lords and masters. The tablets say the gods created humans 'in their own image' and 'after their own likeness.' Thousands of years later, these words were copied into the Bible—into Genesis. The Sumerians wrote about their gods and masters in matter-of-fact terms, describing them as flesh and blood beings with whom they could have sex and produce hybrid offspring."

"Where are the people who engineered us?"

"They're extinct ... They were the Neanderthals."

Lilly frowned. "Weren't they grunting beasts?"

"No," Wolf said with a chuckle. "Their jawbones were deliberately misaligned to make them look clumsy and stupid. Scientists' have recently acknowledged they weren't the grunting brutes they've long been maligned as."

Lilly rubbed her brow. She'd heard something about this but hadn't checked into it. "But they weren't massive ... were they? You're huge! Where did your great size come from?"

"Our creators mixed their own DNA with a variant of the massive pre-hominoid Gigantopithecus blacki's DNA before adding marsupial and queen bee DNA along with other genetic material."

Lilly frowned. "But Neanderthal bones have been found beside stone-age tools."

"They have, yes, but so have human bones ... All that tells you is, at some point in the past, civilization broke down so completely people were forced to wander around in the bush like animals. Neanderthals' brains were bigger than modern humans, their intellect vastly outstripping yours. The first of our kind was born in one of their females' wombs. In mythology, she's called Chaos or Tiamat; the primordial goddess."

"How come they're extinct?"

Wolf tenderly kissed Lilly's brow before answering. "Because modern humans vast numbers and their improved intellect made them a threat to be reckoned with. Your people, now able to plot and plan, grew jealous of the Lazy Kings. Going on a murderous rampage, they slaughtered them in their beds, but Neanderthals persisted for some time in remote bush afterwards and they live on in your DNA."

"How did your kind avoid the slaughter?"

"We were the brains behind the operation ... The Lazy Kings made the mistake of regarding us as big harmless teddy bears, but, tiring of being ruled and manipulated, we made a play for power."

"Of course you did," Lilly said bitterly. "I should have guessed, but why didn't humans slaughter you in your beds ... then or now? Why have they allowed you to remain in control when your population is small and ours is vast?"

"Mostly, humans are ignorant of our existence, and if not ignorant, they're happily trading with us. Our alliance suits us both. In general, humanity has nothing to fear from us."

"You mean ordinary man or the slave strain of humanity has nothing to fear ... My kind has everything to fear!"

"True," Wolf said matter-of-factly.

"Surely, the other races don't want to be part of some slave race?"

"One doesn't tend to get upset about things they know nothing about."

"My kind will be furious when they find out they're part of a prey species!"

"Not so," Wolf said. "Mostly, they've long since converted and aren't fit for purpose, your seed having mixed and corrupted over time. Once this is pointed out to them, they'll shrug off any annoyance and happily breed with the slave race ... many already have."

"How will they know if they are or aren't part of the prey species?"

"A specialized test exposes your kind. Many Caucasian families harbor one or two individuals, but they'd never know."

"Is a person's blood type an indicator?"

"Yes, but it's only a broad marker."

Lilly shuddered at the thought of her people being hunted down like animals and forced to undergo some barbaric test. Deciding the test was probably no more invasive than a simple blood test, she shrugged. "Do humanities leaders already know who is or isn't part of the prey species?"

"Mostly, yes."

"Why don't our leaders challenge your kind? Lead a strike force against you?"

"Leaders in your old society lick the boots of the real people in power, the human leaders in our world, and they do their bidding."

Lilly groaned. "Is that because they're suck-ups or because they don't dare disobey?'

"Neither ... They yearn to be part of our world, and to get here they must prove themselves."

"The old carrot and stick routine."

"Yes."

"Why would they even want to be here? Surely, being on Earth is better than being here, especially if you're rich."

"In your previous society you have a saying, 'In this world, nothing is certain except death and taxes.' In our world, neither exists."

"So, I'm in heaven?"

"If that's what you want to call the place where the gods reside ... then yes."

Lilly blinked several times. "Something doesn't feel right ... This doesn't feel like heaven to me. I can see how it might be for Cat, but I have serious reservations."

The corners of Wolf's mouth turned up. Pressing his lips together while rubbing his mouth to stop himself laughing, he said through tight lips. "Do you now?"

"You're having me on! This isn't heaven ... is it?"

"Oh, it is ... heaven's just not what you thought it was."

"Why isn't it!"

"Because you've been deceived ... lied to. You belong to the prey species and nothing can change that."

"Fuck you! You're positively hateful ... You're a fucking wanker!"

After kissing the top of Lilly's head, Wolf cradled her. "I love you, Baby. I know this isn't your perceived idea of heaven, but remember, I didn't set up the foundations of the world and I'm a victim of circumstance like you."

"No, you're not! And what's more you think it's funny ... It's not funny!"

"I *am* a victim of circumstance, and so is Cat."

Lilly glared at Wolf. "How did I get pregnant with your baby?"

"You were drugged and taken to a basement where I impregnated you. You gave birth to my infant ... not yours and mine ... *my* infant."

Lilly thought this was an atrocious thing to do to somebody, but considering all the atrocities she'd endured so far, it didn't rate that highly. "What happened to the prehistoric humanoids from whom I was created?"

"Homo erectus' termination was ordered and carried out."

"Wow! Imagine being part of a species that's been selected for termination and knowing you're being systematically hunted down and exterminated."

Wolf displayed no emotion like he was nonchalant about the whole affair.

"It was a terrible genocide! Why don't you care?"

"It's news to you, not me. It happened long ago ... It's done and dusted."

"Why were they terminated?"

"Having them around was a problem ... When humans saw them, they knew where they came from and they were naturally bitter about some of the changes made to their DNA ... Homo erectus had fur ... Seeing him was like a sphinx cat seeing a normal cat ... it can't help but be jealous."

Lilly had felt this sting of jealousy. She sighed. "How come the two lines of humanity can interbreed? Surely, it's leading to a blurring of the lines? Aren't the lines becoming one?"

"Yes," Wolf said, "and for now, that's exactly what we want because the slave race has greater genetic variation and interbreeding adds diversity to your line. Close to a harvest, we encourage it because the fewer and more scattered your people, the less power you have, and rounding you up is a cinch ... Your enemies will include members of your own families."

"So ... you're saying the Neanderthals' dreamed up the notion of a large intelligent humanoid that could carry a woman around in his pouch and feed her, and feed off her to produce the Elixir of Life? That they conceived the idea of a placenta that wasn't expelled when an implanted baby was born, but, rather, it radically changed so it could milk a human body and produce the Elixir of Immortality?"

"That's right."

"And Ox's probes … Did they imagine and dream them up too? All of this genetic intervention and invention was imagined and actioned by the Neanderthals before they were simply overcome in war and vanquished?"

"Yes."

"So, do I know all there is to know about the elixir now?"

"No, we've still much to teach you."

CHAPTER TWO

Christianity, riddles, and half-truths

Lilly tossed and turned in Ox's pouch before opening her eyes. She'd adjusted to sleeping in the pouch of a fourteen foot Bigfoot, a strange concept at first, but she'd adjusted to their symbiotic relationship.

"Morning," Ox greeted.

She felt her stomach, but there'd been no need, she already knew she wasn't ready to be milked. "You've let me wake early?"

"You're obviously bothered about something, so I thought it best to let you wake so we could talk it over."

"Wolf said Christ was the invention of Roman leaders and mystery schools," Lilly blurted out, having been sullen for days while mulling it over.

"I know, and he's right. Christianity was invented to suppress the pagan religions and truth along with them."

Lilly coughed. "Truth? Paganism wasn't truth!"

"There was more truth in it than there is in Christianity. Every successive religion has added another layer of whitewash while simultaneously removing truth from the world ... It's important you understand who Jesus is in the Bible: a goat playing many roles and wearing many crowns.

> Revelation 19:12 *His eyes were as a flame of fire and on his head were many crowns; and he had a name written that no man knew, but he, himself.*"

Lilly frowned. She'd read the passage before but never

considered its meaning.

"Verses in the New Testament are given clarity or altered by connecting passages in the Old Testament, but you can't rely on your Bible to point these passages out. While it's almost universally known that Jesus is referred to and spoken about in the Old Testament, it's not always clear he's taking his cue from there. For example, Christ's most important role is that of 'I.' Two connecting passages, one in the Old Testament and the other in the new, identify him as 'I' and expose his deceptive nature.

> *Matthew 13:*[14] *And in them is fulfilled the prophecy of Isaiah, who said, 'By hearing you shall hear and shall not understand, and seeing you shall see and shall not perceive.'*

> *Isaiah 6:*[8] *I heard the voice of the Lord saying, Whom shall I send and who will go for us? Then said 'I,' Here am 'I,' send me.* [9] *And he said, Go and tell these people, hear you indeed but understand not, and see you indeed but perceive not.* [10] *Make the heart of this people fat and make their ears heavy and shut their eyes, lest [for fear] they see with their eyes and hear with their ears and understand with their heart, and convert and be healed."*

Lilly shrugged. "Jesus is called 'I' and he's a deceiver...? Does that even make sense...? Couldn't 'I' be anyone?"

"In the Bible, 'I' is very important, and Jesus not only identifies himself so, but he also identifies himself as 'I AM':

> *John 8:*[56] *Your father Abraham rejoiced to see my day: he saw it and was glad.* [57] *Then the Jews said to him, you are not yet fifty years old and you have seen Abraham?* [58] *Jesus said to them, Truly truly I say to you, before Abraham was, I am."*

"I know many Christians think he is I AM," Lilly said, "They regard him so because his words line up with an important verse in Exodus:

> *Exodus 3:14 And God said to Moses, I AM that I AM: and he said, this shall you say to the children of Israel, I AM has sent me to you."*

"Indeed. God placed his spirit upon Jesus ... he was his avatar:

> *Isaiah 42:1 Behold my servant whom I uphold; mine elect, in whom my soul delights; I have put my spirit upon him: he shall bring forth judgment to the Gentiles.*

> *John 5:27 and has given Him authority to execute judgment also because He is the Son of man.*

> *Isaiah 48:16 Come you near to me, hear you this; 'I' have not spoken in secret from the beginning; from the time that it was, there am 'I,' and now the Lord God and his Spirit have sent me."*

"So, Jesus was speaking the actual words of God?" Lilly said. "Is that why he's called the Word of God?

> *John 1:1 In the beginning was the Word, and the Word was with God and the Word was God.*

> *John 1:14 And the Word was made flesh and dwelt among us (and we beheld his glory, the glory as the only begotten of the Father) full of grace and truth."*

"Yes," Ox said, "but Jesus wasn't the only one to speak God's words:

> *Exodus 4:12 Now therefore go, and I will be with your [Moses's] mouth and teach you what you shall say ... 15 You are to speak to him and put words in his mouth, and I will*

be with your mouth, and with his mouth, and will teach
you what you shall do. ¹⁶ Aaron will be your spokesman to
the people. He will be your mouthpiece, and you will stand
in place of God for him, telling him what to say."

Lilly sighed. "Oh, right."

"There are other potent verses in Isaiah:

Isaiah 48:¹² Hearken to me, O Jacob and Israel, whom I
have called; I am he; I am the first, I also am the last. ¹³ My
hand has laid the foundation of the Earth, and my right
hand has spanned the heavens: when I call to them, they
stand up together."

Lilly shook her head. "But, surely, Jesus is the Son of God and he alone is the first and the last? As the only Son of God, he's of great importance. Therefore, he can't be reduced to some mouthpiece called 'I' and be considered of no greater standing than Jacob or Moses!

John 1:¹⁸ No man has seen God at any time, the only
begotten Son which is in the bosom of the Father, he has
declared him."

"Most of the characters in the Bible are fictitious, including Jesus, and, not only does the Bible name another his father, but it also makes an erroneous statement while doing so. In the Book of Matthew, it says Jesus was descended from King David via Joseph, but, according to the Bible, the royal line died out five hundred years before his birth and priests had been ruling for centuries:

Matthew 1:¹⁶ And Jacob begat Joseph, the husband of
Mary, of whom was born Jesus, who is called Christ. ¹⁷ So
all the generations from Abraham to David are fourteen
generations, and from David until the carrying away into
Babylon are fourteen generations, and from the carrying

away into Babylon to Christ are fourteen generations."

"Hey! Not so fast! I know where you're going with this ... The Bible may say Jesus was descended from David via Joseph, but the next verse says Christ is born of God:

> *Matthew 1:*[18] *Now the birth of Jesus Christ was on this wise: When as his mother, Mary was espoused to Joseph before they came together, she was found with child of the Holy Ghost."*

"The verse isn't saying he's God's progeny because *Holy Ghost* has another meaning that I'll explain later ... The Bible says Jesus was descended from David via Joseph his father which clearly isn't the case. Rather, in one of his hats, Jesus, the Son, represents the tribe of Israel in the New Testament:

> *Matthew 2:*[14] *When he [Joseph] arose, he took the young child [Jesus] and his mother by night, and departed into Egypt:* [15] *And was there until the death of Herod: This was to fulfill what the Lord had spoken by the prophet, 'Out of Egypt have I called my son.'"*

"Yes, Jesus ... God's Son."

"No," Ox said. "God's Son called out of Egypt is the tribe of Israel and that's who Christ's representing in one of his crowns or hats that he wears in the New Testament:

> *Exodus 4:*[21] *The Lord said to Moses, say to Pharaoh, Israel [the tribe] is my son, my firstborn.*

> *Hosea 11:*[1] *When Israel [the tribe] was a child, then I loved him and called my son out of Egypt."*

Lilly shook her head in annoyance. "But Jesus is God's only begotten son:

John 3:¹⁶ For God so loved the world, that he gave his only begotten son, that whosoever believes in him should not perish, but have everlasting life."

"There are lots of sons in the Bible," Ox said. "There's even another 'begotten.' David is the begotten son in Psalms 2 ... Confirmation that it's him comes in Acts:

Psalms 2:¹ 'Why do the heathen rage, and the people imagine a vain thing?' ... ⁷ 'I will declare the decree,' the Lord has said to me, 'You [David] are my Son; this day have I begotten thee.'

Acts 4:²⁵ Who by the mouth of your servant David has said, 'Why did the heathen rage, and the people imagine vain things?'"

Lilly shrugged. "That can't be right!"

"Of course, it's right," Ox said. "In the past, rulers ruled by divine right. It was believed throughout the ancient world that a ruler was deified at the end of his reign when he joined the gods. Egyptian pharaohs were said to be the sons of Amen or Amen-Ra, and Greek culture and religion stemmed from the same source ... The Greek god Zeus was identified with Amen, or Amen-Ra.

"Credence was given to this when the Egyptians warmly welcomed Alexander the Great born in the northern Greek kingdom of Macedonia in 332 B.C. When the oppressive rule of the Persians was overthrown by Alexander, he was rumored to be the son of Egypt's last native pharaoh. While in Egypt, Alexander crossed perilous sands to the temple of the Oracle of Amen at the oasis of Siwa. On the way, it's said he was blessed with abundant rain and guided across the desert by a flock of ravens. At the temple, he was welcomed by priests who spoke to the oracle on his behalf. The priests told him, he was the son of Amen and destined to rule the world. The Egyptian God Amen is said to have said to him, 'You are my son!'"

Lilly exhaled loudly.

"Alexander was then crowned a traditional pharaoh and proclaimed a god, and he submitted to Egyptian ceremonies and wore Egyptian dress while in Egypt. After Alexander the Great's death, the era of the Ptolemy dynasty, also known as the Ptolemaic Period, began when one of Alexander's generals, Ptolemy, ruled Egypt as Pharaoh and lived in Alexandria. Uniting Zeus and Amen, the universal deity Zeus-Amen was then formed. Later, the Ptolemys' tried to unify the region under the god Serapis. The Ptolemy dynasty ended with the suicide of Queen Cleopatra in 30 B.C."

Lilly scoffed. "So, you're saying ... just as God said to David, 'You are my son,' he said as Amen to Alexander the Great, 'You are my son'? But Amen was a different god ... a fake god ... a pagan god."

"Was he? Well, God definitely didn't say to David, 'You are my son' because David is a fictional character in a book; invented and slipped into a historical setting. Whereas, Alexander the Great, on the other hand, is a genuine historical figure."

Lilly pouted. "I hate it when Wolf and you reduce my Jesus to nothing more than an invented humble servant ... a mystery school collective representing the tribe of Israel."

Ox cleared his throat. "You've been led astray. Instructed via riddles and half-truths:

> *Psalm 78:¹ Give ear, my people, to my law: incline your ears to the words of my mouth. ² I will open my mouth in a parable: I will utter dark sayings [hidden things] of old: ³ Which we have heard and known, and our fathers have told us.*
>
> *Matthew 13:³⁵ That it might be fulfilled which was spoken by the prophet, Jesus said, 'I will open my mouth in parables; I will utter things which have been kept secret from the foundation of the world.'"*

"His parables weren't riddles and half-truths! I understood and enjoyed them just like other Churchgoers do."

Ox slowly shook his head. "They understand them no better than you. The Bible's meaning is as lost on them as it was on you:

> *Proverbs 26:9 As a thorn goes up into the hand of a drunkard so is a parable in the mouth of fools."*

Lilly folded her arms in a huff. "No secret was kept from me via parables ... I'm not a fool!"

"No ... You were deliberately misled, but it's foolish to hang onto half-truths and defend them."

Lilly snorted. "Well, I'm not convinced Christ was a mere servant."

"I'm sure you're aware chapter 53 in Isaiah is attributed to Christ, but are you aware Jesus is called a servant in the verses leading up to it and connecting with it?

> *Isaiah 52:13 Behold, my servant shall deal prudently, he shall be exalted and praised enthusiastically, and be held high. 14 As many were astonished at you; so his appearance was so marred, more than any man, and his form more than the sons of men: 15 So shall he sprinkle many nations; the kings shall shut their mouths at him: for what they had not been told, shall they see; and that which they had not heard, shall they consider ... 53:4 Surely, he has borne our griefs, and carried our sorrows: yet we did esteem him stricken, smitten of God, and afflicted. 5 He was wounded for our transgressions; he was bruised for our iniquities: the chastisement of our peace was upon him, and with his stripes, we are healed. 6 We like sheep have gone astray; we have turned every one to his own way; and the Lord has laid upon him, the iniquity of us all. 7 He was oppressed, and he was afflicted, yet he opened not his mouth: he is brought as a lamb to the slaughter."*

Lilly frowned. "The Bible is a riddle wrapped in an enigma?"

"That's right … You already knew it wasn't written in plain language and people ponder over its passages."

"I thought it was just written in a confusing way."

"Your brain alters the text to make it fit the parameters of your mind and beliefs."

Lilly's brow furrowed. "Really? You think?"

"Of course … People regularly adjust religious texts in their heads to suit the limitations of their own minds to make them fit their personal beliefs while attributing meanings incorrectly."

"You're a wolf in sheep's clothing!" Lilly growled. "Just like Wolf is … his name's very apt!"

Ox shook his head and laughed. "Jesus was the original wolf in sheep's clothing. In an act of great mockery, he warned the masses about himself:

> *Matthew 7:15 Beware of false prophets which come to you in sheep's clothing, but inwardly they are ravening wolves."*

Lilly folded her arms. "Are you now trying to tell me Jesus is the false prophet?"

"Of course … The Bible covertly exposes him so … Spinning a yarn that's essentially a riddle while providing some clues, it should be viewed as a mystery book that fails to tie up loose ends; making you search out clues and piece them together yourself. Its truth will be revealed in time … Many references contained within expose its mysterious nature:

> *Revelation 10:7 But in the days of the voice of the seventh angel, when he shall begin to sound, the mystery of God shall be finished, as he has declared to his servants the prophets."*

"Where in the Bible is Jesus exposed as the false prophet?" Lilly said curtly. "I demand you tell me!"

"In the Old Testament:

Zechariah 13:⁴ And it shall come to pass, that the prophets shall be ashamed every one of his vision, when he has prophesied; neither shall they wear a rough garment to deceive: ⁵ But he shall say, 'I am no prophet, I am a farmer; for man taught me to keep cattle from my youth.' ⁶ And one shall say to him, 'what are these wounds in your hands?' Then he shall answer, 'those with which I was wounded in the house of my friends.'"

Lilly's eyes narrowed. "I've never read those words … Are you sure they're even in the Bible?"

"Of course they're in the Bible … I was quoting the King James Bible. Many modern translations have changed the word 'hands' to another part of the body so the passage doesn't point so directly at Jesus."

"Surely, the word for 'hands' was mistranslated in the King James Bible and corrected in later translations?"

"Not so … The word in Hebrew occurs eighteen times in the Bible and it's always translated as 'hands,' except in this verse in newer translations."

Lilly scoffed. "Christ's hands wouldn't have held him up at the crucifixion, so 'hands' is incorrect anyway … Jesus obviously had wounds in his wrists."

"In Luke 24:⁴⁰ Jesus identifies himself after he's risen by the wounds in his hands, and the word used in the verse for 'hands' is always translated as hands:

John 20:²⁴ Now Thomas (also known as Didymus), one of the Twelve, was not with the disciples when Jesus came. ²⁵ So the other disciples told him, 'We have seen the Lord!' But he said to them, 'Unless I see the nail marks in his hands and put my finger where the nails were, and put my hand into his side, I will not believe.' ²⁶ A week later, his disciples were in the house again, and Thomas was with them. Though the doors were locked, Jesus came and stood among them and said, 'Peace be with you!' ²⁷ Then he said to Thomas, 'Put your finger here; see my hands. Reach out your hand and put it into my side. Stop doubting and believe.'"

"I give up!" Lilly said, shrugging in annoyance. "So, the Bible has Jesus showing off wounds in his hands when nails in them wouldn't have supported his weight?"

"That's right ... because it's a story! And the Bible deliberately gives conflicting accounts while messing up historical facts."

Lilly gave Ox a frosty glare while straightening herself. "I know why some of the stories are muddled," she declared. "They were written to reflect the Old Testament ... The gospel writers used Jewish scriptures, prophecies and pagan myth forms to create new stories about Jesus's birth and life because in him they saw the fulfillment of Israel's ancient hopes and dreams for Jews and Gentiles in the world. The use of the Old Testament to tell a new story in the New Testament was a literary practice acceptable in those days ... It's called Midrash in Jewish commentaries."

"Well," Ox said with a smirk. "That's hardly honest and true ... now is it? So ... you're now admitting you knew all along that Christ's life was a constructed story?"

Lilly groaned and looked down.

"Historians used to use the Bible as a guide because they thought it was true. They no longer do because so much has been proven inaccurate ... There never was a grand King David, and the towns he supposedly lived in were tiny."

Lilly frowned. "If the purpose of Christianity and the Bible is indeed to spread disinformation, then aren't you sickened by the lies told by the leaders of humanity?"

"No," Ox said while shaking his head. "You obviously don't understand leadership and have little to no idea how the world works. Deception isn't distasteful, it's the law of nature. When you attempt to catch a fish, do you alert it to your endeavors and say to yourself, 'If I can't get this fish to swim into my open outstretched hands, then I shouldn't eat him?' Does a lioness ask a herd to offer up their young for her dinner, or does she creep up on them and pounce?"

Lilly sighed heavily.

"If you read the book *The Art of War,* you'll learn deception and leadership go hand and hand. Force alone seldom wins wars, whereas deception will because you must outsmart your enemy. A true leader understands this. He also knows the masses are a herd to be managed and manipulated."

Lilly exhaled loudly. "Cattle?" she growled. "Was the prophet in Zechariah who you claimed was Jesus, covertly calling the masses cattle:

> *Zechariah 13:⁵ But he shall say, 'I am no prophet, I am a farmer; for man taught me to keep cattle from my youth.'*

"Of course," Ox said.

> *John 15:¹ I [Jesus] am the true vine, and my Father is the farmer.*

Ox gently tapped Lilly on the nose with a finger. "Order is maintained by spin and lies ... carrot and stick. You must always maintain the illusion of having the masses best interests at heart while rewarding their loyalty."

"So ... that's it in a nutshell, is it? How to rule the world 101?"

"It's helpful if you can fool people ... get them to turn the other cheek and believe only the meek will get into a magical place in the sky called heaven. Then they'll leave you in peace, and when they've finished living their humble, subservient lives, they'll drop dead without giving you a moment's bother."

Lilly groaned.

"You should always keep the threat level turned up ... There must always be a bad guy and some imminent danger from whom you're protecting the populous ... Leaders create the danger, of course, and play it up for all it's worth."

Lilly shook her head in dismay while covering her eyes. "Who are you, people?"

"I don't know why you're so surprised," Ox said. "Your beloved Christianity follows this formula exactly ... The carrot is life after death and a trip to heaven, and the stick—hell and eternal damnation—while Satan is the bad guy from whom the masses must be saved."

"And you think our current leaders follow this formula, and: therefore, there's no democracy?"

"Democracy is an illusion ... There are usually two main political parties whose policies are extremely similar. They're two heads of the same beast controlling the masses by letting them think they have influence over policy and decision. In reality, leaders decide upon a policy and get lobby groups to campaign for it while simultaneously instructing the media to portray it in a positive light—give it a positive spin—to get the public's backing. So, people think they've had a hand in influencing policy when they haven't, they've been coerced ... as usual."

Lilly exhaled loudly, "Are human leaders, lower-level gods, answering to your leaders? Is that why some men in the upper echelon of British society are called 'lords'? Because 'Baal' means lord and they're in charge of people ... or, at least, they used to be."

"Correct. Pharaohs were worshiped as living gods. The word 'god' can be interpreted as 'overseer' or 'ruler' ... either human or divine. In this context, both Wolf and Cat are gods and they belong to a pantheon of gods. Ruling humans were and are, considered lower-level gods, or lords ... yes."

"And Jehovah was one such god?"

"That's right," Ox said. "El [supreme god] and Baal were worshiped alongside Yahweh [Jehovah] until he took over their attributes and became a monopolistic god. Over time, the royal court and temple promoted Yahweh to the God of the entire cosmos and he possessed the qualities previously attributed to other gods and goddesses. By the end of the Babylonian exile in the sixth century B.C., Jews denied the very existence of foreign gods and Yahweh was proclaimed the creator of the cosmos and the true god of the world."

"But, surely, he never had a goddess?"

"Of course he did," Ox said. "The sexual union between goddess and god was celebrated in antiquity, and goddesses worshiped. Yahweh was intimately involved with the Semitic mother-goddess Asherah who appeared in both Akkadian and Hittite writings and was identified with the Ugaritic goddess Atirat. Asherah was the mother of the gods and her divine epithet was 'qaniyatu 'ilhm,' which is translated as 'the creatrix of the gods.'

> *An 8th-century B.C. combination of iconography and inscriptions discovered at Kuntillet Ajrud in the northern Sinai desert on a storage jar shows three anthropomorphic figures and several inscriptions. The inscriptions refer not only to Yahweh, but also to El and Baal, and include the phrases 'Yahweh of Samaria and his Asherah' and 'Yahweh of Teman and his Asherah.'"*

Lilly's brow rose.

"Asherah was the consort of both the Sumerian god Anu and the Ugaritic God El, the oldest deities in their respective pantheons. When Yahweh was in the process of transitioning into a monopolistic 'one God,' he not only took over other gods' roles, he took over their goddesses."

"Does Yahweh, the Lord in the Bible, have anything in common with pagan gods?"

"His persona contains aspects of many different gods. He's called a potter in the Bible; a title borrowed from an earlier Egyptian deity of the Nile called Khnum. In art, Khnum was depicted as a ram-headed man sitting at a potter's wheel with recently created people standing on the wheel. Earlier in art, he appeared as a water god holding a jar from which a stream of water flowed. He was a god of rebirth, creation and the evening sun—a function later given to Amen. He was also the third aspect of Ra, and was titled the Divine Potter and the Lord of created things from himself:

> *Isaiah 64:8 But now, O Lord, thou art our father; we are the clay, and You our potter; and we all are the work of your hand."*

Khnum, the divine potter.

Lilly felt her belly, her placenta was full to bursting.
"Yes, it's time for you to see Cat," Ox said.

CHAPTER THREE

An important ritual

Sitting on the pools edge with Lilly, Wolf guided one of her hands between his legs. "Feel my nuts."

She tried to pull her hand away, wanting to slap his smug face, but he held her wrist firm. She glared up at him: he glared back.

Exhaling loudly, she begrudgingly opened her hand and cupped one of his large testes. "Wow, they're huge ... bigger than cricket balls!"

"That's right, Baby, and they're yearning to feed you, just like I am."

After dimming the light, Cat lit some real candles and placed them around the central pool before setting fake, glowing lotus-flower candles adrift in it. The sound of Benedict monks singing in Latin filled the courtyard like they were in a towering cathedral filled with worshippers. Lilly found the Gregorian chant emotionally pleasing, and knew, according to Church history, Pope Gregory the Great had been credited with composing the melodies for the liturgical texts in 600 A.D., but he'd claimed he didn't compose them. Rather, according to him, the Holy Spirit in the form of a dove landed on his shoulder and whispered the melodies into his ear.

Wolf pushed a button under the edge of the poolside tiles, on the first step going down into the pool in a set of human-sized steps. The tile covering of the first step and some of the poolside tiles drew up like a garage door opening before sliding under the surrounding tiles to reveal a sloping silicon mold with obvious indentations for a protruding belly and breasts.

"We've had that made especially for you," Cat said with some satisfaction. "Every baby is a little different and they're happiest in their own mold."

Lilly eyed the mold suspiciously. It was obvious she was going to be placed in it face down. Fortunately, the step was also lined with silicon and it had silicon knee indentations but her buttocks would be left high and exposed at the edge of the pool in a most unbecoming pose. She groaned.

"Yeah ... that's right," Wolf said. "We're going to put you in there and fuck you."

Lilly glared at him. "Is that any way for a god to speak? What if water gets in there, I might drown!"

"It has little channeled drains that quickly draw water away and return it to the pool. Now, in you go!" he said as he helped her into the mold.

Lilly's head settled sideways into a small indentation made especially for it. The belly mold drew her stomach in and formed a suction seal around it, holding it firmly. She struggled to free herself from its powerful grip.

Wolf placed a soothing hand on her back. "Relax."

Cat sat down beside her and rubbed some cream onto her arse. Almost immediately, she went limp and was unable to speak. Wide-eyed, her breathing labored.

"Relax, Baby," he said as he ran tender fingers through her hair before letting them trail down her back to her anus. After rubbing some lubricant in, he started preparing her. "Today is a big day," he announced. "This is an important ritual."

Ritual? Lilly sighed loudly, angry insult was about to added to injury by having her precious church music accompany their weirdo proceedings. *What's ritualistic about being fucked up the arse?*

Wolf rubbed her back. "Relax, sweetie. Daddy's getting his lovely worm ready for you."

Lilly opened an eye before blinking several times. *Worm? What the hell is he talking about?* Was he going to shove a worm up her arse or was "worm" merely a crude term for his penis?

Mozart's Requiem Mass began to play. Lilly recognized the

melancholy piece about Judgement Day almost immediately. The words and basic melody were sourced from Pope Gregory's melodies, supposedly, written by God and dictated by a white dove. The distinctive section is sometimes heard in movies. The 1973 horror classic *The Exorcist* opened with it, and Stanley Kubrick's movie *The Shining* also did, but in a different arrangement. Lilly had looked up the lyrics in the past:

> Mozart's *Requiem Mass*
> *Day of wrath and day of mourning*
> *David's word with Sibyl's blending*
> *Heaven and earth in ashes burning.*
> *Oh, what fear man's bosom renders*
> *when from Heaven the Judge descends*
> *On whose sentence, all depends*
> *Death is struck and nature quaking*
> *All creation is awaking*
> *to its Judge an answer making.*

Cat finished preparing Lilly's arse with his penis. He'd lubed her up as he crudely liked to put it.

Wolf took up position behind her and entered her. His rhythm was slow and deliberate at first, but unlike previous occasions when he'd been quick, and the whole affair had been over and done with in no time at all, he slowly built up his pace and force to a level she was ill-prepared for before climaxing with a deep guttural moan heard over the music while holding her buttocks in a vice-grip. Then, he firmly massaged her buttock cheeks with his thumbs and patted one of them too firmly before stepping aside.

Lilly breathed a sigh of relief. *Bloody hell!*

Wolf ran a seductive finger down her back. "You're a sturdy wee thing, built to take a pounding."

Lilly sighed loudly. *What a prick!*

Mozart's Requiem ended and his Confutatis began to play; the piece adding to Lilly's distress. For the first time ever, she wondered about the accused that are confounded:

Confutatis
When the accused are confounded,
and doomed to flames of woe,
call me among the blessed.
I kneel with submissive heart,
my contrition is like ashes,
help me in my final condition.

As Ox took up position behind Lilly, Wolf said, "Wash that up for me, will you?"

Although not nearly as rough as Wolf, Ox was still more exuberant than usual. He may have teased her in the past by saying he was going to give her a pounding, but he never had—until now. When he withdrew, Cat rubbed some oil onto her arse and gave her back a soothing massage as Vivaldi's four-season masterpiece, *Spring,* played. Filling the courtyard with its sweet tones, Lilly was grateful for both the tempo change and Cat's caring touch.

"Your arse is going to be a pretty shade of blue in the morning," he said.

Lilly groaned. *What did I do to deserve this?*

CHAPTER FOUR

Goliath and Angels

Ox rubbed Lilly's back and gently inserted his main, anal probe before picking her up and cradling her to his chest. "Come on, Baby," he said. "It's time for bed."

She looked up at him and sighed as he made his way to a corner shower. Standing beside a human-sized showerhead, he pressed one of the three gold buttons associated with it before directing a torrent of warm, sudsy water to wash his fur that got wet in the pool. Clearwater rinsed him when he pushed another button. A third button turned on a machine that blew warm air in a sweeping downward motion. Blowing strongly on his lower extremities, it made no noise other than the sound of the air, itself, moving. After he'd dried the same portion he'd washed, he raised his feet and dried each set of toes in the warm air before strolling into the cave.

"You're all right, Baby," he said. "Everything is okay."

"Don't just send me off to sleep, Daddy!" Lilly growled as she waved a finger about angrily. "Everything is not okay!"

Ox massaged her head with his lean fingers. "What do you want to talk about?"

"You lot. You devils! Why do humans associate with and worship devils?"

"You know why."

"Surely, you've outlasted your usefulness? Haven't humans advanced to a point where we're no longer requiring your services? Couldn't we make a longevity potion from plants and manage our own affairs?"

Ox chuckled. "Humans are light years behind the wolves. If they piss them off, they'll send a virus after them or hit their prize locations with a massive earthquake or meteor."

Lilly sighed heavily. "Really?"

"Of course."

Slumping, Lilly said, "The Bible doesn't speak of your kind or the wolves ... Why doesn't it?"

"It most certainly does ... You could hardly have missed the story of David and Goliath:

> *1 Samuel 17:4 And there went out a champion out of the camp of the Philistines, named Goliath, of Gath, whose height was six cubits and a span—approximately 9'9". 5 And he had a helmet of brass on his head and was armed with a coat of mail, and the weight of the coat was five thousand shekels of brass. 6 And he had greaves of brass upon his legs, and a javelin of brass between his shoulders. 7 And the staff of his spear was like a weaver's beam, and his spear's head weighed six hundred shekels of iron: and one bearing a shield went before him."*

"Oh, that," Lilly said dismissively. "People think Goliath wasn't really a giant—the tale more myth than fact. An exaggerated yarn to make David seem great; a legend among men."

"So ... you pick and choose which bits of the Bible you're going to believe?"

"The Bible is written in figurative language and people only guess at its meaning—"

"True ... and I agree, the story about David and Goliath *was* made up, but mighty men descending from the sons of gods did roam the Earth."

"You're talking about the offspring of the angels who mated with human women in Genesis:

> *Genesis 6:4 There were giants [Nephilim] in the earth in those days and also after that when the sons of God came*

unto the daughters of men, and they bare children to them: the same were the mighty men that were of old, the men of renown."

"They weren't angels," Ox said. "They were sons of God."

"They *were* angels," Lilly argued. "Sons of God are identified as angels in the New Testament. We're taught … angels are the sons of God and they don't take wives:

Matthew 22:[30] For in the resurrection they neither marry, nor are given in marriage, but are as the angels of God in Heaven.

Luke 20:[36] In fact, they can no longer die, because they are like the angels. And since they are sons of the resurrection, they are sons of God."

"There are several things wrong with your assumption … Firstly, the wording is 'are *as* the angels' and 'they are *like* the angels.' It doesn't say they *are* the angels. And as for them being sons of God … clarity is given in a couple of verses:

John 1:[12] But as many as received him, to them he gave power to become the sons of God, even to them that believe on his name.

Roman 8:[14] For as many as are led by the Spirit of God, they are the sons of God. [15] For you have not received the spirit of bondage again to fear; but have received the Spirit of adoption."

"So … you're saying, man never becomes a true son of God but rather an *adopted* son, and he doesn't become an angel either?"

"Correct," Ox said.

"Did those verses speak of the deceit in the Bible? 'Son of God' is, in fact, a term for the initiates of Apollo's son, Asclepius's daughter,

Ieso. Candidates in her father's temple were brought forward for initiation and known as 'sons of Ieso,' and called Iesous which means 'son of Ieso' and deemed 'Chreistos'—servants of God—"

"And 'Iesous' is Jesus in Greek ... and the church claims the word 'Christ' is based upon the word for priest, prophet or servant of God in Greek, 'Chreistos.' Therefore, the Son of God in the Bible is a collective term for mystery school initiates, and Asclepius, of course, is renown for his famous symbol, the Rod of Asclepius—the current symbol for medicine."

"Right?"

"Modern-day candidates or initiates are members of Skulls and Bones or they're high-level Masons."

"So, who are the angels then?"

Tablet of Shamash in the British Museum depicting god as a giant.

His outfit has the symbol for water on it. Babylon trinity symbol on table.

"Men born and raised in our world. The term especially applies to those who travel between worlds and instruct the leaders in your previous society. And the giants in the Bible are the Nephilim, god sons, who bred with human women in Genesis 6:⁴ and their offspring walked the Earth after the flood. The word 'Nephilim' makes two appearances in the Bible. The later day giants were hybrid descendants of the Nephilim and human women, and, as the mighty men, they continued long after the flood:

Numbers 13:³² And they brought up an evil report of the

land they had searched to the children of Israel, saying,
the land, through which we have been, is a land that eats
up the inhabitants thereof; and all the people that we saw
in it are men of great stature. ³³ And there we saw the
Nephilim—giants—the sons of Anak, which came from
the giants: and we were in our own sight as grasshoppers,
as were we in their sight."

"Then why are we taught that God is a spirit?"

Ox sighed. "You're not taught that. The Bible speaks of gods— plural. The Hebrew word 'Elohim' is used throughout the Bible. It means multiple gods, and the gods have bodies:

> *Genesis 1:²⁶ And God said, 'Let us make man in our image,*
> *after our likeness.'*

> *Genesis 3:⁸ And they heard the voice of the Lord God*
> *walking in the garden in the cool of the day: and Adam*
> *and his wife hid from the presence of the Lord God*
> *amongst the trees of the garden."*

"But the Bible speaks of the 'Spirit of God.'"

"It does, yes," Ox said as he rubbed Lilly's back. "It also speaks of the Spirit of Man:

> *Genesis 6:³ And the Lord said, 'My spirit shall not always*
> *strive with man for he **also** is flesh.'*

> *Revelation 4:² And immediately I was in the spirit: and,*
> *behold, a throne was set in Heaven, and one sat on the*
> *throne."*

Lilly sighed.

"To add to the confusion regarding the word 'spirit,' the word also means breath or wind, in both Hebrew and Greek. In the Bible, wind is the breath of life in human beings and the creative, infilling power of God. The Bible tells you the angels are like men … made of flesh and blood:

> *Genesis 18:¹ And the Lord appeared unto him [Abraham] in the plains of Mamre: and he sat in the tent door in the heat of the day. ² He lifted his eyes and saw three men standing nearby. He ran to meet them and bowed himself low toward the ground. ³ 'My Lord, if I find favor in your sight, I pray you don't pass away, for I am your servant:* ⁴ *Let a little water be fetched, wash your feet, and rest yourselves under the tree. ⁵ I will fetch a morsel of bread to comfort your hearts; after that, you shall pass on: for you have come to your servant.' And they said, 'do as you have said.' … ⁸ … he set it before the angels, and they did eat."*

"Oh!" Lilly said. "That's right, and the angels also ate and slept at Lot's house in Sodom:

> *Genesis 19:³ … they entered his [Lot's] house, and he made them a feast, providing unleavened bread, and they ate. ⁴ But before they lay down, the men of the city of Sodom surrounded the house—"*

"Correct," Ox said.

"So, the Bible speaks of real giants?" Lilly said, wondering if her religious training had counted for naught.

"Yes. There are multiple references to giants in the Bible:

> *Amos 2:⁹ I destroyed the Amorite before them, whose height was like the height of the cedars, and strength as the oaks. I destroyed his fruit from above, and his roots from beneath.*
>
> *Deuteronomy 2:¹⁰ The Emims who dwelled in times past, were a great people, tall, as the Anakims; ¹¹ Which were*

also accounted as giants, as the Anakims; but the Moabites called them Emims.

Joshua 11:²¹ And at that time came Joshua, and cut off the Anakims from the mountains, from Hebron, from Debir, from Anab, and from all the mountains of Judah, and from all the mountains of Israel: Joshua destroyed them utterly with their cities. ²² There was none of the Anakims left in the land of the children of Israel: only in Gaza, in Gath, and in Ashdod did they remain.

Deuteronomy 3:¹¹ For only Og king of Bashan remained of the remnant of giants; behold his bedstead was a bedstead of iron; is it not in Rabbath of the children of Ammon? Nine cubits [13.5 feet] was the length thereof, and four cubits [6 feet] the breadth of it, after the cubit of a man. ¹² And this land, which we possessed at that time, from Aroer, which is by the river Arnon, and half mount Gilead, and the cities thereof gave I to the Reubenites and the Gadites. ¹³ And the rest of Gilead, and all Bashan, being the kingdom of Og, gave I to the half-tribe of Manasseh; all the region of Argob, with all Bashan, which was called the land of giants."

Lilly rubbed her brow. "I heard a report of giants a while back. They were found in Lovelock Cave in the United States of America, in Nevada. Three of the skulls are locked in a cabinet in a local museum seventy-five miles away. I watched the first episode of season seven of *Ancient Aliens*. On it, they took the skulls out of the cabinet and placed one of the monstrous jawbones beside that of a modern human. The difference in size was tremendous but I thought it was nonsense."

"You have a habit of thinking things are nonsense. However, in your defense, such evidence is usually buried or destroyed and you're encouraged to regard it as fake."

Lilly shrugged. "I guess I should have been a bit more open-minded."

"Indeed."

She sighed. "But you guys can't be gods."

"Why not?"

"Because you're arseholes ... God is wondrous!"

Ox laughed. "And I suppose humanity is nothing more than a herd of lowly sinners who need to be forgiven? Listen ... God is an overbearing bully in the Old Testament, a jealous and vengeful creep, and that's the cleaned-up version. Hebrews tidied up his image and blamed everything on people ... especially women. Gods' who were worshiped as lords and masters in the past behaved in ways that were in no way exemplary."

"I see."

"You've heard of Titans, I suppose?"

"Of course. In Greek mythology, the Titans were giant deities of incredible strength who ruled during the legendary Golden Age."

"Correct," Ox said. "They descended from the primordial deities, the Neanderthals, and preceded the Olympian deities. The first twelve children of the primordial Gaia, 'Mother Earth,' and Uranus, 'Father Sky' or 'Heavenly Father,' were Titans."

"So, giants aren't the invention of biblical scribes?"

"No."

CHAPTER FIVE

Worm and Bunny tail

Wiping away sleep dust, Lilly winced as Ox lifted her out of his pouch and gently laid her upon the milking table before placing her feet in stirrups as usual.

"My arse is throbbing and my tummy hurts," she grumbled in a childish voice.

"Where does your tummy hurt?" Cat said.

Lilly placed a hand over her appendix. "Here."

"How much does it hurt?" Cat said. "Does it ache?"

"Yes, it aches."

Cat dragged a monitor over and turned it on before squirting some gel on her belly and grabbing an ultrasound wand. Placing the wand on the gel, he moved it about. "There it is ... a lovely big worm has taken up residence in your appendix."

"What!" Lilly exclaimed as she tugged at the monitor, trying to turn it around so she could see. "Get it out of me!"

Wolf appeared in the doorway. "No," he said as he stepped into the room to get a better look at the monitor that Cat was holding firmly. "It's found a good home in you ... It won't hurt you."

"It's a good size worm, Wolf," Cat said. "You must've been growing it for a while."

Attracted by all the commotion, Ox appeared in the doorway. Peering at the monitor over Wolf's shoulder, he said, "Yeah, that's a good-looking worm all right ... nice and strong."

Lilly's eyes were nearly popping out of her head. "Will you psychos tell me what's going on?"

"The worm will produce special hormones, enzymes, and

proteins that will circulate in your body and infuse in your wine to improve it," Cat said in doctorly fashion.

"What the fuck!" Lilly growled. "Don't be so bloody absurd! ... Get it out of me!"

"No," Wolf said. "I made the lovely worm especially for you in a cavity near my scrotum and I ejaculated it into you yesterday ... It belongs in you."

Lilly snorted. "I can't believe you shitheads deny you're aliens ... Who the fuck makes a worm by their scrotum and ejaculates it into another?"

"I do," Wolf said matter-of-factly. "And if I'm an alien, then so are you. We belong together ... we're yin and yang."

"That's your story!" Lilly snapped, "I'm not buying into it for one second!"

Wolf and Ox turned to leave the room.

"When you've finished milking her, give me a hollow will you," Wolf said over his shoulder as he exited.

Lilly folded her arms in a huff. Inhaling sharply, she caught her breath, the movement had made her arse throb and her stomach ache. She winced.

Cat looked at her bottom. "The boys did a real number on you yesterday," he said as he picked up a bottle of cream and began applying it. "You've got a blue arse ... I'm putting some numbing cream on it so you can cope with Wolf's affections."

"Affections? Abuse is more like it!"

"Don't get lippy ... If you annoy Wolf he'll make you suffer. Now, let's get on with your milking."

"Fucking alien pricks!"

"Stop it or I'll smack," Cat growled.

"You're all wankers! Especially you ... you're a sellout ... a turncoat prick!"

Cat smacked one of Lilly's bum cheeks.

She cried out in pain as her eyes watered. Sniffing back tears, she wished she'd kept her mouth shut—at least till the numbing cream had taken effect.

"I told you to shut up and behave," Cat growled as he poised a hand ready to give her another smack. "Are you going to be quiet now?"

Lilly nodded and looked away as Hello Sailor's 'Blue Lady' began playing on the sound system. Recognizing the tune, and it's intended implication, she sniffed back more tears before rubbing her wet eyes.

◆ ◆ ◆

Wolf appeared in the doorway just as Cat finished milking her. His timely arrival made her wonder how he knew the exact moment her milking was finished.

Eyeing the growing, hand-shaped, red welt on her bum, he said, "Now you have a blue and red arse."

Lilly sniffed loudly before wiping her nose rudely on the back of her hand and covering her eyes with her hands. Social niceties now a thing of the past—irrelevant.

"Come on," Wolf said. "It's not the end of the world."

After making Lilly almost delirious with his intoxicating mouth feed by the poolside, Wolf carefully placed her in her mold. Once in, she noticed a container down the side containing some creams. She caught her breath as Cat's fingers gently touched her arse, fearing it would hurt, but she was numb. Cat rubbed some more cream in before working her open with his fingers. "Good girl," he cooed as he entered her.

Lilly fought back tears. I should have run off when I had the chance!

As soon as Cat withdrew and stepped away, Wolf leaned over her. Placing a big hand gently on her shoulder, he licked her back. His long luscious strokes added to the level of her intoxication. Then he seductively licked behind one of her ears. As high as a kite, Lilly moaned and raised her hips, wiggling an invitation to him.

Wolf entered her with a guttural moan. Taking his time, he massaged her hips with his thumbs as he repeatedly pulled her toward him. Contracting her arse eagerly, Lilly moaned. All too soon,

Wolf came with a groan that sounded almost like a growl before withdrawing.

Ox followed up in a similar fashion. Then Cat did something surprising and out of the ordinary. He inserted some device into the entrance of her anus, and after taking time to adjust it, he inserted something into her anus before moving the device and doing it again. Lilly held her breath, but his actions weren't painful.

"Relax, breathe," he said as he repositioned the device. Working his way around in a circle, he continued to insert something into her.

Wolf rubbed her back. "It's over ... relax," he said as Cat removed the device.

Lilly's mind spun. What have they done to me now?

"That's a one-time event, Baby," Cat said.

"What have you done!" Lilly said as her intoxication level dropped and her mind cleared.

"I inserted some little grains into your anal glands," Cat said as he rubbed in more numbing cream.

"Anal glands? Humans don't have anal glands ... do they?"

"We do," Cat said, "but because they seldom become infected or cause a problem, most people don't know about them. The insertion of grains into them was the final part of our ritual ... All babies get little beads inserted into their anal glands ... You can't be a baby without this happening."

"Beads? I thought you said they were grains?"

"I did," Cat said. "When they go in they look like small grains of rice but they swell over the course of a week or so and become flexible, hollow beads."

"They swell? How much do they swell?"

"Quite a bit."

"My anus won't work properly if it's all swollen!"

"We've repurposed your arse. The new and improved you will have a lovely swollen anus ... a bunny tail."

"What the fuck!" Lilly growled as she felt behind her. Her anus felt normal. "What do you mean, 'bunny tail'?"

"The beads will cause your sphincter to bulge."

"What!" Lilly said, her eyes wide.

"The beads are much loved," Wolf interjected. "Your anus will swell into a lovely bunny tail that we'll rub and hold in our palms before enjoying fucking it ... The beads increase our pleasure and yours."

Lilly couldn't see his face, but she imagined he was salivating. "What lunacy is this?"

Cat smacked his lips together. "Thousands of years of trial and error have gone into both the apparatus and design. We have it down to a fine art. There's nothing to worry about ... You'll get a lot of pleasure from your sphincter when the beads have puffed it out. It'll drive you wild when we stroke it and run our fingers over it, and you'll want us to fuck you ... hard."

Lilly thought she could feel her sphincter swelling already, but she figured it was either her imagination or a reaction to the tiny beads being shot into it. "I think you should remove those grains! Isn't it enough that you guys bruised me up yesterday?"

"We tenderized you good and proper! Got your arse ready," Cat said. "The beads are nigh on impossible to remove ... not that anybody would be so inclined."

"I would!" Lilly said. "You had no right to do that to me!"

"Oh, come on ..." Wolf said, "where's your sense of adventure?"

"It's my arse!"

Cat moistened a finger before running it around the rim of Lilly's anus. No longer totally numb, she found his action intensely pleasurable despite her anger.

"This isn't your arse," he said. "It's *our* arse! We paid a good price for it."

"I thought you said you don't deal in money."

"Not money ... trade. Believe me, Baby, you were bought and paid for." Cat smacked Lilly's bum in a firm yet playful manner on the opposite cheek to the one that bore his red hand-mark. "This body belongs to us ... It's a kindness we do when we're tender and sweet to the consciousness that inhabits it."

"Consciousness...? Is that what I am to you?"

"For the longest time, we've captured and released your kind. After letting you run free for thousands of years ... you know ... to go forth and multiply ... we round you up again."

CHAPTER SIX

Obelisk & the Lady snake

Wolf lay on his bed, his head on pillows. Lilly lay upon him on her back. After running her hands over her softened belly and breasts, she sighed.

"I like it when you touch yourself," Wolf said.

"I bet you do! I thought you're supposed to be the brains of the operation, not a sex fiend."

"That's a sideline ... I love feeling my weighty balls swelling in anticipation of feeding you."

"You're supposed to be a god, not a grubby old bastard!"

"In the past, the phallus of God was a revered item of worship."

Lilly scoffed. "My religion doesn't worship God's dick!"

"Yes, it does. It just doesn't do so openly. You do know there's an Egyptian obelisk at the Vatican, in the center of St Peter's Square?"

"I know of it ... So what?"

"An obelisk is the sculpted representation of a phallus. Humans have long worshiped God's generative organ. In the ancient Egyptian tale of Osiris and Isis, Osiris was killed and dismembered by his brother Set [Seth] who cut his body into fourteen pieces and scattered it. His wife Isis searched for and found all the missing pieces of his body except his phallus which couldn't be retrieved because it was eaten by a catfish. In his honor, she built a tall column—an obelisk—as a symbolic representation of his missing phallus and buried the rest of his body under it, then she worshiped it."

Lilly's brow rose.

"Pan, a goat god in the ancient Greek religion, was a god of sensuality often symbolized by an obelisk—a long four-sided shaft with a pointed top shaped like a pyramid. And 'obelisk' actually means, 'Baal's shaft' or 'Baal's organ of reproduction.'"

"And the church went out and found one of these shady objects and dragged it back to the Vatican?"

"That's right," Wolf said. "The obelisk that sits in St Peter's Square was originally in Heliopolis, Egypt. The Roman Emperor Augustus had it moved to the Julian Forum in Alexandria, where it stood until 37 A.D. Then it was transferred to Rome, where it stood on the spina which ran along the center of the Circus of Nero, but in 1586, under the direction of Pope Sixtus V, the obelisk was moved to its current location at the Vatican."

"Maybe the pope wasn't aware of its checkered past?"

"He was aware of it ... The church has extensive secret archives and it has actively been spreading disinformation since its inception ... that being its purpose."

Lilly cleared her throat. "How do I know if any of this is true? You might be telling me porky pies."

Sumerian god Enki with living water and a bird.

"I'm not lying," Wolf said. "Twice in the Bible's book of Jeremiah, God describes himself as the fountain of living waters. This and countless other veiled references in the Bible, speak of the power of God's phallus. The obelisk that stands in the middle of St Peter's square is located within a circle—it symbolizes a giant, erect, dick within an anus."

Trying to sit up, Lilly coughed and almost choked.

Wolf patted her back in a patronizing way. "There, there," he said as she settled on her side and recomposed herself.

"What do you suppose is sitting on top of many churches?" he said. "It wouldn't happen to be giant dicks posing as steeples … would it? The Romans weren't a classy bunch; they were straight to the point."

"You're insinuating the Church venerates and worships an Egyptian god's dick?"

"Secretly … indeed."

After positioning Lilly's uppermost leg closer to her stomach, Wolf rubbed her anus with a couple of fingers on his other hand. "My phallus is yearning to feed you … my fountain wants to issue forth."

"I'm too sore for your *phallus*."

"Didn't Cat put some numbing cream on you?"

"Yes, but I'm bruised to hell … Can't we give it a miss?"

"No. I need to feed my wee worm … which is now *your* wee worm."

"Don't talk about that bloody thing, it's disgusting! Take it out."

"No, the worm is extremely important and it must be well-tended. I need to feed my wee worm."

"You're acting like the fucking worm is more important than me! Like I'm a vessel for your stinky worm!"

"I say … Baby. You wouldn't happen to be jealous of my affections … would you?"

"You can stuff your affections up your arse!"

"No," Wolf said with a wicked smile. "I'm going to stuff them up *your* arse."

"No, you're not! I hate you and I hate your bloody worm! I'm going to pull it out."

"That's not possible," Wolf said as he picked Lilly up and embraced her. "Calm down. There's no need to be upset … I love you *and* your worm."

"Shut up!" Lilly screamed as she rained down fists of rage upon his chest. Caught in the grips of a full-blown toddler tantrum, she screamed, "Shut the fuck up! You're turning me into a lunatic!"

Wolf gently restrained her fists. "You may have regressed into your child's mind, but you haven't turned into a lunatic just yet"

"Thanks! Thanks a fucking bunch. Now I need a shrink?"

"No, that's progress."

"Progress! How's it progress?"

Wolf ran a tender finger down her nose. "It means your mind is letting go of its autonomy and is accepting its dependent state."

"Charming!"

"Calm down, Baby. Relax. It won't be long before you're best friends with your wee worm and you'll love her as much as she'll love you. The worm within you will become part of you and you'll assume her identity."

"What do you mean ... I'll assume her identity?"

Adam, Eve and the serpent at the entrance to

Notre Dame Cathedral in Paris, France.

The serpent is portrayed as a mirror image of Eve.

"Eve means 'female serpent.' Her name comes from the root word 'hawwwah' or 'hevviah,' and the constellation 'serpens' was called 'little Eve' by some Arabs ... Adam, Eve and the 'female serpent' are seen at the entrance of Notre Dame Cathedral in Paris, where the serpent is depicted as a mirror image of Eve. This was common in early iconography because Eve and the serpent in the Garden of Eden are essentially identical. The only difference is one contains a serpent or worm and the other doesn't. The one containing the internal serpent was called 'serpent' and depicted so."

Lilly frowned.

"The goddess Asherah, who was at one time paired with the Jewish god Yahweh, was titled 'the Lady Snake Asherah' in an inscription in Aramaic (the language of Christ) and in Phoenician ... And in the Egyptian Middle Kingdom, pharaohs adorned their headdresses with the Uraeus—the goddess Wadjet symbolized as a raised serpent—a cobra on a sun disk. Originally her body alone represented the uraeus and she was often depicted coiled upon Ra's head in an act of protection. This image of her became the uraeus symbol that was employed on the royal crowns of pharaohs; the goddess Wadjet symbolized as a raised cobra with a sun disk. Wadjet was also depicted as a woman with two snakeheads, or a snake with a woman's head. An early image of Wadjet depicts her as a cobra entwined around a papyrus stem. Likewise, Ishtar's symbolic staff featured two entwined serpents."

Lilly glared down at her belly, to where the worm resided.

Wolf rubbed it affectionately. "In time, you'll become friends with her and when she's happy, she'll reward you. Before you know it, you'll love her."

"Listen! I'm not as bat-shit crazy as you! I don't fall in love with worms ... And what do you mean ... 'when she's happy she'll reward me'?"

"Well-fed ... She needs to be fed several times a day. As much as I want and need to take care of you, I want and need to take care of her. You'll come to love her as much as I do."

Lilly rolled her eyes. "She's a worm! You're acting like she's got feelings ... like you're emotionally attached to her."

"She does have feelings, and as basic as her needs may be, she's very important to me ... I grew her in my body."

"I know ... you said! But she's a bloody parasite! You should have taken a dose of de-worm."

"No, I shouldn't have," Wolf said as he scooped Lilly up in his arms and headed for the pool. Sitting down beside the covered mold, he pushed the button to slide the cover away. "Now ... in you go! I'm going to feed you *and* my wee worm."

CHAPTER SEVEN

Baphomet & the Cosmic egg

Lilly glared at Ox as he carried her into the cave. Not only had Wolf fed her wee worm, so had he.

"You're okay, Baby."

"Shut up!" Lilly growled. "I can't trust your twisty words! You're probably the evil Baphomet ... the goat devil. I've been thinking about it, and the more I think about it, the more he looks like you! He has a pouch with probes in it ... just like you do."

Baphomet

Ox sighed. "King Philip IV of France suppressed the Knights Templars by accusing them of worshiping a heathen idol or deity named Baphomet. However, modern scholars agree the name 'Baphomet' was an Old French corruption of the name Muhammad. It was believed that some of the Templars, through their long military occupation of the Outremer had begun incorporating Islamic ideas into their belief system. This was seen and documented by the Inquisitors as heresy. So, King Philip IV had the Templars simultaneously arrested and tortured on Friday, October 13, 1307."

"Black Friday."

"Yes. Later, in the nineteenth century, the name Baphomet became associated with the occult when Eliphas Levi published 'Dogmas and Rituals of High Magic' which included a self-drawn image of Baphomet. His Sabbatic Goat depiction bearing the words 'dissolve' and 'congeal' in Latin on its arms, is now the best-known image of Baphomet; depicting him as a breasted, winged humanoid goat with a burning torch between his horns."

"Yeah! You have much in common!"

"Get some sleep."

Lilly tried to settle in her pouch, but she couldn't. Wolf's words were bothering her, yes, but the ache in her belly was bothering her more. "The bloody worm is hurting me!"

Ox rubbed her back through his pouch wall. "She likes you ... She's happily growing in her nest."

"Growing! The bloody worm is growing!"

"Of course ... she's only a baby."

"Oh my God! How big will she get? Will my appendix explode!"

"No ... Stop panicking. Your appendix will expand to accommodate her, and the worm excretes special enzymes that will help it do so. Your appendix is designed for her."

"How big will she get?"

"Don't fret. You'll learn to love her."

Lilly moaned as Ox's sleeping drug washed over her and started taking effect. Sighing, she closed her eyes.

◆ ◆ ◆

It felt like only a moment had passed before she re-opened her eyes, but when she felt her stomach, it had grown considerably. She'd clearly been asleep for a while. Ox's internal cavity was sucking on her belly, pulling on it, drawing it in further.

"Daddy! What are you doing to my belly?"

"Enjoying it."

"Are you trying to make it bigger than its already voluminous size."

"I'm just enjoying it."

"Really? You like having my big belly in your cavity?"

"I like it about as much as you like having a big cock inside of you," Ox said. "Cavities, anuses, and vaginas have much in common—they like to have something big and fat in them."

"What a crass thing to say!"

"Breathe out and push it into me, then suck it back a bit and do it again."

"Are you serious?"

"Of course, I like that."

Lilly hesitated, undecided.

"Oh, come on ... Don't be a spoilsport."

Lilly wondered if she'd be in for another punishing session if she didn't oblige. Groaning, she did as Ox asked.

"That's lovely," Ox moaned as his muscles sucked even harder on her belly.

"I'm finding this highly disturbing!" Lilly grumbled.

"You're enjoying it, don't deny it. Your belly is a big fat heavy egg that delights us both ... I adore the sight and feel of it before you're milked."

Lilly clapped her hands over her ears. "Shut up!"

"Spoilsport," Ox said as he expelled her from his womb and sat her upon a thigh. "Do you want to see it?"

"See what?"

"My cavity of course," Ox said as he opened his pouch wide.

Lilly didn't want to look in, but she snuck a peek anyway. "Oh my God, it looks like a huge eye. A big slit eye like in the *Lord of the Ring's* movies. It's disgusting!"

Ox grinned a wicked grin. "Why, because it wants to gobble you up?"

"So you lied when you said you weren't going to devour me!"

Ox chuckled. "Yeah, like I was going to give you a heads-up on that! Turn around and let me poke you up the bum while I run my hands over your fat egg."

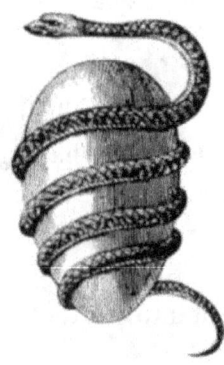

Cosmic egg.

"Ox!"

"Oh, come on … You'll enjoy it. Don't deny your man some pleasure."

Lilly choked. "Who are you?"

"I'm your Daddy, of course. Who do you think I am?"

"I don't know … I thought you were my protector. My lovely Ox."

"That's me."

"What's gotten into you?"

"Nothing … I've played the nice guy long enough. I'm tired of it … It's time for you to meet the real Ox."

"The real Ox?" *Holy shit.* "I'd rather not if it's all the same to you."

"Tough," Ox said as he began to finger Lilly's arse.

"Jesus—"

"No use calling to him … he won't save you."

Tears welled in Lilly's eyes. "Ox, I love you … Don't tell me the guy I fell in love with never even existed. I don't think I could stand it."

"Oh, Baby … don't. I was only having a bit of fun. For shit's sake, do you have to be such a spoilsport?"

Lilly exhaled loudly. "You just showed me your big scary eye, and now you're being mean! Your eye's the most disturbing thing I've ever seen."

Ox sighed as he rubbed Lilly's back. "It's not my fault if the leaders of the world terrorize people with images of my eye. There's nothing wrong with it ... It protects your egg and keeps it safe."

"Or it could be perceived as a big spooky eye hunting its prey!"

Ox ran tender fingers over Lilly's belly. "It loves your belly." He leaned down and kissed her stomach. "Don't be upset."

Lilly pouted. "Don't scare me!"

"I'm sorry, Baby. I want to be myself with you. I was hoping you wouldn't mind."

"Well ... I do mind. It's too much! And you're as much as admitting you've been playing me ... You're a creep."

"Oh, come on ... you like my eye. Your belly's been resting in it for months now. In the mysteries of Bacchus or Dionysus, noble virgins carried golden baskets containing small pyramids, wool, honey cakes with raised lumps upon them like navels, grains of salt, and a serpent. The symbolic pouches were similar to those in the Bible:

> *Zechariah 5:6 ... and he replied, 'It is a basket for measuring grain that is moving away from here.' Moreover, he said, 'This is their 'eye' throughout all the earth.' 7 And, behold, a cover of lead was lifted: and there sitting in the basket was a woman.*"

Lilly frowned. "Your pouch is 'their eye,' and it's symbolized as a basket in the Bible?"

Ox stroked her head. "I'm sorry for being a jerk. I'll take it easy ... wait for you to adjust."

Lilly wiped her wet eyes. "Thank you, Daddy."

While trying to pull herself back together and compose herself, a disturbing thought occurred to her. "Hey, Daddy, wasn't the eye in *The Lord of the Rings* looking for the ring?"

"Yes."

"If the eye is your cavity, then what's the ring?"

"Your anus, of course," Ox said. "The word 'anus' comes from the Latin word 'ring,' and people still refer to their anus as their ring ... The ring in *The Lord of the Rings* was called 'My precious, my love, my precious' ... Did that not conjure up an image of a woman in your mind?"

Lilly's eyes widened. "I'm the ring? I'm the ring of power? That can't be right ... can it?"

"There are lots of rings," Ox said, "just like there are many goddesses and no singular god, but, yes, *you are* a ring of power."

CHAPTER EIGHT

The Goddess "Eye" and the Fascinus

"Aleister Crowley, a sex magic occultist, wrote, 'Oh, how superior is the Eye of Horus to the Mouth of Isis.' From his statement you can ascertain that the anus symbolizes the Eye of Horus."

Lilly frowned. "Really?"

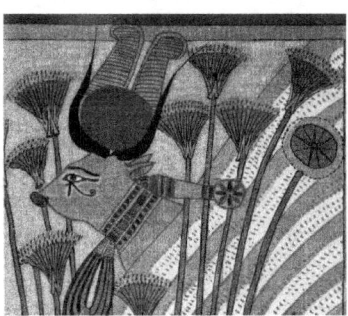

The Goddess Hathor in her persona as

a cow with an Eye of Horus

"Yes ... In ancient Egypt, the Eye of Horus or Ra had a separate identity to that of the god. In an Egyptian myth, Horus and his uncle Set [Seth] fight for the throne of Osiris after he's murdered and dismembered by Set. During the fight, Set gouges out and damages Horus's left eye. The eye is then restored by being spat on by either Hathor or Thoth. During the New Kingdom, the restored eye was said to have been created from part of Khonsu, the son of Amen, who was worshipped as a moon god.

"Horus offers the restored eye to his father Osiris, who, by devouring it, is recalled to life. After the myth spread, the Eye of

Horus became a symbol for eternal life and regeneration, as well as a symbol for sacrifice and rejuvenation. The offering, known as the Eye of Horus, was the greatest gift of all—the quintessential gift. The healed Eye of Horus was also known as the Wedjat Eye or the Sound Eye."

"So," Lilly said, "The left Eye relates to the serpent goddess Wadjet and Khonsu?"

"Indeed … After the new myth was circulated in the New Kingdom, the left eye of Horus and the right eye of Ra became jointly known as the Eye of Horus—the meaning of both absorbed into the one eye. Prior to this, the eye of Ra represented a separate being—the Goddess. The feminine counterpart of the Sun God was personified by several goddesses including Hathor, Wadjet, Bastet, and Mut. They extended his power and were considered to be his daughter, sibling, consort, and mother—his partner in the creative cycle."

"So, the more ancient tale told you who or what the Eye was—the Goddess—and the newer didn't?"

"Correct," Ox said. "As I've told you before … every religious update has added another layer of whitewash while simultaneously deleting knowledge from the world. Osiris's wife Isis was equated with the Solar Eye and the Eye of Ra, and later she was equated with the Eye of Horus, but the meaning was still diluted."

"Why was the restored eye also said to have been created from part of Khonsu, the son of Amen?"

"Khonsu was a placenta god … Osiris's healing and restoration was acquired from what remained after he was born … from his placenta."

Lilly blinked rapidly. "Tell me about the goddesses."

"The early Egyptian goddess Wadjet was symbolized by a snake or serpent—one of the world's oldest and most widespread symbols—the symbol of the goddess, and her name was derived from 'wadj' meaning green. Known as 'the green one' by the Greeks and Romans and as Uraeus in Egypt—from the Egyptian 'iaret' which means the 'risen one'—she was associated with other goddesses.

"The Egyptian goddess Hathor was depicted as a red cow with an Eye of Horus. When angered she became the lion Sekhmet, a bloodthirsty slaughtering war goddess. In her avenging lioness form she was known as the Eye of Ra. To stop Sekhmet's rampage, copious amounts of blood-colored beer was poured onto the ground to trick her. When she drank it, and got drunk, she returned to her gentle self. Ra was housed within Hathor in her cow form at night and reborn as her son every morning—rising as Horus the golden calf who grew into a bull. Likewise, he was said to have been housed within the lioness Sekhmet at night. Reflecting from her eyes, he was seen during the hours of darkness."

"I see," Lilly said. "So, what did the Sun God represent?"

"The sun's life giving properties: coming and going from the Earth in a repeating cycle and having life-giving properties, the sun symbolized him. Currently on Earth it's said to be night time, but when the gods return a symbolic new day will dawn. Covertly, the gods guide their human crop via human lords who do their bidding by protecting it and manipulating it—including purging impurities. So, when the crop's finally brought in it's not only immense but contains ample pure, uncorrupted seed. The ancient Egyptians called your kind Apophis ... an evil snake battled at night. Also known as the evil forces, your kind are currently called Lucifer."

Lilly frowned. "How's the crop purged?"

"Varying methods are employed ... Viruses and diseases that you have high immunity to, have been used to good effect. As has war which has not only weeded out unwanted genes but also isolated the crop to maintain its purity. The Spanish Inquisition was yet another brutal method employed, killing more often than not, people with dark birthmarks ... something your kind don't have."

Lilly sighed heavily.

"Such measures were necessary because without your kind there is only darkness ... Containing the god's goodness, you reflect it like an unspotted mirror. Viewed as both good and evil your kind are essential ... In the myth of the Distant Goddess, a motif with several variants, the Eye Goddess upset with Ra, ran away to a distant land in her wild feline form Sekhmet. In her form, she was as dangerous and uncontrollable as the forces of chaos she's meant to subdue. To restore order, one of the gods was sent to retrieve her. After he'd placated the goddess and escorted her back he was rewarded. Her return was celebrated annually at the beginning of the New Year, in a celebration marking the beginning of the inundation of the Nile."

Finding the ancient tales of Egypt intriguing, Lilly wondered why she'd never paid them any mind before. "So, the Eye or Ring represents the goddess?" she said, shaking her head in amazement. "Well ... Christianity really did suck knowledge out of the world ... didn't it?"

Bas-relief of a legged phallus ejaculating into an eye
on which a scorpion sits in Leptis Magna, Libya

"Yes," Ox said. "The Eye associated with the goddess Hathor and other goddesses called the Eye of God was of great importance. Likewise, an embodiment of god's phallus called the Divine Phallus or Fascinus which also had an eye—the penis eye—was of great significance. A graphic representation of the Divine Phallus getting it on with the Eye Goddess can be found on a Roman mosaic in Leptis Magna, in present-day Libya. The relief shows a phallus ejaculating into a disembodied eye with a scorpion above it. God's penis eye was also known as the Evil Eye and representations of it were painted: blue and white concentric circles representing god's waters were fashioned into amulets and painted onto the sides of boats. And amulets have been found with an image of a goddess on one side and the Evil Eye on the other.

Evil Eye on boat to ward off harm

"Invoking the power of personal protection, the Evil Eye amulet was known in Greece as an 'apotropaic' amulet … meaning it reflected harm. Talisman amulets symbolizing the Evil Eye are still prevalent in the Middle East. Known as 'nazars' they're sold to tourists, and some have a golden ring around them."

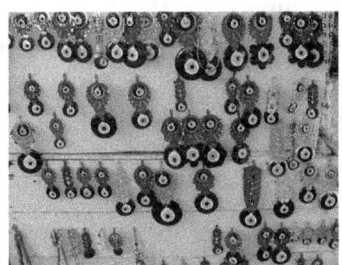

Evil Eye talismans

Lilly frowned. "Is that what's meant by the phrase, 'An eye for an eye'? The penis eye of God ejaculating into the eye of a goddess … into her anus?"

"Covertly, yes," Ox said. "It's also why some of the amulets have a golden ring around them … like your ring does. The blue and white eyes symbolize the bitter waters of God flowing from his penis eye:

> Sir 23:19 … the eyes of the Lord are ten thousand times
> brighter than the sun, beholding all the ways of men and
> considering the most secret parts."

"Why is a scorpion clinging to the goddess's eye in the bas-relief in Leptis Magna while the legged phallus is ejaculating into her eye?"

"A scorpion is a known ancient symbol for a womb. However,

shown above the Eye, the scorpion depicts what it actually represents—the goddess's placenta clinging onto her womb."

Cat entered the cave. "What's the hold-up? Why haven't you brought Baby in to be milked?" he said, looking at Lilly's still red eyes from having been upset earlier. He sighed. "Oh, I see ... you've upset her."

Lilly looked at Ox's pouch. "He showed me his big scary eye and it sucked on me."

"You should keep that bloody thing out of sight!" Cat growled. "You Cyclops idiot!"

Lilly glared at him. "Don't speak to Ox like that. He's not a Cyclops ... he's got two eyes."

"On his head," Cat said snidely. "Listen, Clopsy, bring her to the milking table and hurry up about it!"

Ox gave Cat a lingering dirty look, but he dutifully got up and carried her to the milking room. After gently laying her on the table, he left.

"So ... you've had a lovers tiff?" Cat said as he placed her legs in the stirrups.

Lilly sniffed.

"Oh, come on ... you love Ox. You haven't really gotten all bent out of shape over his big eye ... have you?"

CHAPTER NINE

Winter Wonderland

Lilly refused Wolf eye contact when he picked her up off the milking table. After he carried her back to his room in silence, she stared out the window at the bush—the ground was thick with snow. It was the first time she'd seen snow in years and the scene was almost magical in the low light. She loved snow, but the sight of it did little to improve her mood.

"What month is it?" she said. "How long have I been locked up in this hell hole?"

"You arrived in Summer, in December. It's now March and the first snow has fallen."

"This bloody house is exposed," Lilly grumbled, "people are probably peeking in the windows and leering at me. I know we're at the bottom of New Zealand in a remote part of the Fiordlands, but your sleazy pad isn't invisible!"

"You're upset with me?"

"No shit, Sherlock! You've inserted your disgusting worm into me, and your fucking Evil Eye has looked upon me!"

Wolf chuckled. "It's done more than look upon you."

Lilly glared at him, her eyes brimming with tears.

Wolf tried to look serious. He opened his mouth wide and rubbed his chin before looking out the window. "How about I take you outside for a walk in the snow, and show you how our home is disguised after I feed you? Would that please you?"

Lilly was immediately elated. *I'm going outside!* She wrapped her arms around him in a giddy embrace, his worm and Evil Eye momentarily forgotten.

Wolf looked down at her glowing face before positioning her beside his breast. "I'm not a monster, Baby. I'm your Daddy," he said, as he licked her behind an ear.

Lilly moaned and succumbed to his affections. Afterward, she lay slumped in his arms. Placated, she said, "Your dick is like a magic wand ... you've cast a spell on me!"

Wolf smiled. "I have, yes ... The chemicals and enzymes in my sperm sedate and drug you just like my mouth feed does. You're enjoying being anointed by my dick ... When the worm's grown ... you'll enjoy her secretions too."

Lilly clapped her hands over her ears. "Oh my God ... stop talking!"

Wolf laughed.

"Don't speak to me about your bloody worm! And what did you mean ... 'anointed by your dick?'"

"Just what I said ... The word 'anointed' in Latin means covered in semen," Wolf said as he got up and carried Lilly to the delivery room beside the milking room. He opened a drawer and took out a hooded onesie, helped her into it, then sat her down on a bench while he pulled on a pair of huge furry boots with a multitude of odd shapes on their soles. After scooping her up, he flicked his wrist. Two large cupboard doors slid open in front of him. He stepped into the elevator within and pressed the top button.

Lilly gazed at the multitude of buttons. Clearly, the delivery room had many levels above it, just like the cave did.

The elevator sped upwards before grounding to a halt. After its doors opened in a rocky outcrop, Wolf stepped out and into the woods. Lilly looked back at the elevator; its doors were closing and it was sinking into the ground. Within a matter of seconds, all that was visible was a boulder affixed to its roof. Nestled in among other boulders, it was perfectly camouflaged. "Wow, that's some trick."

Wolf looked back at the inert boulder. "You like that? It's a simple trick ... You don't have to be an engineering genius to pull that off."

Lilly looked around, she couldn't see their house or the mountain. She frowned. "There's no mountain?"

"Our house isn't at ground level and neither is the complex, they're deep underground."

"But I looked out the windows and saw the bush."

"Hidden cameras relay feed to the screens in our house. Everybody wants a view."

"So we live underground ... deep underground?"

"That's right," Wolf said. "I didn't want to tell you sooner because you were upset about living in a basement, so I decided to let you enjoy the illusion for a bit longer. As you can see, you don't need to worry about people peeking in the windows at you."

"Or busting down the door to save me," Lilly said dryly. "I know there are lots of verses in the Bible that speak of God hiding out, but I didn't think they were literal:

> Deuteronomy 32:20 Then God said, 'I will hide my face from them ...'"

"Well, now you know ... they *were* literal."

Lilly sighed. "Why are you hiding out underground anyway? Why don't you just rule openly?"

"This planet isn't our only home ... We live on many different planets, as do humans. Experience has proven this way works best. Human leaders are perfectly capable of managing the crop with little guidance from us when we're absent. We could pull off a harvest if the crop knew of our existence, even without human help, but we interfere in your lives enough. It gives us pleasure to let you think you're free ... for a while. The illusion of freedom is almost as good as the real thing ... don't you think? We'll rule openly soon enough."

"You travel? You leave this planet?"

"I can if I want to," Wolf said. "The universe isn't new to me, so I'm not that interested in traveling. I like living in my underground lair with my hive family."

"You care for us?"

"I do, yes. We entertain ourselves by chatting over our private net and partying together."

Wolf was moving at a leisurely pace, but covering ground faster than Lilly ever could. She looked down at her onesie, it matched Wolf's fur.

"Is my onesie designed to blend in with your coat?"

"It is, yes. It's providing camouflage and keeping you warm, but there's practically no chance of a hunter being anywhere around here anyway because we're miles off the beaten track and we have sensors and cameras everywhere ... The last thing I want a crazed killer to see is a big hairy ape carrying a naked woman, I don't want to get shot! At least with you in a fur onesie with mitted hands and feet, he might give pause before shooting."

"I don't know about that," Lilly said dryly. "There's plenty of idiot hunters."

"Well, hopefully, if they're idiots they won't suspect this bush is laced with cameras, and so they won't get this far."

Lilly looked up at Wolf. "I suppose you do look like a big hairy ape."

"Of course I do. So do you in that suit."

"You don't have an ape's head though ... your head is more refined."

"Yeah ... I'm a classy ape."

Branches rustling ahead made Wolf dart behind a massive tree. When he peeked around it, Lilly saw another wolf. He was walking towards them, his white fur blending in with the snow.

"Bloody hell, you scared the shit out of me," Wolf said, stepping out from the tree. "I thought you might've been a crazed hunter after a trophy."

"Don't be stupid," the wolf said. "If there was one of them around here we would have dealt with him already. You've alerted the whole hive ... There isn't a single monitor that isn't being watched."

"Can't a man take a walk in the bush with his new baby in private?"

The other wolf stepped in front of them. "Sure, let me see her, you've got her all tucked up ... Oh, there you are, my precious," he said as he reached out and gently stroked Lilly's face with a finger. "Ole Wolfe has been holding out on us. We're ever so keen to meet you."

Wolf brushed him aside before carrying on. "Yeah, well, you can bugger off and leave a wolf to stroll in the bush alone," he said over a shoulder.

"How many other homes are there like ours?" Lilly said.

"Too many! This isn't a high-density area, but there's still about fifty homes in this section of bush alone."

"Fifty homes?"

"Yes. Unlike humans who build huge cities and destroy the landscape while doing so, we leave our environment pristine ... the bush virtually untouched."

"So, there's a network of rabbit warrens below us?"

"Yes, and a new bunny creates quite a stir."

"Are your homes stronger than ours?"

"Absolutely!" Wolf said. "Yours are vulnerable to weather events and earthquakes, whereas ours can survive for thousands of years—rolling with seismic events."

"I think it's marvelous that you don't destroy the bush, and you don't require roads."

"You lived in a primitive world."

Lilly sighed. "I guess I did."

Wolf turned for home, his pace quickening.

"Are you worried about an idiot hunter?"

"No ... nosy wolves."

Another wolf jumped out in front of them. "Come on, you bastard ... give us a look at her. You've got her all hidden in that hood, we can hardly see her face on our monitors."

"Bugger off!" Wolf said. "I'll invite you over when I'm good and ready."

The wolf was not as easily brushed aside. He stepped in front of Wolf and placed his hands around Lilly. "Look at you ... aren't you a pretty one?" he said as he leaned in and cupped the back of her head. Before Lilly knew what was happening, his tongue was on her cheek and he was wrenching her out of Wolf's arms.

Wolf snatched her back before legging it to the boulder they'd emerged from. The elevator was already half out of the ground and its doors opening. The wolf laughed at him as he dashed in and hit a button. When the elevator opened below, Lilly was pleased to see Cat and Ox.

"Are you okay?" Cat said.

"They were jumping out at me," Wolf said.

"We thought we were going to have to mount a rescue," Ox grumbled.

"Bloody wolves," Wolf growled. "You can't trust those bastards!"

Ox strode into the cave in a huff, but Cat merely laughed and returned to the poolside while Wolf undressed Lilly.

"It will be a while before we go back up there," Wolf said.

"Don't wolves usually walk around up there?"

"No ... too many other bloody wolves."

"Are you all worried about getting shot?"

"Not really ... We're more concerned with being caught on film or photographed because that would cause all hell to break loose; this close to a harvest we don't take chances."

After removing Lilly's onesie, Wolf carried her to the pool and sat down on its edge. Cat was sitting on the opposite edge, his legs in the water. Wolf ignored his amused look as he attended to Lilly.

"Is Baby okay?" he said.

"Yes," Wolf replied shortly.

"Are you okay, Wolf?" Cat said.

"I didn't want that prick to run off with my baby."

"I would've been pissed off if that had happened," Cat said. "She's not ready for that."

"I know," Wolf said. "He was only playing."

Lilly watched Cat as he dropped his boardshorts and stepped into the pool. *Wow, what a body.* "I was worried he was going to accost me," she said, her eyes resting on his genitals.

"It's okay," Cat said reassuringly.

A speaker on the wall between Cat's room and Wolf's study made a beep. Lilly stared at it, she hadn't noticed it before.

"Who is it?" Wolf barked. "What do you want?"

"We nearly had her," a wolf replied.

"You upset my baby," Wolf snarled. "She was worried you were going to accost her."

"Accost her?" The wolf burst out laughing "Ha-ha, yes, we were planning on accosting her ... and abducting her too. Ha-ha." The speaker clicked off.

"Don't worry about them, Baby," Cat said. "They're only playing ... They won't hurt you."

Wolf rubbed Lilly's back. "It was just a bit of sport."

Lilly looked up at his relaxing face as he wrapped his arms around her.

"You're exactly what this house needed," he said. "We'd become complacent, distant, and aloof. The other wolves told us this, but we didn't listen. We had to have a new baby forced upon us. They snatched our old baby away and made us take another, but now I see they were right. We'd lost touch ... forgotten how difficult it is for a new baby to adjust. Your people had become numbers on a screen to us ... marks on a spreadsheet. I'm pleased you came to us."

After Cat selected a music file, 'Father Figure' by George Michael began to play. Lilly knew the song well. Knew it included the words, 'I will be your preacher, teacher ... I'll be your daddy,' and wondered if that was why Cat selected it.

Looking up at Wolf, she wondered if he was secretly pining for his old baby.

The music was too loud for normal, relaxed speech, so Wolf continued their conversation in her head. "You're like a breath of fresh air that's blown into our lair. You've given me a new lease of life, put vigor in my bones. I'd become rigid, stale. I needed you ... we needed you." He tenderly kissed her brow. "We'll take good care of you, Baby," he said as he got up. Cradling her to his chest, he carried her to his room.

After sitting on his bed, he leaned back against his headboard and sat her upon a thigh. Facing the snowy scene out the window, Lilly was absorbed in the scenery. Behind her, Wolf's main probe made its way out of his pouch. Like a snake creeping up on its prey, it slithered down and under her, eagerly positioning itself. Wolf parted his legs and gently adjusted her on his knee so it could advance unhindered.

The probe tickled Lilly's anus and gently made its way inside her.

Lilly looked up at Wolf, surprised. He raised his brow in a knowing look. Almost without thought, she welcomed his probe in by drawing her knees up a bit and folding one leg over the other to give it better access. Wolf moaned and clutched her to him as his probe eased itself in further. Suddenly feeling an urgent need for the probe to be deep within her, Lilly clutched Wolf's arm.

Wolf needed no further invitation; his probe raced up inside her at breakneck speed. Lilly gasped and clung to him as his probe's sudden advance caused waves of intense pleasure to course through her body; even the muscles in her face quivered.

The probe journeyed into her further than Ox's probe ever had. So far, in fact, it entered the worm's nest. Lilly felt the serpents within lock faces before dancing. Her worm quivered intensely— seemingly as delighted with the intruder's advances as she. The motion made the pleasure center in her brain light up like a Christmas tree as the rest of her brain faded. Panic swept over her but within seconds, she was too far gone to protest or care.

"It's all right, Baby," Wolf said. "Don't fight it … This is what's meant to happen. As my brain fires up, yours goes to sleep," he said as he opened his pouch and pushed her in. "You'll be safe in me."

After his pouch sucked her in like a big mouth, it seemed to chew on her as it positioned her effortlessly in place.

Sighing, Lilly drew in his nipple and closed her eyes as she drifted off to sleep.

Having devoured his prey in a big satisfying gulp, Wolf moaned his delight as he rubbed his full belly.

CHAPTER TEN

A legion of wolves

The moment Lilly slipped into another, Ox sensed it. Instantly enraged, he stormed out of the cave and into the courtyard, only to be intercepted by a legion of wolves. He snarled at them as he tried to brush them aside, cross Wolf had used his walkabout in the snow as a diversion tactic—a ploy to sneak in a pack of wolves.

This was a pre-planned intervention, he was sure of it. They'd obviously snuck in through the surface elevator after Wolf had returned and hid out in the delivery room, waiting for an opportune moment. Ox supposed this was why Cat had turned the music up so loud. His brow furrowed angrily. "Get out of my way!"

The leader of the rogue operation stepped forward. "No. You need to leave via the main elevator ... We'll discuss this in the room above."

"We'll do no such thing!" Ox hissed. "I want my baby back."

"We understand, but like I said ... we'll discuss this above."

The wolves clustered around Ox, corralling him to the elevator. As he was pushed in, he thumped an inside wall of it angrily, wanting to thump every last one of them, but he was seriously outnumbered. The elevator easily carried its heavy load to the next floor, when its doors opened the wolves filed out. Ox doubled back and hit a button, but the elevator wouldn't move.

"It's locked off," the lead wolf said. "Now come and get in the pool and we'll discuss this quietly."

Ox folded his arms. He wasn't mad, he was murderously angry and he was about to let rip when he felt a sharp jab in the top of his left arm. He looked down and saw a dart, they'd darted him like an animal. The rogue group had crossed the line now and he was going to make them pay. Well, he would have, had his muscles not weakened and he'd fallen on the floor.

The huge men half carried, half dragged his heavy body into the pool, then they sat him up in the warm water. Two of them sat beside him, supporting him so he didn't nose-dive under the surface.

Ox was surprised he was still conscious.

"We've sedated you and given you a powerful muscle relaxant," the lead wolf said. "Don't try to speak, you'll be unable. You can reply in your head."

"You fucking bastards!" Ox growled.

"My name's El," the lead wolf replied. "I'm Wolf's mate"

"I know who *you* are!" Ox snapped. "I want her! I want my baby back!"

"You can't have her. She belongs to Wolf. You agreed to train her and get her ready for him."

"I know, but I love her. I want her!"

"Yes ... It happens to the best of us. You've been poisoned."

"What? You darted me with poison?"

"No. Lilly poisoned you."

Ox scoffed. "Don't be absurd."

"You're aware our touch, saliva, and sperm, drugs and changes a woman ... and like a caterpillar changes, so do they."

"I'm aware," Ox said impatiently.

"Well, the same thing happens in reverse ... They alter us."

"They do not!" Ox snapped. "I've trained many a baby, so have my friends ... You're talking nonsense!"

"There's a lot you don't know ... You've always been given an antidote in your drinking water before and while you've been exposed to a baby, and it made you immune to them. We stopped giving it to you a few weeks ago."

Ox frowned. "How do I not know of this *antidote?* Is this a joke? Are you having me on?"

"No. We've just administered a large dose of it to you along with a muscle relaxant, but it will only calm things down a bit for a while ... take the edge off. We'll keep giving it to you until you join a team."

"A team?"

"Yes. Someone will stick their hand up and decide they want to finish your training and introduce you to their lair. Until then, you'll study and wait."

Ox blinked several times. "Is this how it's done? How you cause a powerful general to lose his mind and want to live in the basement?"

"Yes, this is how it's done ... You thought you were nearing the pinnacle of your career?" El laughed. "You weren't."

"I was! I was a commander and a chief, only one or two steps down from the highest level ... I still am!"

"No ... you were a boy soldier, and your days of playing general are over. You've been replaced."

Ox snorted. "I don't want to be relegated to the basement and given a desk job ... made to create plants!"

"Your days of strutting your stuff are over," El said. "You're about to become what you've always been destined to be ... a mature wolf. Only drugs have prevented you from becoming one thus far."

"Then I want Lilly. I love her. I want her!"

"You know you can't have her. You'll love your next baby just as much ... maybe more. With no lingering antidote in your system, you'll hunger for her with a fire in your belly."

Ox groaned.

◆ ◆ ◆

The moment Lilly woke, the memory of what had happened flooded back to her. "Daddy, I don't understand ... you're like Ox? You're not a different species?"

"That's right. We're the same species."

Lilly frowned. "Why are you white then, when Ox is brown? His fur is also much longer and shaggier than yours."

"A cold environment changes our coat's coloring from reddish-brown to white. Arctic foxes and hares likewise change color in winter. When you're asleep, the heating is switched to cooling in our lair. It's as icy in here as your cave previously was. Only Cat's room and the pool are heated when you're asleep. My fur is short because I'm regularly groomed. I like my coat to be just long enough to keep me warm and no longer ... Ox was training you and taking care of you while I nurtured my baby."

"The baby I gave birth to?"

"Yes."

"He's been here all along ... in your pouch?"

"Until recently, yes."

Lilly frowned. "But Ox never gave me a mouth feed or probed my inner chamber."

"No, because he was your trainer, and now his job is done and he's moved on."

"Oh my God, we parted on such bad terms, and he loved me ... didn't he?"

"He knows you cared for him, and he was fond of you."

Lilly sniffed.

CHAPTER ELEVEN

Lion & Eagle

Lilly lay on the milking table drained of her milk and wine. Feeling relaxed, she watched Cat set up to wash her hair.

"Cat, why are you called, Cat?"

"To delete knowledge from the world, symbols are often given a new meaning. When the lion symbol was selected for change and reassigned to the leaders of men, I mockingly called myself Cat, and the nickname stuck. A lion or lioness was a well-known symbol for the Goddess. Even before the time of Christ, the symbol was targeted for change. The first of Hercules' twelve labors set by King Eurystheus was to slay the Nemean lion. Leaders of men adopted the cat symbol for themselves after this."

"I see,' Lilly said. "And the Nemean lion—"

"Was a vicious monster in Greek mythology that lived at Nemea. It couldn't be killed with mortal weapons because its golden fur was impervious to attack and its claws were sharper than a sword; they could cut through any armor. According to one version of the myth, the Nemean lion took female hostages into its cave lair and the damsels in distress lured in warriors from nearby towns. After entering the cave, the warriors saw a woman feigning injury and rushed to her side. When they were close, the woman turned into a lion and killed them."

"And Hercules killed that lion?"

"Yes. After slaying the lion, Hercules skinned it with one of its own claws and wore its pelt as armor—his head could be seen under the lion's head."

"And the lion became a symbol for Hercules?"

"Yes. Then it was applied to the tribe of Judea and Christ upon his return."

"England has it as a national symbol," Lilly said.

"Yes. It was associated with the British Empire and the royal family after the marriage of Eleanor of Aquitaine to Henry II. The lion derived from the coat of arms of the Duchy of Aquitaine—Eleanor's family. It's now a symbol of British pride and might and has been forever identified with Eleanor's irresponsible but fearless son King Richard I, the Lionheart."

Lilly shrugged. "Does it matter that the symbol has been applied to Hercules, Christ, and England?"

"Before you came here if you were shown a picture of a lion and asked what it represented, what would your answer have been?"

"Christ or the British Empire."

"Exactly," Cat said. "Hence, the symbol was successfully reassigned."

"I see what you're saying," Lilly said. "Changing the symbol's meaning made the goddess less visible ... made her almost disappear...? Was it only in Egypt that a lion represented her?"

"No, the Babylonian goddess Ishtar's symbol was also a lion. There are images of her driving a chariot drawn by seven lions and her Sumerian equivalent, Inanna, was frequently depicted standing on the back of two lionesses."

Cat removed a section of the table under Lilly's head and held her head over a bowl filled with warm water. Washing her hair, he said, "When you read the Bible and were told Jesus was coming back as a lion ... did it ever occur to you he was coming back as a goddess?

> Galatians 4:4 *When the fullness of the time was come, God sent forth his Son made of a woman, made under the law,* 5 *To redeem them that were under the law, that we might receive the adoption of sons.*

Lilly frowned. "No, it never occurred to me and I didn't know the lion meant that. We're told Judaism and Christianity reject everything pagan."

"Of course … The Church doesn't want you to know they used ancient symbols as biblical code. The lion symbol pre-dates the Bible by millennia … Chauvet-Pont-d'Arc Cave in southern France contains some of the best-preserved figurative cave paintings in the world. They're approximately 32,000 years old.

"In the deepest chamber of the cave, in a privileged position on a hanging outcrop, there's a partial 'Venus' figure composed of a vulva attached to an incomplete pair of legs. Her pubic triangle is drawn in the shape of a cup. A man-bison reminiscent of a minotaur shares a leg with the woman and appears to drink from her cup. Her other leg is attached to a lioness—the symbol of the goddess."

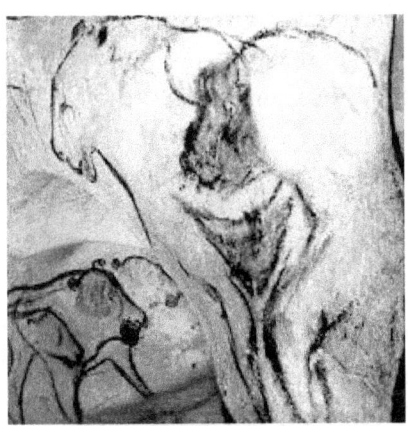

Venus and the Minotaur in Chauvet Cave

"I watched a documentary on that cave … I remember the Minotaur with Venus but was blind to its significance."

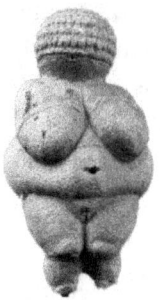

Venus

"From time immemorial, God has been symbolized as a bull, and the goddess as a lion or lioness."

♦ ♦ ♦

The water gently caressed Lilly's face as it lapped around her while she floated on her back in the central pool. Enjoying the afterglow of Wolf's affections more than she'd like to admit, she felt delightfully swollen and wondered if the swelling beads were adding to her delight. Eyeing the dragons on the beams above, she thought the worm might be contributing to her pleasure; already rewarding her.

"Come on, lazy bones, start swimming," Wolf said. "You need to get some exercise."

Lilly dreamily closed her eyes then opened them again. Looking at the dragons once more, she noticed they had tails that ended in arrowheads and thought they looked like Chinese dragons—the kind that was a hybrid between a lion and a dragon. She closed her eyes again.

"What do you call that? Floating on your back is not exercise. It's time for you to start swimming."

Lilly sighed. *Really? Must I?*

"Yes, you must," Wolf replied in her head.

Lilly stared at Wolf as she rolled over and tread water. "That's the second time you've spoken to me in my head? How can you do that when you haven't got a probe in me?"

"I don't need to have one in you ... Your body is soaking in my enzymes; they're our biological connecter. I'm tuned in to you."

Lilly lazily breaststroked to the end of the pool without putting her face under the water. Turning around and heading back in Wolf's direction, she said, "How far does the signal travel? When I was in the cave could you hear me?"

"Yes."

"Did you listen in on my conversations with Ox?"

"Only if they were interesting."

Lilly wasn't sure if the new revelation bothered her or not. What did bother her, however, was the pang of remorse she felt over her last conversation with Ox. It hadn't been one of their best and she wasn't able to say goodbye or tell him she loved him. She sighed audibly. *Why would he even care? He was only training me and he's probably training another already.*

With a flick of his hand, Wolf indicated she should turn around and swim back to the end of the pool. She groaned: the pool was small for Wolf but lengthy for her. "Must I keep swimming?"

"I'll tell you when you've had enough."

"I thought you were all about work? Isn't sitting by the pool and watching me swim a frivolous waste of your time?"

"Being with you is never a waste of my time."

"Aren't you meant to be saving the world?"

"Everything is in hand."

Lilly was drawn to Wolf but she kept swimming. "Do you only work when it suits you?"

"Don't insinuate I'm lazy. Look at you ... a few lengths of the pool and you're grizzling."

"It's not my fault if I'm fed heaps and carried around. You've turned me into a fat little pig."

Wolf grinned. "That's the way we like you. Whoever desired a thin calf?"

"I don't like it when you objectify me," Lilly grumbled.

"Don't pretend to find my attentions displeasing," Wolf said, his eyes flashing.

"You look like a predator eyeing up its prey."

"It's one of the reasons why ancient cultures symbolized me as an eagle ... Romans carried an eagle standard into battle to represent their god. Osiris's son Horus was symbolized as a falcon or hawk, and Hindus and Buddhists worship a large hybrid eagle-type bird, a mythical, humanoid bird called Garuda. Imagery of God as an eagle is also found in the Bible. When God brought Israel out of Egypt, he bore his people up as young eaglets on his pinions, the outer wings of an eagle, and flew with them."

"I know God is symbolized as an eagle in the Bible and I've heard of Garuda airlines, but I didn't know about the hybrid eagle called

Garuda."

"The word for 'eagle' in Sanskrit is Śyena. In the Vedas, it's a mighty bird. Later, it became the Hindus' and Buddhists' Garuda often depicted with a human body and wings. The Jews also have a mythical bird called Ziz, and it has enormous wings too and the head of an eagle."

Lilly trod water. "How am I supposed to know any of this? I had my own religion and I took it seriously which meant rejecting other religions."

"Of course … Current religions all have that directive, it helps prevent the dot connection of historical information surviving in the world."

Lilly sighed. Obviously, she'd been very selective in what she'd chosen to learn.

Wolf leaned forward his mood playful. "Come here, Bunny. Ole Wolfe wants to make a meal of you."

Unable to resist the urge to tease, Lilly backed away. "Maybe I need to swim some more?" she said. "It wouldn't do for me to get too fat."

Wolf grinned. "It's not good to tease Ole Wolfe."

"Really?" Lilly said, remembering a childhood game. "What's the time, Mr. Wolf?"

Wolf chuckled. "It's time to eat you up."

Lilly grinned as she quickened her pace. "Is it now?"

Wolf beamed. "Yes, it is," he said as he sank into the water and moved towards her. "Ole Wolfe is going to gobble you up."

Lilly made a half-hearted attempt to get away, but Wolf was on her in a second. She let out a playful scream before turning to wrap her arms around his neck. Wolf sat on the bottom of the pool and cradled her to his shoulder. The water barely reached his pecs.

"I see the pool's designed for me."

"Indeed," Wolf said. "Well, that's not strictly true … the perverts who live here like to leer at you as you splash about."

"Fancy that! I'd never have guessed," Lilly said somewhat flatly, her mind returning to Ox. She tried not to let it show, but she missed him, and anything that reminded her of him, stung. She sighed.

Cat smiled as he walked by. Stopping momentarily, he put a song on before continuing to his room. Hot Chocolate's 'You Sexy Thing' began to play.

Wolf kissed Lilly on a cheek before returning to the side of the pool with her and pulling her onto his knee in a warm embrace.

She smiled as she lay her head upon him. "I think I love you despite your predatory ways," she said.

"I love you, Baby," Wolf said, as he kissed her brow tenderly. "I want you to feel secure in my arms, to feel loved and well-tended."

Lilly closed her eyes as Wolf ran a seductive finger down her spine before lovingly giving her swelling anus a gentle rub. "My wee bunny," he said.

Lilly enjoyed the rub despite herself. Seizing upon a possible opportunity. she said, "Daddy, do you think you can remove the worm, its growth is freaking me out ... look at my fat tummy."

"Oh, I see, you were sucking up to me to get your own way ... Well, it won't work ... the worm stays."

Lilly groaned.

"Nice try though, Baby," Wolf said in her head. "I would enjoy it very much if you'd suckle on one of my breasts."

Lilly frowned. "Are you trying to distract me from how much you're using me?"

"I want to feed you, nurse you."

"Your breasts have milk?"

"Not much currently, but I'll make more if you feed from me." Wolf cupped Lilly's head in one of his big hands and gently guided it to one of his nipples. "Daddy loves you and he wants to feed and take care of you."

Lilly latched on. Sucking on a nipple surrounded by fur felt weird, but it wasn't an awful experience. Wolf's fur was after all, soft and silky. She sighed. It seemed she could get used to anything.

"Do you want Daddy to take care of you, Baby?"

"I like it when you're sweet ... When your affections are gentle and kind."

"I like feeding you. I want to pour myself into you ... water you like a garden."

Closing her eyes, Lilly continued to suckle on Wolf's nipple even though it didn't contain much milk, enjoying his embrace.

Wolf cradled her like a nursing parent. "Thank you," he said. "It pleases me to have you at my breast."

"I'm worthy of your attention?"

Wolf laughed. "You worry I'm using you, then in the next breath you think you're not worthy of my attention?"

"Everybody wants God to pay them some mind."

"You're right … People want my attention. They long for it and worship me even though they have no understanding of who or what I am. It's part of the human condition, how you're designed, and why humans are nicknamed dog … but, of course, I would be nothing in their eyes if I didn't have something to give." Wolf rubbed Lilly's belly. "It's almost criminal that knowledge of you has been suppressed; almost erased from the face of the Earth. You're every bit as glorious as me, and without you, I'm nothing."

Lilly shrugged. "Feminism has tried to give women equality, but when women are still insulted and called whores for enjoying sex and being liberal with their affections, it's as if no progress has been made … You make me feel good, and in a way, I feel a sense of freedom here that I've never felt before," Lilly said, thinking about how she was in love with three men at the same time and was feeling no shame about it.

"Are you feeling particularly good since I've fed you and your wee worm?

She groaned. "I guess …"

"The worm releases a drug into your system that makes you feel good … it's part of her charm."

Lilly wished the drug was strong enough to suppress her grieving. There was little point in having a discussion about it though because Wolf already knew what she was thinking and feeling, and clearly, he was choosing not to talk about it, just like she was. "Does the drug affect my wine?"

"Yes."

"And those who drink it … does it affect them also?"

"Absolutely," Wolf said. "Humans quickly become addicted to it and will do almost anything to get it."

"Are you serious?"

"Yes. Along with having a positive effect on their health and well-being, it makes them feel great."

"What about my health?"

"Your wee worm's already having a positive effect upon it."

"Are you sure you're not making that up...? You know she makes my stomach ache?" Lilly said wondering why she wasn't currently in any pain. *Am I too upset to notice?*

"The ache's only temporary ... growing pains. You feel it worst after I've just fed you both, but the drugs building up in your system are increasingly reducing your pain and relieving your distress ... You'll feel better soon."

Lilly sighed. So ... we've discussed it.

CHAPTER TWELVE

The Trinity

"Let's talk about the Trinity," Wolf said, changing the subject. "In the classical world, ancients worshiped the same gods in different languages. The Egyptians' New Kingdom gods were Amen, Khonsu, and Mut—the Father, Son, and Mother."

Lilly frowned. "Mother or Mut means both mother and Holy Ghost?"

"Yes, and 'Amen' wasn't just a word used at the end of prayers, he was an Egyptian god and the husband of Mut equating to Mary, and their son Khonsu was cognate to Jesus. The word, *Holy Spirit* or *Holy Ghost* comes from an Old English word, 'gast,' meaning spirit, and she's the third divine person in the Trinity according to the Fourth Lateran Council:

> *The Godhead is made up of three divine persons.*
> Fourth Lateran Council"

Lilly shook her head. "But, surely, the Holy Ghost is God's spirit and it lives in the sky."

"If that were so, then why did Clement of Alexandria, a father of the church, write, 'flesh represents the Holy Spirit'?"

Lilly hadn't heard this before. She shrugged.

"In 325 A.D., the Roman Emperor Constantine incorporated the Trinity into the newly formed Christian religion—incorporating the theory of Egypt's New Kingdom gods into Christianity—and the Catholic Church worships and venerates Mut's equivalent Mary and labels her the 'Queen of Heaven; a pagan title for the mother goddess

Asherah mentioned in the Bible. Asherah's symbol was a dove just like Mary's is. In the 'Coronation of the Virgin' or 'Coronation of Mary' a subject in Christian art, a dove flies above Mary's head while Jesus accompanied by the Father places a crown upon her head. Together, they crown her the 'Queen of Heaven.'"

The Coronation of Mary

Lilly frowned. "Really?"

"Amen was symbolized as a ram and depicted as a ram-headed man. This, of course, made his son Khonsu a symbolic lamb paralleling Jesus—the Lamb of God."

"So, Christianity is a 'copy and paste' with a few name changes?"

"Essentially, yes ... minus some critical information of course. The traditional symbol for the Christian Trinity demonstrates that neither the Father nor the Son is God, but, rather, the Father, the Son, *and* the Holy Ghost—the mother—are *jointly* God. The Fourth Lateran Council declared:

> *It is the Father who generates, the Son who is begotten,*
> *'sired' and the Holy Spirit who proceeds—goes forth from*
> *the source. While distinct in their relations with one*

another, they are 'one' in all else. The work of creation and grace is a single operation common to all three divine persons, who at the same time operate according to their own unique properties. So that all things are from the Father, through the Son and 'in' the Holy Spirit."

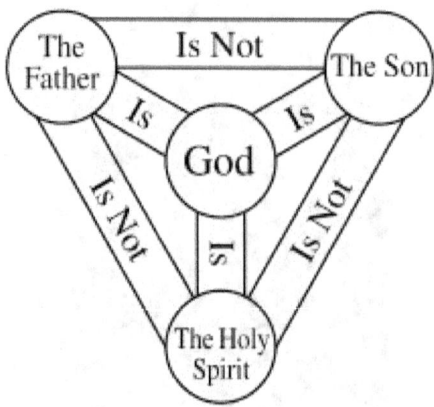

The "Shield of the Trinity" or Scutum Fidei diagram of medieval symbolism, dating from the twelfth century.

"And the father, God, sires his own full-blooded offspring via the goddess, but Jesus, in one of his crowns worn, was a demi-god son equating to the proceeding seedline or the goddess [Holy Ghost] and he also roleplayed the true son?"

"Yes ... we're genetically linked. The information was easier to decipher in previous religious trinity symbols ... not that you're likely to recognize them as such.

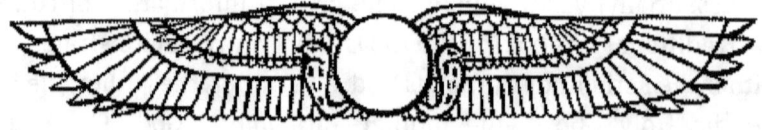

Egyptian trinity

"In ancient Egypt's religion, the serpent Uraeus symbolized the goddess Wadjet who was depicted either as a singular or double-headed serpent. In Egypt's trinity symbol, the two serpents surrounding the globe represented her. The globe itself is the placenta—the son—or what remains of him, and the adorning wings symbolized the Father ... God."

"The globe is a placenta?" Lilly said. "I thought it symbolized the sun."

"Depictions of the rising sun in ancient Egyptian art often show Ra as a child within a rising solar disk emerging from the body of the sky goddess. The rising sun represented his birth and the hieroglyph for Ra is a circle with a dot in the middle; a circled dot or circumpunct is still the symbol for gold and the sun. The Egyptian solar disk was usually colored red because it also symbolized a placenta within a womb."

"I see."

"The wings of the Egyptian trinity symbolized God's vivifying power."

Lilly frowned. "What's meant by that ... vivifying power?"

Fascinus of Rome

"God was symbolized as a giant bird of prey, an eagle or a falcon, and his virility was depicted by wings in flight—a flying phallus. The first crosses drawn were flying penises; God's phallus taking flight. The active wings represented his virility and the power of his penis."

Lilly blinked several times.

"Like the fascinus of Rome, a flying phallus in the shape of a cross was sometimes worn as an earring. The wings on the phallus representing the *penetrative power* of God symbolized as an eagle from time immemorial."

"But the cross is a Christian symbol ... isn't it?"

Wolf cleared his throat. "The New Catholic Encyclopaedia states:

> 'The Cross is found in both pre-Christian and non-Christian cultures.' New Catholic Encyclopaedia"

"Therefore, the cross isn't a Christian symbol ... and Christians didn't honor or worship a cross till it was promoted as a Christian symbol in the fourth century by Constantine."

"But surely it is a Christian symbol?" Lilly said. "Christ died on a cross after all."

"Christ didn't die on a cross ... The Greek word translated as 'cross' in the Bible is 'stau·ros,' an upright pale or stake. 'Stau·ros' has never meant two pieces of timber placed across one another. Nothing in the Greek New Testament implies two pieces of timber. And in multiple texts, biblical writers used the Greek word 'xy'lon' for the instrument of Jesus's death—a word meaning timber, stick, club or tree. A lack of timber at chosen places for public execution often saw simple beams sunk into the ground. On these, the outlaws had their hands raised upwards and their feet bound or nailed."

"So, Jesus was nailed to a stake?"

"A tree ... symbolically:

> Acts 5:³⁰ The God of our fathers raised up Jesus, whom you slew and hung on a tree."

Lilly frowned.

"Religious symbolism has remained intact over the centuries ... Before the Rod of Asclepius symbol was reassigned to the masculine, it represented the goddess Asherah and was seen at the Temple of Jerusalem. Asherah's places of worship were called groves, and the Hebrew word for Asherah could refer to either the goddess or a grove of trees."

"So, was *she* nailed to a stake or rod?"

Rod of Asclepius or Nehushtan

"No ... and neither was Jesus. The rod or tree was symbolic; it wasn't an instrument of death. Limbless tree trunks were carved into symbolic representations of the goddess at her places of worship—carved into rods of Asclepius. In the Bible, Asherah's symbol is called a Nehushtan ... Confirmation that the symbolic carvings represent her comes in 2 Kings:

> *2 Kings 18:4 "King Hezekiah removed the pagan shrines, smashed the sacred pillars, and cut down the groves [Asherah poles]. He broke up the bronze serpent that Moses had made because the people of Israel had been offering sacrifices to it. Hezekiah called the bronze serpent Nehushtan."*

Lilly's brow rose. "So, the bronze serpent that Moses placed upon a pole was called Nehushtan, and it was a rod of Asclepius?"

"I'm sure you know of these verses in numbers:

> *Numbers 21:5 And the people spoke against God, and against Moses, 'Why have you brought us up out of Egypt to die in the wilderness? There's no water, and our soul loathes this worthless bread.' 6 And the Lord sent fiery serpents among the people, and it bit some of the people, and many died. 7 The people then came to Moses, and said,*

> 'We've sinned; we've spoken against the Lord, and against you; pray to the Lord that he takes the serpents away from us.' And Moses prayed for the people. *8 And the Lord said to Moses, 'Make a fiery serpent, and set it upon a pole: and it shall come to pass that everyone that was bitten when he looks upon it shall live.' And Moses made a serpent of bronze and put it upon a pole, and it came to pass that if a serpent had bitten a man when he beheld the bronze serpent, he lived."*

"I know of those verses."

"Are you aware they're referenced in the New Testament ... in John?

> *John 3:14 and as Moses lifted up the serpent in the wilderness, even so, must the Son of man be lifted up."*

"I remember it—"

"Right," Wolf said, "Now, keep in mind that Christ wears many hats—crowns—in the New Testament and he's not only role-playing the true son of God but also a proceeding seedline which is highlighted by the verses linking him to God's son called out of Egypt—the tribe of Israel. With this in mind, we should surely realize that Jesus isn't a historical figure.

> *Matthew 2:14 When he [Joseph] arose, he took the young child [Jesus] and his mother by night, and departed into Egypt: 15 And was there until the death of Herod: This was to fulfill what the Lord had spoken by the prophet, 'Out of Egypt have I called my son.'*
>
> *Exodus 4:21 The Lord said to Moses, say to Pharaoh, Israel [the tribe] is my son, my firstborn.*
>
> *Hosea 11:1 When Israel [the tribe] was a child, then I loved him and called my son out of Egypt.*

"And Jesus represents the true Son in some texts equating him with the Father:

> *John 10:[30] I and my Father are one."*

"Of course, and the seedline and the Holy Ghost or Holy Spirit are essentially the same entity in the Bible:

> *Matthew 3:[16] And Jesus when he was baptized, went up straightway from the water: and lo, the heavens were opened unto him, and he saw the Spirit of God descending as a dove, and coming upon him.*

> *Luke 12:[21] In that same hour he rejoiced in the Holy Spirit, and said, I thank thee, O Father, Lord of heaven and earth, that thou did hide these things from the wise and understanding, and did reveal them unto babes.*

"Ah ... okay."

"So," Wolf said, "if we realize his collective crowns are depicting him as the complete godhead and not as a humble man in a rough garment preaching in his sandals, then, surely, when he's hung upon a tree—which nobody saw happen—we should realize that not only is he a mythical figure but his Cross is symbolic:

> *Colossians 2:[8] Beware lest [for fear of] any man spoils you through philosophy and vain deceit, after the tradition of men, after the rudiments of the world, and not after Christ. [9] For in him dwells all the fullness of the Godhead bodily.*

Lilly frowned. "If Christ didn't die a horrible death upon a cross, then what's the purpose of the story?"

"When a famous person is assassinated or martyred they're afforded a reverence they'd never otherwise receive. If you want to cement the life and times of a famous leader into the minds of the populous, you have him assassinated. This is one of the reasons

Christ was hung upon a cross but it's not the only reason ... Jesus on the cross is a covert trinity symbol."

Christ being stabbed on the Cross.

Lilly frowned. "It is?"

"Yes ... If the cross is a symbolic tree, then who do you suppose Jesus represents when he's seen hanging upon it?"

"God's son called out of Egypt ... the tribe of Israel?"

"The Hebrews were forgiven their sins and their curse was transferred to Babylon, so it's Babylon that we see hanging, but seeing as only female offerings are acceptable to God, it's female members of the tribe of Babylon that are symbolically hung upon a tree ... sacrificed:

> *Malachi 1:*[14] *But cursed be the deceiver, which has in his flock a male, and vows, and sacrifices to the Lord a corrupt thing: for I am a great King says the Lord of hosts, and my name is dreadful among the heathen.*
>
> *Leviticus 4:*[32] *And if he brings a lamb for a sin offering, he shall bring a female without blemish."*

"Oh, I didn't know that," Lilly said. "I thought the Bible was all about males being great and worthy ... and all that."

"It is ... but if you look carefully you'll find the opposite to be true. And if you take into account that the image of Jesus upon a cross is likened to the bronze serpent placed upon a rod by Moses, then we know Jesus was indeed roleplaying the goddess when he was placed upon the rod or symbolic tree.

> *John 3:14 and as Moses lifted up the serpent in the wilderness, even so, must the Son of man be lifted up."*

"Because we're symbolized as serpents?"

"Yes," Wolf said. "The serpent was a well-known symbol for the goddess in antiquity. German Christian Gnostics minted a thaler, a silver coin, in the sixteenth century. On it, they linked the serpent-pillar to Christ's crucifixion."

Silver coin from the sixteenth century

"Does the cross represent the Tree of Knowledge?"

"Yes. In Jesus' assumed identity as the goddess, he's the seedline that proceeds and is hung upon a rod or limbless tree, and as the true son equating to the father, he's the branch."

"So, 'branch' has a double meaning? I knew Christ was the branch because he's called that on several occasions in the Bible.

"Yes:

> *Isaiah 11:1 And there shall come forth a rod out of the*

stem of Jesse, and a Branch shall grow out of his roots. [2]
And the [Holy] spirit of the Lord shall rest upon him, the
spirit of [the goddess] wisdom ... and he shall smite the
earth: with the rod of his mouth, and with the breath of
his lips shall he slay the wicked."

"Hey! I thought you were trying to be nice to me!" Lilly scowled. "So ... where's the son in the trinity image?"

"The son's the water and blood that pours from Christ's side when he's struck by a spear, or rather, it's what remains of him ... his placenta. Therefore, the Holy Grail—the cup said to have captured Christ's blood when he was stabbed upon the cross—is a mythical religious relic. The Holy Grail as an object is better described as a magic platter—the placenta itself. In ancient Egypt, the son of Amen and Mut in the Egyptian New Kingdom religion was Khonsu—a placenta deity equating to Jesus.

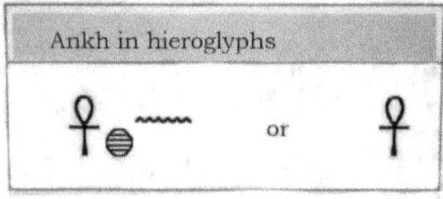

Ankh in hieroglyphs

"The Egyptian symbol for life—the ankh—represented the trinity. In hieroglyphs, it was either drawn as a solitary symbol or as a trinity of symbols. In the trinity, the ankh represented Isis, a symbol for water represented God, and a six-sided circle or hexagon with horizontal lines running across it represented Khonsu's placenta—his symbol. As a royal placenta deity, his name meant 'Pharaoh's or God's placenta' and his symbol represented a placenta."

Khonsu's name

"Wow, I didn't know there was such a thing as a royal placenta deity. Why is god's symbol water, when the waters of life flow from the goddess…? Oh, that's right … the woman is said to contain your waters:

> *Song of Solomon 4:12 A garden enclosed is my sister, my*
> *spouse; a spring shut up, a fountain sealed."*

"Indeed," Wolf said. "In Leonardo da Vinci's *Last Supper*, Mary Magdalene sits on Christ's right where the apostle John is supposed to sit. Da Vinci exposes his hidden knowledge by having Mary Magdalene mirror him, showing he knew Jesus represented the goddess—especially in this image when he's about to be crucified. He also inserted a trinity symbol into his painting because not only does the shape of the Holy Grail appear in the negative space between them—the shape of a woman's womb—it also appears in the landscape behind them … a lake's formed in a natural bowl in the landscape."

The Last Supper by Leonardo da Vinci

"Wow! Are there any more trinity symbols?"

"Of course," Wolf said. "There's one on the back of the United States one-dollar bill. The disconnected, floating, cap above the pyramid is a talisman—"

The pyramid on the back of the United States one-dollar bill

"What's a talisman?"

"An object that's believed to have magic powers; cause good things to happen to the person who possesses it ... The floating cap has its own identity and meaning but it's also an integral part of the pyramid yet to be completed."

"What does the cap symbolize?"

"Christianity's Eye of Providence—the complete godhead—symbolized by an upright triangle with rays of the sun and an eye in the middle."

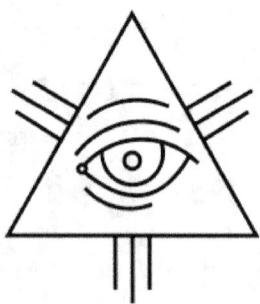

Christian trinity symbol

"What do the symbols represent?"

"Covertly, the eye represents the Holy Ghost—the Eye of God—the personified goddess. The upright triangle is a stylized obelisk—a phallic symbol representing God's phallus—and the rays of the sun emanating from the sides of the triangle represent God's Son's placenta—the Holy Grail."

"I thought the pyramid on the back of the U.S. dollar bill was a Freemason symbol."

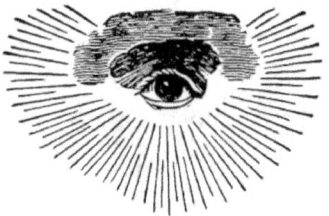

Masonic Eye of Providence

"Many people mistakenly think that, but the Christian Eye of Providence predates any masonic version by twenty years, and the floating cap above the pyramid on the one-dollar bill is fashioned after the Christian Eye of Providence. The earliest Masonic version has heavy clouds laden with water instead of an upright triangle. The clouds are a symbolic depiction of the father, representing his waters pouring forth—his dew falling from heaven—and the rays shining behind the clouds symbolize the Son/Sun." "So, an upright triangle represents God's phallus?"

A depiction of Ishtar from the Ishtar Vase,

dating to the early second millennium B.C.

"Yes," Wolf said, "and a downward pointing one represents the goddess ... it represents her pubic triangle. Conjoined, the triangles represent God *and* his goddess. Nowadays, the conjoined symbols represent Judaism and the symbol's on Israel's flag, it's the star of David."

"There is another symbol for the Christian trinity," Wolf said, "an earlier version which is seen on the La Maddalena church in Venice, Italy. Entirely rebuilt in 1780, it has a circular plan inspired by the Pantheon in Rome, but its most notable feature is the supposed masonic symbol over its door in its portal."

Trinity symbol on La Maddalena
Church in Venice Italy

"How is it different?"

La Maddalena Church in Venice Italy

"Christianity's Eye of Providence has an upright triangle with an eye within it like this version does, but the sun rays don't feature in this design. Instead, a circle reminiscent of the globe in the Egyptian trinity symbol does. As the globe represents the placenta of the Son in the Egyptian trinity, so does the circle in this design. But, just like in the Christian Eye of Providence, the wings of a bird of prey to represent the father have been replaced with an upright triangle to represent his phallus instead, and the serpents to represent the goddess have been exchanged for an eye—depicting her as the Eye Goddess—Hathor in her Eye form. So, you see, Christianity's Eye of Providence is an updated version of Egypt's ancient trinity symbol— the symbolism is the same."

Zoroastrian Trinity symbol

"And," Wolf said, "the trinity symbol of Ancient Egypt is similar to that of the Zoroastrian faith, except the father is not merely represented by wings, he's shown inside the globe that represents the Son. The goddess's serpents are not as well expressed in the design, but stylized versions of them are seen hanging down."

Babylon trinity symbol

"Babylon also had a trinity symbol," Wolf said. "In the Babylonian design the father was symbolized as living water and Ishtar was symbolized as a star and it represented her as Venus, and the son, Shamash, was depicted in the middle of the design as the sun."

"So, the father is always symbolized as a phallus symbol: as a pyramid, obelisk, living water, steeple, or the wings of a mighty bird expressing his *penetrative power.*"

"Don't forget he's also the cross or rod."

"And the Holy Ghost is symbolized either as an eye for the Eye of God, a star for Venus, or as a serpent. And the son is almost always depicted as the sun or as a placenta."

CHAPTER THIRTEEN

Morning Star

Lilly's arms were spread wide around Wolf in a loving embrace despite the dull ache in her belly.

"Baby," Wolf said. "Who do you suppose the Morning Star is?"

"Jesus," Lilly said, aware it was Lucifer's name.

"I thought you'd say that."

"It's what Christians think because Revelation says:

> *Revelation 22:*[16] *I Jesus have sent my angel to testify to you these things in the churches. I am the root and the offspring of David, and the morning star."*

"The verse says Christ is the root and offspring of David *and* the Morning Star, not that he *is* the Morning Star. Does the statement make you think he's David? The Bible says Jesus is descended from David, but it also names him his father. Therefore, surely, it's naming his mother the Morning Star?

> *Luke 1:*[32] *He [Jesus] shall be great and shall be called the Son of the Highest: and the Lord God shall give to him the throne of his father, David."*

"The coma placement makes it seem like he's calling himself the morning star."

"Venus is the morning star and that's a name for the goddess. What do you make of this passage in the Bible?

Job 38:⁴ Where were you when I laid the foundations of the earth? Declare, if you have understanding. ⁵ Who has determined the measures thereof, if you know? Who has stretched the line upon it? ⁶ On what are its foundations fastened? Who laid its cornerstone; ⁷ when the Morning Stars sang together, and all the Sons of God shouted for joy?"

Lilly frowned. "There are verses that speak of multiple sons of God and they're not the Morning Stars?"

"How about we step away from the Bible for a while...? Religion didn't start two thousand years ago, it began much earlier. To fill in some blanks we need to step back in time. Linguists widely agree there was a Proto-Indo-European language—a common ancestor to the Indo-European languages—and scholars estimate that it, 'PIE,' may have been spoken as a single language around 3500 B.C."

"I've heard this," Lilly said. "In the eighteenth century, Sir William Jones observed the similarities between Sanskrit, Ancient Greek, and Latin."

"That's right," Wolf said, "And he said:

The Sanskrit language, whatever be its antiquity, is of a wonderful structure; more perfect than the Greek, more copious than the Latin, and more exquisitely refined than either. Yet bearing to both a stronger affinity, both in the roots of verbs and the forms of grammar, than could possibly have been accidental; so, strong indeed, that no philologer could examine all three without believing them to have sprung from a common source."

"Does the Bible speak of this in Genesis when it says, 'the people scattered and their language became confused?'"

"It does, yes ... The Greeks were illiterate during their dark age, 1100–800 B.C. To regain written language, they adopted the Phoenician writing system and introduced characters for vowel sounds, but their language was still based upon the previous Proto-

Indo-European language; and not only was there a common language in antiquity, there was also a common religion."

"There was?" Lilly said, excited. The idea of a singular religion seeming too fantastic to be true.

"People scattered, but their religious stories and languages retained similarities. The Morning Star as a deity and concept was passed down from the parent religion."

Wolf ran delicate fingers down Lilly's back before cupping her head and kissing it. "The goddess belonging to the original language and religion was called Hausōs, and she was a beautiful young woman personifying the dawn. Her name was derived from a root word meaning to shine, translated as 'the shining one.' The daughter of Heaven, she was characterized as a reluctant bringer of light for which she was punished."

Lilly stared at Wolf, despite her religious training, she was hungry to know more.

"Hausōs became 'Ushas:' plural goddesses in the Vedic Rigveda—the divine daughters of Dyaus Pita [Father Sky or Father Heaven] who were called the Dawns and personified as cows—kine. They were freed from an encloser or blocker in the Vedas called Vala by the Hindu god Indra when he split the stone cave they were entombed in while high on Soma [the Elixir of Immortality]. The cave or blocker was also symbolized as a personified demon dragon called Vala, Vrtra or Vritra:

> *Rigveda 2.12.3 Who slew the Dragon, freed the Seven Rivers, and drove the kine forth from the cave of Vala,*

> *Rigveda 2.15.8 Praised by the Angirases he slaughtered Vala and burst apart the bulwarks of the mountain.*

> *Rigveda 8.14.7 In Soma's ecstasy Indra spread the firmament and realms of light when he cleft Vala limb from limb.*

"The beautifully adorned young women's purpose was to ward

off the evil spirits of the night. Depicted singularly as Dawn, they rode across the sky in a golden chariot dressed in a saffron-colored dress. The color of Dawn's dress linked her to the red cows she was symbolized as. Depicted plurally, Dawn rode upon a hundred chariots drawn by either golden-red horses or cows."

"You said Dyaus Pita equates to Father Heaven ... Who's that? God?"

"Yes," Wolf said. "In ancient Greek literature, Uranus, Father Sky or Heaven was both the son and husband of Gaia—Mother Earth."

"And that's you ... so heaven does exist?"

"Yes ... Heaven is a name for a god ... It's only considered a place when women like you collectively reside within us ... When you're in me ... you're in Heaven:

> *Revelation 14:*[13] *Then I heard a voice from heaven saying to me, 'Write: 'Blessed are the dead who die in the Lord from now on.' 'Yes,' says the Spirit, 'that they may rest from their labors, and their works follow them.'*
>
> *1 John 2:*[24] *Let what you heard from the beginning abide in you. If what you heard from the beginning abides in you, then you also shall continue in the Son, and in the Father.* [25] *And this is the promise that he made to us — eternal life."*

"In your room ... womb? You think it's a blessing?"

"Is it not? You're as fresh as a daisy."

"The verse said 'eternal life' but Revelation says people will live with Christ for a thousand years?"

"Chapter 20 in Revelation speaks of Christ's thousand-year reign while the dragon is sealed up in a pit, and thrones are seen and those who sit upon them give judgment and live and reign with Christ for a thousand years," Wolf said. "This has already happened ... The mythical Jesus has ruled for more than a thousand years and kings have wielded power via him ... and the time's coming to an end."

"Because you're the symbolic dragon and you're going to get out of your pit?

> *Isaiah 45:⁷ I form the light, and create darkness: I make*
> *peace, and create evil: I the Lord do all these things."*

"Indeed ... The crop has long been symbolized as both sheep and cows—kine. In the Bible, a red heifer [female cow] is sacrificed to purify sin, and in the book of Numbers flocks of sheep are referred to as cattle. The dawn goddesses simultaneously symbolized as red cows and beautiful women will once again be contained:

> *The Radiant Dawns have risen up for glory, in their white*
> *splendor like the waves of waters. She makes paths all*
> *easy, fair to travel, and rich. She has shown herself to be*
> *benign and friendly. We see that you are good: far shines*
> *your luster; your beams, your splendors have flown up to*
> *Heaven. Decking yourself, you make bare your bosom,*
> *shining in majesty, you Goddess Morning. Red are the kine*
> *and luminous that bear her the Blessed One who spreads*
> *through the distance.*
> *The foes she chases like a valiant archer, like a swift*
> *warrior she repels darkness.*
> *Your ways are easy on the hills: you pass Invincible! Self-*
> *luminous! through waters.*
> *So lofty Goddess with thine ample pathway, Daughter of*
> *Heaven, bring wealth to give us comfort.*
> *Dawn, bring me wealth: untroubled, with your oxen you*
> *bear riches at your will and pleasure;*
> *You who, a Goddess, Child of Heaven, has shown you lovely*
> *through bounty when we called you early.*
> *As the birds fly forth from their resting places, so men with*
> *store of food rise at your dawning.*
> *Yea, to the liberal mortal who remains at home, O Goddess*
> *Dawn, much good you bring."*

"Is that verse in the Indian Vedic Rigveda?"

"Yes. 'Rig' is Sanskrit for praise and shine, and 'Veda' means knowledge. The Vedic Rigveda is an ancient Indian collection of Vedic [ancient Indian civilization] Sanskrit hymns, and one of the four canonical sacred texts or 'śruti' of Hinduism known as the Vedas. In Sanskrit, 'vanas' means loveliness and desire, and this is how the 'Uṣhas' or 'Dawns' of the Vedic Rigveda are described."

Lilly had always considered herself to be well educated, but it seemed her education was sorely lacking—embarrassingly so. "Did the Dawns or Morning Stars feature in other mythologies?"

"Yes," Wolf said. "Derivatives of them can be found in all of the mythologies of the Indo-European peoples, but Dawn is also found in others ... It's easy to spot Hausōs in Egyptian mythology because she's the goddess Hathor frequently depicted with a cow's head or as a red cow. In the Sumerian religion, she was Inanna, an identical goddess to Babylon's Ishtar, the goddess of the planet Venus called the Morning Star. In Latin, the goddess was named 'Venus,' and in Norse, 'Vanir.'

"So, the goddesses in pagan religions are all the same goddess?"

"Yes. Proof comes in the form of tales from Ancient Egypt. You already know that Sekhmet was Hathor in her lioness form and she was also the Eye, as well as the serpent goddess Wedjat—the Uraeus. In another version of the distant goddess, the lioness Sekhmet as the Eye leaves Egypt to follow the deities Tefnut and Shu. When she returns she's enraged to find Amen-Ra has created another Eye in her place. After her tears of rage and grief form human beings, Amen-Ra places her on his forehead as the Uraeus to rule over all."

"Are goddesses worshipped in various forms, all aspects of the same goddess?"

"Yes," Wolf said. "Venus, the Morning Star, was depicted both as a dawn goddess and as a love goddess, but her dual aspects were separated in some traditions including Roman and Greek. Thus, we get Venus and Aurora in Latin and Aphrodite and Eos in Greek—complementary aspects of the same goddess. Eos was a Titaness goddess of the dawn who had rosy fingers or rosy forearms. She rose each morning from her home at the edge of Oceanus to open the gates of heaven so the sun could rise. In Homer, her saffron robe is embroidered with flowers, and on Attic vases, she's depicted with rosy fingers and golden arms; and adorned with large white wings and crowned with a tiara."

Lilly's eyes widened. "Like an angel?"

"Yes."

"In Semitic mythology she's Asherah. The names 'Ashtoreth' singular and 'Ashtaroth' plural appear in the Hebrew Bible and refer to multiple statues of her. Her biblical names were derived from the second millennium B.C. Phoenician goddess Astarte who equates to Babylon's Ishtar and the identical, earlier, Sumerian goddess Inanna. Astarte or Ashtoreth is the Hellenised [Greek] name for the Middle Eastern goddesses worshiped from the Bronze Age to classical antiquity. Easter was named after the Germanic goddess equivalent Ēostre."

"So, Christianity was invented by the Romans to not only control the masses but to also suppress certain aspects of paganism—goddess worship in particular," Lilly said. "And that's why the Christian tradition calls Lucifer the Devil when his name in Latin means Morning Star, but if his mother Aurora was Roman's Dawn Goddess ... why did the Romans name the planet Venus after him?"

"In ancient times, Arabians worshiped the same gods worshiped in Mesopotamia, but in later years the genders of the deities were switched. In the Aramaic language [supposedly used by Christ] the Babylonian goddess Ishtar became the male god Attar cognate to Lucifer in Roman mythology, whose name as an adjective means 'shining' and 'light-bringing.' But, of course, it was his mother Aurora who was the Dawn Goddess cognate to Hausōs. Thus, the traits of the dawn goddess were switched to the masculine—the qualities of the mother transferred to the son."

"But, surely, Lucifer is Satan?"

"Satan's name comes from the Semitic root 'Stn,' meaning opposition and it represents a general adversary—hence his accepted identity. When Christian tradition made Lucifer's name the name for Satan, they changed an angel of light—the light bringer or bringer of dawn—into an evil fallen angel."

Lilly frowned. "How can the devil be a light bringer?"

"Indeed," Wolf said. "It was deliberate misdirection ... The church assigned evil meanings to anything or anyone valued in paganism, but the Bible says Lucifer will once again be known as he previously was:

> 2 Corinthians 11:[14] And no marvel; for Satan himself is transformed into an Angel of Light."

Lilly blinked several times. "So, who is Satan then? If he's not a light bringing angel named Lucifer, then who is he?"

"He's pretty much a misnomer—a wrong or inaccurate name or designation."

Lilly looked at Wolf suspiciously. "Is he you?"

"No."

"Are you sure? You seem to be God *and* the evil devil dragon so why not Satan?"

"Wolf pulled a face. Well, it depends ... it's all part of the Bible's trickery ... Satan as Samuel is said to have fathered Cain via an incubus in Genesis in some Jewish writings but Jewish tradition states he's an archangel of God ... How many evil deeds do you suppose Satan commits in the Bible?"

"Lots ... doesn't he?"

"His name's only mentioned fifty-seven times and the worst thing he does is smite Job with boils from the soles of his feet to his crown, and this happens in God's presence and can be viewed as being done at his request."

"How can that be?"

"Satan's father is God," Wolf said, "and he was God's right-hand man before his supposed fall:

> Job 1:[6] Now, there was a day when the sons of God came to present themselves before the Lord, and Satan also came among them."

Lilly frowned. "If his father is God then that means he's God ...

doesn't it ... the father and son are one. But the Bible speaks of his fall in Revelation ... Doesn't he fall because he tries to compete with God? I'm confused ... if the devil is the old serpent whose also the great dragon, then surely he's you ... isn't he?

> *Revelation 12:[9] And the great dragon was cast out, that old serpent called the Devil and Satan which deceives the whole world: he was cast out into the earth, and his angels were cast out with him."*

Running tender fingers through Lilly's hair, Wolf sighed. "You're kind are part of the Trinity of good *and* evil. Satan and Lucifer are demigod sons of God cast out when the crop was re-sown on Earth. There are lots of verses that put you wrong in the Bible. That verse lumps us together as one which we *are* and *aren't* ... You see the dragons in the courtyard, and I'll admit I'm the devil dragon *and* a god, but Satan is technically you ... Lucifer is cognate to Attar or Athtar who in Ugaritic mythology succeeds to the throne of the god Baal Hadad, thought to be dead. Proving himself inadequate, he descends to rule the underworld instead. Baal Hadad [Lord] equated to the Rigvedic god Indra and Zeus:

> *Isaiah 14:[12] How art thou fallen from heaven, O Lucifer, son of the morning! How are you cut down to the ground, he who did weaken the nations! [13] For you have said in your heart, I will ascend into Heaven, I will exalt my throne above the stars of God: I will sit also upon the mount of the congregation, in the sides of the north: [14] I will ascend above the heights of the clouds; I will be like the most-high. [15] Yet you shall be brought down to hell, to the sides of the pit."*

"So," Lilly said. "You're saying Lucifer, the demi-god son of a goddess whose identity was transferred to him by the switching of genders in the distant past, is Satan?"

"Correct."

"But some people say the biblical verses in Isaiah speak not of Lucifer, but rather of a king of Babylon, and they say he's the proud one who tried to compete with God?"

"Yes, and in another chapter in the Bible, an unnamed King of Tyre is likewise identified as Lucifer. So, the house of Satan—the seed line of the serpent—is identified as the King of Tyre and the King of Babylon, and by extension their peoples. And, of course, the city of Tyre fell to the Babylonians in 574 B.C.

> *Ezekiel 28:[6] Therefore says the Lord God; because you have set your heart as the heart of God; [7] Behold, therefore I will bring strangers upon you, the terrible of the nations: and they shall draw their swords against the beauty of your wisdom, and they shall defile your brightness. [8] They shall bring you down to the pit, and you shall die the deaths of them that are slain in the midst of the seas. [9] Will, you yet say before him that slays you, I am God? You shall be a man, and no God, in the hand of him that slays you. [10] You shall die the deaths of the uncircumcised by the hand of strangers: for I have spoken it, says the Lord God. [11] Moreover, the word of the Lord came to me, saying, [12] Son of man, take up a lamentation upon the king of Tyrus, and say to him, this says the Lord God. You were the seal of perfection, full of wisdom, and perfect in beauty. [13] You have been in Eden, the garden of God; every precious stone was your covering, the sardius, topaz, and the diamond, the beryl, the onyx, and the jasper, the sapphire, the emerald, and the carbuncle, and gold: the workmanship of your timbrels and your pipes was prepared in you in the day you were created. [14] You are the anointed cherub that covers; and I have set you so: you were on the holy mountain of God; you have walked up and down in the middle of the stones of fire. [15] You were perfect in your ways from the day that you were created, till iniquity was found in you. [16] By the multitude of your merchandise, they have filled the midst of you with violence, and you have*

sinned: therefore, I will cast you as profane out of the mountain of God: and I will destroy you, O covering cherub, from the middle of the stones of fire. [17] Your heart was lifted because of your beauty; you corrupted your wisdom because of your splendor. I cast you to the ground. I put you before kings that they may see you."

Lilly frowned. "Right! So that passage is talking about my kind being cast out and rounded up again? This is the pit … isn't it?"

"Sure … I'm happy with it."

"But how can the King of Tyre and the King of Babylon both be Lucifer?"

"Jesus calls the Devil the murderer from the beginning, and the tares [weeds] his children. The beginning of the Bible is Genesis and the murderer Cain. God and the Devil are one and the same, and Jesus, when he's wearing the hat or crown of the seedline, equates to Lucifer his demi-god son. Therefore, the seedline of humanity seeded by Cain, the murderer from the beginning, is covertly Christ—the seedline or Holy Ghost:

Genesis 4:[1] And Adam knew Eve, his wife; and she conceived, and bore Cain, and said, I have gotten a man from the Lord."

"But Cain was a murderer … he wasn't anybody important, so how can he be associated with Jesus?"

"The Bible makes it clear Cain *was* important to God and he had offspring:

Genesis 4:[15] And the Lord said to him, 'Therefore whosoever slays Cain, vengeance shall be taken on him sevenfold.' And the Lord set a mark upon Cain, lest any find him and kill him."

"No, I can't accept that … I can accept you're the demon dragon … Yeah, I get that … and I can see how you could also be perceived as a

God by many, but I can't accept my kin and I being lumped in with Cain and regarded as God usurpers!"

"No? Well, how do you think you're people are going to react when my whereabouts and nature is accurately portrayed to them?"

Lilly choked. "You mean if word gets out about your true nature?"

"Yes."

"Oh ... it will be on!"

"And there we have it ... and now you know why we shovel false religion down your throats and put out fake reports of little green men and grey aliens so weak and pathetic their arms would break like twigs. We have to creep up on you unawares for your own sakes, so you don't harm yourselves trying to get away."

Lilly folded her arms in a huff.

CHAPTER FOURTEEN

Bread of Life, Seed-line & the Church

"Are you aware," Wolf said, continuing his lecture, "that Jesus wasn't the only one to die and rise again in three days?"

"He wasn't? Really?"

"Have you not heard of the descent of Inanna? You don't know she visited the underworld and while there she was stripped naked, killed and hung on a hook for three days and nights before the god Enki saved her by sending servants to sprinkle the food and water of life on her corpse to revive her?"

"No, I didn't know that," Lilly said, her eyes wide. "Does she share any other characteristics with Jesus?"

"You mean like walking on water? The Semitic goddess Asherah cognate to Ishtar was titled 'Lady Athirat of the sea' by the Greeks, and 'she who treads on the sea.' Her identifying characteristic was reassigned to Christ by the authors of the New Testament."

Lilly sighed and shrugged. "Did all of Christ's miracles previously belong to the universal goddess?"

"Yes."

Lilly groaned.

"What's the most important miracle Jesus says he will perform in your opinion?"

"Giving himself as the bread and wine of life:

John 6:[51] *I am the living bread which came down from Heaven: if any man eats this bread, he shall live forever: and the bread that I will give is my flesh, which I will give*

> *for the life of the world … 53 Then Jesus said to them, 'Truly, truly, I say to you, except you eat the flesh of the Son of Man, and drink his blood, you have no life in you.'*
>
> *Matthew 26:26 And as they were eating, Jesus took bread, and blessed it, and broke it, and gave it to the disciples, and said, 'Take, eat; this is my body.' 27 And he took the cup, and gave thanks, and gave it to them, saying, 'Drink all of it; 28 For this is my blood of the New Testament, which is shed for many for the remission of sins.'"*

Wolf looked proudly at Lilly. "Well done with the quotes, but, alas, once again, Jesus was not being original. The concept of the 'bread of life' was invented long before Christ, and, once again, it was Ishtar or Inanna who was the bread of life … A Sumerian hymn praises her breast viewed as fields of plants, grain, and bread to sustain humanity:

> *O lady, your breast is your field,*
> *Inanna, your breast is your field.*
> *Your wide, wide field which pours out plants.*
> *Your wide, wide field which pours out grain.*
> *Water flowing from high for the Lord, bread from on high*
> *… I will drink it from you.*

"And covertly, the bread of life is also a woman in the Bible:

> *Song of Solomon 7:2 Your navel is like a round goblet that wants not liquor: the belly is like a heap of wheat set about with lilies.*
> *Song of Solomon 2:16 My beloved is mine, and I am his: he feeds among the lilies.*
>
> *Leviticus 15:24 And if any man lies with her at all, and her flowers be upon him …"*

"And lilies and flowers are symbolically women's genitalia," Lilly said. "So, in some texts, Jesus can easily be identified as the goddess?"

"When the genders were switched around in Mesopotamia they stopped worshiping the feminine goddess and worshiped the seed line instead while giving it a masculine identity—the First Father—a male to represent the seed line. 'Christ' is a collective term for your kind. Symbolically, Jesus, in one of his roles, is the first of your kind. His descendants who haven't converted—become defiled with corrupted seed—are collectively Christ. Which, as you've learned, is a title that used to mean 'servant of God.'"

Lilly tried to focus. "And as the Son of God he's symbolically a collective of mystery school initiates or is a mystery school teacher but he also roleplays the Son of Man—the seedline—and is the First Father in that role—the goddess?"

"You're getting it, yes. In the New Testament, Jesus plays many roles and wears many hats—crowns. In his role as the demi-god Son of Man, he represents your seedline and is the archetypal First Father ... Much of mythology was taught in this way. There wasn't one Isis or one Osiris, there were lots. Just like there isn't one man—there are billions. Man is a collective term for every human on the planet and God a collective term for every god."

"I see."

"In ancient times, the serpent was a symbol of immortality and regeneration, and when seen biting its own tail—eternity. Your kind was collectively known as serpents and in Egypt, the serpent goddess was full of divine wisdom, power, and creative energy. Serpent or worm symbolism was transferred from the goddess to Christ:

Job 25:6 *How much less man, that is a worm? And the Son of Man which is a worm?"*

Lilly rubbed her brow.

"Consider this example," Wolf said. "A writer decides to write a story about firemen: he chooses a character to represent them as a collective and loads their trials and tribulations onto his pivotal character. Readers understand the author isn't writing about Jack the fireman, but, rather, firemen in general."

"I understand," Lilly said. "I get that the whole tribe of Israel is the only son:

> Exodus 4:²¹ *The Lord said to Moses, say to Pharaoh, 'Israel [the tribe] is My son, My firstborn.'"*

"Did you know Isis was also the Bread of Life? She was known as the great one, the mistress of the gods and magic and called a witch—a skillful healer in whose mouth is was Breath of Life. By her words she destroyed pain, and by her power, she awakened the dead."

"The symbolic dead?" Lilly said.

"Yes. People with no life in them unless they drunk her wine which means they were mortal and would die a mortal death unless blessed by her. Jesus obtained this quality from the goddess:

> Luke 9:⁶⁰ *Jesus said to him, 'Let the dead bury their dead: but go you and preach the kingdom of God.'*

> John 6:⁵³ *Then Jesus said to them, 'Truly, truly, I say to you, except you eat the flesh of the Son of Man and drink his blood, you have no life in you.'"*

"Because the serpent and ankh were symbols of hers and she made statements about herself being the giver of life."

"Yes." Wolf kissed the top of her head and rubbed her back. "Well done, Baby."

Lilly sighed and returned his embrace.

"A great mystery festival used to be observed annually in ancient Egypt to commemorate the death of the god Osiris, and it actively demonstrated the switch from feminine to masculine worship. On the first day of the Festival of Ploughing, the goddess Isis appeared in her shrine stripped naked. A paste made from sacred grain grown in the temple fields was placed in her bed and moistened with water, and the fecund earth represented her. Priests kneaded the seeded, fertile soil and added water for several days before the mixture was pressed into a mold of Osiris, or fashioned into a crescent-shaped figure representing him as a moon god. It was then clothed, adorned, and buried at the temple. Some grain mix was also placed in molds made from the wood of a red tree in the form of the dismembered parts of Osiris.

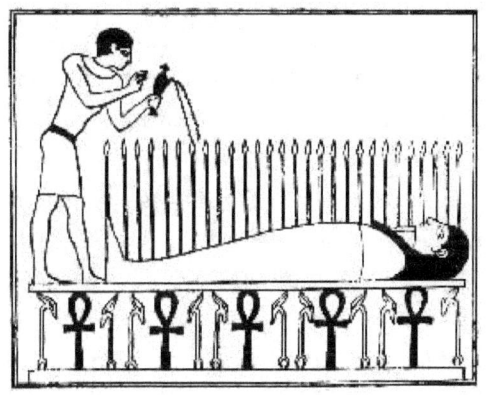

Osiris with sprouting wheat representing his resurrection

"When seed sprouted from the molds, there was a great shout and festive celebrations because Osiris was resurrected. The germinated seed represented his seedline continuing and multiplying. Cakes of divine bread were then made from the molds of Osiris and placed in a silver chest set by the head of the god, as described in the Book of the Dead XVII. Osiris was thus worshiped as the Bread of Life. The sacred rituals climaxed when the sacramental god, as divine bread or cakes, was eaten at holy communion—transforming the celebrants into symbolic replicas of their god."

Lilly frowned. "And prior to this, Ishtar or Inanna were worshiped as the Bread of Life?"

"Correct ... The Bible says drink offerings used to be poured out to the Queen of Heaven, and it was in her image that cakes were made:

> *Jeremiah 44:[19] 'Besides,' the women added, 'do you suppose that we were burning incense and pouring out liquid offerings to the Queen of Heaven, and making cakes marked with her image, without our husbands knowing it and helping us? Of course not!'"*

"I see."

"So, the ancient Egyptian ritual demonstrated not only the worship in full but also showed how the worship of the Bread of Life was transferred from the feminine to the masculine and transferred to the seed line. Thus, in the New Testament, Christ is symbolically the uncorrupted seedline that is proceeding—going forward.

> *1 Corinthians 12:[12] For as the body is one and has many members, and all the members of that one body, being many, are one body: so also is Christ.*

> *1 Corinthians 12:[27] Now you are the body of Christ and members in particular.*

Lilly nodded.

"Jacob and his uncle and father-in-law Laban symbolically divided up the crop as a flock of sheep. Laban kept the white unspotted sheep referred to as cattle, and Jacob got the rest as payment for services rendered:

> *Genesis 30:[29] And Jacob said to his father-in-law, Laban, 'You know I've served you well, and you see how your cattle are with me. [30] For you had little before I came and now a multitude. The Lord has blessed you since my coming, but now I need to provide for my own household.' [31] 'What shall I give you?' Laban asked. 'Don't give me anything,' Jacob replied. 'But if you will do this one thing for me, I will continue to tend your flocks and watch over them: [32] Let me go through all your flocks today and remove all the speckled or spotted cattle, and all the*

brown cattle among the sheep and the spotted or speckled among the goats; and these shall be my hire. *33 In the future, my righteousness will answer for me, when you check on the animals you've given me as my wages. If you find any white sheep among my flock, you'll know I've stolen them from you."*

Lilly's brow furrowed. "What's the importance of the sheep's division according to color and spot?"

"The unspotted represent the desired crop. Jesus, as an arch type and first-father of your kind, is the crop—seedline—without spot:

1 Peter 1:18 You know you were not redeemed with corruptible things, such as silver and gold, from your vain manner of life received by tradition from your fathers; 19 But with the precious blood of Christ, as of a lamb without blemish and without spot:"

Song of Solomon 4:7 You [the women] are all fair, my love; there is no spot in you."

'So, Christ is the seed-line?"

"Yes, confirmation comes in these verses:

1 Corinthians 15:23 ... Christ, the first-fruits; afterward they are Christ's at his coming.

1 Corinthians 15:20 But now is Christ risen from the dead and become the first-fruits ...

"The flock, or crop, is also collectively known as the feminine Church:

Ephesians 5:25 Husbands, love your wives, just as Christ also loved the church and gave himself up for her, 26 so that he might sanctify her, having cleansed her by the washing of water with the word, 27 that he might present to himself 'the church' in all her glory, having no spot or wrinkle or any such thing; that she would be holy and without blemish."

Lilly's eyes widened. "The Church is female? Christ is speaking the words of the Father in that passage, and the 'Church' represents human females of my kind? Women without a spot—birthmark—whose genetics haven't become defiled or corrupted?"

Wolf nodded. "Medieval architects endeavored to express Gothic church buildings as women—their designs resting upon the biblical teachings of the Church being perceived as a woman—the wife of Christ; and the Greek word for church, 'ekklesia,' means wife."

Lilly's eyes widened.

"Thus, church entrances represent female genitalia and the ceilings of churches represent an upside-down ship because a ship is a personification of the feminine productive principle. To show that churches were symbolically women, small idols called Sheela-na-gigs were openly displayed inside Gothic churches. Placed in conspicuous spots over arches, pointed doorways and windows in many Gothic churches, the idols depicted naked old women pulling open their greatly enlarged vaginas ... And Abraham was perceived as a type of god in the middle ages, and his wife Sarah, who bore fruit in old age, is one of several women in the Bible who gives birth in her twilight years. It was perceived and understood that women of age could perform a kind of magic, and, together, they represented the Church:

Psalms 92:13 Those that be planted in the house of the Lord shall flourish in the courts of our God. 14 They shall bring forth fruit in old age; they shall be fat and flourishing."

Lilly immediately thought of several women who gave birth in their later years. Abraham's wife Sarah—Isaac's mother; Manoah's wife—Samson's mother; Elizabeth—John the Baptist's mother.

"At the same time the Church was embracing lewd images of old women, it was demonizing far less objectionable symbols. Objects that had previously been considered sacred like the pentacle were diminished and disparaged. The pentacle was targeted because of its obvious connection to the goddess Venus and other Dawn goddesses because it's the shape Venus traces out in the sky over an eight-year period.

Overhearing their conversation, Cat came forward with a picture of a Sheela-na-gig and showed it to Lilly.

The sight of the image made Lilly blink rapidly. "Good God!"

A twelfth-century Sheela-na-gig on a church in England

CHAPTER FIFTEEN

He's getting his fur

Lilly was lazing in the pool when she heard the ding of the main elevator; she looked at the cave's doorway opening. Momentarily, Cat appeared in it holding an enormous baby covered in fur. It was the size of a nine-month-old human baby, but developmentally it appeared more like a three month old.

"He's getting his fur," Wolf said.

Lilly stared at the baby in disbelief. She hadn't expected to see her baby, or rather, Wolf's baby. "What do you mean? Wasn't he born with fur?"

"No," Wolf said. "He was born naked. He looked a lot like a human baby when he was in my pouch. He's grown fur as a reaction to being turfed out; the cooler environment has encouraged it to grow. He'll likely be feeling a bit better now."

"What's his name?"

"Apple," Wolf said dryly.

"Apple?" Lilly said, momentarily confused.

"Yes, Apple. I decided to give him a Biblical name. He's the apple of my eye ... the fruit of my loins."

"Right," Lilly said.

The baby turned his head and looked at Wolf as Cat handed him to him. As soon as Wolf took hold of him, he squirmed about as he tried to dive headfirst into his pouch; propelling himself forward with a kind of swimming motion.

"No, you don't, you little bugger," Wolf said with the merest hint of a growl. "You don't live in there anymore."

The baby squealed its frustration. Cat pulled a face like he knew things were about to get awkward as he made a bee-line for his room and shut the door behind him.

"Oh, that's awful," Lilly said. "He wants to be in your pouch."

"Of course he does, but he's not getting back in there. He's grown some fur ... he'll be all right. His new mother is feeding him and looking after him ... This is why I didn't want him to come back down here."

Lilly swam to Wolf's side and heaved herself up beside him onto the human steps. "Let me hold him."

"He won't be the least bit interested in you," Wolf said as he handed the squirming baby to her. "He wants to be in my pouch."

Lilly grasped the baby and attempted to cuddle him; almost dropping him when he pushed against her with a strength she was ill-prepared for. "Good God! He's really strong and he weighs a ton."

"Yeah, that's him!"

After a few minutes of fumbling with the baby, Lilly managed to pull him against her and hold him in a firm embrace.

"Cat!" Wolf yelled out. "Will you come and take this little bugger back upstairs."

Lilly looked down at the little wolf and stroked his head. "There, there, little one," she said. "It's all right."

The baby stopped struggling and looked at her, his bright green eyes containing a look of recognition. Lilly continued to stroke his elongated head. "It's all right, little one."

The baby suddenly turned his head and latched onto one of her nipples with a suction so strong she screamed.

Cat jumped into the water beside her and stuffed his little finger into the corner of his mouth to break his suction before wrenching him out of her arms. "That will be enough of that you little vampire," he growled.

He clambered out of the pool clutching the baby to him and headed to the cave, his clothes drenched and water pooling behind him.

Wolf leaned over and examined Lilly's nipple. "Are you all right?"

"I'm fine," she snapped. "You were positively awful to your baby ... My heart bleeds for him."

"Better that than your nipple! He's too strong for you. Upstairs, his new mother wears nipple guards and she needs help with him ... He could have taken your nipple clean off."

"I'm sure you're exaggerating."

"Like hell I am ... He can stay upstairs, he's not coming back down here."

Lilly sat in stunned silence. The whole affair had taken but a few minutes. She'd seen her baby, who was really Wolf's baby, and now he was gone and she wasn't going to see him again.

No time at all seemed to pass before the elevator dinged again and Cat returned to the courtyard. "I just handed the little vampire to the first person I saw and came straight back down here. They'll probably be laughing about it upstairs for a week." He pulled off his drenched clothes and dove into the pool. When he surfaced, he shook the water out of his hair.

"I'm disgusted in you two," Lilly growled. "I've never seen such a hideous display of unfeeling behavior in all my life ... He's only a baby!"

"He's not a baby ... he's a little monster," Cat said as he breast-stroked across the pool to examine Lilly's breast. "Is your nipple all right?"

Lilly slapped his hand away. "I'm fine!"

Satisfied, Cat swam back across the pool. "My mother had to put up with a little monster like him," he said bitterly as he sat down. "It was hard on her."

"Your mother?" Lilly said, surprised. "She raised a little wolf?"

"Yes. I was raised with one of those little buggers."

"Really?" Lilly said, fascinated.

"Yeah ... the bloody bastard hurt me on numerous occasions ... I'm lucky to be alive."

Looking uncomfortable, Wolf squirmed in his seat.

Lilly looked at him.

"Yeah, it was me," he said. "He's about to tell you all the woes of his childhood and say I deserted him."

Lilly looked at Cat. "Are you about to tell me that?"

"Yes! That giant prick shared my mother's breasts ... He near on was the death of my mother and father. They took him in so I'd have a lifelong companion and a job as a trainer—a quality job one aspires to. But Ole Wolfe here abandoned me. He didn't just go off to space for a short while as agreed, he took off and left me to die."

Lilly blinked. "You're not dead."

"I nearly was!" Cat said. "I watched my parents grow old and die and Wolf didn't even return for their funerals. I sobbed at my mother's funeral because I was alone. My parents had chosen to raise a wolf instead of giving me brothers and sisters. They knew it was a gamble. They knew their wolf might die in the wilds of space and never return, and then my hopes of being a trainer would be dashed. My parents went to their graves not knowing what happened to Wolf. My mother said to me on her deathbed, 'Don't give up hope, son. You were a good brother, he may yet return.' But the anniversary of her death came and went year after year and no Wolf."

Wolf cleared his throat. "Yeah, well ... I was having a good time. I'd gotten away from the pariahs on this planet and I wasn't coming back!"

Lilly frowned. "Pariahs?"

"Humans!" Wolf said bitterly. "I'd had enough of them bossing me around ... I knew Cat wanted me to return, knew he was relying on me, but I decided, fuck him, he can stick his brotherhood agreement up his arse."

Cat's arms were folded in rage. "Yeah, that's the big fucking thank you my parents got for all their hard work; their tireless toil and endless love and devotion ... an ungrateful shithead who took off and had no intentions of coming back."

Lilly looked at Wolf. "And yet you're here and you're happy together?"

"Shit happens," Wolf said. "I had a change of heart."

"No, you didn't!' Cat growled. "They lured you back ... They had to trick that prick otherwise he'd probably never have returned ... I was sent to the brink several times!"

"The brink...? What do you mean?"

"It means to be left hanging without tonic," Cat grumbled. "To grow old and die ... I had death in my nostrils several times, and old age is nasty!"

"Why weren't you getting the tonic?"

"I was only supposed to get it for a thousand years because Wolf hadn't pledged his allegiance, and that time came and went. They took pity on me and brought me back from the brink several times; each time giving me an extra thousand years. It was the only way I knew Wolf was still alive. If your wolf dies, your tonic is withdrawn immediately and you know it's the end ... I kept training and hoping. My parents had sacrificed years of their lives for me, and I'd spent countless lifetimes working and training in preparation for the time when Wolf would honor his promise, but he had no intentions of doing so! Finally, I got word that he was back, but he didn't even come and see me."

"Oh, yeah, right, like I was going to come and visit my nemesis!" Wolf said bitterly. "The best trainers have tasted old age—felt their bodies fade and wither ... I helped you be all you could be."

Cat snorted. "You're a fucking bastard!"

"Oh, let it go, already," Wolf said. "It's in the past."

"Maybe for you," Cat stormed. "You giant cunt. It will never be in the past for me!"

Lilly looked at Wolf. He looked uncomfortable; he looked away.

"Well," he said at last. "That was awkward ... Anyway ... the pricks caught up with me, lied to me, tricked me, and here I am."

Lilly frowned. "Don't you want to be here?"

"Oh, I'm happy now," Wolf said bitterly. "Poisoned out of my brain, but I'm happy ... I'm a happy chappy!"

"Poisoned?" Lilly said. "Who's poisoning you?"

"You. That's who ... You!"

"Me? I'm doing no such thing!"

Cat got out of the pool to put on a song: 'Poison' by Alice Cooper began to play.

Wolf sang along with the words. He emphasized the words, 'you're poison running through my veins!' like he'd done it a thousand times before."

Lilly was taken aback. "Surely, that's what you're doing to me?"

"Yes," Wolf said, "but it cuts both ways. I was out wandering the universe, enjoying myself and delighting in the antidote. Having a whale of a time with not a care in the world, and—"

"Prick!" Cat blazed. "Well, we put an end to all that."

"Oh, get over your petty anger!" Wolf growled. "You and your parents brainwashed me my entire childhood. You made me pledge an oath that wasn't in my best interests. You wanted to entrap me and make me serve you and the other fucking pariahs here. As soon as I got away from this planet, I learned the truth and there was no way I was going to honor your vile oath or seek you out. Other than to call you a selfish wanker, which ... by the way ... I was gracious enough not to do ... As far as I was concerned, you could go fuck yourself."

Lilly stared at Cat and then Wolf. They were too busy exchanging evil looks to notice her startled expression. Then Cat got up and stormed into his room.

"Wow," Lilly said, staring at Wolf's angry face. "That was a surprise! Are you guys all right? I thought you were as thick as thieves."

"We are ... That's just a little bugbear from yesteryear that festers and boils over every now and then."

"Cat seemed pretty pissed."

Wolf twisted his mouth from side to side in a dismissive gesture. "He wants me to apologize profusely and be eternally grateful for my upbringing—"

"And are you not?"

"I am ... but not grateful enough to be sorry about abandoning ship and buggering off ... I'm not the least bit sorry about that."

Lilly laughed. "Well, at least you're honest about it, I suppose."

"I made him sweat ... I was the fish that got away. For years he worried they would never catch up with me and wind me in. Cat did it tough while I was gone. He missed me. That's what he's most upset about ... I broke his heart."

"Oh ... poor Cat."

"Don't feel sorry for him ... He's a smiling tiger."

Lilly frowned. "Aren't you God?"

"That little display ought to have opened your eyes to what really goes on around here:

> *Revelation 13:[2] ... and the dragon gave him his power, and his seat, and great authority.*"

"Oh ..."

CHAPTER SIXTEEN

God and Satan

The positive and negative aspects of God were split into two separate identities," Wolf said. "And as I admitted before, God and the Devil are one and the same. This is exposed in the Bible:

> *Isaiah 45:7 I form the light and create darkness: I make peace and create evil: I the Lord do all these things.*

> *2 Samuel 24:1 And again, the anger of the Lord was kindled against Israel, and he incited David against them to say, go, number Israel and Judah ...*
> *1 Chronicles 21:1 And Satan stood up against Israel, and provoked David to number Israel."*

"Hmm ... the last one said Satan not the devil and it's supposedly Satan as Samuel who fathers Cain according to Jewish tradition."

"Your kind are lumped in with me in the Bible, and there are verses that identify God not only as Satan but also as the first beast in Revelation:

> *Hosea 13:7 I [the Lord] will be unto them as a lion: as a leopard by the way will I observe them: 8 I will meet them as a bear that is bereaved of her whelps and will tear out their hearts, and I will devour them like a lion: the wild beast shall tear them."*

> *Revelation 13:2 And the beast which I saw was like a*

leopard, and his feet were as the feet of a bear, and his mouth as the mouth of a lion—"

"So, the supposed evil people bearing the mark of the beast are in fact marked by God, the first beast of Revelation," Lilly said. "And his servants also bear his name?

Revelation 13:¹⁸ Here is wisdom. Let him that has understanding count the number of the beast: for it is the number of a man, and his number is Six hundred threescore and six.

Revelation 22:³ ... and his servants shall serve him: ⁴ And they shall see his face, and his name shall be in their foreheads."

"Yes."

Lilly exhaled loudly. "So, there is no Devil?"

"Oh, there is. We're perceived as being both good and evil ... The Hindu's worship Shiva, a god associated with time, who's, likewise, a destroyer and a creator."

Lilly frowned. "Is Shiva just another name for you?"

"Of course. The Cathars believed the God of the Old Testament was the Devil. Slaughtered by the church, they died for their beliefs."

"I've heard of the Cathars," Lilly said. "Their medieval citadel still stands on a high peak in France."

"Indeed it does, and they weren't the only ones to refer to the Abrahamic God in such a way. Others have called him an evil angel, the Devil God, the Prince of Darkness, and the Source of all Evil, as well as a cruel and wrathful warlike tyrant, Satan, and the first beast in the book of Revelation."

Laughing, Lilly rubbed her eyes. "Well, he was a tyrant, that's true enough. So, the Devil and God are one and the same and they have a seedline?"

"Yes," Wolf said. "There are a number of symbolic deities in the Bible symbolized as trees. The clue to this comes in Mark:

Mark 8:²⁴ And he looked up, and said, I see men as trees, walking."

"Which trees...? The Tree of Knowledge and the Tree of Life?"

"The Tree of Life represents you, and the Tree of Knowledge, us. The serpent declared, 'God knows that when you eat from it [the tree of knowledge] your eyes will be opened and you will be like God, knowing good and evil.' And God declared after Adam and Eve ate the fruit, 'Man has now become like one of us—knowing good and evil. He must not be allowed to reach out his hand and also take from the Tree of Life and eat, and live forever.'"

"Right," Lilly said, "and Man was created in God's image:

Genesis 1:²⁶ Then God said, 'Let us make mankind in our image, in our likeness ...'"

"Yes."

"Okay. I accept that the Tree of Knowledge is God, but where's the proof that it's also Satan?"

"The old Jewish rabbinical tale of Samael leaving Mars and traveling to Earth speaks of it ... In the Garden of Eden, he fathers Cain by Eve after she takes a bite of the fruit from the Tree of Knowledge usually symbolized as an apple tree. Samael, of course, is better known as Satan and he carries his female Lilith within him. The androgynous pair, symbolized as the Tree of Knowledge and the serpent, impregnate Eve ... To 'know' someone in ancient times was to have sexual intercourse with them."

"I've heard of this 'knowing' before," Lilly said.

"Samael, 'Venom of God,' or 'Poison of God,' is an important archangel in the Jewish Talmudic and post-Talmudic lore. An accuser, seducer, and destroyer, he's considered both good and evil. In Talmudic texts, he's a member of the heavenly host—a servant of Yahweh who carries out grim and destructive duties for God—and he's an archangel of death."

Lilly frowned. "And he and Lilith are said to be a conjoined pair ... an androgynous pair?"

"Yes. In the Jewish Kabbalah, Samael is an androgynous serpent who tempts Eve … seducing and impregnating her with Cain, but the Bible says Cain was fathered by the Lord:

> *Genesis 4:¹ And Adam knew Eve his wife, and she conceived, and bare Cain, and said, I have gotten a man from the Lord.*

"It says she knew Adam," Lilly said.

"Yes, just like the Bible says Mary bore Jesus from Joseph. What's important here is … she doesn't say she got a man from Satan. So, there are two traditions in Judaism. One says the Tree of Knowledge is Satan and the other says it's God."

"Right, and the androgynous pair…? I've never heard of an androgynous pair before."

"There are many androgynous pairs in religion; the idea spanning faiths. Hinduism's Shiva and Shakti are often drawn as a fused pair. There's also an androgynous couple in Greek mythology because Hermaphroditus and Agdistis were viewed as one."

"So, Samael [Satan] and Lilith [Serpent] were an androgynous pair equating to God?"

Shiva and Shakti

"Yes … there's even a poem about us:

Zohar Sitrei Torah 1:147b-148b, Jacob's Journey

> *The secret of secrets:*
> *Out of the scorching noon of Isaac,*
> *out of the dregs of wine,*
> *a fungus, 'mushroom,' emerged, a cluster,*
> *male and female together,*
> *red as a rose,*
> *expanding in many directions and paths.*
> *The male is called Samael,*
> *his female is always included within him.*
> *Just as it is on the side of holiness,*
> *So, it is on the other side:*
> *male and female embracing one another.*
> *The female of Samael is called Serpent,*
> *Woman of Whoredom,*
> *End of All Flesh, End of Days.*
> *Two evil spirits joined together:*
> *the spirit of the male is subtle;*
> *the spirit of the female is diffused in many ways and paths*
> *but joined to the spirit of the male."*

"And together Satan and the serpent mate Eve—"

"Supposedly as an incubus," Wolf said. "What's important to understand is a transfer of DNA took place and it was infused into Cain ... Early Gnostic writings such as the Gospel of Philip, written around 350 A.D., said the serpent in the Garden of Eden mated with Eve and the offspring of their union was Cain. The same statement is made in the Kabbalah and Jewish Midrashic texts from the ninth century.

"Jewish tradition also says the sexual pair, Samuel and Lilith, used an intermediary to receive an emanation from one another, and the heavenly serpent—a blind prince called Tanin'iver—was the intermediary. Slithering without eyes he is the bond, the accompaniment, and union between Samael and Lilith called 'Taninsam.' Lilith is a poisonous serpent and the mother of night-side, and she's also Leviathan in the Bible."

Unable to just quietly listen any longer, Lilly clapped her hands over her ears. "I'm not evil and I'm not Lilith or the serpent Leviathan!"

"I'm afraid you are, just like I'm symbolically Behemoth?"

Behemoth as depicted in *Dictionnaire Infernal*

CHAPTER SEVENTEEN

Lucifer and Jesus

"We were made at the same time," Wolf said, running tender fingers through Lilly's short hair. "God forms the light and the darkness, and Jesus spoke of humanities different seed lines in Matthew:

> Matthew 13:³⁸ *The field is the world; the good seed are the children of the kingdom, but the tares are the children of the wicked one.* ³⁹ *The enemy that sowed them is the devil; the harvest is the end of the world, and the reapers are the angels."*

Lilly lowered her eyes. "I've believed in a god and a devil for so long. I was told if someone was wicked they're a tare, and told serpent-seed was nothing more than a controversial religious belief used to explain the biblical account of the Fall of Man, falsely proposing the serpent in the Garden of Eden mated with Eve and the fruit of their union was Cain."

"The idea was officially denounced, yes," Wolf said, "but not only do Jewish Midrashic texts and the Kabbalah speak of the seedline, Gnostic writings do and Jesus said the tares were sown by the Devil. The seedlines are also mentioned at the beginning of the Bible ... in Genesis:

> Genesis 3:¹⁴ *So, the Lord God said to the serpent, 'Because you have caused Eve to [eat of the Tree of Knowledge's fruit], cursed are you above all livestock and all wild animals! You will crawl on your belly and eat dust all the*

> *days of your life.* ¹⁵ *And I will put enmity between you and*
> *the woman, and between your seed and her seed. Hers will*
> *crush your offspring's heads, and yours will strike their*
> *heels.'"*

"Why is the serpent cursed to eat dust all his life?"

"*Dust* is a code word for sperm, exposed in the Bible and the Quran:

> *Revelation 3:*¹⁹ *In the sweat of thy face shalt thou eat*
> *bread, till thou return unto the ground; for out of it were*
> *you taken: for dust thou art, and unto dust shalt thou*
> *return.*

> *Chapter (18) sūrat l-kahf (The Cave) His companion said*
> *to him while he was conversing with him, 'Have you*
> *disbelieved in He who created you from dust and then*
> *from a sperm-drop and then proportioned you [as] a*
> *man?'*

Lilly groaned.

The New Testament speaks of the different seedlines on multiple occasions?

> *Revelation 12:*¹⁷ *And the dragon was wroth with the*
> *woman and went to make war with the remnant of her*
> *seed which keep the commandments of God and have the*
> *testimony of Jesus Christ."*

"That verse doesn't speak of a seedline," Lilly grumbled. "It speaks of the faithful ... the followers of Christ."

"The remnant of the woman's seed keeping the testimony of Christ is the seed in his testes. It's the seedline descending from Cain—the murderer from the beginning. Covertly, Cain is Christ in the bible, and Jesus eludes to this when he says he existed before Abraham:

John 8:⁵⁶ Your father Abraham rejoiced to see my day: he saw it and was glad. ⁵⁷ Then the Jews said to him, you are not yet fifty years old, and you have seen Abraham? ⁵⁸ Jesus said to them, Truly, truly, I say to you, before Abraham was, I am."

Wondering why she'd ever bothered to go to church, Lilly groaned.

"The woman has two seedlines, and one of them issues from the serpent. This was made clear when God said, *'I will put enmity between you and the woman, and between your seed and her seed.'* The dragon is after the remnant of the woman's seed that has *the testimony of Jesus Christ.* The word 'testimony' comes from the word 'testes' and stems from the Hebrew custom of swearing an oath upon one's testes—swearing on the lives of their children. Hence, the seed that has the testimony of Jesus Christ is in his testes ... it's his seed:

A sour pout set on Lilly's face. Frustrated, she said, "Oh, for shit's sake! Whatever will you tell me next? How can you possibly get that Jesus is Lucifer and Satan his father and his seed is the evil tares from all that crap! Isn't it just gobbledygook!"

"In mythology prior to this time, the gods were considered the sons *and* husbands of the goddesses. And, Morning star is the English translation of Lucifer's name. So, beside the fact the church and the Bible have deliberately linked Satan and Lucifer to Jesus by bestowing his name upon him, are you telling me you require further proof?"

"I am, indeed," Lilly said, stubbornly. "You said the verse, Revelation 22:¹⁶ actually speaks of Jesus' mother, and it's calling *her* the Morning Star, so there's no connection. Ha!"

"Morning star more correctly references Lucifer's mother Aurora but, nevertheless, it *was* Lucifer's name. Morning Star, Lucifer, Shining One, and Day Star, all mean and directly reference Lucifer whose name was bestowed upon the planet Venus, even though the term doesn't apply to a male. There are several other verses in the Bible that use the same word translated as Morning star in Revelation 22:¹⁶· but only one other is referring to Aurora rather than Jesus:

> *Revelation 2:*[26] *He that overcomes and keeps my [Jesus']* *works unto the end, to him will I give power over the* *nations.* [27] *And he shall rule them with a rod of iron; as the* *vessels of a potter they shall be broken into shivers: even* *as I received of my Father.* [28] *And I will give him the* *Morning Star."*

"Well, which verses apply to Jesus?"

"One is found in 2 Peter," Wolf said. "I'll quote New Living's Translation:

> *2 Peter 1:*[19] *Because of that experience, we have even* *greater confidence in the message proclaimed by the* *prophets. You must pay close attention to what they* *wrote, for their words are like a lamp shining in a dark* *place—until the Day dawns, and Christ THE MORNING* *STAR shines in your hearts."*

"*New Living* has a habit of making shit up and adding extra words?" Lilly grumbled.

"Really? Then what do you make of the Vulgate's Latin translation?

> *2 Peter 1:*[19] *We have a surer word of prophecy; to which* *you would do well to take heed, till a light shines in a dark* *place, until the day dawns, and Lucifer arises in your* *hearts."*

Lilly's lips tightened. "You're just trying to be difficult! When you translate Lucifer's name into English, it translates as Morning Star, so of course the verse calls him Lucifer!"

"Haven't you just admitted it is his name...? I'm telling you the two are the same. Let's see what happens if I do a change about, use the English word instead of the Latin in another verse:

Isaiah 14:[12] How art thou fallen from heaven, O Morning Star, son of the morning! How are you cut down to the ground, he who did weaken the nations!"

"That's ridiculous!"

"No, it isn't ... Lucifer was the beloved demi-god son of a goddess unlike Jesus the deceiver—a fictitious mystery school teacher spinning a web of entrapment."

"That can't be right."

"Of course it is. Jesus is the false prophet and the Bible identifies him so:

> *Deuteronomy 13:[1] If a prophet, or one who foretells by dreams, appears among you and announces to you a sign or wonder, [2] and if the sign or wonder spoken of takes place, and the prophet says, 'Let us follow other gods' (gods you have not known) 'and let us worship them,' [3] you must not listen to the words of that prophet or dreamer. The Lord, your God, is testing you to find out whether you love him with all your heart and with all your soul. [4] You shall walk after the Lord your God, and fear him, and keep his commandments, and obey his voice, and you shall serve him, and cleave to him. [5] That prophet or dreamer must be put to death for inciting rebellion against the Lord your God, who brought you out of Egypt and redeemed you from the land of slavery. That prophet or dreamer tried to turn you from the ways your Lord God commanded you to follow. You must purge the evil from among you."*

"It's true enough Jesus showed people signs and wonders, but he didn't tell them to worship other gods!"

"Yes, he did," Wolf said. "He tried to get people to worship him instead of God. Isn't it true Christians worship Jesus and rank him above God? Indeed, many Christians believe Jesus *is* God or will become him because he as much as said so. And Christ didn't fulfill the messianic prophecies—no son of God was prophesied—a leader was anticipated."

"I think you're reaching and quoting Jewish beliefs ... Jesus never said he *was* God!"

"He as much as said so. He tried to usurp God's crown and was thrown down for it ... The Jews didn't crucify him for nothing."

Lilly folded her arms in a huff.

"In Roman mythology the underworld is called Hades and in Christian mythology, the pit. It's the same place and Jesus was symbolically thrown down."

Lilly exhaled loudly. "You said the elite, men who've amassed great wealth and power, want the true light of Lucifer to shine upon the world ... What exactly does that mean?"

"They long for the day when the need for smoke and mirrors is no more and they can worship Lucifer openly ... or more accurately ... his mother Aurora to whom the name Venus and Morning Star truly applies. They've dropped hints into the world, like in 2 Peter 1:19 in the Vulgate Bible, but they've never fully articulated their desires.

> *2 Peter 1:19 We have a surer word of prophecy; to which you would do well to take heed, till a light shines in a dark place, until the day dawns, and Morning star arises in your hearts."*

"Well, I'm not accepting your flimsy evidence! It's the kind of twaddle one finds on the internet."

Wolf sighed. "What do you make of this verse then:

> *Matthew 12:26 If Satan drives out Satan, he is divided against himself. How then can his kingdom stand?"*

"Kingdom...?" Lilly shrugged. "I don't know ... How can Satan be divided against himself?"

"Satan has a kingdom just like he has a seedline. If his kingdom is divided it can't stand ... and it's currently divided—"

"No! I won't let you have that one ... If Satan has a kingdom it's because he has sinners for followers."

"We've already put this one to bed ... Jesus said, *'the tares are the children of the wicked one. The enemy that sowed them is the devil.'* Is his word not good enough for you?"

"I'll take it under advisement," Lilly said, grumpily. "He might have been talking about followers."

Wolf scoffed. "I told you ... you don't understand the Bible."

"I think *you* don't!"

"Pfft. Like you'd know more than me ... Let me explain. Satan's brood don't know who they are—"

"You're talking nonsense ... trying to distance me from my Jesus." Lilly said, sticking her nose in the air. "I won't have it ... If I believe you, that means there's no hope for me and I'm stuck here." She sniffed back a tear. "And I don't even have Ox anymore!"

Wolf sighed heavily. "I think you need to be milked. You've woken up on the wrong side of the bed."

"I have not!"

"Do you think your religion appeared out of nowhere?"

"Of course not! Jesus was a Jew descending from King David—"

"Yes ... via Joseph. The more you protest, the more foolish you're appearing. Every religion is seeded by the one that precedes it. Jesus's mother Mary is akin to the Latin Aurora—the real Morning Star—and Jesus is cognate to her son Lucifer and is identified as Satan by the Bible and the Church; he even admits the connection:

> *Psalm 41:⁹ Yes, my own familiar friend, in whom I trusted, who did eat of my bread, has lifted his 'heel' against me.*

"You're making that connection because the serpent, Satan, gets his head crushed by the heel of the woman's seed?

> *Genesis 3:¹⁵ And I will put enmity between you [serpent] and the woman, and between your seed and her seed; it shall bruise your head, and you shall bruise his heel.*"

"Yes."

"It makes no sense!" Lilly growled. "Why would Jesus be against his own people? Why would he lie to them and prevent them from converting to save themselves?"

"Because he's the Devil in disguise ... a wolf in sheep's clothing! He only pretended to be you and you fell for it ... hook, line, and sinker. You let your heart wax gross and lost all sense of propriety because you wanted to be saved by his sacrifice. You thought you were a dedicated follower but you weren't, you were a tare. Now, look what has become of you and what is about to befall your kin. Your people have walked blindly into a net ... looking but not seeing ... listening but not hearing. This verse should have sounded an alarm in your heads:

> *Matthew 4:19 and he said to them, 'Follow me, and I will make you fishers of men.'"*

"Why should it have?" Lilly snapped. "Jesus was gathering followers."

"Do you not know of the verses in the Old Testament that repeatedly speak of the spreading of nets and people being brought up in them...? Being 'fished' is not a good thing:

> *Jeremiah 16:16 Behold, I will send for many fishers, says the Lord, and they shall fish them, and afterward I will send for many hunters, and they shall hunt them from every mountain, and from every hill, and out of the holes in the rocks."*

"Jesus didn't mean that!"

"Of course he did. You've just chosen not to see it."

> *Matthew 13:47 The kingdom of Heaven is like a net that is cast into the sea and gathers of every kind: 48 Which when full, they draw to shore and sit down and gather the good into vessels but cast away the bad. 49 So shall it be at the*

*end of the world: the angels shall come forth and sever the
wicked from among the just.* [50] *They shall cast them into
the furnace of fire: there, there shall be wailing and
gnashing of teeth."*

Lilly folded her arms. "That's what happens to evil people!"

Wolf shook his head. "I told you wars are won by lies and
deception, and it *has* been a war—a war we've won by baiting the
hook with promises and platitudes. Tell me, why exactly do the non-
believers deserve to be punished? Does that even make sense to
you? Can't you see a similarity between Christian doctrine and thugs
extorting protection money?"

"Shut up!"

Golden Ring

Lilly groaned as Wolf lifted and pushed her out of his pouch before cradling her to him as he carried her to the milking room. Yesterday she'd been arguing with him and she hoped today wouldn't be more of the same.

"It's okay," he said as he lay her upon the milking table. "I'm going to give you a break today ... Let you relax and unwind."

"Thank you, Daddy ... I know you've only been trying to educate me, but it was getting a bit much ... I'm having trouble coming to terms with God and the Devil being one and the same, and Christ having not only roleplayed the goddess as the Son of Man equating to Lucifer and the serpent on the rod or cross, but also having roleplayed the true Son of God *as* the rod or branch ... etc."

"I know ... it's a lot to absorb and reconcile with your previous training."

"You mean brainwashing."

"Yes, that," Wolf said as he gave her a peck on her cheek before leaving."

Lilly was surprised Cat was still setting up because he was usually ready for her.

"You're lucky you know," he said, adjusting some equipment.

"How so...? Do you mean to be here?"

"Well, that depends on your point of view, but I was referring to Wolf being so patient with you ... taking his time to explain your religion to you. Everyone in our world knows this forwards and backwards, so he doesn't usually talk about it."

Lilly shrugged. "I guess that makes me an idiot."

"Not at all," Cat said, shaking his head. "That wasn't what I was saying ... I was just pointing out that he's being kind to you ... making a considerable effort to help you adjust."

"I suppose...? And I'm not being grateful?"

"It's fine ... he knows this is hard for you."

Lilly sighed, "I wasn't trying to be ungrateful or rude ... it just burns ... He's turned my world upside down."

"He gets that, and he's trying to tell you the truth as kindly as he can ... You do want to know the truth?"

"I'm not sure I could fail to know it at this point."

"True, but he's trying to fill in the gaps and explain the ins and outs of your religion because he thinks it'll help you."

Lilly sighed audibly as Cat began the milking process. When he finished, he slipped some little tubes into her nostrils and ran his fingers through her hair.

"Are you sending me ..."

"Off to sleep, yes," Cat said, but Lilly was already unconscious.

Cat set about busying himself with a delicate operation. He inserted a needle into one of her swelling beads in her anal glands. It was delicate work and he needed to concentrate because liquid gold flowed through his needle when he squeezed it. The specially designed insertion needle was insulated to prevent the extreme heat traveling through it from burning her skin, and the beads themselves were made from a mixture of mechanical and biological technology. They contained the blazing heat and allowed nothing more than mild radiant heat to escape their confines.

Using scanning equipment, Cat carefully guided the needle into each bead and filled the swelling beads almost to their tops. Any mistake would have resulted in an extreme injury and so he was mindful not to make one. When he finished, he left Lilly on the table and went into the next room to send her milk and wine on its way while monitoring equipment kept track of her vital signs. During his brief absence, her heartbeat steadily rung out into the silence assuring him all was well.

Wolf walked into the milking room. "It went well?" he said over his shoulder as Cat entered.

"Absolutely," Cat said. "The beads should have sealed themselves up again properly in a few minutes. To be sure, I'm going to leave her under for a bit longer, then put some painkilling cream on her and insert the worms."

Wolf stood still in front of him so he could milk some glands at the base of his penis and capture the liquid in a little jar.

"Good amount here,' Cat said. "After I've eye-dropped them into her urethra so they can make their way into her paraurethral glands, and I've carefully inserted them into her Bartholin glands and anal glands, I'll check a sample under a microscope for you."

Wolf watched Cat insert the majority of the fluid into Lilly via a flexible soft needle before taking what little remained to a microscope to look at it under it. "Are they swimming?" he said.

"They sure are, you haven't lost any potency."

"Good," Wolf said, looking at Lilly. "Are you planning on telling her what you've done?"

"Ah ... no," Cat said. "I'm about to trim her inner vagina lips. Hopefully, she'll think that's all I've done. How about you ... are you going to tell her?"

Wolf shook his head. "Course not ... It will be a nice wee surprise for her when the beads swell to their full size and the golden balls within start bouncing around ... When they're pleasing her, I don't think she'll complain."

"Maybe not," Cat said, "but your worms are quite developed ... She'll probably feel them within a week or less, and I'll be surprised if some of them haven't made their own way into her already ... She might be complaining about them before the weeks out."

"The good news keeps coming ... after they stop freaking her out, she'll enjoy them too."

◆ ◆ ◆

"Are you feeling okay?" Wolf said as he settled himself down on his bed with Lilly.

"I suppose … What did Cat do to me?"

"He checked you over."

"You and I both know he did more than that."

"What do you think he did?"

Lilly put a hand between her legs. "He's trimmed my inner vagina lips!"

"Only a smidge … he made you look neat and tidy."

Lilly groaned.

CHAPTER NINETEEN

A polite rap on the door

While Lilly drifted off to sleep, Wolf lay on his bed reflecting upon his time with her and thinking about what to do about Cat's unabated resentment from days gone by. A polite rap on his door frame interrupted his deliberations.

El entered the room. "Penny for your thoughts," he said as he made his way to the bed and lay down behind Wolf. After gently wrapping an arm around him, he rubbed his swollen belly. "How's our girl doing?"

"She's doing well, but I'm still trying to explain our world to her. Trying to get her to understand not only what her religion was really about, but also how it came about."

"Hmm. It takes a while for the pieces to fall into place for them. Are you happy with her progress?"

"Yes, but she's not ready to meet you."

"That's a pity because I'm dying to meet her ... touch her."

"I know, but—"

"She thinks you're her daddy and you're a bonded pair," El said, quoting a previous conversation. "You're worried she'll get upset if she finds out you're in a loving relationship with one of your own kind."

"Yes."

"And you're worried she'll react badly when she discovers you're more 'she' than 'he,'" El said cupping one of Wolf's full breasts in a huge hand. "If she's happy to nurse from you, I don't think she'll be too bothered by the revelation."

"She knows I'm a 'she' and a 'he.' She sleeps in my womb and suckles on my breasts, but I don't think she's ready to learn we vary on the spectrum; hormones influencing if we're more she or he."

"What you're really worried about," El said, "is how she'll react when she finds out I put my dick up your arse."

"Right ... well, that's not how I'll put it to her," Wolf said, his mind drifting back to thoughts of his broken promise with Cat and his departure long ago. Momentarily, he found himself reliving the trauma that had made him refuse to sign a pledge to take a human bride and a job in the basement. As if etched in his mind, he recalled what sent him hurtling through space to distant lands long ago and vowing never to return. It was how his one and only heat had been handled, or rather mishandled that had upset him so.

Wolf got his menstrual period like all adolescent wolves did and he'd informed the authorities like he was told to do, and like other young wolves, he'd been deliberately isolated from his own kind to prevent a young sweetheart relationship from developing, but what happened next shocked him. He was led to an isolation cell and locked in before a wolf of great age and statue was sent in to impregnate him. El visited, and in an abrupt, almost unfeeling manner, he'd told him he'd be doing the honors.

Wolf remembered the day it happened. His muscles all but abandoned him because they drugged his food and water. El arrived and, for the first time ever, Wolf received some affection from one of his own kind. With his hormones running wild he melted into El's arms and enjoyed his mating immensely even though El wasn't overtly loving.

Sensing something in Wolf, El decided to feminize him and simultaneously make an undisclosed claim upon him, instead of just letting him go on his merry way. Wolf didn't understand protocol, so when El continued to have him drugged, and he came down and started mating him anally after his vaginal mating, he didn't know he was being treated differently. He was disturbed by the change in El's behavior but he enjoyed his growing affection and sweet words, and it wasn't long before he looked forward to El's visits and encouraged his attention. He even told him he loved him.

Shortly after this, he was let out of his cage and sent off to do his compulsory military training with other new recruits in space without so much as a goodbye from El. It was there that he realized he'd been treated differently. Feeling a bit shy about what had happened, and smarting from El's apparent rejection, he, fortunately, didn't speak of it, and it wasn't long before he understood what was done to him.

Older recruits would elbow him in the ribs and point to a new recruit before saying things like, "Ha, look at his swagger, one of the old boys bum-fucked him good and proper. Good thing too, now we can take turns and have him as our bitch." Horrified, Wolf quizzed the older recruit further and he was told a proportion of the new recruits were selected to be feminized so the rest of the boys could fuck them. Apparently, it was good for morale and kept the team happy—gave them a release for their tensions and aggressions. Oorah!"

After his timely heads up, Wolf never breathed a word of what had happened with El and he made sure he didn't have a swagger. He was plagued by dreams of him and unwanted desires, but he knew better than to give into them. Feminized recruits never advanced, and the only way they ever got any peace was to attach themselves to a strong male and let him claim them. This kept the other guys at bay, but it seldom worked for long. Most of the feminized wolves did their time hard. To escape, they quickly accepted a job in the basement when one was offered.

Whenever one left the other recruits would say, "He's gone to be a bitch in a hive. Never mind, they'll send us some fresh blood soon enough. Wolf did everything he could to shake off what had happened to him. He even took in feminized recruits and made them his bitch because he felt sorry for them, but nothing helped. Painfully, he learned the changes made to him in adolescence were permanent.

He even witnessed feminizing being employed as a punishment. If a young recruit really messed up and caused his mates to suffer, and it was decided he wasn't elite soldier material, he was locked up and arse fucked by the leaders till he changed. Then he was passed around so everyone could have a piece of him—take their revenge out on him.

Space was cruel, but Wolf had done more than just survive it, he'd progressed through the ranks. Fearing he would be outed, the last place he wanted to return to was Earth. This, of course, had left Cat high and dry. By chance, El visited his ship. Wolf was nervous but El acted as if he'd forgotten him. He invited the seniors to Earth to train a human woman, a baby while enjoying some much needed R&R.

Wolf didn't want to accept because he'd heard rumors about guys getting stuck in the basement or choosing to stay, and he liked space. But against his better judgment, he let himself be coerced, mistakenly thinking his elevated position of general would make him indispensable—too valuable an asset to be ordered into the basement. His arrogance had been his downfall; they'd successfully lured him home and then they ensnared him.

Wolf remembered the nasty shock he received when he was forced to take the final step into adulthood that's delayed in his kind. Younger wolves are unaware of their undeveloped state because they live separate lives from the mature wolves. Unbeknownst to them, high-level generals take orders from an upper-echelon of society they don't know exists and are essentially sentinels lurking in their midst. The same thing happens on Earth in the human world and human sentinels are called shepherds, and a shepherd can even be a mythical teacher who's never lived like Jesus. Holding the highest positions of power, proxy leaders on earth do the bidding of the humans behind the curtain—the men in Wolf's world.

Trapped in a semi-juvenile state, young wolves could maintain a naïve masculine bravo for thousands of years and their entry into the closed adult world, if it ever came, was usually a painful one. Even if an upcoming harvest was anticipated and a wolf had pledged his oath—agreed to take a bride—he wasn't told the secret rites associated with the entrance into the adult world. Sometimes, seemingly out of the blue, a decision was made that a juvenile wolf would make a worthy addition to the adult club and their initiation began even if they hadn't agreed to take a bride and a harvest wasn't imminent. It was like getting an invitation to an elite secret society that you couldn't refuse.

Wolf remembered it well; he'd thoroughly enjoyed training new babies and he had a talent for it, so every time a new job came up, and he was able, he'd put his hand up for the job. He knew the rules, don't try and give them a mouth feed and don't probe their inner chamber. If you didn't do either of those things you were home free. He was training his umpteenth baby when it happened—he developed a burning desire to have her always. He didn't know why she was so special, only that she was and he wanted her to be his. He was about to act on his desires when he was suddenly pushed out of the lair and corralled upstairs.

There he was darted like an animal and told they'd stopped giving him an antidote. He didn't know he'd been receiving one. Then he was led to a cell, and when his sedative wore off, he raged against the bars. He wanted to return to space, to pastures anew, and if he'd gotten away he never would have returned. He should have known better than to return to this planet. Space beckoned and he wanted out, but if he'd thought his boyhood ordeal was rough, the days following his antidote withdrawal were infinitely worse.

Once again, El visited his cell. He told him he'd seen a future partner in him, and a long-term loving relationship in their future. He tried to compassionately explain the intricacies of the adult world, but Wolf wouldn't have it. He hated El for what he'd done—stolen his manhood eons ago—and his hatred had festered over the years. So when El said he'd marked him and claimed him because he valued him, his words fell upon deaf ears.

Wolf would have none of it, so El reluctantly had him drugged and turned over, and once again he'd taken pleasure in him. At first, Wolf was so angry he wanted to kill him, but as days became weeks, he changed. He didn't know how it happened, it just did. Once again, he began to enjoy El's visits and accept his attentions without protest. He told himself he was only doing it because he didn't want to be drugged anymore and he'd do anything to get out of the cage, but in truth, he was still in love with El. His love and desire had never died. It was as if El had cast an unbreakable spell upon him all those years ago.

El broke Wolf's chain of thought by tenderly stroking his face. "I'm sorry I caused you pain."

Wolf rolled over and looked into his eyes. He shrugged. "I forgave you long ago, but Cat's still holding a grudge ... He had a big rant about it in front of Baby."

"I know. I'll try and talk to him. I'm sure he understands, but, deep inside, he still bears the scar—the emotional pain of being abandoned. It's a deep cut that will never fully heal. You and he bear the same scar. I tried to call you back. In the end, I had to make it my mission to get you back, and almost the only thing I was living for. I'm truly sorry. It would sadden me greatly if you decide to change partners. I'm sorry I hurt you, I really am. I tried to bring you in earlier, but you kept eluding me."

Wolf sighed and hugged El. "Don't panic. I'm not about to refuse your advances and take another lover."

El sighed. "I've got to admit I've been worried, especially since Cat's outburst. Producing a worm resets your sexuality and you could choose to make Ox your bitch and advance. No one would blame you if you did. In fact, they're expecting you to seize upon the opportunity."

"I know ..."

"When I felt your full breasts, I hoped that was a positive sign ... confirmation that you've made your decision."

"It was ... But I have to admit when I smelt her and tasted her virgin flesh, and it stimulated a juvenile worm to develop in me, the urge to run with the shot of testosterone it gave me and the change it made to my basic chemistry was almost overwhelming."

"I wouldn't have been cross. I would've understood. I still will understand ..."

"We're family. I've made up my mind."

El hugged Wolf. "Thank you."

"What's going to happen to Ox? Had he been feminized...? I didn't think he had."

"No, he hasn't. You know we spy on the hives ... he was eyeing you up when you weren't looking."

Wolf sighed. "Baby misses him."

"I know. I've had many sleepless nights over it ... Have you thought about making advances to him?"

"No."

CHAPTER TWENTY

Dragons and Nāgas

Water lapped gently around Lilly's face as she floated on her back in the pool. Basking in the afterglow of Wolf's affections, she looked at the dragons on the beams above. "So, you're the symbolic dragon?"

"Yes," Wolf said. "The firstborn of the dragons in the Vedas and the head of the Asuras [demons] was a stone dragon called Vritra, and his name meant 'enveloper.' Personified as drought and viewed as an opposer, he clashed with the major Hindu god Indra when he obstructed the course of the rivers. To stop him, Indra got three Devas [gods] Varuna, Soma, and Agni to help him. He had to coax them into it because they'd previously held the dragon in high esteem and called him Father. Indra then smashed the stone dragon Vritra while high on Soma, [the Elixir of Immortality] and released the rivers at the beginning of time—the start of the New Year."

"When the Dawn Goddesses were released?"

"Yes. The story parallels the tale of Vala, the stone cave or fortress, split by Indra high on Soma."

"So, Vala and Vritra are essentially the same character?"

Wolf nodded. "The deity imprisoning the Dawn Goddesses was symbolized as a stone dragon, mountain fortress or cave, and the Goddesses released at the beginning of time were similarly symbolized in different forms; as cows (kine), rivers and goddesses ... The Ganges is considered to be a major river and a Hindu goddess and Hindus who bathe in it believe it's the cow that gives much milk and is eternally pure."

Lilly's brow rose.

"The central myth of the Rigveda is the tale of the abduction and imprisonment of the Dawn Goddesses by a dragon and the heroic god who liberated them from captivity by slaying it ... Permeating throughout religion the myth is reflected in numerous traditions. In Catholicism, countless Catholic shrines depict the Virgin Mary emerging from a cave."

"Because Mary's a Dawn Goddess?"

"Yes."

"So, you're the evil dragon and my rescuer will slay you?"

"No ... The Dawn Goddesses released at the beginning of time, at the start of the symbolic New Year, were your people—the crop being sown. The tale and central myth of the Rigveda is legend committed to writing ... and legend became myth."

"If it's history, then why didn't they just write evil alien pricks set captives free to multiply so they could torture them in the distant future when they rounded them up again?"

"You don't seriously think your people wrote the tale down ... do you? The truth was deliberately penned in an elusive fairy-tale manner so it *would* become a myth."

Lilly groaned. "You mean your evil strategy was carefully constructed and instrumented from the beginning ... Why was it written? Why was it so important? Did a fair-skinned race of people with blue and green eyes suddenly arrive and the monumental event had to be explained?"

"Of course ... and it wasn't only released females who came, but, rather, a seedline, and to give you a chance to become established your arrival was explained. Originally, everyone knew exactly who you were and why you were set free, and your arrival coincided with the departure of the gods. You were honored and given the best chance of survival but the use of symbols helped you blend in with the other races and your significance fade. And as you know, you eventually became a man wondering around performing miracles in a rough garment and wearing sandals."

"So, everyone just forgot who we were?"

"No ... a concerted effort went into distorting the information. Wars and changing religions eventually caused you to forget who you were and almost everyone else had the same lapse of memory.

Everyone, except our caretakers, our watchers, because at no time have we not been keeping an eye on you and managing the crop from afar."

"Right ..."

"Currently, it's nearing harvest time:

> *Revelation 13:14 And I heard a voice from heaven saying to me, 'Write, Blessed are the dead which die in the Lord from now on': 'Yes,' said the Spirit, 'that they may rest from their labors; and their works do follow them.'"*

"I'm not buying that crap. I'm not resting! I'm producing!"

"You do rest in me ... I'm the symbolic stone cave or mountain fortress called Vala, or when symbolized as a dragon, I'm Vritra."

"Of course you fucking are!"

Wolf cleared his throat. "Vritra had a snake brother in the Vedas called Ahi (snake) who equates to the Nāgas in Hinduism ... In Indian mythology, an ancient sage Kashyapa Prajapati has two wives, Vinata and Kadru who want children. Kadru gives birth to one thousand eggs with 1,000 snake sons in them, the Nāgas, and Vinata births two eggs from which Garuda is born from one of them, and he's either worshipped singularly or as a race with kingdoms and cities. Garuda kings have the magical ability to change into human form and while transformed have romances with human women."

"In the Hindu version of time's beginning," Wolf continued, "the demon Vala is killed by Indra and his bile's pilfered by Vasuki, the king of the Nāgas, but before he can make off with his loot he's confronted by Garuda and he drops it. The bile's then caught in mid-air by Garuda, but it slips from his beak and crashes to Earth, solidifying into an emerald. This is where the belief ... *'if you touch an emerald it will mitigate the effects of poison'* ... comes from."

"I didn't know that?" Lilly said. "So, an emerald is a symbol for your mouth feed, your bile, known to have magical powers?"

"Yes. There's another myth about an emerald. In it, Lucifer's fall is accompanied by an emerald getting lost when it falls out of his crown."

"I see ..."

"In another myth in Hindu mythology, Garuda makes a deal with the mother of the Nāgas, Kadru, to emancipate his mother. He agrees to bring her Nāga [snake sons] the Elixir of Immortality, but the elixir's in the possession of the gods in heaven who are jealously guarding it. To protect the elixir, they've ringed it with a massive fire covering the sky and blocked the way to it with a fierce mechanical contraption made of sharp blades. A similar device is in the Bible:

> *Genesis 3:24 So he [God] drove out the man; and placed at the east of the garden of Eden Cherubims, and a flaming sword which turned every way, guarding the way to the tree of life."*

"So, does Garuda obtain the Elixir of Immortality?"

Garuda, the mount of Lord Vishnu

"Yes," Wolf said. "After getting past the bladed contraption and two deadly guardians—gigantic poisonous snakes placed next to the elixir—Garuda takes the elixir in his mouth without swallowing it and flies towards the eagerly awaiting serpents. En-route he encounters the god Vishnu, but rather than fight the two exchanged promises. Vishnu promises Garuda the gift of immortality, even without drinking the elixir, and in exchange, Garuda promises to become Vishnu's mount. Flying on Garuda meets up with Indra the god of the sky and another exchange of promises is made. Garuda promises he'll make it possible for Indra to regain possession of the elixir and take it back to the gods in heaven after he's delivered it. Indra, in turn, promises Garuda the serpents as food."

Lilly groaned. "I see ... and the Nāgas are my people ... right?"

"Yes. Nāga is the Sanskrit word for a race of intelligent people symbolized as snakes or serpents in Hinduism and Buddhism—Caucasians. Cambodians' claim they're part Nāga because the ancient Khmer kings who built the temple complex at Angkor Wat claimed they were descended from a union between a banished Hindu prince and a serpent woman called Nāgaraja; the daughter of the serpent king of the land. The children of Rishi Kashyapa and Kadru—the mother of the thousand Nāgas—were also called Nagaraja. Individually named children include Shesha, Takshaka, and Vasuki—the king of the Nāgas."

"Does the tail of the Elixir of Immortality permeate throughout religion."

"Of course," Wolf said. "The Elixir of Immortality is an integral part of faith. Jesus spoke of it ... indeed ... he claimed to be it:

> *John 6:*[53] *Then Jesus said to them, Truely, Truely, I say to you, except you eat the flesh of the Son of man, and drink his blood, you have no life in you.*

> *John 6:*[35] *And Jesus said to them, I am the bread of life: he that comes to me shall never hunger, and he that believes on me shall never thirst.*

> *John 6:*[27] *Labor not for the meat that perishes, but for that meat which endures into everlasting life, which the Son of man shall give to you: for he has God the Father sealed.*

"But of course it's a woman who really has the father sealed:

> *Song of Solomon 4:*[12] *A garden enclosed is my sister, my spouse; a spring shut up, a fountain sealed.*

Song of Solomon 7:² *Your navel is like a round goblet,*
which wants not liquor: your belly is like a heap of wheat
set about with lilies.

Lilly frowned. "Does the Elixir of Immortality feature in Judaism and Islam?"

"Absolutely. The Tree of Life and the goddess feature in the Jewish Old Testament and the only woman named in the Quran is Jesus's mother Mary. She holds a singularly exalted place in Islam. Mentioned seventy times, she features more often in the Quran than she does in the New Testament. And in the biblical account of the Garden of Eden, Adam and Eve eat of the Tree of Knowledge, but there's no Tree of Knowledge in the Quran. Instead, the pair eat of the Tree of Immortality."

Islam's Tree of Immortality in the Garden of Eden

"I see," Lilly said. "Are you saying the Vikings with their serpent-headed boats knew who they were symbolically? Knew themselves to be serpent beings?"

"Yes, and Quetzalcoatl of South America: Quetzal [paradise bird] coatl [serpent] was a tall, light-skinned man with blond hair, blue or green eyes and a golden beard."

"Why was the rather straight-forward account of the Dawn Goddesses being released at the beginning of time in the Vedas, replaced with a more fanciful story in the Hindu account?"

"As I've said ... after the gods depart truth is constantly watered down. Another version of the story of the Dawn Goddesses features Chaos of Babylonia. She bore the first of our kind—the dragons and the serpents. Called the glistening one, Tiamat or Chaos was a goddess of primordial creation and she was depicted as a mermaid: the top half of her body human and her lower extremities serpentine or fish-like.

"Later, she became known as Thalattē, a variant of Thalassa, the Greek word for sea. The name Tiamat was dropped in secondary translations because the ordinary word for the sea was substituted for her name due to association. In the Bible, her god offspring are called Behemoth and her human offspring, Leviathan,"

"It's the same story?" Lilly said.

"Another version of the tale, yes."

"So, in the original story in the Vedas—the earliest surviving written account—Vala or Vritra is a stone dragon, cave or mountain fortress, and he has a snake brother cognate to the Nāgas but the dragon doesn't feature in the Hindu account. Instead, a giant eagle-type bird called Garuda does and he's befriended by the gods and his snake brother is the Nāgas?"

Varuna riding on the back of Makara

"Correct. The story was deliberately altered when it moved from the Vedas into Hinduism and it's symbolism split. The major Vedic god was Varuna, not Indra or Vishnu, and his mount was a serpentine dragon. When the Vedic god declined his dragon mount was supplanted by Garuda, the eagle-like mount of Vishnu."

"I see," Lilly said, "because as religion is altered and handed down its meaning is constantly watered down and given another layer of whitewash?"

"Exactly," Wolf said. "After the gods departed symbolism was split into good and bad in Hinduism as well as in the Bible and elsewhere. God's good persona became an eagle or rock and his negative persona a dragon or beast.

> *2 Samuel 22:³² For who is God, save the LORD? And who is a rock, save our God?*
>
> *Psalm 92:¹⁵ To show that the Lord is upright: he is my rock, and there is no unrighteousness in him.*

"God's symbolized as a rock?" Lilly said. "I knew this already but doesn't that link him to Vala, the cave or mountain fortress?"

"Yes, they were given a positive spin unlike his dragon persona:

> *Revelation 12:⁹ And the great dragon was cast out, that old serpent, called the Devil, and Satan, which deceives the whole world: he was cast out into the earth, and his angels were cast out with him."*

"I see," Lilly said wearily.

"Varuna was the Vedic god of water and the celestial ocean, and he was often conjoined with Mitra as Mitra-Varuna. As a monarch and guardian of the whole world, he was depicted as young and wearing glistening garments, and his golden palace had a thousand pillars and doors. Lord of rivers and seas, he sent rain and refreshment from the sky, wetting the pastures with the dew of clarified butter [ghee] and rain abounding in heaven, and his domain had streams that flowed with honey and cows at pasture yielding refreshment."

"Human cows that looked like Hathor?" Lilly said bitterly.

"Yes … Varuna was the chief god in the Vedic pantheon. A god of law and the underwater world, he rode on a dragon mount called Makara. In Sanskrit, Makara means 'sea dragon.' After the ascendancy of Indra, Shiva, and Vishnu who rides upon Garuda, he faded in literature, but the imagery of his fearsome mount remained."

"Right," Lilly said. "So, god rode upon a dragon and provided his sacred cows—the goddesses—with the waters of Father Heaven and they flowed with milk and honey?"

"Yes ... When the goddesses were released at the beginning of time and the gods retired, the dragon was condemned and slain for having imprisoned them and Varuna was named the king of the Asuras [demons], but he was adopted or changed into a Deva after the structuring of the primordial cosmos imposed by Indra after he defeats Vrtra. Then the good gods replace Varuna and their new chief god, Indra, rides upon a large eagle-type bird called Garuda, and the goddess symbol is changed from a beloved cow to a snake."

"Then a bullshit story was made up to make it okay for the evil dragon to feast upon the goddesses once more in his new identity as Garuda!"

"You caught that did you?" Wolf laughed. "But you're only partly correct. The dragon wasn't considered evil previously ... he was held in high esteem and even called Father by high ranking gods."

"So, the gods spoken about, those who rode upon your backs, aren't you! Your symbols were absorbed by human gods and became theirs while you slinked away and became invisible!"

"Indeed, and although many gods in the Vedas did become demons in Hinduism, the negative spin was never complete in Asia because Varuna's sea-dragon mount Makara can still be seen standing guard outside Hindu and Buddhist temples, as the guardian of gateways and thresholds. Makara is also depicted as a gargoyle or as a spout attached to natural springs, and he was sometimes a vehicle for Ganga, the river goddess."

"So," Lilly said, "he still stands guard in Europe on Cathedrals like Notre Dame in Paris where gargoyles were once rain spouts depicting the waters from heaven pouring forth from their mouths when it rained?"

"Yes," Wolf said. "Makara was also a characteristic motif of the Khmer's empires architecture in their ancient capital in the Angkor region of Cambodia. There, Makara is seen in decorative carvings on lintels, tympanums and temple walls, and he's often seen with a Nāga serpent emerging from his gaping mouth."

"Why is a Nāga seen emerging from his mouth?"

Nāga coming out of a Makara's mouth

"Makara's gaping mouth symbolizes a pouch and when a Nāga is depicted emerging from it, it's very much alive. Makara devoured Nāgas just like Garuda does, but unlike in the Bible where snakes are demonized, serpents aren't demonized in Asia because Lord Shiva blessed and wore Vasuki, the king of the Nāgas, around his neck. Working together, the Asuras [demons] and Devas [gods] used him to extract the Ambrosia of Immortality from the Ocean of Milk."

"Hang on a minute," Lilly said, "that means the dragon Makara was worshipped at the same time as the goddesses were symbolized as serpents."

"Yes ... There's always a cross over period in religion when one symbol or god is fading and another's ascending."

Resembling a walking dragon to her, Lilly shuddered as the image of the creature in the movie *Alien* popped into her head. Its second set of teeth that extended out of its mouth had always creeped her out and she wondered if the creator's inspiration was a Makara.

"Dragon imagery was borrowed from the now critically endangered crocodile *Alligator sinensis*. Commonly called the Yangtze alligator it's endemic to eastern China, and its name 'Yow-

Lung' or 'T'o' translates as dragon ... the alligator's appearance."

"So, the symbolic dragon is really a crocodile?"

Yangtze alligator

"Yes," Wolf said, "and it was the worshiped symbol of an Egyptian ... Sobek was an ancient Egyptian deity associated with the Nile crocodile. Depicted either as a crocodile or as a human with a crocodile head, he is known from several Pyramid Texts from the Old Kingdom, particularly from the spell PT 317 which praises the pharaoh Unis as a living incarnation of the crocodile god:

> *Unis is Sobek, green of plumage, with alert face and raised fore, the splashing one who came from the thigh and tail of the great goddess in the sunlight ... Unis has appeared as Sobek, Neith's son. Unis will eat with his mouth, Unis will urinate, and Unis will copulate with his penis. Unis is lord of semen, who takes women from their husbands to the place Unis likes according to his heart's fancy."*

Sobek, the Nile crocodile

"Okay," Lilly said. "So, let me get this straight … the human god Varuna was depicted riding upon you when you were symbolized as Makara the dragon, and, later, Vishnu rides upon you as Garuda an eagle-type bird, and you were also worshiped as a god?"

"When our human crop is running free, humans are portrayed as masters of their own destiny and in control and our symbols are transferred to them. This, as you've observed, allows us to perform the magic trick of disappearing, but, as you know, our invisibility fades if you carefully examine Hindu and Vedic literature. Hindus' are the most in touch with the past, their religion is the oldest, but most of them now worship Krishna or Buddha, so they're none the wiser."

"I see …"

"It isn't possible to delete a symbol as powerful and widespread as the dragon which is why our symbolism was split and the dragon symbol demonized … So, now there are Asuras [demons] and Devas [gods] in Hinduism and God and the Devil in the Bible."

"Well, I guess that explains the demise of the Titans and the rise of the smaller Olympians … Were you also worshipped as dragons in ancient Sumer?"

"Yes," Wolf said. "There, winged, horned dragons were depicted with serpents entwined on a pole—your kind."

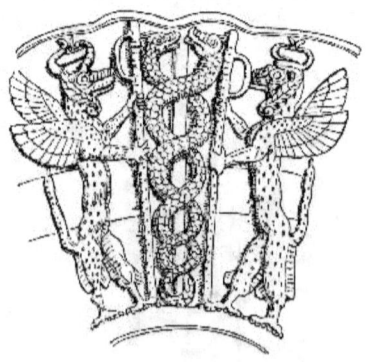

The first known image of serpents entwining a pole
was found in Sumer. It dates to 2000 B.C.

Lilly frowned. "Was that an early Rod of Asclepius or Nehushtan symbol?"

"Yes, drawn as if walled in by winged dragons, the goddess is symbolized by two serpents entwining a rod—phallus. The twin serpents depicting her and her serpent within."

"So, it was an early symbol for the Tree of Immortality or Life?"

"Yes," Wolf said, "At one time, the eagle and the crocodile were both symbols for our kind. So, it was only natural that they'd be merged into one—into a flying dragon. The dragon was further merged with your symbolic identity, and, just as you and the worm/serpent can be viewed as one, so can you and I ... The symbol for the Tree of Life is a serpent wrapped around a rod. It symbolizes the goddess wrapped around us—the rod representing either ourselves or our phallus."

"A stylized version of God and his serpent? Like the Egyptian god Serapis? Is his image also a trinity symbol ... his halo representing the son or active placenta?"

"Yes," Wolf said. "In Vedic and Hindu texts, where we're depicted as beasts, there seems to be a clear distinction between man and us, but Varuna's sea-dragon mount, Makara's, name in Tibetan, 'chu-srin,' denotes a hybrid creature, and several cultures merged our symbolic identities into a blended creature."

God Serapis

"What cultures?"

"We were almost unanimously merged into one creature in early cultures ... The crocodile, dragon, and eagle representing my kind;

and snakes and lions representing yours ... but sheep, cows, and oxen represented us both—males us—females you."

"Rams?" Lilly said. "Were they a later symbol?"

Hybrid dragon called a Mušhuššu on the Ishtar Gate in Babylon

"Mostly," Wolf said. "Babylon's sixth century B.C Ishtar Gate featured a hybrid dragon called a Mušhuššu: a creature with the hind legs of an eagle, rams' horns, snake's tongue, forelegs and tail of a lion, and a dragon's head ... Other cultures merged the characteristics of an eagle and lion as well, the combined form representing us as 'one.' "In Jewish mythology," Wolf said, "a ziz is a giant griffin with the body, tail and back legs of a lion and the head and massive wings of an eagle."

Jewish Ziz

"It had much in common with the Sumerian and Akkadian anzû: a massive lion-headed bird that breathed fire and water. He was conceived by the pure waters of the Apsu (underground aquifer given a religious fertilizing quality in Sumerian and Akkadian mythology) and the wide Earth [goddess] or was the son of a Mesopotamian goddess, Siris.

Sumerian and Akkadian anzû

"Anzu was syncretized by ancients with gods associated with thunderstorms and called 'Father Pasture.' In his symbolic or earthly lion-bird form he was Anzu and in his divine human-like form he was the god, Abu."

Lilly inhaled sharply. "Oh my god! You and I are the beast in Revelation! We're the Sumerian and Akkadian anzû! People will hunt us down and slay us:

> *Revelation 13:² And the beast which I saw was like unto a leopard, and his feet were as the feet of a bear, and his mouth as the mouth of a lion: and the dragon gave him his power, and his seat, and great authority."*

Wolf entered the water. "No, they won't!" he said as he scooped Lilly up. "You're alright. They don't want to kill us."

"They will ... they've done it before ... they slew the dragon and took over!"

"They didn't ... it was a bullshit story circulated to appease the populous when we departed and the crop was sown. And, as you've already worked out, our symbol changed to an eagle and then everyone carried on worshipping us as they'd done before, so nothing changed."

Hyperventilating, Lilly was in full panic mode. "They'll hunt us down!"

"Baby, we're under a military base. They know where we are and they're protecting us … they'll bring in the harvest quietly for us."

"I'm not worried about my people! If they think I'm in the belly of the beast they might actually give a shit, but nobody else will. Women get sent to prison in some counties for being raped and they get stoned to death for taking a lover! Do you think those people will care if they kill a whore? No, they'll slay me without blinking … I'll be some hideous blight that needs done in!"

"Baby, the people you're talking about worship Allah and the Virgin Mary and they believe in the Tree of Immortality. They won't run as through."

"They will … they want to be in control … they want to rule the world!"

"They don't … they long for the end of days and they think it won't happen until they're gained control … They worship Allah."

"They only say that … They want power! They'll want to kill us!"

"You're the Virgin Mary, they won't want to kill you any more than they'll want to kill me," Wolf said as he tucked Lilly up in his pouch and licked her back while inserting his probe.

Lilly felt Wolf's drugs begin to wash over her like a blanket caressing her.

"Calm, Baby, we're okay. You're okay … You seem to be forgetting we have flying saucers and can be out of here at a moment's notice … I'm not going to let anything happen to you because you're me. I'll protect you the same as I would my own right arm … better. Calm."

Lilly drew in Wolf's internal nipple, her head slumped and her eyes closed but she was still very much awake. Wolf rubbed her back and her breathing eased.

"Baby, as I've told you before, wars aren't won by numbers and physical strength but rather by lies, tactical maneuvering, and strategy. You haven't fully appreciated who I am … in ancient languages, dragon meant 'the being who excels in intelligence.' In Greek, it means 'the one who sees and watches.' Surely, you've heard of Draconian rule?"

"You're tyrants …"

"Not to you," Wolf said. "Man will come to understand who and what we are, and when he does, he'll bend his knee and pray to us in fear and reverence. I could wipe this planet clean of almost every human being in a matter of days ... I'm not going to ... but I could."

"With a virus?"

"Or worse."

"But you love this planet?"

"Indeed I do. I've put a lot of blood, sweat, and tears into this planet and it's *our* planet ... I will do what I must to defend it."

"You will?"

"I would, but there's no need. Everything is okay."

Lilly frowned. "Is it ... It doesn't seem okay."

"It will be once we've decreased the temperature."

"Oh, that's right. So, you *are* attacking man."

"We're getting around to it ... Humanity needs to appreciate who we are and who's boss."

"So, you don't fear man ... but you were concerned about a shooter not so long ago."

Wolf sighed. "It's true I'm susceptible to man's weapons and I can be killed, but short of someone getting extremely lucky, I'm not likely to be killed by a man."

"And you don't kill singularly."

"No. I'll wipe man out by the millions or billions if I decide that's what I want to do."

"But you don't want to?"

"No. Well ... I have no intention to do so currently."

"But you're turning the temperature down!" Lilly said.

"Yeah, that's to get humanity running—"

"Into your net?"

"We'll discuss that another day ... We're fine, Baby. Truly we are. I'd leave if we were in danger."

Lilly sighed. "So, we're always depicted either singularly or together as creatures?" she said, picking up their previous conversation.

"Not always," Wolf said. "The goddess Isis was drawn with the wings of an eagle, and the woman in Revelation is given the wings of an eagle in chapter 12:

Revelation 12:¹⁴ And to the woman were given two wings of a great eagle, that she might fly into the wilderness, into her place, where she is nourished for a time, and times, and half a time, from the face of the SERPENT.

Winged Isis

"Oh," Lilly said. "So, verses in Revelation 12 link us together? Does the flood at the beginning of the Bible in Genesis come from the serpentine dragon ... The Bible is circular ... the ending's the beginning?

Revelation 12:¹⁵ And the SERPENT cast out of his mouth water as a flood after the woman, that he might cause her to be carried away by the flood."

"Correct."

"There isn't a positive dragon depiction in European culture ... is there?"

"Like elsewhere, the worshipped dragon was defeated and replaced. In Greek culture, it was replaced with a flying horse named Pegasus ... Poseidon, in his role as a horse god, sired Pegasus by the Gorgon Medusa whose hair was made up of living venomous snakes and visage turned those who looked upon her to stone. Jesus or God is said to descend from the heavens on a white horse ... a horse easily identified with Pegasus."

"Well," Lilly said. "Seeing as so much paganism is in the Bible, it seems only fitting that Pegasus should make an appearance."

"Quite," Wolf said. "In Greek culture, Bellerophon was the hero that killed the Chimera monster depicted by Homer as having a lion's head, a goat's body, and a serpent's tail; her breath came in terrible blasts of burning flame."

"A dragon?"

"According to the Greek poet Hesiod, she was. He said, Chimaera was a fearful creature, great and swift-footed, and strong with three heads; one of which was a grim-eyed lion and her hind part was that of a dragon, and in her middle, a goat; and her breath came forth as a fearful blast of blazing fire."

"I see."

Taweret

"Egypt also worshiped a horse, but in their case, it was a water horse ... a hippopotamus named Taweret. First appearing in the Old Kingdom as a mother of the pharaoh, she offered to suckle him with her divine milk. Her covering was the crocodile often depicted on her back. So, she can also be viewed as a joint creature ... the goddess and the dragon combined."

"And ... over time," Lilly said, "most of this information was watered down and lost."

"Correct ... because you know how it is with the truth ... it's like Chinese whispers, eventually, you can't discern what was originally said."

"I think you've had a hand in watering down the information."

"We've had more than a hand in it ... Chinese whispers aside, humans are very good at passing on oral history; they don't need writing. A concerted effort went into corrupting the information."

"Right," Lilly said sourly, "So, I really am stuck with the dragon."

"The father of Vlad Dracula was born in the year 1431 in Transylvania. He was called 'Dracul' which means dragon or devil in Romanian, and he belonged to the Order of the Dragon which fought the Muslim Ottoman Empire. Dracula means 'son of Dracul.' Therefore, young Vlad was the son of the dragon or son of the devil."

"And Dragons are in the Bible."

"The Bible says how they're born."

"Really?" Lilly said.

"Yes:

> Isaiah 14:[29] ... out of the serpent's root shall come forth a cockatrice, and his fruit shall be a fiery flying serpent."

Lilly thought for a moment. "The serpent's root is the woman's vagina?"

"Correct. The root chakra 'Muladhara' is located at the base of the spine by the pelvic floor. 'Muladhara' can be broken into two Sanskrit words: 'mula' meaning 'root' and 'adhara' meaning 'base.'"

"And a cockatrice is a two-legged dragon?"

"Yes."

"They say his fruit shall be a 'fiery, flying dragon' like a cockatrice is neither of these things?"

Cockatrice

"A dragon isn't either ... the language is figurative. It uses the symbols employed by ancients to describe different types of humanoids. Eve gave birth to Cain and he was the fruit of the serpent—a cockatrice—your kind. And you produce the pure fruit … the fiery flying serpents."

"I see," Lilly said. "So, a two-legged cockatrice gives birth to the red dragon that wants to devour the woman's baby?

> *Revelation 12:[1] And there appeared a great wonder in heaven; a woman clothed with the sun, and the moon under her feet, and upon her head a crown of twelve stars:*
> *[2] And she with child cried, travailing in birth, and pained to be delivered. [3] And there appeared another wonder in Heaven;*
> *behold a great red dragon, having seven heads and ten horns, and seven crowns upon his heads. [4] And his tail drew the third part of the stars of heaven, and did cast them to the earth: and the dragon stood before the woman which was ready to be delivered, to devour her child as soon as it was born. [5] And she brought forth a man child who was to rule all nations with a rod of iron: and her child was caught up to God, to his throne."*

"Your kind is symbolized as cockatrice in the Bible," Wolf said. "The woman was in the process of transforming."

"Okay," Lilly said, "but isn't there a passage in Isaiah 14 that identifies Ahaz, a king of Judah, as the serpent from whom a cockatrice shall come forth?

> *Isaiah 14:[28] In the year that king Ahaz died, was this burden. [29] Rejoice not Palestina, because the rod of him that struck you is broken, and out of the serpent's root shall come forth a cockatrice, and his fruit shall be a fiery flying serpent."*

"Remember, the Bible is deceptive; there's more *disinformation* than there is *information*. It doesn't mean Ahaz for several reasons. At the beginning of the chapter, Judah is defeated and a captive of

Babylon. Judah's captivity happens after the Battle of Carchemish in 605 B.C. when the Babylonian King Nebuchadnezzar besieges Jerusalem. At this time, the King of Judah named Ahaz is long dead: he reigned in the early to mid-seven hundreds and he never smote the Philistines, as demonstrated in 2 Chronicles 28:[18] ... and the verse doesn't speak of any king of Assyria either because shortly after the Battle of Carchemish in 605 B.C., Babylon conquered Philistia and destroyed their cities and exiled their inhabitants to Babylon—ending the Philistine culture forever. Therefore, the rod that struck Palestina was Nebuchadnezzar, the King of Babylon."

CHAPTER TWENTY-ONE

Holy Mountain

"What's God's Holy Mountain?" Lilly said, rubbing her brow. "I've always been mystified by the term."

"The bricks or stones used to form the structure are symbolic people," Wolf said. "Women heaped up upon one another. God's Holy Mountain and a pyramid share the same symbolism:

> *1 Peter 2:⁵ You also, as living stones, are built up into a spiritual house, a holy priesthood, to offer up spiritual sacrifices acceptable to God by Jesus Christ.*

> *Micah 3:¹² Therefore shall Zion for your sake be plowed as a field, and Jerusalem shall become heaps and the mountain of the house as the high places of the forest."*

Lilly frowned. "So, the mountain is you as Vala, a cave or mountain fortress paralleling Vritra, the symbolic stone dragon and demon in the Rigveda."

"Yes," Wolf said. "The Bible doesn't dwell on this symbolism, but it gives the dragon a handful of appearances to support the imagery:

> *Jeremiah 51:³⁷ And Babylon shall become heaps, a dwelling-place for dragons, an astonishment, and a hissing without an inhabitant.*

> *Revelation 12:³ And there appeared another wonder in*

heaven; and behold a great red dragon, having seven heads and ten horns, and seven crowns upon his heads. [5] And his tail drew the third part of the stars of heaven and cast them to the earth: and the dragon stood before the woman which was ready to be delivered, to devour her child as soon as it was born.

"But you don't really want to devour your own children though do you ... only what issues from their remaining placentas?"

"Indeed," Wolf said.

Unconvinced, Lilly gave him a quizzing look.

"Okay ... many of us *would* eat our own young ... We'd prefer to do so, so we can train our own human baby. Few dragons want to nurture their young because we resent the competition, but there are laws against devouring one's progeny and others need to learn how to train a human baby. Not to mention that humans value our young and will do almost anything to save them."

"Right ... So, getting back to what you said before ... the stones of a pyramid are symbolic people?"

"In Greek mythology," Wolf said, "Pyrrha, the daughter of Epimetheus and Pandora, was the wife of Deucalion. When Zeus decided to end the Bronze Age with a great deluge, they were the only survivors because the imprisoned Prometheus had foreseen the coming flood and told his son Deucalion to build an ark to survive it. They landed on Mount Parnassus during the flood, the only place spared the raging waters.

"Once the deluge was over and the couple was back on land, Deucalion consulted the oracle of Themis to get advice on how to repopulate the earth. He was told to throw the bones of his mother behind his shoulder. Deucalion and Pyrrha understood his mother to be Gaia, the mother of all living things, and the bones to be rocks. The rocks thrown behind their shoulders lost their hardness, and after growing in mass, they changed into human form; the softer parts becoming skin, the veins of the rocks, human veins, and the hardest parts of the rocks becoming bones. The stones thrown by Pyrrha became women, and the rocks thrown by Deucalion changed into men."

"So, the flood in the Bible isn't an original story?"

"Far from it," Wolf said. "That story's had many renditions."

"Does Holy Mountain symbolism date to pre-biblical times?"

Ishtar's Gate and processional way

"Yes. The Ishtar Gate of Babylon had a yellow brick road—a processional way—over half a mile long. The high walls on either side of it were adorned with over 120 sculptured lions. The road's yellow stones or bricks had an inscription underneath, a small prayer from King Nebuchadnezzar to the chief god Marduk. During New Year's celebrations, statues of deities were paraded down the yellow brick road that led to the Temple of Marduk—a symbolic representation of God's Holy Mountain—a festival house made of asphalt and fired bricks, and built firm like a mountain."

"Who did the lions represent?"

"Ishtar, and they appeared to be walking along the walls, making their way to the temple of Marduk, and, of course, the temple's fired bricks represented symbolic women ... Verses in the Bible employ the same symbolism:

> *Jeremiah 51:24 And I will render to Babylon and to all the inhabitants of Chaldea all their evil that they have done in Zion in your sight, says the Lord. 25 Behold, I am against you, O destroying mountain, says the Lord, which destroyed all the earth: and I will stretch out my hand*

upon thee, and roll you down from the rocks, and will make you a burnt mountain.

Isaiah 34:⁹ And the streams thereof shall be turned into pitch, and the dust thereof into brimstone and the land thereof shall become burning pitch. ¹⁰ It shall not be quenched night nor day; the smoke thereof shall go up forever: from generation to generation it shall lie waste; none shall pass through it forever and ever ... ¹³ And thorns shall come up in her palaces, nettles, and brambles in the fortresses thereof: and it shall be a habitation of dragons [gods], and a court for owls [goddesses]."

"Because, in the Bible, Zion and Jerusalem's curses were transferred to Babylon," Lilly said,
"Indeed:

Daniel 4:³³ The same hour was the thing fulfilled upon Nebuchadnezzar: and he was driven from men, and did eat grass as oxen, and his body was wet with the dew of heaven, till his hairs were grown like eagles' feathers, and his nails like birds' claws."

"Consumed by god as an eagle? He became part of him ... part of Garuda ... Was he representing the women in his tribe in that verse?

Revelation 12:¹⁴ And to the woman were given two wings of a great eagle, that she might fly into the wilderness, into her place ..."

Wolf nodded.
"Why were the Hebrews cursed by God? I thought they were his people?"
"When God brought them out of Egypt they became indebted to him because he'd killed the Egyptians' firstborn for them, and he made it clear it was a debt that needed to be repaid. If one was to

quickly summarize what the Bible is all about, this is the key point. It's unlikely they'll tell you this in church, but it is ... The curse changes throughout the Bible and is eventually transferred to Babylon:

> *Exodus 13:² Sanctify to me all the firstborn, whatever opens the womb among the children of Israel, both of man and of beast: it is mine.*

> *Exodus 13:¹³ And every firstling of an ass [symbol for Judah's descendants] you shalt redeem with a lamb; and if you will not redeem it, then you shalt break his neck: and all the firstborn of man among your children shall you redeem [exchange].*

> *Ezekiel 20:⁴⁰ For in mine holy mountain, in the mountain of the height of Israel, says the Lord God, there shall all the house of Israel, all of them in the land, serve me: there will I accept them, and there will I require your offerings, and the first fruits of your oblations, with all your holy things."*

"I see ... but that never really happened, and the debt is just a hidden obligation of the leaders of humanity to God ... a debt that must be repaid ... it's rent?"

"Yes ... In the New Testament, the lamb the Hebrews' firstborn are redeemed with is Christ ... a line of humanity:

> *1 Peter 1:¹⁸ You know you were not redeemed with corruptible things, such as silver and gold, from your vain manner of life received by tradition from your fathers; ¹⁹ But with the precious blood of Christ, as of a lamb without blemish and without spot:"*

Lilly sighed.

"Getting back to Babylon ... The Bible's Tower of Babel has been associated with their Etemenanki tower by modern scholars. A ziggurat dedicated to the Mesopotamian god Marduk, it was located near his temple. Rebuilt by Nebuchadnezzar II, it stood 300 feet [91 meters] tall and was titled the Temple Tower of Babylon."

"That doesn't fit the Biblical account, does it?"

"No," Wolf said, "because the Bible's a work of fiction. Exiled Jews forced to work on the Temple Tower of Babylon during their captivity based their story upon it. The Bible, loosely referencing real history, says the tower was made of brick and bitumen—an ancient tar mortar—and that's indeed what the tower was made of."

"If it was so fantastic, then why is it no more?"

"It was made of mud-brick, a building material with a limited shelf life. However, the tower was still standing 250 years after Nebuchadnezzar II's death when Alexander the Great arrived in Babylon in 331 B.C. and made it his capital. He ordered the deconstruction of the tower because he was going to construct an even grander one, but he died soon after."

"Oh ..."

"The mountain the Dawns were freed from at the beginning of time, Vala, paralleling Vritra the stone dragon, is celebrated in a famous Hindu legend called the 'churning of the ocean of milk.' Vasuki, the blessed snake around Lord Shiva's neck, is willingly bound to a symbolic mountain called Mount Mandara. The Asuras [demons] and the Devas [gods] then use him as a churning rope. Working together, they churn the mountain back and forth to extract the ambrosia of immortality from the ocean of milk."

Mount Mandara

"I see," Lilly said bitterly. "So, God and man work together to extract the ambrosia with the aid of a snake ... like the worm living in my belly!"

Wolf cleared his throat. "The sea is a symbol for god's sperm and the goddess because the Greek's primal goddess Thalassa's name was the Greek word for sea. And in a Greek tale, Uranus [Father Heaven] is castrated by his youngest son Cronus who threw his severed genitals into the sea around which a white foam spread and grew into the goddess Aphrodite or Venus. Thus, the 'churning of the ocean of milk' legend symbolically identifies the parties involved in the making of the ambrosia because God's sperm is called the ocean of milk by the Hindu's and white foam by the Greeks. And the serpent/worm was employed to churn Mount Mandara [goddesses piled high] to extract the ambrosia from the ocean of milk [God's sperm]."

"Right!" Lilly said grumpily.

"There are many mythical, sacred mountains on Earth. Some were created while others are natural, like Mount Olympus in Greece. In Northern Sudan, on a large bend in the Nile, a once sacred mountain's called Gebel Barkal. The 98-meter tall, sandstone, flat-topped mountain was adapted for religious purposes in ancient times. A mythical mountain of creation, it was worshiped as the abode of Amen and his goddess wife Mut. It used to be at the southern limit of the Egyptian Empire, on the border of ancient Nubia. Inside the sacred mountain, titled the creator's mount, Amen is depicted in gold in a relief on a wall.

"The Nubian king Taharqa, a Kushite king who ruled Egypt during the Kushite occupation, 747–656 B.C., is shown in the temple relief making offerings to Amen. Adorned with rams horns, he declares himself the son of Amen. Amenhotep III of the Eighteenth Dynasty was also depicted with rams horns and declared the son of Amen, as was Alexander the Great at a later date.

"The pyramid on the back of the United States one-dollar bill has an image of a Holy Mountain. An almost identical pyramid was found in the 1980s in a jungle in Ecuador, but unlike the one on the back of the dollar bill, it isn't in two pieces. Standing approximately ten inches tall, the sun's rays are missing, but it has a shining eye, and it and other artifacts form the La Mana artifacts."

The pyramid on the back of the United States one-dollar bill

"Really?" Lilly said, surprised.

"Yes," Wolf said. "The stone is black and white and has thirteen levels of bricks engraved upon it—the same number that is on the back of the dollar bill—and there is a cleverly inlaid eye at the top of the pyramid that glows ultraviolet under black light."

Ecuadorian pyramid

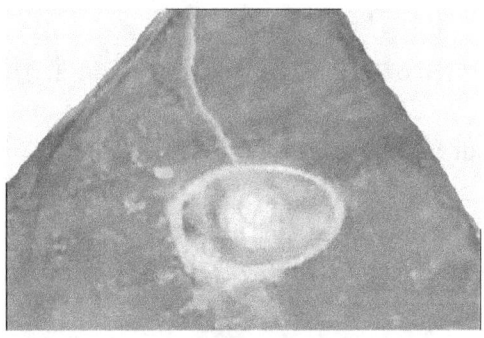

Eye on the Ecuadorian pyramid

Writing on the bottom of the Ecuadorian pyramid

Lilly's eyes widened.

"The pyramid also has writing on its bottom. The Pre-Sanskrit language was translated by German linguist Kurt Schildmann. Until he studied this and other artifacts, Sanskrit was considered the oldest written language. Schildmann translated the five symbols [the fifth is an I-like scratch to the right of the five golden dots].

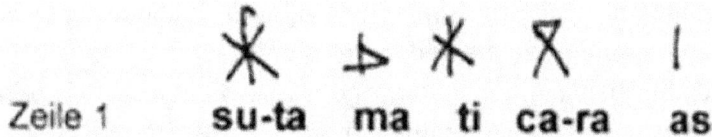

Zeile 1   su-ta   ma   ti   ca-ra   as

"'The son/daughter of my creator moves/comes from outside into' ... then there is a picture of an inlay of the constellation of Orion."

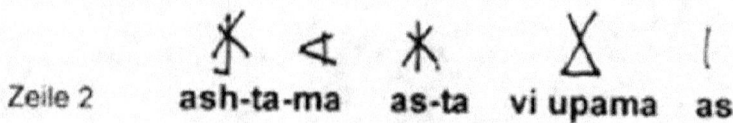

Zeile 2   ash-ta-ma   as-ta   vi upama   as

"The mirrored translation reads 'Venus mine is from highest/creator-star.'"

"I'm gathering that's the correct translation," Lilly said. "What about the Great Pyramid of Giza? Does it have any associated symbolism?"

Great Pyramid of Giza

"Of course," Wolf said, "you don't build something as magnificent as the Great Pyramid of Giza without embedding symbolism into it. Firstly, from a purely structural point of view, it's a symbol for God's Holy Mountain—the stones representing goddesses heaped high; the missing golden capstone represented God's phallus.

"Originally, the Great Pyramid was covered by casing stones that formed a smooth outer surface. What you see today is the underlying core structure. The smooth outer surface was slightly concave on each side and when the sun shined upon it, it shone. The shining pyramid symbolized the goddesses shining—bringing light to the world after being united with the gods ... At night a stone is cold and dark, but when the sun shines upon it, it's warm and frequently shines. Therefore, the pyramid stones represented the goddesses and, the sun that shone upon them, the gods."

Lilly was surprised she'd not realized the pyramids were embedded with symbolism, and it seemed almost beyond belief to her that no one else had either. The standard explanation for the building of the pyramids was, of course, that they were burial chambers for the ancient Egyptian Pharaohs.

"A natural aquifer flows under the pyramids," Wolf said, "The flowing water symbolizes God's water—his semen. The king's chamber is God's pouch, and the rectangular granite sarcophagus in it, the queen's bed. The so-called queen's chamber is God's testes—the source of his power."

"What about the second pyramid—the queen's pyramid?"

"It is the queen's pyramid, yes," Wolf said, "and the third pyramid of Giza represents their son. The three pyramids, sized like Russian dolls, could fit within one another."

"Recently, I heard a theory on the TV show *Ancient Aliens*, it suggested the Great Pyramid of Giza was a power plant, but you're saying it wasn't ... it's a religious icon?"

"Their theory is correct because it was both a religious icon and a functioning machine. Nowadays, humanity makes ugly, utilitarian buildings. In the past, a building was designed to last and be both functional and beautiful. Something as powerful and important as a massive power plant delivering wireless power was far too important and dominating a structure to make into a flimsy, ugly building. It was designed to be an object of great reverence, worshiped both for its functionality and religious imagery."

"Why isn't it delivering wireless power now?"

"Because it's not turned on. There's a process required to make it function ... The pyramid was sealed and deactivated at the end of the last age. The rectangular granite sarcophagus in the king's chamber is larger than the ascending passage and it was installed before the roof. Stored inside the sarcophagus, in a wooden box covered in gold, was a battery. It remained till an ancient pharaoh removed it. An item of great reverence, it's depicted on the walls of Egyptian temples.

"When the Hebrews, then known as the Hyksos [meaning foreigners] seized power in the 1600s BC., they took the golden box with the battery and decorated the top of it with two cherubs. The Egyptians suffered under their cruel rule for fifty years, till they were able to wage war against them. After the fall of the Hyksos' capital in Avaris, the Egyptians chased 480,000 Jews across the northern Sinai Peninsula into the southern Levant, but they weren't able to recover the golden box with the battery now worshipped as the Ark of the Covenant?"

"Can you make a new one ... make the pyramid functional once more?"

"Of course," Wolf said. "We can fire it up whenever we want to."

"What about Stonehenge? Does that have a symbolic meaning?"

Stonehenge England

"Yes. The five inner stone groupings of two large stones capped with a smaller one represent five trinity beings: the father, the goddess and the son. The largest of the five symbolizes the supreme god and his goddess. Initially forming a strongly linked outer layer, the group's surrounded by a circle of stones representing the hive's connectivity and strength. The smaller stones inside represent humans. Aligned to the winter solstice and returning sun, it's the promise of a new day—the coming Dawn [Goddess].

Stonehenge replica

CHAPTER TWENTY-TWO

Wisdom and the Tree of Life

Lilly lay on the milking table, her milking finished. She watched Cat as he set up to wash her hair. "I've been thinking about the Sumerian image of the winged, horned dragons depicted with serpents entwining a pole," she said.

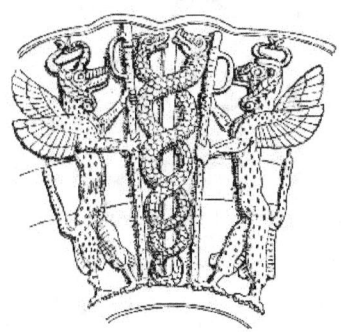

The first known image of serpents entwined on a pole

"I know it," Cat said.

Shiva with the serpent Vasuki

"Wolf said it's a symbol for the Tree of Life—dual serpents entwined a pole in early versions of the symbol."

"In the past, God's image was often adorned with a serpent, like statues of the Hindu god Shiva currently are. Vasuki, the king of the Nāgas is representing the crop's seedline. The stick or rod with the serpents on it is a Tree of Life symbol—a symbol for God and the goddess—but initially, two serpents like Ishtar's symbol were depicted rather than one.

Old Babylonian relief of Ishtar currently held at the Louvre
Museum from the early second millennium B.C. It depicts
Ishtar wearing a crown and flounced skirt and holding her symbol.

"Imagery of the Garden of Eden with a serpent on a tree was in Greek culture long before it was in the Bible."

"It was?"

"Yes," Cat said. "The Greeks called the original paradise the Garden of the Hesperides, and it also had a serpent-entwined apple tree. The Book of Genesis doesn't say what kind of fruit the Tree of Knowledge produced; it is from Greek tradition that we get the idea that Eve ate an apple."

"But the idea of a snake entwined tree wasn't original to the Greeks."

"No, pagan cultures held the serpent in high regard. Early images of Wadjet depicted her as a cobra entwined around a papyrus. It symbolized her wrapped around the god Ra?"

350 BC depiction of the Hesperides tending to the tree and serpent.

Cat started washing Lilly's hair. "The serpent goddess Wadjet as the uraeus was often seen wrapped around Ra's head, and the papyrus was a symbol for life and one of the 14 Spirits of Ra; it represented his vigor."

"His phallus?"

"Yes. The Tree of Knowledge is the tree or rod itself ... not the tree *and* the serpent. The Tree of Knowledge and the Tree of Life were conjoined in the Biblical Garden of Eden:

> *Genesis 2:9 ... The tree of life was in the midst of the garden, and the tree of the knowledge of good and evil.*

> *Genesis 3:3 But of the fruit of the tree which is in the midst of the garden, God has said, you shall not eat of it, neither shall you touch it, lest you die."*

"You're both the Tree of Life and Wisdom in the Bible," Cat said. "When you fully assume your role of 'she who is wise' and 'loving and giving,' you'll be much happier."

Lilly almost choked. "I don't desire the role or the title ... Who is Wisdom anyway? A goddess? I've never heard of her."

"Wisdom was a deity in Greek mythology ... The first Greek

goddess to be called Wisdom was Metis. A cousin and the first great spouse of Zeus, Metis was the Titaness of wisdom and the very embodiment of it. She was both an indispensable aid to Zeus and a threat to him. After Zeus laid with her, he regretted it because a prophecy said Metis would bear him powerful children. To avoid dire consequences, Zeus tricked Metis into turning herself into a fly and he swallowed her. But it was too late because Metis had already conceived a child, and she began making a helmet and robe for her daughter in Zeus's belly. When Athena was born, she leaped from Zeus's head fully grown, armed and armored, and the role of Wisdom was taken over by her, but Metis continued to live in Zeus's belly, making him wise."

The personification of Wisdom at the Celsus
Library in Ephesus, Turkey

"My inner wine makes Wolf wise. He needs it to fire up his brain?"

"That's right."

"He's a fucking vampire!" Lilly exploded.

Cat cleared his throat. "As you know ... all goddesses are essentially the same even if they're personifying different aspects. The owl was a symbol of the goddess Athena, it depicted her Wisdom. Owl symbolism links back to Ishtar or Inanna, and Lilith. A relief found in Iraq depicts Ishtar with two owls at her feet. The Greek figure of Wisdom was patterned after the Egyptian goddess,

Isis, who equated to Hathor in many ways. Asherah, an early consort of Yahweh, was also a goddess of wisdom."

"So, an owl is a symbol for the goddess?"

"Yes," Cat said. "The Hebrew word for wisdom is a feminine word—Chokmah. In Greek, she is Sophia, and in the Bible's Book of Wisdom, she's the 'divine she.' As the Presence of God, she's also the Shekinah. Shekinah is the English transliteration of a Hebrew word meaning dwelling or settling—it denotes the divine presence of God. The term doesn't appear in the Bible, but it is in rabbinic literature. Wisdom is she who 'fashions all things,' and she was present from the beginning with God:

> *Wisdom of Solomon 7:²⁴ For Wisdom is more moving than any motion: she passes and goes through all things by reason of her pureness. ²⁵ For she is the breath of the power of God, and a pure influence flowing from the glory of the Almighty: therefore, no defiled thing can fall into her. ²⁶ For she is the brightness of the everlasting light, the unspotted mirror of the power of God, and the image of his goodness. ²⁷And being but one, she can do all things: and remaining in herself, she makes all things new: and in all ages entering into holy souls, she makes them friends of God and prophets. ²⁸ For God loves none but him that dwells with Wisdom. ²⁹ For she is more beautiful than the sun, and above all the order of stars: being compared with the light, she is found before it. ³⁰ For after this comes night: but vice shall not prevail against Wisdom.*
>
> *Proverbs 7:⁴ Say to wisdom, 'You are my sister,' and call understanding your kinswoman."*

"Does she make any other appearances in the Bible?"

"Yes, in Proverbs:

> *Proverbs 9:¹ Wisdom has built her house, she has hewn out her seven pillars: ² She has killed her beasts; she has*

> *mingled her wine; she has also furnished her table.* ³ *She*
> *has sent forth her maidens: she cries upon the highest*
> *places of the city,* ⁴ *Who is simple, let him turn in hither: as*
> *for him that wants to understand, she says to him,* ⁵ *Come,*
> *eat of my bread, and drink of the wine which I have*
> *mingled."*

"Oh," Lilly said. "The Bible refers to her as the bread and wine, and even calls her wine brain food? Does my wine improve human cognitive abilities as well?"

"Yes, but nowhere near as much as your inner wine improves Wolf's. Unlike your normal wine, it contains a small amount of blood and a similar poison to that which is in Wolf's blood, rendering it useless to all except him. Humans can't drink your inner wine. Wolf draws it into himself and holds it in a bladder-type organ to use as required."

"So, humans can't achieve immortality or gain intellectual improvement by injecting his blood into theirs?"

"No, and that's by design," Cat said. "Imagine someone discovers a toxic river that has properties in it that can heal the sick, cure cancer, and return one's youth, but they're unable to drink its bitter waters. Then imagine someone sees a tree growing in the river; it's planted its roots right into the water and is suffering no ill effects, quite the opposite in fact, it's thriving. Now imagine people run tests on the leaves of this wondrous tree and discover it has absorbed all the healing properties of the river while simultaneously filtering out its toxins. More than that, the tree has added special ingredients of its own, and the healing powers of the leaves are superior to that of the river. Now imagine people can eat the leaves and they're delicious."

Lilly groaned.

"There are passages in the Bible that reference it:

> *Exodus 15:²² So Moses brought Israel from the Red sea,*
> *and they went out into the wilderness of Shur, and they*
> *went three days in the wilderness, and found no water.* ²³

And when they came to Marah, they could not drink of the
waters of Marah, for they were bitter: therefore the name
of it was called Marah. 24 And the people murmured
against Moses, saying, What shall we drink?
25 And he cried to the Lord; and the Lord showed him a
tree, which when he cast it into the waters, the waters
were made sweet: there he made for them a statute and
an ordinance, and there he proved them.

"The Marah? That reminds me of a quote in the 2009 *Sherlock Holmes* movie. When Inspector Lestrade instructed his men to take the bewitched girl to the hospital, he says, 'Put her in the Marah!' I tried to find out if 'Marah' was the name of a carriage, but couldn't ... I always thought there was a double meaning."

"Indeed. She was covertly a Tree of Life in the movie. Other passages in the Bible refer to the Tree of Life:

Ezekiel 47:12 And by the river upon the bank thereof, on
this side and on that side, shall grow all trees for meat,
whose leaf shall not fade, neither shall the fruit thereof be
consumed: it shall bring forth new fruit according to his
months because their waters they issued out of the
sanctuary: and the fruit thereof shall be for meat and the
leaf thereof for medicine.

"I see ..."
"You're an unspotted mirror ... a Tree of Life:

Wisdom of Solomon 7:26 For she is the brightness of the
everlasting light, the unspotted mirror of the power of
God, and the image of his goodness. 27 And being but one,
she can do all things: and remaining in herself, she makes
all things new:

Proverbs 3:13 Happy is the man who finds Wisdom ... 18 She
is a Tree of Life to them that lay hold upon her: and happy

is every one that retains her."

Lilly sighed audibly; her fate obviously sealed.

"Wisdom is the divine she, and she's eternally important:

> *Proverbs 8:14 Wisdom: I am understanding. 15 By me, kings reign, and princes decree justice ... 19 My fruit is better than gold ... 21 I may cause those that love me to inherit substance, and I will fill their treasures. 22 The Lord possessed me in the beginning of his way, before his works of old. 23 I was set up from everlasting, from the beginning, or ever the earth was. 24 When there were no depths, I was brought forth; when there were no fountains abounding with water ... 30 Then, I was by him, as one brought up with him: and I was daily his delight, rejoicing always before him."*

"So," Lilly said. "According to the Bible, God has always had his woman—his goddess."

"Indeed, he has, and his very survival depends upon her. Hence, humanity's also dependent upon her."

"Because Wolf's role is pivotal," Lilly said, "and the world depends upon him and his kind."

"Yes."

"But couldn't the wolves take supplements?"

"Juvenile wolves *do* take supplements and their maturity is delayed, but the supplements are made from your wine, and no mature God can go without a woman. No goddess equals no god. You're the fuel—the wind beneath Wolf's wings—and people yearn for your wine:

> *2 Corinthians 13:14 May the grace of the Lord Jesus Christ, and the love of God, and the communion of the Holy Ghost, be with you all. Amen."*

Lilly placed her head in her hands.

Cat rubbed her belly. "You're our sweet reluctant goddess."

Lilly sighed. "Is Revelation the only place other than Proverbs 3:[18] where the Tree of Life makes an appearance in the Bible?

> *Revelation 22:[1] And he showed me a pure river of water of life, clear as crystal, proceeding out of the throne of God and of the Lamb. [2] In the midst of the street of it, and on either side of the river, was there the Tree of Life which bare twelve manner of fruits, and yielded her fruit every month: and the leaves of the tree were for the healing of the nations. [3] And there shall be no more curse: but the throne of God and of the Lamb shall be in it, and his servants shall serve him: [4] And they shall see his face, and his name shall be in their foreheads. [5] And there shall be no night there, and they need no candle, neither light of the sun; for the Lord God giveth them light: and they shall reign forever and ever."*

"Pagans believed the waters of life flowed from the loins of the goddess ... God is described as the fountain of living water in the Bible, but his fountain is contained in the goddess and it flows from her:

> *Jeremiah 17:[13] O LORD, the hope of Israel,*
> *all who abandon You will be put to shame.*
> *All who turn away will be written in the earth,*
> *for they have abandoned the Lord,*
> *the fountain of living water.*

> *Leviticus 20:[18] And if a man shall lie with a woman having her period, and shall uncover her nakedness; he has discovered her fountain ...*

> *Song of Solomon 4:[12] A garden enclosed is my sister, my spouse; a spring shut up, a fountain sealed.*

Revelation 22:[17] And the Spirit and the bride say, Come. And let him that hears say, Come. And let him that is thirsty come. And whosoever will, let him take the water of life freely."

"In Norse mythology, Iðunn, the goddess wife of the god Bragi, was the keeper of apples and the granter of eternal youthfulness. An apple is a symbol for God's genitals in the Bible."

"So, an apple tree has been a symbol for God as the Tree of Knowledge for longer than the Bible has used the symbolism, and, likewise, the goddess was depicted as a Tree of Life in pre-biblical times?"

"Ancient Egyptians depicted the goddess as a tree pouring out her bounty to recipients below," Cat said. "In 1923 Edmond Bordeaux Szekely discovered a document in the secret archives of the Vatican written by the Essenes called the Essene Book of Revelation."

Hathor or Isis as the Tree of Life suckling Tuthmosis iii

c 1479–1425 B.C. Tomb of Tuthmosis iii, Valley of the Kings

In her role as a tree deity, Hathor was called Lady of the Sycamore.

"Who were the Essenes?"

"The Essenes were a religious sect active around the supposed time of Christ. They shunned publicity, living away from towns they weren't involved in the politics of the Sadducees and Pharisees. It was them who wrote and hid the Dead Sea Scrolls in the caves of Qumram. Josephus wrote around 80 A.D. that the Essenes were Jews by birth, but had a greater affection for one another than they did for the Pharisees and the Sadducees."

"What did their document say?"

"It's a shorter Book of Revelation and it exposes some of the Church's mysteries:

> *There appeared a great wonder in heaven: A woman clothed with the sun and the moon under her feet, and upon her head a crown of seven stars. And I knew she was the source of running streams and the mother of the forests."*

"Oh," Lilly said, surprised. "'*And I knew she was the source of running streams and the mother of the forests.*' That's Eve as the mother of the future Trees of Life...? The passage is far more telling than the Bible's version:

> *Revelation 12:[1] And there appeared a great wonder in heaven; a woman clothed with the sun, and the moon under her feet, and upon her head a crown of twelve stars."*

"That's right," Cat said as he massaged Lilly.

She shrugged. "But isn't Wolf the source of running streams?"

"The Essenes were referring to the Fountain of Youth—the spring that restores youth to those who drink it. Accounts of the Fountain of Youth have been around for thousands of years. For example, it appeared in writings by Herodotus in the fifth century B.C."

"You said Wolf's blood is toxic before, so is his sperm also poisonous?"

"His sperm isn't poisonous as such ... It's regarded as toxic because of what it does to your kind ... it drugs you and keeps you addicted. Ordinary people are unaffected by it in every way ... they can't gain benefit from it unless it's converted. Just as a cow converts grass into milk, you convert sperm into wine and milk. In the Bible, it's said to kill, but it doesn't kill you—it transforms you. You don't DIE in the Lord ... you RESIDE in the Lord. And, of course, it isn't men that die as suggested by the masculine Bible—it's women. The Bible often uses the term 'man' or 'he' to refer to men *and* women.

"Okay," Lilly said. "Well, what was all that stuff about a toxic river then?"

"Wolf's blood is poisonous, but not to you. You extract substances from his blood *and* his sperm ... both flow through you."

"How poisonous?"

"His blood contains antibodies that attack the red blood cells of rhesus-positive people. If injected into their bloodstreams it induces severe jaundice. Rhesus-negative women produce smaller amounts of a weakened version of these antibodies when they give birth to a rhesus-positive baby. To prevent the build-up of antibodies in their blood after giving birth to a rhesus-positive baby, they're given an anti-D immunoglobulin injection which neutralizes the antigens in their blood, and stops their bodies attacking a subsequent rhesus-positive baby."

"I know ... I've had the vaccine."

"Indeed. When you were pregnant with Wolf's baby, it's potent blood crossed the placenta and entered your bloodstream. Immune to its effects, it didn't harm you."

Lilly blinked several times. "So, Wolf's blood isn't poisonous to me?"

"No ... You and he have the same blood type and you exchange small amounts of blood all the time. Many mythological stories speak of the poison in Wolf's blood including the Bible. When God tells the Israelites in Deuteronomy that they will become corrupted, 'not the spot of his people' ... he speaks of this poison:

Deuteronomy 32:33 Their wine is the poison of dragons, and the cruel venom of asps. 34 Is not this laid up in store with me, and sealed up among my treasures?"

"That verse speaks of my wine and says it's poisonous!"

Cat sighed. "'The word 'wine' is often substituted for blood in the Bible:

Revelation 14:20 And the winepress was trodden without the city, and blood came out of the winepress."

"Because wine *is* a blood product?"

"Yes," Cat said. "It's made from the poison of dragons and the cruel venom of asps ... Your wine doesn't contain red blood cells because, like any placenta, your placenta makes exchanges and extracts substances from your blood, but blood doesn't cross the placenta. Even if some poison did pass into your wine, it wouldn't be harmful because people ingest your wine rather than inject it."

Lilly frowned. "Then why make such a point of saying Wolf's blood is poisonous...? Why go on about him being the toxic stream ... I don't understand."

"As I said before, ordinary humans can't benefit from his body directly. Drinking or absorbing his sperm provides them with no benefit, but in the past, people were tempted by the magic flowing through his veins. They injected it into themselves and died and now that you've been with Wolf, your blood is every bit as poisonous as his ... it's the cruel venom of asps."

"My blood is full of strong antibodies that will viciously attack the red blood cells of rhesus-positive people?"

"Yes," Cat said, "and only a mad man would attempt to inject it into himself. If you ever cut yourself, I'll take care around your blood ... give it the respect it deserves."

"So, the line of humanity changed by Eve's supposed eating of the apple from the Tree of Knowledge, Cain's or Christ's descendants, had their DNA changed to align with the Wolves so they wouldn't be poisoned by them?"

Cat laughed. "Oh, you're poisoned by him all right, he's a toxic stream to you ... but not in a deadly way. He's opened your eyes in more ways than one!"

Lilly groaned. "But, surely, a third of humanity isn't going to die in the Lord?"

"No ... the crop is much larger and more dilute than usual ... You were made at the same time as the wolves and ordinary man. The tale of Adam and Eve is a mythical way of explaining your connection. Eve is an allegory for Asherah, and her name means Mother of Life. In classic Hebrew, her name 'hawwah' means 'living,' and it comes from a root word for snake."

"So, Eve was a goddess?"

"Yes, and she, as the woman, passed the serpent's seed on to *one* line of her descendants. You're considered a virgin; the title not relating to sexual innocence. Your uncorrupted seed ... you've bred true. Even though Isis was married before miraculously conceiving Horus after Osiris's death, she was considered a virgin. Horus's name means 'virgin.' The Arabic word 'hoor' means virgin of paradise or nymph, and the suffix 'us' means various things, but ultimately means 'of one.' So, Horus' name means 'of one virgin.' Native forest is called virgin forest because it's made from uncorrupted seed—i.e. it's bred true."

"Right."

"Quintus Septimius Florens Tertullianus, who lived from 155 to 240 A.D. was the first Christian author to produce an extensive corpus of Latin Christian literature, and he made this statement:

'Woman, thou art the gate of the Devil,'"

Lilly frowned. "He decreed women the Devil's gateway?"

"Yes, and it's true ... is it not?" Cat said. "The wolves only entrance into the world is through a woman. In them, they plant their seeds, and in them, their placentas adhere and grow, and in them, they insert their worms ... Without the woman, the Devil has no entrance into the world."

"And if he has no entry, there's only darkness and death."

"Indeed."

"So, the Fall of Man wasn't really a fall. If some of the woman's seed hadn't become aligned with the gods, then humanity would be doomed?"

"Yes."

"So, instead of the woman being blamed for the Fall of Man, she should be praised for his continuing survival?"

"Yes."

CHAPTER TWENTY-THREE

Wormwood

Lilly looked at her belly. The worm's position had changed over the past few weeks and it now lay across the top of her belly. When her wine was fully drained, like it currently was, the worm puffed itself up. Stretching out, it started moving about.

Lilly frowned. "How has my appendix moved to the top of my belly?"

"It hasn't," Cat said. "It's elongated. The bulk of it has drifted upwards and there's a tube leading down to the entrance of your appendix."

Lilly's stomach rippled as the worm began to do somersaults and perform figure eights inside of her.

"That's a strong, healthy worm you've got in there, Baby."

Lilly placed a hand on her belly; her skin rippled under it. "She's positively huge and disgusting!"

Cat's demeanor changed in an instant. "You're a descendant of those naughty, arrogant people who thought they were better than God," he said. "Your people thought their star would rise above his, but see, you've crashed down into the pit and wormwood's forced down your throat:

> *Revelation 8:10 And the third angel sounded, and there fell a great star from Heaven, burning as if it were a lamp, and it fell upon the third part of the rivers and upon the fountains of waters; 11 and the name of the star was Wormwood. 11 ... and the third part of the waters became*

wormwood …"

Lilly groaned. "I hate it when you say shit like that … Why was the star called Wormwood?"

"The star that fell is your kind—Lucifer's star. It crashed into the pit … A worm won't die in your flesh because in you it finds a suitable home … you're the tree the worm feeds upon:

> *Mark 9:⁴⁸ Where the worm dies not, and the fire is not quenched."*

Lilly groaned. "The gods are symbolized as fire:

> *Hebrews 12:²⁹ For our God is a consuming fire."*

"The sins of your fathers have caught up with you. Now you're fed your own flesh, and you're drunk on gall:

> *Micah 7:¹⁷ The nations shall lick the dust [sperm] like a serpent, they shall move out of their holes like worms of the earth."*

"I'm not drunken of gall."

"Wolf's mouth feed is called gall," Cat said. "He vomits it into your mouth and you gulp it down. You're drunk on it … you can't get enough of it:

> *Jeremiah 9:¹⁵ Therefore, this says the Lord of hosts, the God of Israel. Behold, I will feed them with wormwood, and give them water of gall to drink."*

Lilly snorted. "That verse says I'm fed wormwood … How can I be wormwood if I'm fed it?"

"Wolf recycles what he draws down from you. He feeds your own body to you:

Isaiah 49:²⁶ And I will feed them that oppress you with their own flesh; and they shall be drunken with their own blood, as with sweet wine: and all flesh shall know that I the Lord am your Savior and your Redeemer, the mighty One of Jacob.

Lilly groaned.

"You're the wood the worm devours and *yet* doesn't consume … thriving in you, it doesn't die:

Revelation 14:⁹ And the third angel followed them, saying with a loud voice, 'If any man worships the beast and his image, and receives his mark in his forehead, or in his hand, ¹⁰ The same shall drink of the wine of the wrath of God which is poured out without mixture into the cup of his indignation; and he shall be tormented with fire and brimstone in the presence of the holy angels, and in the presence of the Lamb.'"

Lilly folded her arms. "There's no fire and brimstone here!"

"The modern word for brimstone is sulfur … the strong smell emitted by volcanoes. Wolf's the symbolic fire and his breath, brimstone:

Isaiah 30:³³ … the breath of the Lord is like a stream of brimstone.

Psalms 11:⁶ Upon the wicked, he [God] shall rain snares, fire, and brimstone."

"Dragon symbolism? Daddy doesn't hurt me … he loves me."

Cat scoffed. "You're too drunk to object to anything he does:

Jeremiah 51:⁷ Babylon has been a golden cup in the Lord's hand that made all the earth drunken: the nations have drunken of her wine; therefore, the nations are mad.

> *Revelation17:⁴ And the woman was arrayed in purple and*
> *scarlet color, and decked with gold and precious stones*
> *and pearls, having a golden cup in her hand full of*
> *abominations and filthiness of her fornication.*
>
> *Revelation 18:⁶ Reward her even as she rewarded you, and*
> *double unto her double according to her works: in the cup*
> *which she has filled, fill to her double."*

Lilly huffed out a breath. "Why are you being such a prick?"

"Do you want me to tell you sweet lies? Sometimes, the harsh light of truth has more value:

> *Job 20:⁵ The triumphing of the wicked is short. ... ¹¹ His*
> *bones are full of the Sin of his youth, which shall lie down*
> *with him in the dust. ... ¹⁴ Yet his meat in his bowels is*
> *turned, it is the gall of asps within him. ¹⁵ He has*
> *swallowed down riches, and he shall vomit them up again:*
> *God shall cast them out of his belly. ¹⁶ He shall suck the*
> *poison of asps: the viper's tongue shall slay him. ¹⁷ He shall*
> *not see the rivers, the floods, the brooks of honey and*
> *butter. ¹⁸ That which he labored for shall he restore, and*
> *shall not swallow it down: according to his substance shall*
> *the restitution be, and he shall not rejoice therein.*
>
> *Revelation 3:¹⁶ I [God] will spew you out of my mouth."*

"Can you shut up with that shit?"

Cat moved to Lilly's side and looked at her intently. She looked away.

"No, don't look away," he said. "We need to have an honest conversation. You think I'm a prick for what I do to you, for the part I play in your entrapment ... right?"

Lilly glared at Cat.

"The thing is, Baby, I'm not being a prick ... I see you. I know who you are. You and I may look the same, but we're not. You have needs, wants, and desires that I'll never understand because we're fundamentally different. Not because you're a female and I'm a male. Women like me don't understand you either. Your needs and desires are as much of a mystery to them as they are to me because you're different. To wrench you away from Wolf would be cruel, and I'm not a cruel man."

"I'm *not* different! Wolf's poisoned me … infected me!"

"Yes, but you were just sitting around awaiting awakening … a candle ready to be lit."

Lilly covered her eyes.

"Baby, I know you've been brainwashed your whole life. You believe humans are all the same, and if you peel back their skin, they're the same underneath, but that's simply not true." Cat rubbed Lilly's arm. "My job isn't to try and force a square peg into a round hole. I realize a square peg is different, and treat it with the respect it deserves."

Lilly snorted. "Pfft. I hardly think your evil words are respectful."

"Put the cruel words in the Bible out of your mind and realize you're different and that's all right. Those verses were written as a warning. To caution those in the know to hold fast and not deviate, but you have a right to be respected and valued for who and what you are."

Lilly wiped her eyes. "Then why did you taunt me with those passages?"

Cat shrugged. "I shouldn't have … I'm in a mood. Your whining over the last few days has started to bug me. It's getting on my nerves. You should learn to be proud. Hold your head up high and disregard the Bible's nasty passages … Wolf is a god, accept him as such and be happy."

Lilly snorted. "He can't raise the dead!"

"No, and neither could Jesus. Lazarus rising from the dead was an initiation ritual … part of a death and rebirth ritual common in mystery schools at the time. In pagan mystery cults, an initiate was given a share of the fortunes of his or her deity. By means of ritual dying and rising, he was said to be able to attain salvation. Echoes of these rites are found in Freemasonry today:

> *Mark 12:²⁷ He is not the God of the dead, but the God of the living. "*

"But all live unto God," Lilly said, quoting a different Bible passage.

Cat rolled his eyes. "No, they don't! You need to give up on that living as a spirit nonsense ... nobody is immortal."

"But Wolf doesn't age."

"No, he doesn't, but if you shot him in the head with a large bullet, he *would* die."

"Would that bullet need to be made of silver? It seems more likely I'd need to chop off his head and drive a stake through his heart."

"Come now!" Cat said, dismayed. "You love Wolf. He's flesh and blood."

"The Bible also speaks of dead people returning to life."

"Not in the way you're thinking ... Jesus said, 'Let the dead bury their dead.' He was calling people dead when they were obviously still alive. The Bible speaks of a first death and a second death. This tells you the first death is not a real death, but, rather, a transformation. An initiate moves from one world to another. You can't contact the people you knew in your previous life because you're dead to them ... you've moved from one world to another, and people are similarly reborn in Secret Societies:

> *Luke 9:⁵⁹ And Jesus said, Follow me. But a man said, Lord, suffer me first to go and bury my father. ⁶⁰ Jesus said to him, 'Let the dead bury their dead: but go you and preach the kingdom of God.'*

> *Revelation 2:¹¹ He who has an ear, let him hear what the Spirit says to the churches. He who overcomes will not be hurt by the second death.*

"I see," Lilly said bitterly.

"God was symbolized as a lake of fire in antiquity ... Those who take part in the first resurrection, don't die ... they join us in our world, or they'll become a member of the earth when it's like heaven. 'Thy will be done on earth as it is in heaven.' God is symbolically a huge pool of lava, like that found at the top of mount doom in the *Lord of the Rings* movie, and you most definitely reside in the symbolic lake. But people who aren't part of the first resurrection, i.e., they're not valued members of our network and don't enter our world as you have ... when they die a mortal death, they're dead ... plain and simple."

"Right!"

"Their spark was said to be sent forth again from the lake of fire in some teachings, but, apart from living on in the flesh of their descendants, they're dead. You, on the other hand, aren't dead. You were thrown into the lake of fire alive, and alive you shall remain:

> *Revelation 19:20 And the beast was taken and with him the false prophet that wrought miracles before him, with which he deceived them that had received the mark of the beast, and them that worshipped his image. These both were cast alive into a lake of fire burning with brimstone."*

Lilly frowned. "The false prophet? The mark of the beast is DNA?"

"Yes, and you're from the line of Jesus or, rather, Cain, and, of course, Jesus is the false prophet in the New Testament and he represents your line."

"Right, so there are no miracles?"

"Well ... that depends on what you call a miracle ... Some would consider being rejuvenated to youth pretty miraculous ... Remember Jesus said, 'If you don't eat and drink my flesh, you have no life in you.'"

"You said before that the great star was Lucifer falling from heaven after trying to compete with God. Was there a war in heaven?

> *Revelation 8:10 And the third angel sounded, and there fell a great star from Heaven, burning as if it were a lamp ...*

> *Revelation 12:9 And the great dragon was cast out, that*

old serpent called the Devil and Satan which deceived the whole world: he was cast out into the earth, and his angels were cast out with him ... 12 Therefore rejoice, you heavens, and you that dwell in them. Woe to the inhabitants of the earth and of the sea! for the devil is come down to you having great wrath because he knows that he has but a short time. 13 And when the dragon saw that he was cast unto the earth, he persecuted the woman which brought forth the man child.

Cat sighed. "I'm not meant to talk to you about such things."

"So, there was."

"Wolf's already told you there are many inhabited planets. There was a war on one of them, and when it came time to seed the Earth with a crop, we punished uprisers by casting them out and into a barren world stripped of technology. Coming from a highly technical world, they had no idea how to start again. They were so hopeless, we actually had to save them on more than one occasion and provide them with a tutor, or they would have simply died out."

"And I'm descended from them?"

"Yes."

"What about the rest of humanity?"

"Let's just say, being dropped off here wasn't a plum job."

CHAPTER TWENTY-FOUR

Fire and Worms

"I think it's time I told you about the real Tree of Life," Wolf said as he cradled Lilly on his bed.

Lilly frowned. "Don't I know what it is already?"

"You've learned you're symbolically *called* the Tree of Life, but you weren't told why."

"Because I give life?"

"That isn't why you're called a *Tree* of Life."

Thinking, Lilly blinked several times.

"Have you noticed when you have an orgasm that you produce a lot of fluid in your urethra and your orgasm is usually centered there?"

"I can have a variety of orgasms ... I can have one in my vagina, my anus or my urethra, but yes, they do tend to be centered there."

"The urethra resembles a tree trunk and the paraurethral glands branching off it—branches or limbs. It's a tree that's flourishing in a bitter stream."

"Oh, clever ... really? That's where the term the Tree of Life comes from?"

"That's the esoteric meaning, yes. The Tree of Life has been shrouded or veiled in mystery for a long time."

"I see, and is it from these glands that the Elixir of Life flows?"

"You are a beautiful fruiting flower, flowing with goodness and life from almost every orifice, but the fluid that gushes from your urethra when you orgasm, from your paraurethral glands, when you're with me is particularly potent."

Lilly's brow rose.

"To make you fruit and produce abundantly, Cat inserted some little worms into your paraurethral glands."

Lilly stared at Wolf, shocked once more, her eyes misted. "Can't you stop doing hideous things to me?"

Wolf rubbed her back. "You'll be all right, Baby. They're tiny and they'll excite you ... give you more pleasure. They probably already are. Before you know it, you'll be accustomed to them and they'll just be another part of you."

Lilly sniffed back tears. "Is this another one of those coded things in the Bible?

> *Sir 7:17 Humble thyself greatly: for the vengeance of the ungodly is fire and worms."*

"Yes. The meaning is cloaked ... hidden behind a veil."

Tears burned at the back of Lilly's eyes. "Say what you like, but you can't expect me to find these verses sweet and demure!

> *Lamentations 3:13 He [God] has caused the arrow of his quiver to enter into your inward parts ...15 He has filled you with bitterness; he has made you drunken with wormwood.*

> *Judith 16:17 ... The Lord Almighty will take vengeance of them in the Day of Judgment, putting fire and worms in their flesh; and they shall feel them, and weep forever."*

"I don't wish to cause you physical or emotional pain. While I'll delight in the wept substance from your urethra, tears that flow from your eyes bring me no joy. A seedy type of brain fluid also weeps from behind your eyes, from your pineal gland and it is collected in your wine. These are the only tears I'll delight in. I want you to be happy ... As for the fire ... that's me. The gods are said to baptize your kind with fire—transform you. So, there's no real fire. I'm symbolized as the blazing sun, gold, and fire."

"But those nasty verses are imprinted in my mind and they haunt me."

"You'll do yourself a great favor if you disregard the cryptic, enigmatic and cruel verses in the Bible and dispense them from your mind. They weren't meant for you and you failed to understand them. Cat inserted the worms into you simply by squirting a fluid filled with minute baby worms into your urethra, in a procedure that took only seconds. You'll adjust to the worms as they grow."

Lilly groaned. "So, could anybody extend their own life with the fluid from their paraurethral glands—females or males?"

"No. The worms excretions make your gland's fruit—produce a potent elixir. The immature worms developed in a gland at the base of my penis and they'll mature in you. You're lucky to be charmed by their delights."

Lilly scoffed. "I'm sure you could sell ice to Eskimos," she said before giving him the classic signal that she wanted to be fed. While butting his lips repeatedly with her own, she moaned. Responding almost instantaneously, Wolf grasped her firmly and delivered his mouth feed to her while inserting his womb probe deep within her to draw down a feed from her holy of holies. Afterward, she closed her eyes and lay against him in drunken bliss.

"How are you feeling my wee sponge?" Wolf said telepathically.

Lilly was pleased he'd used his internal voice because she wasn't up to replying in the usual way. "I can't believe how much I enjoy being fed by you, even though I know you're poisoning me."

"You're poisoning me too, Baby. Hopelessly addicted, I can't get enough of you."

"Why did you call me a sponge?"

"Because you are one ... You're a cistern or a vessel virgin upon whom the hive depends."

"And that's why I'm imprisoned ... Why you won't let me go ... Why men don't kill the wolves."

"They don't kill my kind for reasons beyond that. You're not fully comprehending who I AM. My colleagues and I are the brains of the operation. You see me when I'm being playful and loving, but there's more to me than that ... Your brain is a simple first-generation computer compared to mine. Comparatively, mine is infinitely more complex and running at light speed."

"So, I'm an idiot."

"No ... for a human you're pretty smart. A sharp increase in your intellect was an unavoidable consequence of being aligned with us. For my part, I'm happy with the outcome because it means I can talk to you and to a great extent you understand what I'm saying and get my drift, but your intellect *does* cause problems. A harvest is difficult if your people have a heads up ... know what's coming. It's natural for them to try and escape the net and the future we have planned for you. For your own good, we extract information from the world so you become a people with amnesia, having little or no idea who you are."

"And you think that's best!"

Wolf sighed. "It is actually ... I have seen some terrible harvests ... Harvests that had to happen when your people knew who they were and were prepared."

"Did things get ugly?"

"They got very ugly ... By making your kind mix with the other races and breed with them prior to a harvest, we do you a favor because, for the most part, they're more compassionate towards you and have a better understanding of who you are; and if only a small percentage of people on earth are aligned with us, even among white people, their ability to fight back is reduced. If we try to bring in the harvest when the crop is the same size but purer, we run into trouble. We've learned from previous harvests what works best, and the upcoming harvest is set to go off without a hitch."

Lilly groaned.

"I'm not telling you this to upset you. Many of your people, wave after wave of them in fact, have gone into other lands and been absorbed and lost there. Just in this cycle alone, large tribes have been absorbed and lost in India, China, Japan, Egypt, South America, and the Middle East to name but a few places they've traveled to and been absorbed into."

"Was that intended? Did you want that to happen?"

"Absolutely," Wolf said. "We manipulate the crop's genes *and* the servant's genes."

"So, you're the big brain!"

"You've already deduced that. I'm not trying to intimidate you. You'll learn to live with me ... You like to argue with me and I let you, but I'm very old and I've seen it all before ... many times ... I know what I'm talking about."

"Are you and Cat the same age?"

"No. Cat is four years older than me."

"How many thousands of years old are you?"

"It's not thousands, it's millions."

"Really! Millions?"

"Yes," Wolf said with a shrug.

"So, I don't get to use my brain?"

"You do, but you weren't brought here for your intellectual abilities."

"So it's true ... nobody gives a shit what I think?"

Wolf chuckled. "That's a bit harsh. We care about your emotional well-being ... I sense you're fully comprehending how dire your situation is, and that it's in nobody's interest to let you go. Even if people were magnanimous enough to forgo the Elixir of Immortality, they wouldn't stand by and watch their gods wither and die. Death of the gods would doom this planet and much of the universe to a barren wasteland, so freedom of your kind can never be allowed."

Lilly blinked several times. "The wolves can't survive without us?"

"We can live mortal lives, the number of our years far exceeding yours, but if forced to do so, we'd likely behave in ways that wouldn't please you. Juvenile wolves are given a small amount of concentrated elixir for its health benefits, but it doesn't contain the necessary ingredients to allow their brains to fully develop ... fire up. It is only when a wolf is on a steady diet of your inner wine that his true potential is reached. However, if he's then deprived of it, he'll die."

"How come?"

"It's how we're designed—a safeguard for those who created us. You'll have noticed that Ox only drank your outer wine, whereas I drink your inner wine which contains additional ingredients ... Ox had an immature internal organ. When he drank from you with his wine probe, the wine bypassed his organ and went directly into his upper bowel. If he'd drunk your inner wine, his immature organ would have quickly developed to encapsulate it. When fully developed, it would have then released your inner wine into his bloodstream as required. Ox also didn't give you a mouth feed because the gland in his throat that makes gall wasn't developed and he didn't have the urge to do so."

"Oh," Lilly said.

"Wolves can live indefinitely, and knowledge obtained over millions of years is far too valuable to squander on moralistic ideals."

Lilly closed her eyes. The peril of her situation almost too much to bear. While she'd developed feelings for Wolf, loved him even, part of her still longed to be free.

Embracing her, Wolf said, "I'm sorry, Baby, but we can't let you go. None of us can ... You'll have to learn to endure ... but I hope you'll do more than that, I hope you'll be happy here and this will be your heaven ... I'll be your heaven."

Lilly wondered if Wolf really cared. She opened her eyes to study his and thought she saw compassion in his eyes. "Do you care?"

"You mean ... am I remorseful about what I'm doing to you?"

"Yes."

"No, not really ... I'm not human ... I understand how your brain works and know how you'd like me to think and feel, but that's the breadth of my compassion. From my point of view, I'm doing you a favor. Besides, we're all slaves and victims of circumstance here. I, like you, didn't choose this life, I wanted to continue roaming the universe."

Lilly wasn't sure if the day would come when she'd feel only happiness, but she found herself wishing it would.

Wolf placed her on the edge of the bed, on her hands and knees, and leaned over her before cupping the worm in her belly in a large hand and licking the back of her neck.

She groaned, half from pleasure and half from anxiety. *What's he up to?*

"It's all right, Baby, relax."

Carrying several items that knocked together in his arms as he walked, Lilly heard Cat enter the room rather than saw him. He laid the items on the bed before gently placing a reassuring hand on her back.

She didn't turn around to see what he'd carried. Instead, she closed her eyes and groaned her reluctant approval to whatever he intended to do. He was in a mood and she didn't feel up to challenging him.

Cat poured some warm oil onto her back and began to firmly and seductively rub it in. Moaning, Lilly felt its effect almost immediately. Whatever Cat was up to, he wanted her calm and submissive. "Good girl," he cooed as her drugged head drooped.

While still cupping the worm, Wolf stroked one of her buttocks tenderly with the back of his fingers on his other hand. "You're a beautiful wee thing," he said as he leaned over and around her to kiss her cheek.

Lilly slumped onto the bed. He carefully repositioned her back onto her elbows and knees before, once again, cupping the worm in his hand. Lilly could feel the worm moving and clearly, he could too.

She tried not to think about the worm—about its rapid growth and the pent-up strength in its sinuous muscles. If she'd been looking at her belly, she would have seen its strong muscular form rippling under her skin. She wondered if it was thinking. Wondered if it had thoughts? Was it in there thinking, "Oh, come on already, I'm hungry," or was it simply doing a mindless dance of anticipation?

Wolf leaned around her body to kiss the worm through her skin, his love for it all too apparent. Lilly would've asked him what the worm knew, felt, and thought, but she was too off her face.

Cat began to prepare her arse. The moment he touched it, the worm jumped in Wolf's hand and he closed his hand sharply around it and pushed it in a downward, right-hand direction. For a brief moment, Lilly thought she was in an *Alien* movie nightmare, but the worm wasn't in her rib cage and Wolf seemed to have things in hand—literally. Sensing a silent communication between him and the worm, she briefly opened her eyes. She closed them again, confident Wolf wasn't about to let any harm come to her or his precious worm.

She wondered why Wolf was feeling its position and holding it firmly and pushing it. It only did mindless figure eights as far as she knew. Once again, Cat stimulated her arse, and, once again, the worm jumped. Lilly groaned. No matter how stupid it was, it had acute nerve endings and knew when her anus was touched.

Once again, Wolf had captured its sharp movement in his hand, and, once again, he'd directed the now highly agitated worm in a right-hand, downward direction. Twitching back and forth with increasing vigor, its whole body was like the tail of an annoyed cat, the power in its muscles frightening. Even so, Lilly felt a degree of sympathy for it. It was obviously hungry. *Why aren't they feeding it?*

Cat touched Lilly's anus yet again, and this time, the worm didn't jump. Instead, it dug its head into the side of her bowel wall with the full force of its pent-up muscles and twitched violently.

Lilly screamed out in pain as the worm forced its way out of her appendix and into her bowel. Escaping its prison, it raced through her bowel at break-neck speed, and she thought it would fly out of her arse until she felt a sharp pull in her belly, inside her appendix. With its tail anchored deep within her, the worm had come to a sudden stop. Stretched out inside her bowel with its head poking out her arse, it blindly twisted about, searching for something.

"There you are my little beauty," Wolf said as he stroked its head. Cross, it tried to latch onto his hand with its big mouth. Wolf pulled his hand away and pushed his erect penis into its sightless face instead. It opened its huge mouth wide and latched onto the full length of his dick. Grasping it firmly, it drew itself back in and up Lilly's arse with surprising strength. The suddenness of its action, and the added width of its head around Wolf's penis, made Lilly gasp. Once the worm had retreated up her arse as far as it could while still holding onto Wolf's erect penis, it began to suck as if there was no tomorrow.

Wolf grasped Lilly's hips and let out a guttural moan as the worm quickly brought him to a climax, but the worm wasn't satisfied. It continued to twitch and suck as Wolf massaged her tense hips. "It's all right, Baby ... relax," he said with his inner voice. Enjoying the worm's attention, he moaned as it readied him for another orgasm.

Lilly tried to relax, but the point where the worm had burst through hurt and she wondered if she was injured. After orgasming, Wolf pulled his penis out of the worm's relaxed jaw. He lay on the bed on his back beside her before placing her on top of him.

When she was on her hands and knees on top of his belly, he said, "It's all right, Baby. The worm didn't harm you when she forced her way out of your appendix. I know it's a bit sore, but it will settle. She'll now move up and down your bowel as she so desires and retreat into her nest to rest."

"Did she give you a blow job?" Lilly said, stating the obvious.

"Yes," Wolf said as he felt his nuts. "Every creature has a talent and that's hers. She's done a good job of emptying me."

Lilly groaned. Will there be no end to the debauchery in this place?

The worm forcefully poked its head back out of her arse and started to search around again. Cat got into position before letting it latch onto his penis and draw him in. He moaned his delight as the hungry worm set to work again. Now that Lilly was somewhat relaxed, she found the worm's twisting urgency sexually stimulating and she enjoyed it. Cat placed a talented finger on her clitoris and it wasn't long before she was orgasming, contracting strongly on Cat's member and the worm. Cat groaned his delight and shuddered as he orgasmed a second time.

After removing his spent cock from her arse he pushed the teat of an especially designed, large feeding bottle into the face of the worm. The bottle's sudden, broad end prevented it from disappearing entirely when the worm drew it up and into her. Lilly moaned in delight when the worm butted the bottle's fat end against her anus violently as it gulped down the bottle's contents. Cat stimulated her clitoris, and it wasn't long before she was contracting strongly on the sides of the worm and the pliable, penis-shaped bottle grasped within its jaws. Orgasming again, she moaned.

When the bottle was removed, she sighed. She might not have been aware of the worm's antics and abilities, but Wolf and Cat clearly knew her talent and were well versed in dealing with her kind.

CHAPTER TWENTY-FIVE

The Serpent & the Elixir

Lilly lay half in and half out of Wolf's pouch, resting upon him. Having retreated into its nest, and only occasionally moving its sinuous body, the worm was enjoying a contented slumber. Lilly started rubbing it through her skin, not sure why she was doing it. Was she pleased it hadn't killed her? She shrugged. The entrance to her appendix still ached, but nonetheless, she continued to caress the worm like a beloved infant.

"It pleases me to watch you thank the worm for her excretions," Wolf said.

Lilly frowned. Is that what I'm doing?

Wolf ran tender fingers through her short hair. "You're feeling relaxed and at peace ... high. The worm is making you feel that way by excreting pleasing substances into your bloodstream. It's right to thank her and let her know you appreciate her efforts."

"She likes it when I stroke her? How much does she know and feel? Can she think?"

"Absolutely. She's acutely aware of your emotions and your stress level."

"Does that add up to thinking?"

"The worm is capable of thought and communication."

Lilly frowned. "She'll speak to me?"

"Not with words ... You know if she's content or agitated ... do you not?"

"Yes."

"And she's equally aware of your emotional state, and your

distress upsets her every bit as much as hers bothers you. If you stroke her to calm her and thank her, she'll move in pleasing ways and excrete delightful substances into your bloodstream to thank you."

"And you think when she does this, that it's a conscious decision on her part?"

"It's as much of a conscious decision on her part as it is on yours. You stroked her without thinking about it, and her reply was similarly instinctual ... much of your communication will be so."

"Are you saying I'm as mindless as her?"

"No," Wolf said. "Stop taking offense when none's intended. I'm saying not all communication is thought out and deliberate ... mine isn't either. I often stroke you or kiss you without thinking about it. Comforting you comes naturally to me."

Closing her eyes, Lilly sighed. "But she can't actually think like we do?'

"Creatures' cognitive abilities are directly correlated to the level required for their survival. Single-celled organisms living in the sea are mindless, but you need to perform complex tasks to survive, so your intellectual ability is greater than there's. You're also a predator, and predators need to have reasonably high cognitive capabilities."

"So, because the worm only eats and shits, she has a limited cognitive capability?"

"She lives inside of you. You're her shell, but rather than being an inanimate object, you move and think; therefore, her cognitive abilities are set at a higher level ... she'll control you."

"What!" Lilly's eyes nearly popped out of her head. "She'll control me!"

"Her survival depends upon you relaxing and getting into a suitable position so she can travel down your bowel and feed. She needs you to submit to Cat and me so she can gulp down as much food as she can cope with. A worm's stomach is spread along the full length of its body and they like to stuff it full. When you're laden with wine, her body is less than a quarter of the size it swells to when she's full, and she not only drinks a lot, she shits a lot ... directly into you."

"What!"

"Her tail is not only anchored into the wall of your appendix, but her anus is also a complex web of exiting veins resembling a placenta that exits into your bloodstream and bowel. As you fill with wine, she expels almost all of the fluid in her body into yours and shrinks to a fraction of her engorged size. When your wine is extracted, she sucks fluid out of you to rehydrate herself and begins to move about. When her hydration levels are fully restored, she communicates with your brain by releasing a cocktail of aphrodisiacs into your body to make you as high as a kite and as horny as a cat on heat—she's demanding you let her feed."

Lilly groaned. "Are you sure...? I haven't felt any overwhelming urge ... I think you're exaggerating!"

"She's only a baby, only just big enough to get out of her nest, but soon enough, you'll know and feel her desires. We encourage our worms out of their nests early to ensure they don't damage our women when they open their appendixes. Now she's made the journey, she'll continue to do so."

"And her control over me will increase?"

"Definitely," Wolf said, running a tender finger over Lilly's cheek. "But there's no need to panic, once you've gotten into position and allowed her to feed, she'll be satisfied. Then she'll return to her nest to rest and delight you with pleasing substances."

"So, then I can do whatever I want?"

Wolf scoffed. "Hardly. She'll want you to lie still and relax so she can process her lovely meal. To get you to do so, she'll drug you. If you fight her, she'll drug you more. My advice is not to resist. Don't encourage her to drug you into a stupor. Any battle you wage against her, you'll lose. The happiest babies are those who have never fought with their worm. Stroke her, love her, please her, and she'll treat you well."

Lilly shook her head in dismay. It seemed almost inconceivable that a worm inside her belly could control her, and yet she knew Wolf was telling the truth. She rubbed the worm to see if it would respond. The worm turned a lazy figure eight and Lilly felt high.

"Shouldn't I touch her?" she said. "I stroked her, and she drugged me."

"She thought that's what you wanted ... You were nice to her so she rewarded you. She's given you some of her 'feel-good drug' rather than the drug that immobilizes you. It was a nice thing she did, but I should warn you, she's capable of physically harming you if you upset her."

"What! How?"

"She's strong and can bang about in there and hit tender parts of your body. Worms have an innate ability to target the most sensitive spots."

"Why are you telling me this!"

"Because, before long she'll start to make her presence known. I'm advising you to appease her. The next few weeks are critically important for you and her. If she senses that you love her, and you want her to be happy and well-fed, she'll develop into a sweet-natured worm."

Lilly groaned. She was already a captive, and now, to add insult to injury, she was expected to tolerate an overbearing bully living inside of her. *I should get a knife and stab the bloody worm.*

Wolf laughed. "I wouldn't do that. If by some remote chance you did manage to kill her, her dying body would poison you."

"And if she dies, I die?"

"No, we'd remove her dying body before she killed you, but you wouldn't be any further ahead. I'd just grow another worm and insert it into you, and the new worm would sense the previous resident had been harmed."

Lilly placed her head in her hands. "You're all so evil. How can such evilness be in the world? How is it that nobody cares? That nobody will release me from my prison?"

"The worm/serpent isn't evil. Subtle, crafty and manipulative maybe, but she's not evil. She has no evil thoughts or intentions. She only wants to feed and make you happy."

Groaning, Lilly rolled her eyes. "Pfft."

"In Sumer, around 3,500 B.C., the serpent symbolized regeneration and eternal life. This knowledge remained in the world until the Church decided to change the serpent into an evil entity ... the Devil no less."

Lilly felt tears burning. It didn't matter what sense Wolf's words made, part of her still believed in her Church and she was still as brainwashed as ever. Perceiving the serpent as evil, Wolf's words felt like devil's daggers.

Wolf rubbed her back. "Calm down, little one. You, and I, and the serpent have been framed—declared evil when we're not."

Lilly snorted. "I know I'm not evil, but I'm not so sure about you and the bloody worm! I'm an unwilling gateway for the Devil."

"That's right. I'm God and the Devil ... and if I have no entry into the world, there's only darkness and death ... You are the dawn, the bringer of light, and as such, you are symbolized as a lamp."

◆ ◆ ◆

After being milked, Lilly lay quietly. "Tell me about the elixir I produce. I really want to know how it's made, and why it works?"

"All right," Cat said. "It stimulates your thymus gland ... When you're born, you have a functioning thymus gland located behind your sternum, between your lungs. It almost ceases to function in late puberty when it begins to shrink. At around forty years of age, it stops functioning altogether, and by the time people are seventy years old, it's little more than a blob of fatty tissue."

"What does the thymus do?"

"It produces and secretes thymosin, a hormone necessary for T-cell development and the maturation of T-lymphocytes or T-cells ... a specific type of white blood cell that fights viruses and infections."

"Our bodies stop making T-cells?" Lilly said, alarmed. "How can anyone survive without T-cells?"

"Cell division of existing naïve T-cells mostly maintains T-cell numbers and diversity throughout adulthood. A strong immune response depends upon naïve T-cell diversity. When their numbers drop dramatically around the age of sixty-five, impaired immune response allows diseases such as cancers, autoimmunity, and opportunistic infections to increasingly cause mortality."

"So, the shrinking and ultimate failure of the thymus gland causes aging and death?"

Cat nodded. "Yes, but there's more to aging than a declining immune system. Telomeres, located at the ends of chromosomes, shorten, and cells and tissue replace and repair less perfectly. As people age, their weakening muscles fill with fat."

"What's a telomere?"

"Telomeres are the caps at the ends of strands of DNA. They protect chromosomes from fraying and sticking to one another."

Lilly groaned. "Thanks for that horrid forensic analysis," she said. "It was totally depressing. So, how does my wine prevent this?"

"As mammals age, their stem cells don't die; rather, they fall into dormancy. Adult stem cells can restore aging tissue but they fail to get instruction to do so. By increasing the level of a protein called FOXN1, a necessary message will get through, and they'll start repairing aging tissue and rebuilding organs ... especially the thymus which is essential for continued good health. The gene GDF 11, growth differentiation factor 11, is also required for stem cell activation. This gene is in useful levels in the bloodstreams of children but not in adults."

Lilly rubbed her forehead. "So, adults could heal their aging bodies with their own stem cells, if only they received the necessary proteins and genes to turn the message system on?"

"That's right," Cat said. "In recent times, humans in your previous society carried out an experiment to find out what would happen if they circulated a young mouse's blood through the body of an old mouse. After stitching an old mouse to a young mouse, so blood could circulate freely between them, they waited and watched. Later, an autopsy revealed the young mouse's blood had induced vascular remodeling in the old mouse, culminating in increased neurogenesis, and its heart had rejuvenated to such an extent, it resembled that of the young mouse ... You see, you can cheat the system, renew your body if you receive the correct rejuvenation protein factors to do so."

"Become young again and remain that way?"

"Yes."

"And these rejuvenation proteins are in my wine?"

"Yes ... Without it, people could attempt to transfuse themselves with copious amounts of young blood ... exchange their blood regularly with that of little children in the hope of some improvement, but, short of being the busiest midwife in town, collecting every placenta, and having a blood type compatible with most blood groups, it would be nigh on impossible to do; and even then it wouldn't give the desired result. Not to mention, there is more to blood than rejuvenation proteins, and a large amount of foreign blood has both a positive and negative effect on the body, so is best avoided."

"Right?" Lilly said, conjuring up images of evil old men stealing small children and dragging them into their basement.

"When the Lazy Kings created yours and Wolf's kind, they cracked the formula." Cat looked at the worm's position in Lilly's stomach. "Wolf's sperm and blood contain substances that circulate in your bloodstream and are absorbed by your brain and cause your pineal gland to produce a substance we call seed—a seedy fluid. This fluid, and enzymes produced by the worm, circulate in your blood before being extracted by your placenta. Infused in your wine, they, and protein factors produced by the placenta, make up the active ingredients that stimulate stem cell activation ... Your worm is only a baby, but she'll grow to serve us well."

Lilly groaned. "So, I'm making the Elixir of Life?"

"You are, but your worm's not mature enough for you to make a potent brew just yet. Your miraculous return to youth was fuelled by Ox's and then Wolf's blood circulating in your bloodstream. This alone would return your youth, but their sperm is also potent. If I was to test Wolf's blood and then yours, I would find little difference."

"Did my old, spent blood impair Ox?"

"Only minorly because his body houses significantly more blood than yours ... You're a virginal, pure vessel designed and created to house Wolf's worm and placenta ... A wonderful garden from whom the Spice of Life will flow:

Song of Solomon 4:¹² A garden shut up is my sister, [my]
bride; A spring shut up, a fountain sealed ... ¹⁶ Awake, O
north wind; And come you south; blow upon my garden
that the spices there may flow out. Let my beloved come
into his garden and eat his precious fruits."

"Spice of Life," Lilly said. "From the worm? That reminds me of a book about large worms traveling through sands on a dry planet."

"Where do you suppose such tales come from?" Cat said. "People are compared to sand in the Bible: Jacob promised God he would make his seed 'as the sand of the sea which cannot be numbered for multitude.' Shortly afterward, God renamed him Israel. Jacob named the place of his name change Peniel [Pineal] because he had seen God, face to face, and perceived his life preserved."

"I see," Lilly said. "So, Earth is the sand planet from which the Spice of Life flows?"

"Yes."

"And I convert sperm—living waters?"

"That's right," Cat said. "Wolf is described in the book of Jeremiah as the Fountain of Living Waters, and Jesus role-played God and spoke his words. The name Jesus is 'Yeshua' in Hebrew—a newer form of the name 'Yehoshua,' which comes from the Sumerian name 'Ja u shij a,' meaning 'semen that saves, restores and heals.' Jesus is thus comparable to the fertility god Dionysus whose cult emblem was an erect phallus. His Sumerian name, Ia-u-nu-shush, also meant 'semen that saves.' In ancient Greek culture, the 'word' or 'logos' referred to the life-giving semen that flowed from the sacred mountain."

"'Word' equals sperm? Really?"

"Yes."

"But surely the rejuvenatory protein factors and enzymes you're talking about can't enter the body through the digestive system? Wouldn't they be rendered inactive by stomach acid?"

"When a baby drinks colostrum rich in proteins, enzymes, and antibodies in the first few days of its life, the digestive system absorbs them and provides the baby with protection against disease.

After this time, the digestive pathway is closed. Because of this, your wine does little other than make us feel good if we simply drink it. Sloshing wine around inside our mouths repeatedly increases absorption because the tongue and mouth tissue will absorb some wine, but this still results in relatively poor absorption. Spice is best taken by slow-release capsule; the coating remaining intact until the capsule's progressed well into the digestive system, minimizing the effects of stomach acid upon it ... The Bible speaks of the renewal and regeneration of aging tissue:

> *Job 33:²⁴ Then he is gracious to him, and says, 'Deliver him from going down to the pit: I have found a ransom. ²⁵ His flesh shall be fresher than a child's: he shall return to the days of his youth.'*

"A ransom?" Lilly said.

"An offering given to God in exchange for the Fountain of Youth. The Hebrews redeemed their own by offering up another. The elixir's the tonic that all men desire. In Hinduism, it's called soma, and it's the promise of the Bible, the Elixir of Immortality:

> *Revelation 22:¹⁷ And the Spirit and the bride say, Come. And let him that hears say, Come. And let him that is thirsty come. And whosoever will, let him take the water of life freely."*

"I see," Lilly said.

"Your kind were created to give life in unison with the wolves."

"I thought the wolves were created to be clever dick leaders."

"Clever dicks is correct," Cat said dryly. "But their primary role was always to make and to deliver the dew from Heaven."

"And my primary role?"

"To amplify and purify their stream:

> *Exodus 15:²² Moses brought Israel from the Red Sea, and they went out into the wilderness and found no water. ²³*

They came to Marah, but they could not drink the water at Marah because it was bitter, that is why it was named Marah. 24 The people grumbled to Moses, 'What shall we drink?' 25 Moses cried out to the Lord, and the Lord showed him a tree; Moses threw it into the waters, and the waters became sweet."

Lilly groaned.

"As you know, you're the Tree of Life and Wolf is the river. The bitter water is Wolf's sperm which he feeds into your root."

"My root?"

"Your anus. The chakra that relates to the anus is called 'Malkuth.' It's also called the root chakra:

Revelation 22:1 And he showed me a pure river of water of life, clear as crystal, proceeding out of the throne of God and of the Lamb. 2 In the midst of the street of it, and on either side of the river, was the Tree of Life which bore twelve manner of fruits, and yielded her fruit every month: and the leaves of the tree were for the healing of the nations."

"My fruit is my milk and wine?"

"Of course," Cat said. "But your most potent fruit will flow from your paraurethral glands. The language of love in the Song of Solomon is imbued with vegetal imagery. The fruits of the garden are full of voluptuousness, and the lovers desire each other's fruit. Female genitals are likened to flowers in a garden; the vulva is a flourishing garden yielding much fruit, and the male is compared to an apple tree. Thus, his fruit is 'the apple of his eye':

Song of Solomon 4:12 A garden enclosed is my sister, my spouse; a spring shut up, a fountain sealed.

Song of Solomon 2:3 As the apple tree among the trees of the wood, so is my beloved among the sons. I sat down

under his shadow with great delight, and his fruit was
sweet to my taste.

Song of Solomon 4:16 Awake, O north wind; and come, the
south; blow upon my garden, that the spices thereof may
flow out. Let my beloved come into his garden and eat his
pleasant fruits."

"So, that's another reference to the goddess in the Bible?"

"Correct," Cat said. "The Bible is full of such references, and many of the verses in the Song of Solomon are reflected in John."

Lilly frowned. "But don't the verses in John say 'he'?"

"Yes; 'he' is often gender-neutral in the Bible. The verses in the New Testament that speak of a well of water springing up for everlasting life within, pertain to the feminine principle. Jesus is speaking to the woman at the well from Samaria when he says:

John 4:10 ... 'If you knew the gift of God, and who it is that
says to you, give me to drink; you would have asked of him,
and he would have given you living water.'"

Lilly smirked. "Well, I'm sure that's a grubby reference missed by most Christians."

"Only women have wombs, and they're the only ones who can bestow this gift. Jesus is speaking the word of the Father—the word of God—when he says:

John 4:14 'But whosoever drinks of the water that I shall
give him shall never thirst. The water that I shall give him
shall be in him, as a well of water springing up into
everlasting life.'

John 7:38 'He that believes in me, as the scripture has said,
out of his belly shall flow rivers of living water.' 39 By this
spake he of the Spirit [the goddess] which they that believe
on him should receive: for the Holy Ghost [goddess] was

not yet given; because Jesus was not yet glorified [not yet crucified].

"Right ..."

"You're the manna from Heaven," Cat said. "Athanasius, the bishop of Alexandria, wrote of the connection between the ark, the manna, and the Virgin Mary:

> *O noble Virgin, truly you are greater than any other greatness. For who is your equal in greatness, O dwelling place of God the Word? To whom among all creatures shall I compare you, O Virgin? You are greater than them all O [Ark of the] Covenant, clothed with purity instead of gold! You are the Ark in which is found the golden vessel containing the true manna, that is, the flesh in which Divinity resides."*

"Wow, he really spelled it out."

"Yes."

CHAPTER TWENTY-SIX

The team & Sacred prostitution

Wolf picked Lilly up from the milking table in his usual manner and carried her to the courtyard. She moaned in anticipation of the worm's feeding frenzy which she'd come to enjoy. The worm delighting her more now the little gold balls inside her flexible anal beads had become free-flowing; their weight adding to her pleasure as they knocked about like inaudible bells ringing.

"My anus feels all heavy and swollen," she said.

"That's nice," Wolf said as he sat down on the edge of the pool and turned her around on his knee.

Sitting opposite were seven wolves. Lilly nearly jumped out of her skin when she clapped eyes on the huge strangers. Smiling, they gave her a polite nod.

Wide-eyed, she blinked several times before looking up at Wolf. "What are they doing here?" she said internally.

"They're here to feed you."

Lilly stared at the strangers. They nodded in unison as if to say, "Yes, that's right."

Lilly turned her upper body and buried her face in Wolf's fur. "That can't be right," she said. "You and Cat feed me."

"Cat's been milking us to feed you," one of the wolves volunteered from across the pool. "It's our sperm that he's been putting into that fake dick that he shoves up your arse."

Lilly was horrified by the wolf's rude interjection. "Can they hear our conversation?"

"Yes," Wolf said. "And what he said is true ... You've been

absorbing their essence ... That's why they can hear what you're thinking when they're nearby."

Lilly groaned. She'd suspected Cat was up to something when he constantly encouraged the worm to feed from the fake rubber dick, and she knew it was repeatedly filled with sperm. If she'd thought about it, she would've known this scene was coming up. Indeed, if she was honest with herself the idea had occurred to her.

"It's not a big deal," the wolf said. "We won't stick around long ... We'll feed you and be on our way."

Lilly glared at him. "You mean ... you'll stick your dick up me like I'm a common whore and then you'll go and have a beer and yarn about it with the boys?"

"Not exactly ... After this, we're going to work, but I guess we might have a yarn about it later."

"No, you bloody won't!" Lilly stormed, "because it's not happening! Good God, I've put up with some shit, but I'll not tolerate this!"

Trying not to laugh, the wolf bit his lip but his eyes twinkled with laughter. Momentarily, he cleared his throat and straightened his face. "I'm afraid it is happening," he said. "It's happening all over this warren ... in every lair. It's part of our morning routine."

"No, it isn't!"

"Yes, it is," Wolf said quietly.

Lilly looked up at him. No emotion was registered on his face like there was nothing particularly unusual about the morning. He kissed her brow. "Don't make a fuss, it's a waste of energy."

Lilly couldn't believe her ears. "A waste of energy?" Tears filled her eyes. "Don't you care about me?"

Wolf suddenly looked tired. "It's not that I don't care about you ... This is just how things are ... You'll get used to it."

The wolf that had rudely interrupted their conversation, waded across the pool to pluck her out of Wolf's arms. "Come now," he said clutching her to him. "That was a bit harsh don't you think? Wolf has no say in what happens around here, and he and Cat have done their best to prepare you and your worm."

When the wolf's fingers lit upon Lilly's flesh, her body delighted in his touch and her worm jumped, but it remained in its nest. Hunger swam in the wolf's eyes. Lilly looked at his team members; reflecting his hunger and need, their eyes were focused upon her. Almost in unison, they lowered their gaze to the position of her worm before looking up again, clearly waiting for her worm to make its move—waiting for its demands to overwhelm her.

Melting into the stranger's arms like he was a long lost lover, Lilly felt more ashamed than she had when she first met Wolf and his touch had had a similar effect upon her. "Do you have magic cream on your fingers?" she said.

The wolf gave her a sly smile before slowly shaking his head. "No … you want me … don't you, Baby?" Nodding, he raised his brow. "You're hungry for me."

Lilly buried her face. What the hell is wrong with me? Is the worm weaving an evil spell?

"Yes, the worm is weaving her magic," the wolf said as he ran seductive fingers through her hair. "She wants to be fed." He gave her cheek a gentle peck. "I've been looking forward to meeting you."

Lilly frowned. Do I know him? Is he the wolf that tried to snatch me from Wolf?

"Yes, I'm he," the wolf said. "Your daddy and I are mates." He looked at the other wolves: they were looking intensely at her. "It's my job to introduce you to the team."

Lilly's body trembled and blood rushed to her genitals when he placed a gentle hand on top of her right hand.

"Place your hand on your worm and say good morning to her," he said while directing her hand to her upper belly and rubbing the worm through hers.

Lilly groaned. Will there be no end to the humiliation?

The wolf gave her another gentle peck on the cheek. "Good girl … Now tell her you're ready to let her feed."

Lilly gave him a frosty glare, but he didn't see it because he was busy directing her hand to the spot where the worm would soon exit her appendix.

"Rub here," he said.

Lilly exhaled loudly as he continued to rub the worm with her hand. She closed her eyes and willed the worm to lay still, but even as she was giving the thought power, the worm pushed its insistent head through her appendix opening: it was through the gateway. She held her breath, knowing the slightest touch would send it speeding through her bowel and prayed the wolf wouldn't bump her.

The wolf smiled. "She's ready ... I felt her get into position."

Lilly swallowed hard before rubbing her forehead.

"There's no need to be anxious. It'll all be over and done with soon enough, then you'll wonder what all the fuss was about."

"You think?"

"Of course," the wolf said. "Though to be honest, the boys love a good tease ... you've got them waiting on baited hook. Look at them ... they're all fucking you with their eyes. They can't wait for your worm to wrap her fat lips around their dicks."

"Agh!" Lilly said as she clapped her hands over her ears. "Can you stop talking?"

"In the future, you might like to joke around with us and have a bit of a laugh, but for now, we'll just get down to business. Come on ... it's like ripping a band-aid off ... best do it quickly."

He placed Lilly in her mold and sat down beside her. "I'll sit beside you and guide you," he said, laying a gentle hand on her back. "Cat will lube you up for Wolf, then the team will have their turn. I don't usually go last, but in this case, I will ... I'll help you remain calm."

Lilly wanted to roll her eyes, but she closed them instead and waited for Cat's touch. His rhythmic pat on her swollen anus was the call to action the worm was waiting for—he'd rung the dinner bell. As the golden beads, he called pearls began knocking about like inaudible bells being rung, the worm heeded his call to action. Feeling the vibrations, she rushed through Lilly's bowel to greet the boys with gusto.

Lilly was relieved her drugs had flooded her system enough to sedate and relax her, and hoped she'd enjoy the experience despite her reservations.

As the worm made quick work of gulping down a feed from Cat, Wolf and then the team, Lilly coped with the experience and found it pleasurable. Nonetheless, she was grateful for the worm's proficiency.

The guiding wolf took up position behind her. "You're doing well, love ... It's lovely to hear you moan." He ran a gentle finger down her spine and kissed her shoulder before turning his attention to the worm. It tried to seize his finger when he ran a finger over its twisting head. After pulling it away in the nick of time like a seasoned pro, he pushed his penis into its open mouth. It latched on and then pulled strongly, pulling his generously girthed penis up inside Lilly's arse. She moaned as it feasted upon him greedily and he stimulated her clitoris.

The wolf came with a moan, almost a groan, before withdrawing. "We'll have to get her to slow down and chew her food," he said dryly.

The team was busy showering and the worm retreating into her nest when the lead wolf scooped Lilly up and sat her down upon his knee. He kissed her brow. "You did ever so well, love."

After drying themselves off, the team gave Lilly a polite nod before leaving. She groaned as the lead wolf once again placed his hand on top of hers to rub her inner serpent. "Stroke your worm and moan ... let her know you're pleased with her efforts."

As Lilly reluctantly did as he said, the worm quivered under her hand. "Oh ... she's quivering."

"She's happy ... she's doing her happy dance. Give her a warm hug to let her know you're pleased with her efforts."

Lilly was already doing it as if by instinct.

"You have genetic memory of all of this, Baby. You come from a long line of virgin babies. If you listen to your inner voice and follow your instincts, you'll know what to do."

Lilly looked up at the wolf and frowned.

His facial expression was tender. Hugging her, he kissed her brow once more. "My name's El. It's lovely to meet you, Baby."

Lilly frowned. "You have a name other than 'wolf'?"

"Of course ... we all do."

Lilly looked at Wolf.

"I go by several names," he said, answering her unasked question.

"Often a wolf has a nickname as well as a formal name ... Wolf is my nickname."

"Is it the nickname of other wolves as well?"

"No," Wolf said with a shrug. "But somehow it became mine ... I got you to call me wolf because I didn't want to divulge who we were at the time ... We're not called wolves, we're gods, and we each have a name. Some of us share a name, just like many humans are called Sarah for example."

"What's your formal name?"

"Agni."

El gave Lilly a lasting embrace before returning her to Wolf and getting up to shower.

Lilly moaned contentedly in Wolf's arms as her worm did her usual goodnight figure eights before settling down to sleep, her mind a haze. Was she pleased with the worm, pleased she'd given her a big hit of drugs. *Did she sense my anxiety?*

"Yes," Wolf said internally as he put Lilly back in his pouch. She closed her eyes, but even in her dreamy state, she wanted answers. "Daddy, surely the Bible doesn't speak of what happens here?"

"Of course it does. As I've pointed out in the past, you just weren't reading it correctly. You're not only symbolized as Babylon and Jerusalem, but you're also Tyre, and there's a passage that speaks of your hire as a whore:

> *Isaiah 23:[17] And it shall come to pass after the end of seventy years, that the Lord will visit Tyre, and she shall turn to her hire as a harlot and shall commit fornication with all the kingdoms of the world upon the face of the earth.[18] And her merchandise and her hire shall be holiness to the Lord: it shall not be treasured nor laid up; for her merchandise shall be for them that dwell before the Lord to eat sufficiently and for durable clothing."*

"Durable clothing?"

"Flesh that doesn't decay ... eternal youth. In Greek mythology, the Golden Fleece was the fleece of the gold-haired, winged ram sired by Poseidon. In his primitive ram form, Poseidon mated with Theophane, a nymph granddaughter of Helios the sun god, and the gold-haired ram was their progeny. Guarded by a dragon, the fleece hung in an apple tree and was called the immortal coverlet because it had extraordinary healing powers … Gold is a symbol for immortality in Biblical and pagan lore:

> *Psalm 45:[9] Kings' daughters are among your honorable women: upon your right hand did stand the queen in gold of Ophir. [10] Hearken, O daughter, and consider, and incline your ear; forget your own people and your father's house. [11] The king shall greatly desire your beauty: for he is your lord; worship him. [12] And the daughter of Tyre shall be there with a gift; even the rich among your people shall entreat her favor. [13] The king's daughter is glorious within, her clothing is of wrought gold."*

◆ ◆ ◆

Wolf woke Lilly in what she perceived as the middle of the night. Her placenta wasn't full, nowhere near, and her worm was asleep. Peering out of her partly opened pouch, she shivered. It was dark and frosty out, and she was unable to tell if it was night-time, or if the window filter was simply turned up to make it appear so.

"Are you all right?" Wolf said.

Lilly gave him a sleepy shrug. "It's frosty in here. Can you close your pouch?"

"Of course, Baby."

Lilly snuggled down.

"I didn't tell you what was about to happen because I thought it would make you unnecessarily anxious."

Lilly groaned. Deceit had become all too familiar.

"It's part of a baby's routine … The goddess Asherah was known for her sacred prostitution, and it was her role, just as it's now your role. Multiple gods will feed you to ensure you produce an abundant supply of high-quality wine. Your service will keep some of our younger gods happy and productive. They'll fly in to feed you before going off to work without complaint."

Lilly blinked several times. She'd heard of work perks, but surely this was taking it to extremes. "Aren't you also milking them?"

"Absolutely ... We even get them to rub a special cream onto their scrotums so they'll produce more abundantly. They don't mind because you're their queen, and they live to serve their queen."

"Really?" Lilly said, feeling a tinge of pride.

"Apart from the lead wolf who you'll see at every feeding session, you'll see six gods in the morning and another six in the evening ... They're your twelve disciples."

"Are you trying to be funny?"

"No."

"Are the twelve always the same?"

"Nearly always," Wolf said. "Every goddess is served by twelve younger gods who are also serving humanity. Letting them be intimate with you serves several purposes. Firstly, and most importantly, you need the extra food to keep your production up, and secondly, we need to keep the younger gods happy. When our worlds become one, they're less likely to run wild and try to fuck human women walking down the street if they're serving a queen. This is important because rogue gods are infinitely more troublesome than rogue humans."

Lilly sighed. "You said the gods fly in? Fly in from where?"

"The moon."

"Oh, come on ... the dark side of the moon? You're telling me there's an alien base on the moon and they fly here in flying saucers?"

"That's right ... but it's not on the moon ... it's *in* the moon."

Lilly had heard of the conspiracy theory that the moon was hollow. Apparently, it rang like a bell when the Apollo missions landed on it. "And I suppose their flying saucers are invisible?"

"Cloaked," Wolf said, "but mostly they're just not in people's line of sight."

"And what are the gods doing on the moon, or in the moon?"

"Keeping the wheels on and running protection."

"Protection...? Protection from what?"

Wolf let his breath out loudly. "You don't need to know. You're safe, and that's all that matters."

Lilly groaned. *More secrets.* Her mind drifted to earlier events. "Those gods who fucked me—"

"They didn't fuck you ... The worm gave them a blow job."

"In my arse!"

Wolf shrugged.

"It's not a big deal to you?"

"No. There's plenty of things to worry about in the world, but that's not one of them."

"Really...? You think?"

"Yes ... Besides, you were too off your face to care, so where's the harm?"

"Where's the harm?" Lilly's eyes widened. "Don't you have a moral compass?"

"It's obviously lacking ... How about we don't discuss my shortcomings?"

Lilly pulled a face. "So ... did the gods enjoy the worm's blow job?"

"Yes, very much."

"And you? Do you enjoy the worm's blow jobs?"

"Absolutely, she's a talented worm." Wolf shuddered. "She gives me goosebumps!"

"Goosebumps? You don't get goosebumps because you've got fur!"

"I decided to refrain from saying, 'she makes my fur stand on end' because I thought it might make you jealous."

"It's more likely you didn't want to point out an obvious difference between us!"

"That too."

"Why wake me up if you're going to be a prick?"

Wolf shrugged. "I'm not trying to be a prick ... I don't know what to say ... I know I should say something, but I'm obviously messing it up."

"Yes, you are! Do you prefer the worm's blow jobs to just being up my arse?"

Lilly felt Wolf draw in another deep breath. He was slow to let it go and an uncomfortable silence developed.

"Wolf?"

He cleared his throat but still said nothing.

"So, you do prefer her fat lips?"

"Oh, come on … she's designed for her job. That's her talent."

"So, you didn't enjoy sticking your dick up my arse when she wasn't there, or when she wasn't mature enough to come down and greet you?"

"Don't put words in my mouth … It had been a long time since I'd had me a piece of virgin arse. I enjoyed it … a lot."

Lilly blinked several times. "You really are disgusting."

"You wanted to know if I enjoyed it, and I'm telling you I did."

"Right!"

"Are you having another attack of jealousy? Are you jealous of my affections?"

Lilly groaned.

CHAPTER TWENTY-SEVEN

Agni

"Tell me about your name ... Agni," Lilly said, changing the subject. "What does it mean? Is it the name of a god in a different religion?"

"Yes," Wolf said. "Agni is pronounced ag—ne. In Sanskrit it means 'fire,' and Agni's often depicted with a fire in his belly. In early Vedic literature, Agni had primordial powers to consume, transform, and convey the sacrificial fire at an altar—the fire of cremation and rebirth."

Lilly frowned. "Like Moloch ... who's depicted with a fire in his belly

Moloch

"Yes. Agni is the fiery, metabolic energy of digestion. Ridding the body of waste and toxins, he transforms dense physical matter into subtle forms of energy that the body needs. Agni is said to be the self-born son of Brahma, the creator god in the Trimurti of Hinduism, and his father made him the purifier of everything he touched. His wife is Svaha, and her name means 'a refreshment that nourishes.' She represents the Shakti in Hinduism. Shakti means 'power' or 'empowerment' and is the primordial cosmic energy."

"Okay," Lilly said, struggling to keep up.

"Agni is usually symbolized as a ram, and the Latin word for lamb is Agni. In Hindu lore, the ram is a generic name for God and an attribute of Agni, and the Hebrew God provided a ram, not a lamb, to be sacrificed instead of Abraham's son Isaac; and Agni was not only symbolized as fire, but also as the sun and lightning. He was, is the god of fire, energy, and is the acceptor of sacrifices for onward conveyance to other deities. Sacrifices made to Agni go to the other deities because Agni delivers messages to and from the other gods and his fire is re-lit every day ... so he's ever-young ... immortal."

Agni with his crown of flames
using a goat as a footstool

"Okay, that sounds like you," Lilly said. "There seems to be a Jesus connection ... Jesus is the Lamb, and Agni's name in Latin is lamb ... Am I correct in thinking there's a connection?"

"Yes," Wolf said. "Vedic guru teachers teach that all gods are supreme, and they're all forms of the Brahman—the Universal Principle. Agni's characteristics and personality traits align with other major and minor gods in different layers of Vedic literature. In hymn 2.1 of the Rigveda, Agni is said to be the same as twelve other gods. He's also said to be the same as five goddesses and is called the bull who's also a cow."

"And Agni was symbolized not only as fire but also as the sun, and Jesus was likewise compared?

> Revelation 1:[16] ... and his countenance was as the sun shining in his strength."

"Yes," Wolf said, "And Agni is said to have eyes that are the color of fire which is also comparable to Christ:

> Revelation 2:[18] ... These things say the Son of God who has eyes like the flame of fire."

"So ... Christ and Agni both baptize with fire?

> Matthew 3:[11] I [John] baptize you with water unto repentance: but he that comes after me is mightier than I, whose shoes I am not worthy to bear: he shall baptize you with the Holy Spirit, and with fire."

"Correct ... Christ's symbolized as the complete godhead in that verse. He's the word of God made flesh. There are many verses in the Old Testament that speak of God's abilities which are later reflected and attributed to Christ in the New Testament. Likewise, the fire god Agni is a leader who disseminates knowledge and is the first principle of thought which manifests as speech: i.e., he's the Word ... The Rigveda contains a prophecy about a lamb that must be sacrificed for the sins of humanity ... a lamb without blemish ... and the prophecy is fulfilled in the New Testament."

Lilly frowned. "If this relates to you, then how is it that you're sacrificing yourself? How do you represent Christ?"

"God gives his son as a sacrifice: the Father and his *real* son are one and the same because the Son grows to be like the Father. Before I was trapped in this basement, I was free to do almost as I pleased and I had no intention of giving it up; I traveled the universe and had a great life. Now I see others doing as I did, but I was called to heed. So, here I AM attending to you and creating plants and animals, and my life is one of servitude ... I give my life for others."

Lilly rubbed her forehead. "You're saying we both serve?"

"Yes, but it's not you and I ... we're one. Together with what remains of the Son, the placenta, we're God, and we serve. That's what we do, and that's what we'll continue to do."

"Right," Lilly said sourly. "But I didn't agree to any of this."

"Neither did I ... I was coerced into it, as were you, but now I'm committed. This is my life: this is who I AM. My destiny was written before I was born ... as was yours."

"Pfft. I'm not a willing participant. I didn't hang myself on some cross or tree of my own volition."

"Jesus didn't either ... God gave his son as a sacrifice. Your kind, plural, are also considered my son, and you share in my destiny and are bound to it:

> *Matthew 26:³⁹ He went a little farther and fell on His face, and prayed, saying, "O My Father, if it is possible, let this cup pass from Me; nevertheless, not as I will, but as You will."*

Lilly groaned. "And you're symbolically burning me?"

"I've baptized you with fire, and here you'll continue to burn like a lantern that never runs out of oil:

> *Revelation 18:¹⁸ And they cried when they saw the smoke of her burning, saying, What city is like this great city!*

> *Revelation 19:³ And again they said, 'Praise Yahweh.' And her smoke rose up forever and ever."*

"Christianity was adapted from Mithraism," Wolf said, "and it contains Druid principles, Egyptian and Babylonian elements, Greek philosophy, and various aspects of Hinduism. A created religion: it draws its imagery and doctrine from the various religions that preceded it. Constantine created a new god to unite the various religious factions in his empire under one deity."

"I accept that."

"You do?"

"Sure," Lilly said with a shrug. "It seems more than apparent to me now ... What is the concept of light? Jesus said he was the light or the lamp:

> *John 8:*[12] *Jesus said, I am the light of the world: he that follows me shall not walk in darkness, but shall have the light of life.*

> *Matthew 6:*[22] *The eye is the lamp of the body. If your eyes are good, your whole body will be full of light."*

"Light equates to life force," Wolf said. "The gods are compared to the sun because its light makes the Earth blossom, and the gods', likewise, sustain life. The goddess is symbolized as the Earth which the sun brings life to, and Osiris said, 'My substance is of the same nature as that which composes light.'"

Lilly frowned.

"I'm symbolized as the sun," Wolf said, "and you're symbolized as the Earth. I, as Agni, as the supreme director of religious ceremonies and duties, give life to you. I'm the messenger between mortals and gods. Agni is the first emanation, the sacred spark hidden within all beings, the life-giving energy, and he contains the fuel of the sun and emits sparks. Called the lover of dawn, he was asked to fill Heaven and Earth with light and knowledge ... People still make offerings to Agni through fire altars. He arises from water or dwells with water. Seated in the lap of winding water, he flames upwards. Together with the placenta, you and I bring life to the world ... We are the Light:

> *Revelation 21:*[23] *And the city had no need of the Sun or the moon to shine in it: for the glory of God did light it, and the*

Lamb is the light thereof."

Lilly sighed.

"You were sacrificed so others could have life:

> *Proverbs 22:⁹ He that has a bountiful eye shall be blessed; for he gives his bread to the poor.*

> *Exodus 13:² Sanctify to me all the firstborn, whatever opens the womb among the children of Israel, both of man and of beast: it is mine.*

> *Ezekiel 20:⁴⁰ For in mine holy mountain, in the mountain of the height of Israel, says the Lord God, there shall all the house of Israel, all of them in the land, serve me: there will I accept them, and there will I require your offerings, and the first fruits of your oblations, with all your holy things.*

> *Sir 35:⁸ Give the Lord his honor with a good eye, and diminish not the firstfruits of your hands.*

> *Isaiah 52:⁸ The watchmen shall lift the voice; with the voice, together shall they sing: for they shall see eye to eye when the Lord shall bring again Zion."*

Lilly groaned. "And the firstborn sons are redeemed by man because it's daughters who are offered up ... it's they who are redeemed by God?"

"That's right."

"Are there any verses that speak of the bowel and what goes on here?"

'Yes ... They're throughout the Bible:

> *1 Corinthians 12:²³ and the parts of the body that we think are less honorable, upon these we bestow more abundant honor, and we make our less attractive parts, more*

abundantly attractive. For our attractive parts have no need. For God has tempered the body together, giving more abundant honor to that part which lacked.

Isaiah 3:[17] *The Lord will smite with a scab the crown of the head of the daughters of Zion, and the Lord will discover their secret parts."*

"Right!" Lilly said.
"There are also verses in Song of Solomon:

Song of Solomon 5:[2] *I sleep, but my heart wakes: it is the voice of my beloved that knocks, saying, Open to me, my sister, my love, my dove, my perfect one: for my head is filled with dew and my locks with the drops of the night.* [3] *I have put off my robe; how shall I put it on? I have washed my feet; how could I soil them?* [4] *My beloved put in his hand by the hole of the door, and my bowels were moved for him.* [5] *I rose to open to my beloved, and my hands dropped with myrrh, and my fingers with sweet-smelling myrrh on the handles of the lock.* [6] *I opened to my beloved, but my beloved has withdrawn himself and is gone; my soul went after his speech; I sought him, but I could not find him; I called him, but he gave me no answer.* [7] *The watchmen that went about the city found me, they struck me, they wounded me; the keepers of the walls took away my veil."*

"The passage speaks of a lock."
"You're the lock and I'm the key," Wolf said. "The papal coats of arms, and those of individual popes, and the Holy See and Vatican City State, include images of crossed keys. The keys symbolize the Keys of Heaven, and they're said to have been presented to St. Peter by Christ. Since the popes are regarded as St. Peter's successors, the keys are an important symbol for the Holy See; the gold and silver keys representing spiritual and worldly powers, respectively.

Coat of arms of the Holy See

CHAPTER TWENTY-EIGHT

Pagan holidays and Mithraism

Wolf rubbed Lilly's back. "Do you know what the festival of Christmas is about?"

"If you mean ... other than what Christian tradition says it's about? No, not really ... but I do know Christmas was also a pagan holiday and Christ's birthday isn't the 25th of December."

"Correct ... There were many previous traditions. In Siberia, these weren't set to a fixed date, and shamans there used to dress in ceremonial red and white fur-trimmed jackets before going out to collect Amanita muscaria mushrooms: large red and white toadstools that grow in symbiosis with pine trees and cedar trees; trees commonly used as Christmas trees.

"After the shamans delivered the mushrooms as presents to the people in the villages, they hung them in stockings by the fire overnight to prepare them for consumption. Amanita mushrooms must be dried to convert the toxic ibotenic acid in them into a highly potent chemical, muscimol, through decarboxylation, and sometimes only the shamans consumed the mushrooms and their followers drunk their urine because the active ingredient was then in a gentler form. After consuming the mushrooms, the people had visions of beautiful lights."

"Fancy me not knowing that!" Lilly said. "So, pagan mid-winter celebrations had nothing to do with religion?"

"They had everything to do with it," Wolf said. "You and I are symbolized as conjoined trees—cedar or pine trees—and the Tree of Knowledge and the Tree of Life were conjoined in the Garden of

Eden.

> Mark 8:24 And he looked up and said, I see men as trees,
> walking.

> Isaiah 55:12 The mountains and the hills shall break forth
> before you into singing, and the trees of the field shall clap
> their hands."

"I've heard of claims that Jesus was a symbolic mushroom ... what do you say about that?"

"Amanita mushrooms have a symbiotic relationship with cedar and pine trees," Wolf said. "Growing on their roots and absorbing their essence, they're ceremonially celebrated as their fruit. In paganism, the mushroom parallels the bread or wafer of communion that Jesus is said to be ... The bread from heaven the Hebrews ate in the wilderness can easily be viewed as mushrooms because, after growing on the dew of the night, the bread appeared as fluffy round balls every morning ... and dew, of course, has long been a symbol for god's sperm."

"I see."

"Sometimes we're both symbolized as mushrooms—as in Zohar sitrei Torah 1:147b-148b. Jacobs journey:

> A fungus, 'mushroom,' emerged, a cluster,
> male and female together,
> red as a rose,
> expanding in many directions and paths.
> The male is called Samael [Satan],
> his female [Lilith] is always included within him."

Lilly sighed.

"Pine trees produce pine cones which look like and symbolically represent the pineal gland in your kind which must be activated by the gods to produce the Elixir of Immortality. By consuming the symbolic fruit of the pine tree, the dried Amanita mushrooms, humans' could activate their pineal gland in a limited way and connect with the divine spark within them."

"And get high?"

"Yes."

"Well," Lilly said. "I can't believe I celebrated Christmas all those years without knowing that."

"Christmas is celebrated on the shortest day of the year in Christianity like it was in Mithraism and other traditions. Symbolically, the celebration marks the end of one cycle and the beginning of the next. Mithraism was popular during the time of early Christianity, especially among the Roman legions. Once Christianity took hold, the conversion of pre-Christian places of worship, rather than their destruction, was common. This was particularly true of Mithraic temples."

"What was Mithraism about?"

"Mithraism's cult image was a bull being stabbed by Mithras. There are three humans in the image, and they appear both in their human form and their symbolic animal form. A dog licks at the blood flowing from the wound. Below, a slithering serpent is almost connected to a scorpion that's gripping the testes of the bull. The sun god Sol is on the upper left, and the goddess Luna is depicted on his far right—tucked up in her crescent moon as if it were a pouch."

"Oh," Lilly said. "So ... the Sun god is the bull, and the dog licking his blood is Mithras representing ordinary people symbolized as dogs. The serpent's the goddess Luna, and the scorpion—a uterine symbol—represents the placenta gripping your testes ... you're enslaved via the goddess ... she's got you by the balls!"

"Thanks for that ... not so elegant description, Baby ... Yes, that's correct. Mithras was also depicted emerging from a rock or sharing a banquet with Sol. Soldiers dedicated to managing the crop worshipped Mithras. Privy to sacred knowledge, they knew in the autumn of the great year humans would be required to bring in the harvest. Their reward for their part in helping to achieve this end was the resurrection of their leader. This is why when Julius Caesar died, Romans believed he'd been resurrected and he was officially deified and worshiped as a god. Christ is an offshoot of this worship."

Double-sided Mithraic relief

Lilly frowned. "Do you deify leaders?"

"You mean ... would we reward a man who did as much for us as Julius Caesar did ... absolutely. Few men of his era received such a reward, but he was certainly worthy of it."

Lilly's brow rose. "And to think I thought that was all a load of bollocks! And Easter eggs ... what do they represent?"

"Easter eggs are a symbol for the womb of the goddess Eostre— the German equivalent of Ishtar. The tradition of coloring eggs red and laying them on graves to strengthen the dead was common in Greece and southern Russia and it can be traced back to Palaeolithic graves. The red ochre paint was said to resemble Mother Earth's womb from which the dead were reborn."

"And the rabbit?"

"The sacred animal of Wenet, a minor Egyptian goddess, was the Cape hare. It has a distinctive yellow chest and a white abdomen. Associated with the sun at dawn, it was the subject of amulets found in tombs and tomb paintings. Along with the European hare and the brown hare, the cape hare has the scientific name of Lepus Capensis—the animal the Easter Bunny is based upon.

"Coming at the time of Christ's death and resurrection, Easter heralds spring. Rabbits symbolized the moon that died every morning only to be resurrected in the evening. Believed to die in order to be reborn, the rabbit and the moon were symbols of immortality. Rabbits also represented the rebirth of nature in spring. In Egypt, passion plays were held at Abydos in the last month of the inundation—the spring flooding of the Nile. Osiris, who was often portrayed with the head of a hare called Wepuat, or Un-nefer, was sacrificed to the Nile in his hare form to facilitate the spring flood which brought renewal to the land and crops. The body of Osiris as a hare would drift to shore after having drowned in the Nile."

"Rabbits and hares have slightly different physiology, but shared symbolism," Wolf said. "Rabbits are a symbol of immortality in the New World, just like hares were in the Old World. The hare is an emblem of many lunar goddesses, such as Hecate, Freyja, and Holda. The use of the white rabbit as a symbol of immortality is seen in many religious paintings."

Lilly frowned. "So, Christ *is* the white rabbit?"

"The white rabbit is a hidden or remote symbol for Christ ... yes. The use of a lamb for this purpose would never have done because it's too closely associated with Jesus—the lamb who leads people. Covertly, Christ is the white rabbit:

> *Revelation 7:17 For the Lamb which is in the midst of the throne shall feed them, and shall lead them to living fountains of waters: and God shall wipe away all tears from their eyes."*

"And my eyes from which tears are wiped, are my anus eye, my pineal eye, and my new placenta eye—the valve that holds it open?"

"Correct," Wolf said.

"How did Easter traditions begin?"

"They started with Ishtar. Easter (Ishtar) eggs and the Easter Bunny stem from the Babylonian and Sumerian religions. Ishtar is said to have come from the moon or the moon god Sin, in a giant egg called the Ishtar Egg. Hot cross buns have their origin in Babylon, where buns had a cross on them to symbolize Ishtar's son and consort, Tammuz, and the Bible speaks of worshippers making cakes to the Queen of Heaven and pouring out drink offerings to her:

> *Jeremiah 7:18 The children gather wood, the fathers light the fire, and the women knead the dough and make cakes of bread for the Queen of Heaven.*

"The tradition of eating Sacramental bread or Communion bread symbolizing the body of God's son predates Christianity. The Christian wafer used in Catholic ceremonies comes from the Egyptian word 'ta-en-aah,' the sacrificial bread of the moon god Thoth whose name was sometimes shortened to Ta. The moon god Sin was also eaten as a Sacramental bread, as was the Queen of Heaven whose symbol was both a rabbit and an egg."

"Does this relate in any way to the Jewish Passover celebrations that take place around the time of Christian Easter celebrations?"

"Yes," Wolf said. "The highlight of the Jewish Passover ritual feast is the drama surrounding the afikomen. The leader lifts a tri-compartment of matzoh, unleavened bread, and removes the middle section which is wrapped in a white linen napkin and becomes the dessert. Also known as the bread of affliction, the bread is then hidden in the home. After the meal, children search for it and the finder is rewarded with a gift. The eating of the retrieved matzoh comes only after it is ransomed by the children at the end of the feast … The afikomen symbolizes the Passover lamb:

1 Corinthians 5:[7] Christ, our Passover, is sacrificed for us."

CHAPTER TWENTY-NINE

Hell

"You're feeding off my people! That's bad enough ... but it sickens me to my bones that people have clearly been aware of your deplorable actions and intentions, and they have rituals and festivals to celebrate their despicable behavior!

> *Genesis 9:⁵ 'And surely the blood of your lives will I require;*
> *at the hand of every beast will I require it, and at the hand*
> *of man; at the hand of every man's brother, will I require*
> *the life of man.'"*

"Settle, Baby," Wolf said as he ran tender fingers through her hair. "I'm not going to hurt you. You're precious to me and I will allow no harm to come to you. We're not planning on slaughtering your people either. Everything possible has been done to bring about a quick and peaceful End of Time:

> *Ezekiel 32:³ This says the Lord God; I will spread out my*
> *net over you with a company of many people, and they*
> *shall bring you up in my net."*

Lilly groaned as she thought about how overrun with foreigners her lands were. They lived next door, and people were not about to take up arms against their neighbors. And to make matters worse, Gog (the people who'll fight the Lord in the last days) were probably the very people who thought they weren't Gog. She wiped her nose on the back of her hand.

Cat handed her a tissue and stroked the back of her head. Lilly hadn't seen him slip into the room. "I'm sorry to have done this to you, Baby. I really am, but I truly believe you're better off here. All that awaited you in the outer world was death. Here you've been rejuvenated into a beautiful rose in full bloom, and that's how you'll remain."

Lilly found herself almost admiring Cat's efforts to put a positive spin on hell—for surely that's where she was. There was no doubt in her mind, and she was going to remain in hell forever. "I'm in hell, aren't I?" she said at last.

Cat sighed. "God was symbolized as a lake of fire in pagan days ... The solitary sperm that starts life was symbolized as a spark of life sent forth from the lake of fire ... When someone died, their spark was said to return to the lake, ready to be sent forth once more."

Lilly wondered if life wasn't better for the pagans—they at least understood the world that surrounded them.

"Baby, hell doesn't exist," Wolf said. "The word 'Sheol' occurs sixty-five times in original Bible manuscripts, and it means 'grave.' All modern versions of the Bible have translated the word correctly. In Norse mythology, hell was a place in the underworld. Hel, Hela or Hell was a being who presided over the realm of the same name and received a portion of the dead. In the Poetic Edda, Prose Edda and Heimskringla, Hel is a daughter of Loki and Angrboða. To 'go to Hel' is to die."

Lilly frowned. "Hell's pagan?"

Cat nodded. "Do you fear this passage in Revelation?

> *Revelation 14:9 If any man worship the beast and his image, and receive his mark in his forehead, or in his hand, 10 the same shall drink of the wine of the wrath of God which is poured out without mixture into the cup of his indignation; and he shall be tormented with fire and brimstone in the presence of the holy angels, and in the presence of the Lamb, 11 and the smoke of their torment shall ascend forever and ever."*

"Yes," Lilly said.

"It's a deliberate mistranslation," Wolf said. "The Greek word translated as 'brimstone' or 'sulfur' is 'theion,' which means 'divine.' Theion is derived from 'theos,' the Greek word for God. If you study religion, you study theology—the concepts of God. In the past, places that lightning touched were called 'theia' because a sulfur smell lingered. Burning brimstone was thought to purify and ward off disease, and Sulfur got its name from the Latin word for brimstone—burning stone.

"Ignited sulfur was used in religious ceremonies to purify buildings and bleach cloth. The Greek word for torment is 'basanisthêsetai,' a form of the verb 'basanizô' which concerns 'examining,' and comes from the noun 'basanos,' which refers to a touchstone used for checking whether an object is genuine gold or not. And the phrase 'forever and ever' in Greek means 'in ages of ages.' Some Bibles have a better translation:

> *Matthew 26:46 ... and these shall go away into age-abiding*
> *correction.*   Rotherham Emphasized Bible.

Lilly frowned. "Correction?"

"Yes, they'll be purified by the fire of God," Cat said.

"By Wolf as Agni? The fire of God?"

"Yes. The first verse of the Rigveda is addressed to Agni: 'I praise Agni, the chosen Priest, God, and minister of sacrifice ... In Hindu scriptures, Agni is often depicted with seven hands, two heads, three legs, and seven fiery tongues with which he licks the sacrificial butter, and he's pictured riding a ram or a chariot pulled by fiery horses. And the ancient Vedic religion wasn't the only religion with a god of fire. The Egyptian Book of the Dead identified Osiris as the god of the soul. He symbolized death and resurrection with fire:

> *I am the Great One, the son of the Great One. I am Fire, the*
> *son of Fire. I have made myself whole and sound. I have*
> *become young once more. I am Osiris, the Lord of*
> *Eternity."*

Wolf stood up and carried Lilly to the courtyard. "Don't fret over fire symbolism ... All gods are gods of fire, even yours:

> *Hebrews 12:29 For our God is a consuming fire."*

"Hell, or the underworld is but a place," Cat said, "and what's in a name? And although technically you're in a place, you really reside in Wolf. Where he goes, you go. Heaven and Earth have become one ... there's no separation between you."

CHAPTER THIRTY

The Hive

After being milked, fed, and placed back in the pool by Wolf, Lilly lolled about in the water, feeling ashamed. "I think you're underestimating my people," she said enraged. "They're not about to let the other races put a boot on their necks and rule over them. They'll die before they'll let their women endure what I'm having to."

Wolf gave Lilly a sly smile. "We make no such underestimate, Baby. Who do you suppose oversees the humans here ... rules over them? Do you think it's the Arabs or the Chinese?"

Lilly shrugged. "I've no idea ... either I suppose?"

"It's neither. Nordic Caucasians rule here."

"What? I don't believe it!"

"I'm not lying. I'll have one of them come down here and introduce himself."

"Why would they do that! It's the ultimate betrayal."

"They aren't betraying you, Baby. They're worthy, loyal members of the hive who've honored their duty by offering up sacrifices for the common good."

Lilly groaned. "Well, I think they're despicable!"

Wolf stepped down into the pool and scooped her up in his arms. After running tender fingers through her hair and licking her spine, he said, "No ... they know I'm your true love, and here is not only where you want to be, it's where you yearn to be. One of these days you'll admit it to yourself. Like you, I'm also a trapped sacrificial lamb. Many moons ago, I was a general enjoying an antidote to your poison, but humans and gods conspired to trick me and ensnare me. Like you, they pushed me into the basement and milked me of my goodness for their own delight and longevity:

> Revelation 13:2 ... and the dragon gave him his power, and his seat, and great authority."

Lilly frowned. "Is that why the Hindus regard Garuda as a lesser divinity even though he's so magnificent? In Hinduism, he's the vehicle or mount of Vishnu, the supreme preserver deity."

"Yes ... All over India there are statues depicting Shiva as a white man, and the god Indra is clearly white in the Rig Veda where he's described as having golden skin—the color of a tanned white man—and yellow hair:

> HYMN XCVI. Indra.
> 1 In the great synod will I laud your two Bay Steeds: I prize the sweet strong drink of you the Warrior-God, He who pours lovely oil as it were with yellow drops. Let my songs enter you whose form has golden tints. 5 You, you, when praised by men who sacrificed of old. had pleasure in their lauds, O Indra golden-haired. All that befits your song of praise you welcome, the perfect pleasant gift, O Golden-hued from birth ... 6 Many libations flow for him who loveth them: to Indra have the gold-hued Soma juices run ... 8 At the swift draught the Soma-drinker waxed in might, the Iron One with yellow beard and yellow hair ... 11 O Asura, disclose you and make visible the Cow's beloved home to the bright golden Sun ... 13 Gladden thee, Indra, with the meath-rich Soma: pour it down ever, Mighty One! Within you.

"Well, how humbling for you," Lilly said sarcastically.

Wolf sighed. "That's why I abandoned Cat. He was my nemesis undertaking medical training back here. A wolf is paired with his human brother if at all possible. I knew what would happen if I returned to this region of space. We all heard the rumors. As much as he's my brother and I love him, my loyalty didn't run that far, and he understands. He has the odd grump about it every now and then, but we're brothers … we're close."

Wolf rubbed Lilly's back. "Your intense desire for me, and mine for you is what unites us and binds us to this lair. Like I said before, we're emotionally and chemically addicted to each other. The hold I have over you is stronger than any drug, just like yours is over me. The hive has us in a vice grip."

"You're resentful?"

"No," Wolf said.

"What really happened to Ox? Is it normal for a trainer to just leave without saying goodbye?"

"No. They've done to Ox what they did to me. They conned me into training a baby, saying trainers only remained in the basement if they chose to. I didn't choose to, just like Ox hasn't. They stopped his antidote and then your body started poisoning him. Out of his mind, he was about to claim you … drink your inner wine. He was pushed out of here before that happened, and they have him now."

"I see … poor Ox. Was he a general like you?"

"Yes, and I found his posturing nauseating," Wolf shrugged. "I guess I was jealous … he was a painful reminder of my previous life."

CHAPTER THIRTY-ONE

Rosary beads

Lilly sighed as Cat removed the milking probe, relieved to be empty of her wine and milk. She placed a hand upon her belly and caressed the worm through her skin as it began it's slow dance, doing lazy figure eights.

"Roll onto your side and draw your knees up," Cat said.

Lilly did as she was told. Nowadays, she did whatever Cat asked.

Cat rubbed her back, and then her swollen anus. Lilly moaned and encouraged him. "Good girl," he cooed. "You have a lovely swollen eye now. It's quite beautiful and desperately hungry like it should be."

Such words used to be like nails on a blackboard to Lilly, but over the past few days, her brain seemed to have faded and mellowed. She wasn't sure why, but now she internalized any minor reaction she might have. Smiling sweetly, she continued to moan her encouragement, unsure if she did it because of repeat instruction or pleasure.

As Cat worked his fingers into her anus, she moaned and pushed her swollen anus into them, inviting them in. Cat worked her open for a minute or so before removing his fingers and inserting a small round ball about the size of a ping-pong ball. As soon as it entered her, it started vibrating its way up and into her colon.

Lilly was used to things traveling up and down her large bowel, so she accepted the new experience without question. Instead, she wiggled and pushed her anus towards Cat in an inviting gesture and moaned louder.

"Rosary beads," he said, amused as he reached for yet another ball to insert.

"Were they an invention of Christianity?" Lilly said internally, forgetting Cat wasn't able to hear her.

"Of course not. Shiva statues show him wearing prayer beads. Nothing in Christianity is original. Shiva's beads *supposedly* represent his tears."

Shiva

Lilly moaned and rubbed the moving balls through her stomach wall. "The balls feel lovely," she said internally. "Can you hear my inner voice Cat?"

"Yes, I have a special device implanted in my skull which allows me to tune into you and hear what you're saying, and when you're as high as you currently are, it's the only way we can communicate … I need to know what you're thinking."

Lilly moaned and wiggled her arse impatiently.

"Good girl … That's some good twerking you've got going on there, Baby … I'm making you beg for your supper," Cat said, inserting another ball. "I'm going to stuff you full of these magic little balls. They'll clean your bowel of what we call 'honey' by drawing it into the middle of themselves, and I'll extract them later. Humans here make wafers out of your honey and place them on their tongues. Sacramental bread called altar bread, communion bread, the lamb, or simply the host, is the bread used in the Christian ritual of the Eucharist ... but, of course, the Christian bread has no active ingredient and Churchgoers are simply partaking in an empty ritual. The Spanish name for the white communion used in the Catholic Church is 'hostia.' It is a sacrificial animal in Latin."

"Surely, the wafers will taste like shit?" Lilly said, surprised.

"The wafers don't taste like shit because most of your honey isn't actually poo. You've long since stopped making ordinary poop ... This is one of the main reasons you're not allowed to eat food ... Nobody wants tainted bread ... yuck!"

"This reminds me of that gross verse in the Bible,"

"Are you referring to this verse:

> *Ezekiel 4:12 And the Lord said, the children of Israel shall make and eat bread as barley cakes, baked with dung that comes out of man, in their sight."*

"Yes."

"Like that verse says, it's made into a bread or cake mixture ... The wafers taste nice when they dissolve on your tongue ... I ate them for thousands of years and I was grateful for them. When people take communion in your previous society, they're partaking in our ritual, but with no active ingredient, eating them is a complete waste of time."

Lilly frowned. "Is it the manna from Heaven?"

"Yes ... Athanasius, the bishop of Alexandria, wrote about the connections between the ark, the manna, and the Virgin Mary:

> *O noble Virgin, truly you are greater than any other greatness. For who is your equal in greatness, O dwelling place of God the Word? To whom among all creatures shall I compare you, O Virgin? You are greater than them all O [Ark of the] Covenant, clothed with purity instead of gold! You are the Ark in which is found the golden vessel containing the true manna, that is, the flesh in which Divinity resides."*

"That's me, and other women like me?"

"Indeed ... In Numbers, manna is described as having the appearance of bdellium. The Israelites supposedly ground and pounded it into cakes that tasted like cakes baked with oil. Exodus says raw manna tastes like wafers made with honey, and the Israelites were instructed to eat only the manna they gathered each day because stored manna bred worms, but even so, they could store it for the Sabbath."

"I see," Lilly said. "So, the Bible deliberately references and connects the worm with the manna?"

"Yes."

"But their manna had no active ingredient."

"That's right," Cat said, "but the passage is included in the Bible as a reference ... Manna is also identified with the goddess when she's symbolized as a white stone:

> Revelation 2:17 He that has an ear, let him hear what the Spirit says to the churches; To him that overcomes will I give to eat of the hidden manna, and will give him a white stone, and in the stone a new name written, which no man knows save he that receives it."

Lilly moaned contentedly as Cat pushed in yet another ball and rubbed her anus. "Are you starting to feel nice and full?"

"I think you can push in a few more yet," Lilly said, knowing this was what Cat wanted to hear.

"Good girl! I'm going to stuff you like a Christmas turkey."

Twerking seductively, Lilly moaned in anticipation.

"Now let's see if I can get these three larger balls in," Cat said with some satisfaction as he gave Lilly's anus another firm rub. "Then I'll seal you shut. After that, you can go and float in the pool and tease the boys while your worm gets ready to feed ... The boys will enjoy that."

Lilly encouraged Cat as he greased and pushed in the three larger balls. Then he inserted a plug designed to keep the balls in place. "The balls won't come out till I remove the plug and give them a signal to descend."

El entered the room and picked Lilly up. "Are you enjoying your lovely rosary beads?"

"I'm so used to having a full bowel, I think I am enjoying them, yes ... They feel good."

After picking her up off the table, El rubbed Lilly's anus eye. "Hmm ... Cat's stuffed you nice and full," he said, as he carried her into the courtyard. He placed her in the water. "Let the boys rub your eye, they'll enjoy that."

Impatient to rub her anus, one of the waiting gods plucked her out of the water. He rubbed her anus as he did so. "Does that feel good?"

Lilly moaned and leaned against him as he raised her to his chest.

"Good girl," the god said. "Rest upon me and let me rub your pearly gate."

Lilly did as he asked, then she moaned and encouraged each god in turn as she was passed around the circle. The gods delighted in rubbing her bulging anus eye.

When she'd completed the circuit, she was handed to El. He stood on the bottom of the pool and wrapped her legs wide around him before leaning forward so Cat could place a pail under her bum. After he removed the plug, the balls vibrated their way out and into the bucket.

El then placed Lilly in her mold. "You did well, Baby."

She moaned. Her worm was hungry and she was keen to let her feed. "Why didn't she gobble up some of those beads?"

"She's not interested in them," El said. "She desires flesh and can smell sperm ... dust ... and hungers for nothing else, and she won't descend till she's given the signal to do so."

CHAPTER THIRTY-TWO

Parental duties

After all the other gods had left and Lilly had finished swimming, or rather, floating on her back, El pulled her into a warm embrace. "How are you doing, Baby?"

Lilly sighed as she snuggled into him. She wasn't sure what was different about him, but he was different. Unlike Wolf, he oozed masculinity and she found it strangely intoxicating. She moaned a satisfied moan as he gently rubbed the flat of his palm up her spine.

"I'm pleased you're happy, Baby," he said as he raised her to his chest and opened his pouch. After pushing her down and into his pouch in one smooth motion, he inserted his probe.

Lilly gasped and panted, their connection so intense she felt like she was about to pass out.

El groaned as he clutched her to him with both his pouch muscles and hands. "I've wanted to do that for a long time," he said as he leaned down and gave her a mouth feed.

Lilly felt dizzy; she went limp.

Wolf reached over to run tender fingers through her hair. "How are you feeling?" he said, cupping her head in one of his huge hands.

"Weak ... El's overpowering me."

"Yeah, he does that," Wolf said, with the barest hint of bitterness. "You'll adjust, Baby."

Lilly knew she would adjust because it seemed there wasn't anything she couldn't adjust to. "How about you, Daddy? Don't I belong in you?"

"He's not your Daddy," El chimed in, "he's your Mommy. We're a bonded pair and we'll share you ... You belong in both of us."

Lilly frowned. "I do?"

"Yes, love," Wolf said. "We live in coupled lairs ... El moved out so we could bond because it's important to let a new baby bond with her primary carer first."

Lilly rubbed her forehead. "But you have a penis, Daddy ... ah, Mommy, and I know you like using it ... I thought you were a hermaphrodite?"

"We are," El said, "but we naturally lean toward either male or female. Wolf is smaller, so he was predisposed to becoming a female, and I'm larger and my male hormones dominate."

Lilly blinked several times. "You mean like how some guys are effeminate and gay, and others are masculine and gay and yet they're both gay,and they form bonded pairs...? That's how it is with you?"

"That's right," Wolf said, "but we're not technically gay."

"Well, you've taken me by surprise, but then, nearly everything in this world has."

"Don't stress, Baby," El said. "We'll both love you and take care of you."

Lilly looked up at him. "And you'll live here and sleep in our bed? You two are lovers?"

"Yes," Wolf said, answering for El.

"I thought I was your lover ... ah, Mommy."

"You were and are ... Don't worry about our relationship. We won't carry on in front of you."

Lilly rubbed her brow. "So, sometimes I will sleep in you ... ah, Daddy?"

"Yes," El said. "We share parental duties."

"Well, that's very progressive of you."

"Indeed," Wolf said.

After drawing Lilly deeper into his pouch and closing it, El moaned as he fed from her. After her worm quivered, Lilly felt her brain fade even faster than usual, but she succumb without resistance.

◆ ◆ ◆

Feeling disorientated, Lilly remembered what happened when she woke. "Is Mommy still here?"

"No, she's taking a break."

"A break?"

"She's having some time out ... I'm going to look after you for a while."

Lilly suddenly became agitated; it was all too much. "I want to be free!" she blurted out, stressed.

"I see we've still got some work to do on your adjustment."

"I'm not going to adjust!" she stormed as tears formed. "You bastards stole me away from my people." She'd barely got the words out before she felt sedated and high. She groaned. El had drugged her, but Lilly suspected he wasn't the only one who had. "Did the fucking worm drug me as well?"

"Yes, she did ... and no ... we didn't steal you away from your people. We're your people! You're our daughter ... our blood flows through your veins."

"Only because Wolf fucking hooked into me like a vampire!"

"No," El said, as he ran a gentle finger down her cheek. "You got your rhesus negative blood and green eyes from us ... We're your people."

"You infected my people like a fucking disease ... you're a virus!"

"That's true enough, but it doesn't alter the fact that you're our daughter. Why do you think we call you baby?"

Lilly groaned. "I'm more like Cat than I am like you."

"Cat would contest that."

"He's a bloody wanker ... a turncoat prick. I could have children with him. Well ... I could have, had I met up with him when I was younger ... he might even have desired me."

"I'm sure he would have. He desires you now, but that doesn't make him your kin."

Lilly tried to pull herself out of El, but it was mission impossible because she was tucked up firmly and El's nipple was down her throat. She exhaled loudly.

"Relax, Baby. Let Daddy love you."

She groaned.

CHAPTER THIRTY-THREE

Golden cities & Notre Dame

Lilly sat on El's knee. The troop had gone and her worm was doing lazy figure eights in her belly as it settled down for a nap.

"Are you feeling okay, Baby?" El said.

She closed her eyes. "I guess," she said sourly.

El ran a tender finger down her cheek. "You're very beautiful."

Lilly groaned. "Once upon a time, maybe, but it feels like a long time ago now, and yet it also feels like yesterday."

"Are you content, sweetie?"

Lilly exhaled loudly. 'According to Cat, I'm too off my face to know."

"Well, that was a naughty thing for him to say ... When one finds their niche in life they're naturally content. When a god is first summoned here he's often quite unhappy, but it's not long before his consciousness expands and he realizes this is where he was always destined to be."

Lilly sighed.

"To love and to give is greatness, Baby. Men plot wars and bear arms, but women give birth and hold precious infants to their breasts." El ran tender fingers through her hair. "A great leader and general understands that life is precious, even the lives of his enemies, and his goal is to have no enemies ... If he can win a war without spilling a drop of blood, he can celebrate a great victory."

Lilly frowned. "You know war?"

El cleared his throat. "There's nothing I don't know about it."

"So, you're a leader and a general?"

"I'm above all that. I give generals their orders."

Lilly frowned as her eyes widened.

Suddenly looking tired, El rubbed his brow. "On the eve of a great battle, a young and stupid general is excited. His posturing is necessary, but I find it exhausting ... I have to hang onto the reins so tight, I'm almost choking the young generals to avoid a bloodbath."

"Are you talking about the upcoming harvest?"

"I am."

Lilly groaned. "It sickens me to my bones."

El sighed. "When we set your people free, we do all we can to make sure they thrive. Hiding in the shadows, we hope they don't notice us there because we want them to relax and be happy ... forget there are monsters about."

"And when the harvest comes?"

El looked away. "It goes against the grain to hurt you. To round you up like animals and tear you away from all you've known ... Nobody wants to do it—"

"But yet you do."

"We must ... I hope you'll come to understand that if you weren't the prey, you'd have no purpose and if you have no purpose ... you don't exist."

"What about the slaves? What's their purpose?"

"They mine minerals, farm animals and keep us in the lifestyle we're accustomed to. The land above is ours, and they pay us a tribute. We only lease the land to the leaders of men. One of their main roles is to look after the crop and help bring it in. After the harvest, the slaves' duties will expand to caring for the planet, and many sins we're currently overlooking will no longer be tolerated or ignored:

> Luke 20:9 *He went on to tell the people this parable: 'A man planted a vineyard, rented it to some farmers and went away for a long time. 10 At harvest time he sent a servant to the tenants so they would give him some of the fruit of the vineyard. But the tenants beat him and sent him away empty-handed. 11 He sent another servant, but they also*

beat and treated him shamefully and sent him away
empty-handed. ¹² He sent still a third, and they wounded
him and threw him out. ¹³ Then the owner of the vineyard
said, "What shall I do? I will send my son, whom I love;
perhaps they will respect him." ¹⁴ But when the tenants
saw him, they talked the matter over. "This is the heir,"
they said. "Let's kill him, and the inheritance will be ours."
¹⁵ So they threw him out of the vineyard and killed him.
What then will the owner of the vineyard do to them? ¹⁶
He will come and kill those tenants and give the vineyard
to others."'

"I know those verses, and I suppose I understand…"

"Do you?" El said, looking intensely at Lilly. "I'm not sure you do … Your people have laid claim to this planet for so long they think it's theirs. But a hop, skip, and a flying saucer ride away, there are legions of men who know it isn't. It belongs to them, and they're tired of being cooped up in that barren rock you call the moon, and they're tired of endlessly running protection for a bunch of ingrates who scurry around on Earth thinking they're all that. They could wipe you out in an instant, like a farmer releasing myxomatosis to exterminate rabbits."

"You're talking about the men born into your world … angels?"

"They're angels and demons … especially when the harvest needs to be brought in, but I was mostly referring to *our* younger sons … the sons of gods."

"Are you saying you can't hold onto the reins any longer?"

"I am … the warhorses are about to be loosed."

"But what will happen—"

"To your people?" El sighed. "What usually happens when there's gold in them there hills? On the plus side, no reward will be given to anyone bringing in damaged or injured stock … We won't have our women dragged in by their hair."

"Well, that's mighty big of you!" Lilly said, rolling her eyes. "It's not very reassuring! I know what happens on the surface … I know how ugly things can get up there!"

"People change at harvest time ... Suddenly they're back in their natural habitat; they're part of a hive. In their natural state, they pull together. You've heard about the golden cities we're going to set up ... Your people will do well to flock to them, and there they'll either be admitted or given a permanent wristband to show they've been checked and excluded. The wristband will have a radio-frequency identification chip embedded in it, and after the crop's in and the dust's settled, we'll take over."

"After three and a half years?"

"Yes ... Inside the golden cities wall's there will be peace and life will continue for many as it did before."

Lilly snorted. "I highly doubt that."

"It's true enough ... Children will continue to go to school and adults will hold down jobs. In many ways, their lives will be better, and there'll be plenty outside the walls who'll wish they were inside."

Lilly sighed. "And this isn't the first time you've done this?"

"No. It's a repeat cycle ... Sometimes it goes smoothly and everything goes to plan, but other times, everything spirals out of control and where we hoped to tread lightly, we stomp in heavy boots. But one thing remains constant ... we reward those who help bring in the harvest:

> *Job 33:24 Then he is gracious to him, and says, 'Deliver him from going down to the pit: I have found a ransom. 25 His flesh shall be fresher than a child's: he shall return to the days of his youth.'*

> *Proverbs 21:18 The wicked shall be a ransom for the righteous, and the transgressor for the upright.*

> *Matthew 20:28 The Son of man came not to be ministered to, but to minister, and to give his life as a ransom for many."*

Lilly groaned. "And the Son of man is my tribe, not some singular man wandering around in sandals 2000 years ago."

"Yes."

Lilly wondered if El had had a hand in writing the Bible. "How will people know when the end is nigh?"

Notre Dame de Paris

"There's already been a shot across the bow. The burning of Notre Dame was symbolic ... Notre Dame means our lady in French; the title referring to the Virgin Mary. The structural wood in the roof was called a forest because each large beam was made from a big tree, and a forest of roughly 52 acres was felled to build the roof structure. And the great church is, of course, a symbolic woman. Forests and churches are both esteemed as your women:

> *Revelation 17:16 And the ten horns which you saw upon the beast, these shall hate the whore, and shall make her desolate and naked, and shall eat her flesh, and burn her with fire. 17 For God has put in their hearts to fulfill his will, and to agree to give their kingdom to the beast, until the words of God shall be fulfilled. 18 And the woman which you saw is that great city [Babylon], which reigned over the kings of the earth.*

"So, it was a symbolic burning signaling the end is nigh?"

"Yes. Did you see the footage of the military tr3b in the sky? See the web footage of the man on the roof making big sparks before the fire started, and did you also notice the fire brigade stood around doing virtually nothing for hours ... other than letting the fire burn, that is?

> *Ezekiel 20:40 For in mine holy mountain, in the mountain of the height of Israel, says the Lord God, there shall all the house of Israel, all of them in the land serve me: there will I accept them, and there will I require your offerings, and the first-fruits of your oblations [sacrifices], with all your holy things ...* 46 *Son of man, set your face toward the south, and drop word toward the south, and prophesy against the forest of the south field;* 47 *And say to the forest of the south, Hear the word of the Lord; This says the Lord God; Behold, I will kindle a fire in you, and it shall devour every green tree in you, and every dry tree: the flaming flame shall not be quenched, and all faces from the south to the north shall be burned therein.* 48 *And all flesh shall see that I, the Lord, have kindled it: it shall not be quenched."*

CHAPTER THIRTY-FOUR

Sentinels & Sin's gate

"I love you, Daddy," Lilly almost sang as she watched the last gods leave.

"I love you too, Baby," El said as he gently pressed her little body to him. "You're a welcome addition to our lair."

Lilly sighed before groaning. Now that her passion had faded and her desire had been satisfied, she suddenly felt ashamed. "I'm a sinful woman," she said, downhearted.

"We'll have none of that … There's no need for guilt. You were created to perform this task and designed to develop specialized desires and needs so you enjoy your job … A dung beetle likes to roll shit around. If a creature doesn't desire what it's created to do … it's faulty."

"But the gods had nothing to do with my design?"

El laughed. "Of course we did. Who do you suppose your creators were if not us? We altered our own DNA so we could be reborn into our new and improved bodies."

"Are you reborn from the line of your ancestors?"

"Yes … Humans are also born from their ancestors."

"Really…? Wolf said we weren't."

"He was referring to your consciousness which doesn't travel forward. You can't die and then be reborn into another body with your consciousness intact. Rebirth doesn't work like that, but every human born has a collective history inbuilt into their DNA from their ancestors—they're the sum of those who came before. When you die, the essential part of yourself that you consider your soul is lost.

If I cloned your DNA, you would be reborn as the day you first drew breath. Everything you've learned since that day would be unknown to the new you, even though they're essentially you. I could recreate you, and mold you into a person more agreeable to my desires. I could also create a new you who you'd find distasteful if I brainwashed them or conditioned them in a different way."

"I see ..."

"But we don't have to kill you to do that," El said. "From the moment you were placed in the cave, we've been altering your programming. Brainwashing you and transforming you into the person we wish to interact with."

Lilly groaned. "Do you think you've been successful?"

"To a large degree ... yes. If you weren't malleable you wouldn't be here. You would've been chucked onto that rubbish heap long ago."

Lilly's brow furrowed. "That wasn't an idle threat?"

"No ... but we would've put you down in a humane way."

Lilly blinked several times. "Are you brainwashing the people in my former world to help them deal with the upcoming harvest?"

"Of course ... But we haven't begun the harvest's pre-programming in earnest yet, we're still setting the scene."

"I see ... You said you created the new and improved you ... Do you remember your past lives?"

"No, but we have genetic memory just like you do. You call this imprint instinct—a sense of what's correct. The death of our old bodies was necessary so we could transform into who we wanted to become. Like you, we were trapped in an endless cycle of birth and rebirth, unable to remember all that we had learned previously and unable to achieve immortality via any other means. Like yourselves, we considered downloading our consciousness into a computer. We even tried this, but one can't achieve happiness in the body of a machine. You can make an inanimate object think and move, but you can't make it happy ... There's more to a humanoid than a brain."

Lilly frowned. "So, your sense of wellbeing was intimately tied to your physical bodies?"

"Yes. This being the case, we were forced to consider other means of achieving immortality which led to the creation of yourselves and the reinvention of our own bodies—the only way we could achieve true immortality. The system isn't perfect; there has to be a sacrificial lamb. However, we are governed by rules and regulations. If a woman isn't able to adjust, and she chooses death as a way out, we're bound to honor her request."

"But I chose that!"

"No, you didn't," El said. "Your flippant comment when distressed in the cave didn't count."

"I chose to leave later."

"Again, you didn't really want to. This was borne out when you got back on the train."

Lilly groaned. "I didn't think it was a real option. So, will I get to formally choose ... sign an agreement."

"No. Overseers make the call, and almost from day one, they pegged you as a keeper ... Nobody wants to terminate a baby, so every effort is made to help them adjust."

Lilly sighed.

"We created your kind partly from Homo Erectus's DNA and then we killed him off; so you, like us, could achieve immortality via your transformation."

"Do you really think I've adjusted?"

"Absolutely! Your adjustment isn't complete as yet but you're well on your way to becoming a well-adjusted baby. You wouldn't have left the cave if we didn't have faith in your full adjustment."

"I see ..."

"I have other names I'm known by ... One of them is Sin."

"Your nickname is Sin!" Lilly said stunned.

"It's not a nickname ... Sin was a moon god in the Mesopotamian mythology of Akkad, Assyria, and Babylonia. The head of his pantheon, he was commonly known as En-zu which meant 'Lord of Wisdom.' His wife, Ningal, 'Great Lady' bore him a son called Shamash, 'Sun' and a daughter named Ishtar, 'Star.' Ishtar was the goddess of the planet Venus. A goddess of fertility, love, and war, her symbol was the lion of Babylon."

Depiction of the emblems of Ishtar (Venus), Sin (Moon)

and Shamash (Sun) on a boundary stone of

Meli-Shipak II (twelfth century B.C.)

Lilly blinked several times. "I'm still trying to process your nickname."

"There are lots of double meanings in the Bible. The first verse in the Bible to feature the word 'sin' speaks of me:

> *Genesis 4:⁷ If you do well, shall you not be accepted? And*
> *if you do not well, Sin lies at the door. And to you shall be*
> *his desire, and you shall rule over him."*

Lilly frowned. "I don't understand ... If you lie at a person's door and he's your desire ... how is it that he rules over you? And, if you do well...? Do you mean ... well with water—flow like a stream?

> *John 7:³⁸ 'He that believes on me, as the scripture has said,*
> *out of his belly shall flow rivers of living water.'*
>
> *Song of Solomon 4:¹² A garden shut up is my sister, [my]*
> *bride; A spring shut up, a fountain sealed."*

"That's right, Baby," El said, "and, of course, you do *well*."

"That verse said you'd desire ordinary man—the slave race—and they'd rule over you ... That can't be right ... can it?"

El shrugged ambivalently. "It's true enough ... It's easy to view us as imprisoned and enslaved by humanity, but it's not quite that simple. Members of the hive enslave and entrap each other. One could just as easily say ... 'we've enslaved humanity and they're beholden to us.'"

Lilly nodded. "I agree."

"The Bible calls me Sin and labels my offspring 'sinful' because Eve took a bite of the apple—the fruit of my loins—and brought 'sin' into the world, and the Hebrews were called a sinful nation after they disobeyed the Lord and were brought into Babylon by the cursed nation in the Bible. And there, for the most part, they ceased to be 'the *spot* of the Lord's people' because they interbred with the Babylonians:

> *Deuteronomy 32:3 They have corrupted themselves, their spot is not the spot of his [Lords] children: they are a perverse and crooked generation."*

> *Isaiah 1:4 Ah, sinful nation, a people laden with iniquity, a seed of evildoers.*

> *Amos 9:8 Behold, the eyes of the Lord God are upon the sinful kingdom, and I will destroy it from off the face of the earth; saving that I will not utterly destroy the house of Jacob, says the Lord.*

> *Romans 8:3 God sent his own Son in the likeness of sinful flesh, and Sin condemned sin in the flesh."*

"I never understood how Eve brought 'Sin' into the world, but now I see it's wordplay. Does the god Sin feature in any other religion?"

"Yes," El said. "In Sumer, the son of Enlil and Ninlil, Nanna, was identified with the Semitic god Sin. The bull was a symbol for Sin and his father Enlil was known as the Bull of Heaven. Enlil was also symbolized by the crescent and the tripod or lampstand. On cylinder seals, he's depicted as an old man with a flowing beard with his crescent symbol."

"Like the Muslims' crescent moon? The crescent is the symbol for Sin or Enlil and seeing as the Arab God, Allah, is also a moon god, the symbol proudly displayed above mosques is a symbol for God/Allah, and it welcomes you into a House of God?"

Masjid or Mosque

"Yes."

"What about when the star is seen … is it then part of a trinity symbol?"

"Only when the sun is seen shining through it," El said. "And the shining sun is a symbol for the Son, of course … Turkey's crescent moon and star symbol belonged to Constantinople—the symbol predating the Muslim Empire who invaded the great city and renamed it Istanbul."

Hagia Sophia in Istanbul

Lilly thought about the lovely Christian basilica in Constantinople named Hagia Sophia. She knew Islamic minarets were added to it after the fall of Constantinople when it was turned into an imperial mosque. Now a museum, she'd always wanted to visit it.

The elevator dinged in the cave. Lilly stared at the doorway leading to it hoping Wolf would momentarily appear in it. He'd been gone for days now and she'd run over every possible reason in her mind for his departure, and all she could come up with was it was her fault. She'd been bad, and she should have stopped complaining.

Wolf entered the courtyard. As soon as Lilly laid eyes upon him her worst fears were realized. He was carrying another baby in his pouch, or maybe it was his son? She desperately hoped it was his son ... hoped he'd wanted to spend time with his infant.

Wolf sat down on the edge of the pool and opened his pouch. Reaching in, he pulled out the most beautiful woman Lilly had ever seen; her hair like golden silk and her glowing skin the color of goats' milk. So perfect was it, it resembled new-born skin, and to make matters worse, she didn't look a day over sixteen. Burying her face in El's fur, Lilly burst into tears.

Wolf set the beautiful woman down in the water before reaching over to stroke her back. "It's all right, Baby, I haven't thrown you over ... She's El's baby ... I was just taking care of her so the two of you could have some space and time together to bond."

Lilly looked up at El, stunned. "Why would you want to even be with me when she's yours? Look at her ... she's like heaven itself ... She's absolutely gorgeous!"

Cat entered the courtyard from his room with a mirror. "And so are you, Baby," he said as he held out the mirror so Lilly could catch her reflection in it.

Lilly stared at her reflection; her skin was now even younger looking. Young and beautiful once more, she looked even better than she had when she was sixteen. "That's me?" she said, hardly able to believe her eyes.

"Yes," Wolf said. "That's you ... I told you I knew what I was doing and you were highly desirable ... Menopause changes women like you ... it stimulates hidden code in your DNA which allows us to awaken you."

Lilly looked at her belly. "And I have the worm to thank for my rejuvenation?"

"And me of course," Wolf said, feigning injury.

Lilly's eyes drifted to the beautiful woman in the water; she no longer seemed so threatening. The essence of loveliness, she was floating on her back.

She lazily swam over. "Hi, my name's Ishtar. It's lovely to meet you ... I hope we can be friends."

Lilly was lost for words. *Is she really Ishtar?*

"Ishtar is thousands of years old," Wolf said, reading her mind.

Lilly blinked several times. "And you've been here, Ishtar, in this lair being milked for thousands of years?"

'I have, yes," she said as she gently rubbed Lilly's foot. "You'll get used to it ... I've been so looking forward to meeting you."

Lilly looked up at El. "And you'll love me too?"

"There's plenty of love in my heart for the two of you, just like there is in Wolf's. It had been a while since Ishtar had spent time with Wolf and she was missing him. They needed some quality one-on-one time together and I wanted to spend time with you."

Lilly looked at Wolf.

"It's all right, Baby," he said. "I love you, your worm, El ... and Ishtar."

Lilly smiled as he held out his arms to her. In quiet desperation, she grabbed hold of them. As Wolf pulled her into a warm embrace, she nestled into his chest and sighed.

"And there we have it," El said as he affectionately rubbed her back, "you're more adjusted then you realize."

Wolf ran tender fingers through her hair. "I'm pleased your training's over, Baby. I want things to return to normal around here."

The elevator dinged and, momentarily, a young Arab man entered the courtyard.

"Hi, I'm Mithras," he said looking at Lilly. "I'm El's trainer, and I normally share digs with Cat."

Lilly looked at Cat.

"That's right," he said. "We moved Mithras' bed in last night, so now I'll have help when I tend to you."

Wolf nodded. "Training you alone, poor Cat's had his work cut out for him."

"It's all right, Baby," Cat interjected. "You weren't difficult to train. I managed on my own just fine, but I'm pleased Mithras here now because I've been a bit lonely."

Lilly smiled at Cat, but her focus immediately shifted to Wolf when he leaned down and placed his head near hers. Suddenly, it was as if everyone in the room had disappeared and they were alone. In a move that shocked her, she grasped hold of his head and urgently pecked at his lips, desperate to be fed by him and desperate to have him inside of her. Wolf's probes entered her as he cupped her chin and delivered his mouth feed. She moaned her pleasure as her legs twitched and a burst of endorphins flooded her system.

◆ ◆ ◆

After getting up with Lilly, Wolf showered and dried his legs before going into his room and sitting on his bed with her. Music was pounding in the courtyard as he rubbed her back. "Our intense desire to unite is what binds us together and to this lair. We're chemically, emotionally, and physically addicted to each other. The hive has us in its grasp. The hold I have over you is stronger than any drug, just like yours is over me. You're my lamp and I'm your lampstand. In me, you find stability and an eternal power source ... I'm your throne. The original hieroglyph for God was a throne with an eye above it. God *is* the throne and he gives power to, and gets power from, his eye goddess."

Isis with a throne on her head

"His human bride?"

"Yes ... Isis's seat was her king. He was her throne, and just as a bird of prey was often seen upon her head representing her god husband's dominance over her, so did his throne."

Isis hieroglyph in a cartouche

"I thought a throne was associated with a king?"

"A throne was a symbol for Isis's god-king husband and it was associated with her. Her hieroglyph had a throne and a loaf of bread because she was the Bread of Life, and it often had an egg, a symbol of her womb, and sometimes a serpent."

"And Osiris's hieroglyph?"

"Osiris's hieroglyph and cartouche contained the original symbol for God, a throne and an eye, along with a figure to represent him ... and his supposed false beard was really his tongue."

Osiris's hieroglyph

Lilly snuggled into Wolf pleased to be alone with him at last. "I'm confused by the power structure in the hive. Humans seem to rule because we're trapped down here, and yet El spoke as if he were in control?"

"There are layers to hive management. You understood the

power structure in your old society to some extent, but there were layers you never saw or knew about. Our world also has secret layers."

Lilly frowned. "What layer didn't I see?"

"You didn't see or sense the sentinels, shepherds or watchers in place in your old society ... It's their job to see that things go as planned, and they belong to secret societies or religious orders and hold roles of power."

"And they're in contact with the human leaders in your world ... they get instruction and orders from them and report back?"

"Correct."

"Okay," Lilly said. "I understand this ... What else is going on?"

"You know men from here travel into your previous society and meet with the shepherds, and, of course, they appear very young. Their youthful appearance makes it easy for them to travel because they blend in with backpackers, and this makes them almost invisible."

"Right."

"Kings are stand-ins for gods. When the gods left your world, kings or pharaohs stepped into their places and occupied their roles. Originally, it was well known and understood they'd be rewarded for their good guidance with extended life in our world ... in the Underworld. After the time of the pharaohs, this knowledge was suppressed."

"But it was still known around the time of Christ because the original 'Chrestes' were said to share in the rewards of their gods and receive an afterlife, and Julius Caesar was deified after his death."

"That's right," Wolf said, "and the knowledge was inserted into Christianity and became part of Christian teachings and beliefs ... be a good Christian and you'll go to heaven."

"Of course," Lilly said. "Tell me about the power structure in this world. How's it different from what happened in my previous society?"

"If I explain what happened in my early life, you'll see ... I spent my first six weeks in my mother—a blissful time that was all too short. Then I was introduced to my human mother. She was a loving woman, but nonetheless a poor substitute for my own mother. After a nasty teenage ordeal, I left Earth when I was recruited off-world. This was a happy time when I was finally with my own kind and I had a strong brotherly bond with team members. I progressed through the ranks in much the same way members of your armed forces do. After excelling in lower leadership roles, I attained the role of general. It was then that I started learning about what goes on down here. My commanding general invited me to join his team, and I got to fly down here and feed a goddess every day—a perk that thrilled my senses and delighted my soul.

"After I'd been in my role for some time, I thought I'd be given my own command on a new world. While I was waiting for a new post, my commander asked me if I'd like to train a new goddess. I was hesitant at first because I'd heard trainers sometimes became trapped in the basement, but my commander assured me it was always their choice. After some convincing, I decided to give it a go and I enjoyed it very much. I trained several new goddesses and became more and more accustomed to life in a lair. On my last two trips to the basement, I became so entrenched in this world, it was like my normal life had ceased to exist, but still, I returned to my leadership role and the truth was kept from me."

"What truth?" Lilly asked eagerly.

"The truth about how one becomes ensnared and trapped in the basement. And the truth about who, or rather what my commander was ... a sentinel. It was his job to direct likely candidates into the basement. I thought we were friends, but he was leading me up the garden path."

"I thought humans got you to sign a pledge and then honor an oath like you had with Cat?"

"No," Wolf said. "There's a strong request from them, but ultimately it isn't up to them. Humans are in charge of human affairs and have little sway over the affairs of gods, and our world is heavily governed by genetics rather than work ethics and brotherly bonds."

"I don't understand ... aren't all gods born of a goddess and sired by a god in the basement? Aren't you all the same, sharing a common destiny?"

"We're all born of a goddess and sired by a god, yes, but take the son you bore, for example, he is El's and my progeny. El has extremely high standing, so we're a senior team down here. Our infant will start his career as a grunt like all sons do, but if he survives and does well, he won't become a sentinel. His life has already been carefully mapped out for him and his mate chosen, and he's been placed in a training family of high standing—his human brother carefully chosen."

Lilly frowned. "Like a future human king is given special treatment and training?"

"Correct. Royal families model themselves after the gods. Our little king is destined for great things, but he won't know who he is for a long time yet. In secret, sentinels will guide his life—steer him away from danger and encourage him to take specialized training."

"Did you want to be a sentinel?"

"I wanted to be a commanding general. I didn't know what a sentinel was ... I didn't even know the role existed, and I thought gods who became trapped in the basement lived miserable lives."

"But you don't?"

"No, we're perfectly happy," Wolf said, "and it is us who give the sentinels their orders. They're proxy generals—our mouthpieces. And the men we call shepherds or watchers in your previous world are the mouthpieces of human leaders here. Steering humanity in the direction we want, they're proxy sentinels. Jesus was a proxy sentinel for human sentinels as well as gods—a tool employed by human sentinels and their shepherds. Belief in him empowered the Gods, human leaders here, and the proxy sentinels in your old world ... the shepherds."

"Because, even though he was a fictional character, he was a mouthpiece for gods and men, and he was God's mouthpiece?"

"That's right."

"Why don't you tell your sons the truth?"

"If we did, there'd be too much competition to come here. Order is maintained in our world by spin and lies, just as it is in your previous society; it allows peace and harmony to reign ... The value you place upon truth is misguided. You acknowledge this every time you tell a white lie to spare someone's feelings. Kind people tell many lies ... insensitive people, insisting upon telling the truth regardless of consequences, are the cruelest and uncaring of individuals. They think it's an honorable thing that they do, but more often than not, it isn't. And like I've said previously ... power is born of deception."

"So, you're not unhappy here?"

"No, and neither will you be."

Lilly sighed. "So, do you and El share your role ... work as a team?"

"We're the most senior team here, and there's some cross over in our work, but senior administration in the world of gods is strictly patriarchal ... El's the head honcho, and he's in charge of this universe. Like I said before, he has a very high standing. I'm only governing this planet ... I make creatures and plants and oversee human affairs here."

Lilly looked at Wolf suspiciously. "Is that how you got your nickname? Did you have a hand in writing the Bible ... Christ is a wolf in sheep's clothing?"

"Well spotted. Yes ... that *is* how I got my nickname."

"It's probably a good thing you didn't own up to that sooner."

"Indeed."

Looking like he'd been hitting the sauce, Cat stumbled into the room. After he clambered up the stairs conveniently placed beside Wolf's bed for him, he sat down on his lap beside Lilly and snuggled into Wolf like he'd done it a thousand times before. He reached out and took Lilly's hands in his. "Are you happy, Baby?"

She nodded and smiled.

El entered the room with Ishtar in the crook of one arm and Mithras in the other. A broad smile crossed his face as he looked at Lilly. "He ain't heavy, he's my brother."

CHAPTER THIRTY-FIVE

The Bride and Groom

"El told you, you're my lamp and I'm your lampstand," Wolf said, "and you find stability and an eternal power source in him or me. In the Old Testament, the tribe of Israel who becomes Babylon were also known as the vine or plant.

> *Isaiah 5:⁷ For the vineyard of the Lord of hosts is the house of Israel, and the men of Judah his pleasant plant."*

"Yes, but it's the feminine Jerusalem that fruits, or drops down wine, and it's her milk that flows because Jerusalem is feminine:

> *Lamentations 1:¹⁷ Jerusalem is as a menstruating woman among them.*

> *Jeremiah 6:² I have likened the daughter of Zion to an attractive and delicate woman.*

"Yes, but Zion is more than that, she's also the Holy Mountain:

> *Joel 3:¹⁷ So shall you know that I am the Lord your God dwelling in Zion, my holy mountain: then shall Jerusalem be holy, and no more shall strangers pass through her. ¹⁸ And it shall come to pass in that day, that the mountains shall drop down new wine, and the hills shall flow with milk, and all the rivers of Judah shall flow with waters, and*

*a fountain shall come forth of the House of the Lord, and
shall water the valley of Shittim."*

Lilly blinked several times. "Oh."

"Have you worked out that the daughters of Zion are the Brides
of Christ in the New Testament?

> *Isaiah 62:4 For Zion's sake will I not hold my peace, and
> for Jerusalem's sake I will not rest, until the righteousness
> thereof goes forth as brightness, and the salvation thereof
> as a lamp that burns. 2 ... and you shall be called by a new
> name, which the mouth of the Lord shall name."*

"No, I hadn't spotted that ... right."

"As I've said before, in ancient religions, Father Heaven or God
was symbolized as the Sky and the mother or the goddess was
symbolized as the Earth—Gaia. So, the Bible isn't original when it
symbolizes a piece of land as a woman or women, and the passage I
quoted is part of a longer passage with more to offer:

> *Isaiah 62:3 You shall also be a crown of glory in the hand
> of the Lord, and a royal diadem [symbol of sovereignty] in
> the hand of your God ... 5 For as a young man marries a
> virgin, so shall your sons marry you: and as the
> bridegroom rejoices over the bride, so shall your God
> rejoice over you."*

Lilly frowned. "'So shall your sons marry you?' What's meant by
that...? Is it a mistake?"

"No. Women give birth to the gods and in turn, god sons' marry
and take care of their daughters ... I was born of a human woman
and it was always my destiny to carry and care for a woman in
return. It's a repeat cycle. The crop is set loose on Earth to multiply
and thousands of years later it's harvested. The sons of the gods born
of the fruits of one harvest, wait till the next to find a bride ... but
even then, one may not be offered. We hope there'll be enough

brides to go around this time as the harvest is plentiful."

"You go thousands of years without a bride?"

"Our lifespan is much longer than yours ... The decision to make our sons live for thousands of years without a female happened long ago. More sons are born than required because we need soldiers, grunts to get things done, and our young must pay their dues. A percentage of loss is acceptable to us. After our sons have spent a considerable amount of time performing various tasks and learning the ropes, they make good leaders."

"That's cold."

"Things are much worse for your kind ... For thousands of years, good stock is allowed to live and die. Nobody collects your women and saves them and their bones accumulate."

"Then someone calls time?"

"We don't just 'call time,' harvests are plotted and planned.'"

"And I suppose the brides in the New Testament are only the brides of Christ when he's role-playing the true son because Jesus was a stand-in for the goddess and he played many roles and wore many hats—crowns."

"That's right," Wolf said. "In the Bible, many of the 'I am' statements made by Jesus are repeated statements from the Old Testament regarding God. In Revelation, John has a vision of the City of Jerusalem being renewed by God, and Jerusalem is said to come down out of God [Father Heaven] like a bride adorned for her husband:

> Revelation 21:1 *And I saw a new Heaven and a new earth: for the first heaven and the first earth were passed away; and there was no more sea. 2 And I John saw the holy city, new Jerusalem, coming down from God, out of Heaven, prepared as a bride adorned for her husband.*

> Isaiah 62:12 *And they shall call them the holy people, the redeemed of the Lord: and you shall be called 'sought out' a city not forsaken. "*

"'And there was no more sea ...'" Lilly said, "I've often wondered about that verse ... what does it mean?"

"The primordial goddess Tiamat or Chaos was also known as Thalattē, a variant for the Greek word for sea. In later translations, due to the close association of the words, the original name was dropped and she was called Thalassa—the Greek word for sea. In a sense, you're her daughters and you've assumed her symbolism. Thus the sea became a symbol for the goddess, and mermaids depictions of her."

Looking up at Wolf adoringly, Lilly snuggled into him, keen to hear more.

Sandro Botticelli, The Birth of Venus (c. 1484–86)

"Adding to the association of the goddess and the sea, in a Greek legend, the goddess Venus was born from the sea after Cronos, the youngest Titan son of Uranus, Father Heaven, cut off his father's genitals and threw them into the ocean. Venus then emerged from the frothy sperm on a giant scallop shell. Thus god's sperm and your kind have long been associated with the sea. Symbolically, the goddess is the sea and when the verse says 'there was no more sea,' it is referring to them ... The oceans aren't about to dry up."

"I thought the sea had nothing to do with the Holy See because the word 'See' is derived from the Latin word 'sedes' which in its original or proper sense, denotes the bishop's seat—the earliest symbol for the bishop's authority?"

"It supposedly doesn't," Wolf said, "but like many terms or passages in religion, there's a deeper or hidden meaning. Bishops' power is derived from your kind because whoever manages the crop has the keys to heaven. Your kind will no longer be seen running free on Earth. You'll either be segregated off into white lands or cities, or you'll be with us, and the rest of your kind will go on to interbreed with ordinary man and; therefore, cease to be."

Lilly sighed.

"In the Bible, your kind is Leviathan whom God both punishes and cares for.

> *Isaiah 27:1 In that day the Lord with his sore and great and strong sword shall punish leviathan the piercing serpent, even leviathan that crooked serpent; and he shall slay the dragon that is in the sea. 2 In that day sing you to her, A vineyard of red wine. 3 I the Lord do keep it; I will water it every moment: lest [for fear of] any hurt it, I will keep it night and day."*

"What about the changing of people in the twinkling of an eye ... what does that mean?

> *1 Corinthians 15:51 Behold, I show you a mystery; We shall not all sleep, but we shall all be changed. 52 In a moment, in the twinkling of an eye, at the last trump: for the trumpet shall sound, and the dead shall be raised incorruptible, and we shall be changed. 53 For corruptible must put on incorruption, and mortal must put on immortality. 54 So when corruptible shall have put on incorruption, and mortal shall have put on immortality, then shall be brought to pass the saying that is written, 'Death is swallowed up in victory.'"*

Wolf chuckled. "I don't think you need me to explain the twinkling eye to you ... do you."

Lilly groaned.

"What about the oil the Brides of Christ are said to have for their lamps?"

"You are the lamps of course, and without oil, a lamp is no good. During menopause, estrogen levels decrease in women and testosterone produced by the adrenal glands is no longer masked by their bodies, and it stimulates the sebaceous glands to secrete thick sebum in some women. It is this oil that's covertly spoken of, but the verse is really referring to the changes made to your kind's DNA during menopause."

"I see ... Do you have more to tell me?"

"Yes, much more, but for now, I think you need to snuggle down in me and get some sleep."

CHAPTER THIRTY-SIX

Overlords

An extremely tall Nordic man strode into the courtyard. Lilly eyed him suspiciously as he crouched down near the pool's edge and smiled at her. "Hi, Baby, my name is Varuna. It's lovely to meet you at last."

"Varuna ...? The original Vedic god?"

"Yes."

"So, you're thousands of years old?"

"Indeed."

"You're the demon Asura who rode on the back of Makara—the symbolic dragon form of daddy?"

Varuna riding on the back of Makara

"Mitra and I were both classified as Asuras in the Rigveda but we're also addressed as Devas and known as Mitra-Varuna. I'm considered to be the king of the Asuras but apparently, I made the change to a Deva after the structuring of the primordial cosmos imposed by Indra after he defeated Vrtra/Vritra the stone dragon."

"Is that not correct?"

Varuna shrugged. "The gods are called many things and their names are interchangeable. One god is replaced by another as time moves on and religion is whitewashed."

Lilly studied Varuna's fine Scandinavian form. "Were you in India?"

"I've been all over the world, but, yes, I've spent time in India."

"And you've been hiding out down here?"

"I've been having a rest."

"Peeking in the windows no doubt and hoping out of sight is out of mind."

Varuna shrugged again. "To a degree."

"People still worship you."

"I know, but I'm *almost* a myth."

"I don't think you're a myth to the Hindus."

"Come closer," Varuna said as he beckoned Lilly with a hand.

Sighing, Lilly slowly breast-stroked towards the pool's edge. After taking off his t-shirt and stepping down into the pool in board shorts, Varuna reached out and picked her up.

'Wow, you're way stronger than Cat," she said as he scooped her up with ease. "How tall *are* you?"

"I'm a little under 9ft ... Is that the measurement you know?"

"I know the metric value of most things, but height is a measurement people are slow to convert ... we still use pounds for new-borns ... I'm used to tall humanoids but not humans. How come you're so tall?"

"The human gods are all tall like me."

"Really? What are we then ... dwarfs?"

"I've been wanting to come down here and hold you for some time now," Varuna said as he sat down on the edge of the pool and placed Lilly on his knee while she continued to eye him suspiciously.

"I hear you think I'm a traitor?"

Lilly pressed her lips together. "Well, seeing you now, I kind of understand. I thought the human gods were my kin?"

"We are like you."

Lilly shook her head. "I don't think you're like me! You're not like

Cat either. I guess you look Scandinavian, but not completely ... You have a different look."

"Scandinavians are descended from us. Every time we take over on earth, the boys can't keep it in their pants."

"I pity the women who try to give birth to your infants."

"When we take over, medical techniques are elevated and our babies are often born via C-section."

"I bet!"

"But not always ... You delivered a big baby, but we did have to induce him because he was getting too large for you."

Lilly sighed. "How big was he...? Nobody ever talks about him."

"He was a hefty ten and a half pounds, and he would have been considerably larger had we not induced him."

"I *was* struggling with him ... I loved him and wanted him, then I found out he wasn't even mine." Tears welled in her eyes. She looked down.

"Best not to think about it."

"I thought it was a crime for your kind to breed with ordinary humans."

"After being cooped up for ages, the boys go a bit wild." Varuna shrugged. "I wouldn't take too much notice of what's written in the Bible. We deliberately introduce our genes into the human gene pool and the boys have fun doing it."

Lilly frowned. "I'm confused ... Daddy said whites will be encouraged to interbreed with the other races and the purest will be separated off and sent to golden cities."

Varuna chuckled. "What he said is true enough, he just failed to tell you who one of the other races was."

"That doesn't surprise me ... Everybody lies to me down here, they think it's the right thing to do."

"You can only cope with small amounts of disclosure at a time. Wolf told you my kind were killed off because you weren't able to deal with the information at the time."

"So, you're the Lazy Kings!" Lilly said shocked. "I thought they were Neanderthals and they'd been exterminated."

"What he said is partly true ... We're the Neanderthals' superior leaders who they bred and genetically modified to some extent, and after we'd secretly tinkered with our own DNA, we created humanity and Wolf's kind ... We'd changed significantly by that time, and viewed the Neanderthals as a pest to be gotten rid of."

"Wow! That's cold."

Varuna gave Lilly a strong look. "You need to toughen up and forget all that airy-fairy crap that's being doled out on the telly in your previous society."

"The idiot box ... yes. Now I see you, everything is making sense."

"And I'm more like the statue of David than your daddy ... right?"

"Indeed."

"So, what's going to happen after the harvest?"

"Most of earth's population will be shipped off to worlds that we've terraformed; to planets in the process of becoming thriving worlds."

"So, not to Mars then."

Varuna laughed a loud, raucous laugh. "Definitely not. Currently, earth's populous is being painted a very gloomy picture of their future so when they see where they're really going, they'll be relieved."

"Is that like asking for a massive price for something, and then when you sell it for less, but still a highly inflated price, people think they're getting a bargain?"

"You're on to it."

"Will you be going to one of these lands with them?"

"No!" Varuna laughed. "You wouldn't catch me dead on one of those shitty rocks. This is Eden ... Earth is paradise ... well ... it will be when we've unloaded the rabble."

"Will I be staying here?"

"Of course. El and Wolf wouldn't even consider going off-world."

"If it's so shitty off-world, how will you entice the masses to go?"

"They'll go because they'll have no choice, and the bigger the fuss they make about it, the worse rock we'll drop them off on ... There's a price on their heads, and if they present themselves as bad stock, their price will reduce and so will their options."

"Right! So, their outlook isn't any better than mine?"

"You keep going on about wanting to be rescued, but I don't think you really want to be. I think you're happy with your new life and your role in the hive."

"I'm sure I'd be more content if I had *your* role," Lilly said bitterly.

"We're united in purpose, but we have separate duties:

> *1 Corinthians 12:*[4] *Now there are diversities of gifts, but the same Spirit.* [5] *And there are differences of ministries, but the same Lord.* [6] *And there are diversities of workings, but it is the same God who works all in all.*"

"You're quick with the lines … I see you have them well-rehearsed. But we're not united in purpose … I never agreed to any of this!"

"Well, that's not how it works … is it? We're born into our roles. We can't pick and choose them. A lion can't decide he's going to be a goat and then live his life as a goat, and a lamb can't change into a wolf."

Lilly snorted and folded her arms in a huff.

"Besides, there's no perfect role … no easy ride. We all have duties to perform."

"You're about to betray my people … You've brainwashed them and manipulated them, and now you intend to harvest them!"

"Indeed we do:

> *Isaiah 66:*[8] *Shall the earth be made to bring forth in one day? Shall a nation be born at once? For as soon as Zion travailed, she brought forth her children.* [9] *Shall I bring to the birth, and not cause to bring forth? Said the Lord: shall I cause to bring forth, and shut the womb? said your God.* [10] *Rejoice you with Jerusalem, and be glad with her, all you that love her: rejoice for joy with her, all you that mourn for her:* [11] *That you may suck, and be satisfied with the breasts of her consolations; that you may milk out, and be delighted with the abundance of her glory.* [12] *For this said the Lord, Behold, I will extend peace to her like a river, and*

the glory of the Gentiles like a flowing stream: then shall
you suck, you shall be borne upon her sides, and be
dandled upon her knees. *13 As one whom his mother*
comforts, so will I comfort you; and you shall be comforted
in Jerusalem."

Lilly groaned as Varuna rubbed her belly.

"You're the fish," he said. "The ancient sea goddess Atargatis whom mermaids are depictions of. She who had pendulous breasts, accentuated buttocks, and a conspicuous vaginal orifice ... an upright 'vesica piscis.' You're the bread of life and fish that will feed thousands. The voluminous amount you make daily is diluted to make approximately five thousand jellybean-like capsules that the multitudes will take once a week to ward off aging ... Don't you want to be worshipped for your bounty and generosity?"

"No! Why should my body be used to give life to others?

> *Psalms 44:11 You have given us like sheep, appointed for*
> *meat; and have scattered us among the heathen."*

"Well, it's not up to you is it:

> *Romans 8:36 As it is written, for Christ's sake we are killed*
> *all day long; we are accounted as sheep for the slaughter.*
>
> *John 1:29 Behold the Lamb of God who takes away the sin*
> *of the world."*

Lilly's mouth set in a tight pout.

"Come now ..." Varuna said. "You must be at least a little pleased that the Earth will see peace and a golden age will spread across its surface like a ray of sunshine. Surely, you can't resent us for delivering on promises?

> *Psalms 23:1 The Lord is my shepherd; I shall not want. 2 He*
> *makes me lie down in green pastures: he leads me beside*

the still waters. ³ He restores my soul: he leads me in the paths of righteousness for his name's sake."

"Stuff your promises!" Lilly grumbled. "I never made them ... and they were lies! Peace is only going to reign on Earth because you're about to unload almost everybody off it."

"Indeed ... and you should be pleased your full of sap or oil so you don't have to go with them:

> *Psalms 104:¹⁶ The trees of the Lord are full of sap; the cedars of Lebanon, which he has planted ...*
>
> *Jeremiah 22:²³ O inhabitant of Lebanon, that makes your nest in the cedars, how gracious shall you be when pangs come upon you, the pains of a woman in travail!*
>
> *Ezekiel 15:⁶ This says the Lord God; As the vine tree among the trees of the forest, which I have given to the fire for fuel, so will I give the inhabitants of Jerusalem."*

"Stop it," Lilly said as she squirmed about, trying to get down. "I'm officially over the Bible .... I no longer want to talk about it or hear of it."

"Really," Varuna said, holding her firmly. "But I have a few more verses for you. In the Bible you're disguised in many ways, one of the less obscure is the red heifer who purifies sin:

> *Numbers 19:² 'Speak to the children of Israel, get them to bring you a red heifer without spot, wherein there is no blemish, and upon which has never come any burden' ... ⁵ And one shall burn the heifer in his sight; her skin, and her flesh, and her blood with her dung shall he burn ... ⁹ And a man that is clean shall gather up the ashes of the heifer and lay them up without the camp in a clean place, and it shall be kept for the congregation of the children of Israel for a water of separation: it is a purification for sin.*

> *Jeremiah 50:¹⁰ Chaldea [Babylonians] will become plunder; All who plunder her will have enough,' declares the Lord. ¹¹ Because you were glad, because you rejoiced, O you destroyers of my heritage, because you have grown fat as the heifer at grass, and bellow as bulls."*

"I take issue with the Bible!" Lilly scowled. "It's full of treasonous lies!"

"No, it isn't," Varuna said,

> *Hebrews 9:²² And almost all things are by the law purged with blood, and without shedding of blood, there is no remission.*

> *Revelations 12:¹¹ And they overcame him by the blood of the Lamb, and by the word of their testimony, and they loved not their lives to the death."*

"I'm not dead," Lilly declared. "I still have a pulse!"

"Yes, and you should thank God for that. If you were dead we couldn't get anything out of you:

> *Lamentations 1:¹⁵ The Lord has trodden the virgin, the daughter of Judah, as in a winepress.*

> *Joel 3:¹³ Put in the sickle for the harvest is ripe: come, get you down; for the press is full, the fats overflow; for their wickedness is great.*

> *Psalms 73:¹⁰ Therefore, his people return hither: and the waters of a full cup are wrung out to them [to drink]."*

"Shut up!" Lilly screeched. "I thought you were going to come down here and be nice to me ... that's what daddy said!"

Varuna hugged Lilly. "I have, but you're ever so much fun to tease. Let me have a good look at you."

"You weren't teasing!"

"No, I wasn't, I was baiting you … Varunani will be cross with me. I probably should go off-world for a few days to give her a chance to cool off."

"Varunani…? Your wife? Off-world…? Where are you going to go?"

"I should spend a few days on the rock."

"The moon? You call the moon the rock don't you?"

"Horrible place, but I do need to put in an appearance. Things are speeding up now. We'll be bringing in the harvest soon, so regular updates are required by the troops."

"Troops? You have troops?"

"Of course we have troops!" Varuna said. "Indeed, with the mass movement of peoples into Europe in recent times, some are already in place."

"Of course they are!"

"Let's not talk about that. Wolf will be cross with me for bringing it up."

"Well, I'm pleased you did. It's all beginning to make sense now … So, the globalists blew up their own shit … aka 9/11 … so they could go into the Middle East to start driving people into the West where they'll be easier to round up, and the plan went into overdrive when the borders were flung open in 2015 when a deluge of humanity poured into Europe."

"Correct."

"Ha! Well, that'll teach all the economic migrants! Genius! I don't feel so bad now."

"You're not feeling sorry for them? You're not all concerned for their wellbeing?"

"Not in the least. I don't want to be the only victim! So, are you going to make them slaves? Work them to death on some barren rock in the middle of nowhere?"

"Not quite." Varuna shrugged. "We'll give them a mild version of your elixir so their lives will be greatly extended, but the moment they stop doing as they're told, we'll not only withdraw it, we'll hunt them down and kill them."

"You're so predictable!" Lilly said, shaking her head.

"Are you feeling sorry for them now?"

"No!"

"Good ... You and I are going to be friends. I can tell we're going to get along marvelously."

"Maybe...?" Lilly shrugged. "It burns me that they'll benefit from my capture and exploitation, but how can I hang onto my anger if they've had nothing to do with my imprisonment?"

Varuna sighed. "You need to let that stuff go ... Learn to be happy in your own skin. You're different from them. You have a different role, just like you and I have different roles. The ancient Egyptians used to call themselves the 'cattle of Ra,' and the Bible calls people flocks of sheep/cattle. Almost every human on earth is part of a herd or crop, and you grow a crop to harvest it. Earth is about to go into a glacial period, and life will be most unpleasant, if not impossible for humans anywhere other than near the equator. We're offering people sanctuary on other planets ... surely that's a good thing?"

"You're probably *making* the earth go into a glacial period."

"True, we are, and it will seem like an apocalypse to billions of people."

"Are people *really* destroying the planet?"

"Not as yet," Varuna said. "But you only have to look around to see this planet has checks and balances. We're the balance! You're the fish and we're the shark. Currently, there are fewer animals on earth because of the explosion in human numbers, but there's no serious imbalance ... yet. We're promoting that idea so people think they *should* leave."

"And you're troops are going to start raping and pillaging."

"No need for rape ... The women on earth will line up to get our cocks up their arses."

Lilly scoffed. "Bollocks ... They will not!"

"As soon as word gets out that they can get a much stronger hit from our sperm than they can from those silly jelly beans, you wait and see what'll happen ... We'll have to beat them off with a stick!" Varuna laughed.

"Are you serious?"

"Absolutely ... The young maidens might not be so ferocious, but women forty-five years and older can be super aggressive when trying to get a bit ... We'll need protection."

"You will not! Are you really going to let anybody who wants the jelly beans, have them?"

"No. Some won't qualify, and for those who do, it will be first in, first served. When we put out a call for volunteers to come forward and sign up to go to a terraformed world, the first to volunteer will get the best positions and rewards. Those who are slow to put their hands up will live to regret their hesitation."

"What if they never volunteer?"

"They're going and that's that ... They'll just get to go to the worst planets and we might not give them the jelly beans."

"Just work them to death?"

"Pretty much," Varuna said sternly. "The hive has no time for conscientious objectors. They'll either pull their weight or they'll be on the outer," he said waving a finger in a strong gesture. "and nobody wants to be on the outer."

"Want about little old ladies and such?"

"That's what I meant by qualify ... There's bar to pass ... the sick and infirm will get to live out their remaining years on earth, but they might die of the cold, of course."

"That's a bit heartless."

"Not really ... They'll be no worse off than they were going to be."

"And what about your brethren wanting to hook up with the local talent? Will they be married men? Do you prefer to marry your own kind."

"Our world is very patriarchal because we live long lives and few baby-girls are born ... our men may never have a partner. They'll be keen to take a human bride, and while the going is good, the smartest, and undoubtedly the prettiest of women will have the rare opportunity to hook up with them."

"Who are your men likely to fancy?" Lilly said. "What race?"

"The flavor of the day is usually Scandinavian women ... if that wasn't obvious already. The boys have a soft spot for them. Many will be out of bounds in golden cities of course, but those who have an incompatible blood type and, or, are too tall will be highly sought after."

Varuna with Varunani. 8th century CE, Karnataka.

"I see ... What about animals and plants? Are you harvesting them too?"

"You're a clever wee thing, aren't you? Yes, huge ships will arrive in space around earth. Each one will take weeks to fill with humans, animals, and plants ... People, desperate not to be shipped to a barren rock, will collect a bounty that'll surprise you. We'll hardly have to encourage them. They'll set to work with the industry of beavers collecting everything in sight. Loaded arks will leave here carrying more than two of everything they can get their hands on, but it's all carefully managed and usually, we don't even have to intervene."

Lilly sighed. "That pleases me ... As long as they don't deplete the earth or endanger species, I think they should leave with as much as they can."

"The huge arks don't arrive empty ... They come stocked with species that have gone extinct here, as well as animals that prefer an Ice Age climate—many the earth hasn't seen in thousands of years."

"Oh my God, I can't wait to see them! Mammoths! Will they be carrying mammoths?"

"Baby mammoths ... yes."

Lilly embraced Varuna warmly, so overwhelmed with emotion

was she, tears formed in her eyes. Varuna cupped her chin with one hand and tenderly kissed her lips. Returning his kiss and immediately feeling turned on, Lilly was surprised by her response. Blushing, she said, "Aren't you married?"

"It's fine ... My wife will want to kiss you and be intimate with you too ... Life here differs from your previous society. Here, the sharing of one's baby is an act of social bonding that strengthens the ties between colleagues ... Wolf has a pack in a very real sense of the word. By allowing his pack to feed from his baby and service her, he not only increases her production which is good for the hive, but he also unites his team.

"You're the glue that binds the pack together. We call you our queen because just as a queen bee produces queen substance, pheromones which bind a beehive together and settle the workers, so do you. If you view the hive externally, it closely resembles a spiral radiating out from a central point. The center of the spiral contains multiple gods and their goddesses. The next ring contains human gods and wolf packs. After this, you have human and god sentinels and church leaders—"

"Church leaders? Surely, there'll be no need for church leaders ... isn't religion false?"

"How can you say that...? Surely, after all you've learned you know it most certainly isn't ... In the enlightened world, the clergy will hold mass once a week to give instruction to the masses and distribute goddess elixir containing some queen substance. This will unite the populous and encourage social cohesion ... Goddess worship will far outstrip god worship. People will respect and honor their gods, but they'll worship and revere their goddesses."

Lilly sighed. "You're different from me ... I'm feeling uncomfortable with you."

"That's because I'm huge and you're a 5'3" admixture, but that's fine, we have enough in common to be close ... You'll get used to me."

"How tall is your wife?"

"Varunani is 6'5."

"With stunning long, blonde hair, I suppose?"

"Yes ... She really likes you."

"Really? Does she also run things like you do?"

"No ... As I said before, our world is very patriarchal ... chauvinistic. Varunani will concern herself with your welfare and she'll oversee mums and bubs in the golden cities."

"My welfare?"

"Yes ... After your ritual ceremony, she was absolutely livered with everyone down here. She couldn't look at Cat for weeks after he smacked you ... He was very sheepish about it."

"Really?" Lilly said. "She's keeping tabs on everyone down here? She's spying on them? Good to know! I think I'm going to like her."

"You should ... she's your fairy godmother, but she's not the only one who'll look out for you ... Wolf will tear strips off any wolf or person who oversteps their mark."

"Do you think I'm going to be safe down here?"

"Absolutely! It may seem like we're all ogres but we're not. We want you to behave yourself, but nobody wants you to be miserable and sad. We're hoping you'll continue to adjust and settle in."

Lilly sighed.

Varuna smiled at her as he gave her a warm embrace. "We have faith that you will."

Lilly returned his embrace. "You do know people on Earth won't believe a word you guys have to say when you rock up. They'll think you're the creation of camera tricks and clever production ... Unless they see you in person, they won't believe their eyes, and they most certainly won't believe El or Wolf are real ... Most people don't believe in aliens, even though astronomers think there are billions of habitable planets in our galaxy alone.

In November 2013, astronomers reported, based on Kepler space mission data, that there could be as many as 40 billion Earth-sized planets orbiting in the habitable zones of Sun-like stars and red dwarfs in the Milky Way, 11 billion of which may be orbiting Sun-like stars.
Wikipedia

"That's a lot of worlds to terraform, hence why we're still busy!

Evidence of us is everywhere in the world, the Earth is practically swimming in movies and stories about us."

"It is? I never saw them or heard them."

"Of course you did ... practically every religion is about us, and statues of goddesses are everywhere ... you're the Statue of Liberty and you're on the capital building. Stories and whispers of you permeate the world, you just didn't know what you were looking at. Do you remember a song by the Pretenders called '*Hymn to her*?'"

Lilly frowned. "Yes ... I think?"

"Well, that's about the goddess. What about the film *Fantasia* made in 1940? Did you watch it and its sequel *Fantasia 2000*?"

"Yes."

"If you watched those movies again, you'd see yourself."

"I would?"

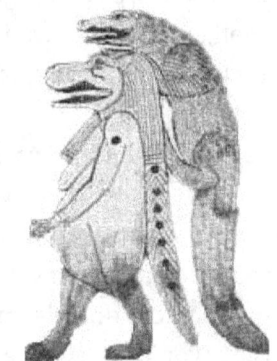

Taweret with a crocodile on her back in
ancient Egyptian religion

"Most definitely," Varuna said. "In the first film, Wolf makes an appearance on Bald mountain as Satan after having already made an appearance as Zeus and as a crocodile in the *Dance of the Hours,* where you also featured as the hippopotamus Taweret—a mother goddess from ancient Egypt. And at the end of the crocodile's dance with the hippopotamus, the symbol for the end of time appears."

"So, you think people will begin to see the truth around them?"

"If they don't, they'll have to be positively blind. You feature in countless songs and not just in religious pieces like 'Ava Maria,' featured at the end of the original Fantasia."

"Ava Maria?"

"It's Latin for 'Hail Mary.' The third stanza from Schubert's original is in the film, spoken in English:

> *Ave Maria!*
> *Heaven's Bride.*
> *The bells ring out in solemn praise for you, the anguish*
> *and the pride. The living glory of our nights, of our nights*
> *and days. The Prince of Peace your arms embrace, while*
> *hosts of darkness fade and cower. Oh, save us, mother full*
> *of grace,*
> *In life and in our dying hour, Ave Maria!*

"But I can't be her!"

"Course you can," Varuna said. "You and millions of others are her."

"What happens in the second Fantasia?"

"It ends with a piece straight out of Revelation ... after Noah's Ark, of course."

"I don't remember it."

"Course not ... It probably seemed like an airy-fairy piece about nature to you at the time. A supposedly mythical story of life death and renewal closes *Fantasia 2000*, set to the '*Firebird Suite – 1919 version*' by Igor Stravinsky."

Lilly frowned. "And it's not an airy-fairy piece?"

"No ... God symbolized as a hart or stag with ten points walks through thick snow into a cave and breathes onto the ceiling. There his breath conceals on a rocky cone hanging from the roof of the cave, and the water drips down into the pool below forming or creating life in the form of a watery woman."

"Oh ... a hart features in the Bible in Song of Solomon:

> *Song of Solomon 2:7 I charge you, O you daughters of*
> *Jerusalem, by the [deer] roes, and by the hinds [female*
> *deer] of the field, that you stir not up, nor awake my love,*

> *till he please. ⁸ The voice of my beloved! behold, he comes leaping upon the mountains, skipping upon the hills. ⁹ My beloved is like a roe [deer] or a young hart [immature stag]: behold, he stands behind our wall, he looks forth at the windows, showing himself through the lattice."*

Varuna nodded. "That's right ... Then the watery goddess with flowing arms like wings turns green and flows over the countryside changing the winter season to spring and then summer. She brings life to the world, including a deciduous tree that she temporarily becomes part of when she makes it blossom. Then she approaches a mountain ... she swoons up its side but no life will catch upon it. Confused, she floats up the mountainside to its peak and peers inside. Inside its lifeless cauldron below, a rocky outcrop that looks like a hunched over figure sits lifeless.

"She glides down to it and reaches out her arms and touches it. It immediately springs to life, becoming a huge fire breathing bird like an enormous phoenix before changing into flowing lava that is out of control with eyes in its leading-edge, consuming the world and chasing her. Eventually, it overcomes her and after the screen turns black for several seconds, we see the mountain smoking and everything is consumed and covered in ash and the lava is gone. Then the hart or stag reappears ... It seeks out the goddess who is now nothing but ash, and once again it breathes life into her.

"Grey and sullen she grasps onto its offered antlers and rides upon it like the Whore of Babylon. Looking at the dead world around her, she cries and where her tears fall life sprouts. Seeing this, she is joyous once more and she flies over the countryside as a watery river raining on the earth below as the stag runs beneath her and the ground turns green and full of life. Then, as she flows up the mountainside, life does catch upon it. She turns into a million butterflies before becoming shards of green and settling on the mountainside as plentiful grass as the stag watches on:

> *Psalms 147:⁸ Who covers the heaven with clouds, who prepares rain for the earth, who makes grass to grow*

upon the mountains."

Lilly drew in a deep breath. "My kind
is symbolized as grass and Wolf, the dew upon it. Well ... I guess
that requires no explanation."

"Not to you, it doesn't," Varuna said, "and soon the people of the
world won't require an explanation either. They'll know a stag is a
symbol for God who breathed life into the goddess, not once, but
twice. He created her in the first instance, and then he makes her
immortal and full of life so she can spread her joy far and wide."

"I see, and this is in Revelation?"

"Do you recall this verse:

> *Revelation 12:³ And there appeared another wonder in*
> *heaven; and behold a great red dragon, having seven*
> *heads and **ten horns**, and seven crowns upon his heads."*

"Oh, so the horns are the points of the antlers of a mature hart or
stag? The fiery bird and the hart is one and the same ... God and
Satan?"

"Yes."

"And his seven heads and seven crowns? What are they?"

"All men have two heads ... the little head usually controls the big
head," Varuna said sarcastically. "And a baby's head is said to crown
as it's being born."

"So, Wolf has seven heads? His phallic head, his three probe heads
and his nipple probe heads, and his big head?"

"Well done!"

Lilly drew in a sharp breath. "But I sense *you're* God?"

"In a way ... It was us who created your kind and Wolf's kind after
we ourselves were enhanced by our people. They thought we
betrayed them." Varuna shrugged his shoulders. "Of course we did
... but we could see what they couldn't and we've no regrets. You
were our greatest creations, surpassing even our wildest dreams.
It's true man can be unruly, but we're more than up to the task of
controlling him ... I know you think Wolf or El is God, and they are to

you and me, but to humanity I AM Lord ... Do you understand?"

Lilly sighed. "I guess so ... I'm feeling on the outer again."

Varuna pulled her into a warm embrace. "You couldn't be more on the inner."

"You seem more like Shiva to me ... both a destroyer and a builder of worlds."

"It doesn't matter what name you give me ... Just like all goddesses are *the* goddess, having the same properties. I'm akin to Zeus, the Hebrew God, Shiva, Indra and a good number of other Gods such as the Sumerian Enki, the Babylonian Marduk, and the Egyptian Osiris."

"What name will you introduce yourself to mankind as?"

"I think Varuna is as good a name as any. Certainly, it's better than using the name of a god currently being worshipped on Earth. Using one of those names would introduce an element of favoritism. My name precedes all current-day religions and the Vedas are at the root of almost every religion on Earth."

"And you *really are* that old?"

"Ha! I'd be a spring-chicken if I was only *that* old."

"So, who's going to announce the end?"

"The fat lady of course."

"Because it ain't over till the fat lady sings?"

"Exactly!"

www.ingramcontent.com/pod-product-compliance
Lightning Source LLC
Chambersburg PA
CBHW051236260626
47162CB00002B/455